This book is dedicated to all of the Medlovians out there. We have had so much fun over the last two years developing characters, plots, blogging up a storm, creating book trailers, having colorful global conference calls and reading about our favorite characters together. We have grown from a mighty group of 50 to over 10,000 women who love our favorite bad boy, Dmitry Medlov and his crew. Thanks for making this such a lively experience. Now we're on to Book Two: Volume 5-8. It's going to be hard to top ourselves.

Acknowledgments

Acknowledgment is due for key people on this project who have displayed exemplary skills and undeniable talent. Karen Moss has done such a wonderful job with proofreading and copy editing this book. Even when I was ill or taking care of sick husband, she committed to this project and worked without me. Kandace Tuggle has done another wonderful job on my cover. My administrative staff, Megan Woods and Crystal Peeples have been instrumental in research, follow-up calls and so much that it takes to develop a true concept for a book. Mark Todd Lenowski, words cannot express my gratitude for uncanny talent to evoke deep thought and inspire awe and creativity. The entire Medlov Crime Family fan base that has sent countless emails about their ideas of how the stories should develop are owed a tremendous debt of gratitude. Adam Nelson, thanks for the push to truly commit myself to this business.

Volume

One

Prologue

The climate in Prague always seemed to remind Dmitry of Russia in the winter. As he sat looking out the picturesque windows of his study, he felt the warmth of the fireplace and listened to the crackle of the embers trickle into his thoughts.

The relentless snowfall made for a beautiful view. As he wrote in his daily journal, he caught a glimpse of his sons running and playing in the light snowstorm with their snowmobiles. Putting down the pen, he marveled at their happiness.

He remembered when he was just a little older than they were, but he and his brother, Ivan, were doing dramatically different things than Konstantin and Maxim. There was no playing in the snow, no hearty meals with the family, no talks of college and respectable dating with girls of a respectable ilk. Instead, for he and Ivan, there was only chaos.

Even the simplest things were pained memories of a time of total hardship. As he looked over at the fireplace, he remembered why he had one in every house that he owned, always one in the master bedroom. A fireplace. A warm space.

It was a memory that he had locked away in the sacred vaults of his mind designed to repress the pain that came with the life that he had struggled to make for himself.

At times, he wondered was it all worth it, but then as he looked out in the snow as his boys played, he knew that it was or at least, he would like to think so. Many had perished since his rise to a new freedom. He was only 15 when he first began his climb...

Chapter One

The heavy rains poured down on Dmitry Medlov's face as he exited prison for the first time in the three years since his conviction. Clutching his soaking wet coat around his protruding chest and the precious release papers hidden in a plastic covering tucked securely inside his pants, he looked up above the shaking halogen lights into the storm.

For most, the sight of such a natural violence would have been depressing or at least alarming, but he smiled at the coming blizzard and gratefully breathed in free air.

No car was waiting for Dmitry, so he began his long walk to the nearest town. Cold and shaking, he inched down the dark gravel road in the silence of his thoughts.

There was a great deal to do in a very small window of time. Kirill had secured a plane ticket out of Moscow in two days time for him and his little brother, Ivan, to get to London, where they would set up shop for a while.

He had learned much while in prison, things he could not have possibly learned on the streets, and he was now anxious to put those things to good use and teach his small crew. Plus, he had to get out of the city for other reasons.

On paper, Dmitry Medlov had been freed for *time served* in the murder of Ukrainian drug lord Hamel Stegnof after a stint of twenty years in prison, but in fact, the papers had been forged at the high price of 300,000 American dollars to the head of the probation board. He still had seventeen years left on his bid, and he wasn't about to spend that amount of time behind bars. When the offer came to hijack him out of jail, he took it.

By the time the prison board realized that they had released him by mistake due to faulty paperwork, he would be gone and a cover would be given for their mistake or pushed under the rug for their protection.

But his freedom had also come with a price. He had twenty-four hours from this very minute to get to his boss's enemy, Sacha Karpenko, and kill him. The thought made him walk faster towards his destination. It would be a small price to pay to gain his absolute freedom.

***

When Dmitry arrived in town hours later, his bones were icy cold and frozen. Walking through the door of a small bar, he was met by warm heat from a nearby fireplace, the smell of beer and the snitch of unwashed men. They all turned to look at him, covered in water, towering in the small space at nearly seven feet tall and covered in a thick, blond beard.

His intense blue eyes scanned the room and saw a woman sitting alone in the corner. Quietly, he walked over to her and kneeled down.

"Do you know where I can get some dry clothes?" he asked in Russian.

She looked up at him, startled by the sheer size of the giant and turned from her mug of lager. "I don't think we have anything to fit the likes of you," she said, greeting his stench with the smell of her own.

She reeked of beer and sweet cologne that made his nose twitch. Her jagged teeth were yellow and stained from cigarettes.

"What size are you?" She looked him up and down.

Dmitry looked down at the puddle of water under his pants. "I don't know really. I've grown a bit since I've been in prison."

The middle-aged woman stood up, barely coming above his waist. "You're a fine specimen. But I don't think we have anything to fit you. Why don't you go in the back room, take your clothes off, and I'll dry them for you, love," she said, pointing towards the doors in the back of the bar past the kitchen.

He nodded gratefully and headed back, ducking under the narrow archways as he went.

Pulling off his heavy, wool coat, he opened the door to the small room housing a twin bed and a wooden desk and looked around. It was a simple place with no hanging pictures or even a mirror, but to him it was heaven.

He quickly peeled out of his clothes, one wet layer at a time, and placed his belongings on the wooden floor. His teethed chattered, and his lips had turned deep blue. It was obvious that if he had been forced to walk much longer in the storm, he might not have made it.

Walking to the fireplace, he dropped to his knees and soaked in the warm heat. It felt so good to his aching body. When he got his own house, he would make sure that it had a fireplace in his bedroom just like this one to always remind him of how wonderful the simple blessing of fire could be on a cold winter night.

The door creaked opened, and the small woman came in and closed it behind her. She looked over at the pile of clothes and quickly went to pick them up. "You're from the prison, *da*?" she asked, looking at the mural of tattoos that covered his entire back. Instantly, she knew that he was Vory. Everyone around the town knew what those markings meant – trouble.

He looked over at her and shook his head without saying a word.

"It's amazing that you were able to keep on so much muscle. I heard that they barely feed you in those places." She gathered the wet clothes in her arms. The excess water ran down on her tattered dress.

"It's survival of the fittest," he explained as he stood up. His deep, baritone voice carried through the small room like thunder. He turned to her and walked over to retrieve the paper that he placed inside of his pants. He did not want her carting off his key to freedom.

The woman was transfixed by the size of Dmitry's naked body and his long, limp penis slapping lazily across his large, hairy thighs. She snaked her tongue around her cracked lips and sighed. "Will you need anything else while you're here? I'm sure that you'll want someone to warm your bed with you tonight," she said, touching his muscular stomach riddled with tattoos and scars.

Dmitry raised his brow. *He hadn't had a woman in three years.* The last time had been for his fifteenth birthday before he had been carted off to jail.   His erection prodded between them only inches from her throat as he looked down at her.

He had been with many women as a young teen, most of them far older than he was. They had treated him as something of a toy, *which most of the time he didn't mind.* But they had never looked as rough as this woman did.

She was a barmaid with wiry brown hair and wild eyes. Dmitry thought that she looked like a witch from the children's stories of his youth.

Without approval, the older woman dropped his clothes and took his thick penis into her weathered mouth. Her warm touch caused a small excitement in him. He watched on a little surprised by her actions. He had been told a hundred times that older women liked a big man *and he was that*, but he didn't know if he liked them.

He thought back on his past experiences. The older woman who had allowed him and his brother to stay in his mother's apartment after she was murdered made him pay for their rent through sex *twice a week*. The butcher's wife allowed him to buy their meat with sex *once a month*, and even the first car he owned came from an older woman who liked his sex.

His mother, a slain prostitute who always stunk of cigarettes, sex and vodka, had shown him bartering of this type early in his life, and he had used the skill when necessary. It never made him feel dirty to have sex for what he needed, but it did make him feel the loss of control. He had grappled with the feeling for a long time, and it still bothered him, even now.

A warm wave came over him quickly as he held the older woman's shoulders, moving in and out of her hollow mouth with the sucks and sounds that made his toes curl. Her small hands gripped his rock-hard buttocks, and he felt her nimble tongue on the tip of his shaft.

Sitting back on the bed, he looked up at her and wondered why he was doing this. She was not attractive, but the oral pleasure that she provided was enjoyable. *Could he give into her?*

Cursing, the woman pulled up her dirty dressed and pulled down her dingy underwear. A musty odor seeped from below her, and her hairy vagina peeked out from under her garments. A thought flashed in his mind.

The woman in her grimy lust suddenly reminded him of his mother with the many *Johns* she had provided service. He had been responsible for protecting his mother from them but had failed.   He had been her pimp. It was he and his brother that she worked for – to provide for them.

A flash of her bloody, beaten face flashed before him.   He flinched involuntarily from the painful memory of his mother and the pleasure of this woman's touch.

With little effort, his large hands grabbed the woman by her chubby waist and raised her off his mountainous erection. He spoke gently, looking into her desperate eyes.

"Stop, please," he said, moving her. "Stop."

A familiar surge started to grow below him. He didn't want to climax for her. He didn't want to see *it* spring forth from his loins with a woman of this ilk.

"Well, what's wrong with you, boy? Don't you like women?" She wiped her mouth and panted heavily. She wanted more than anything to feel him inside of her – having never been with a man like him before.

"*Da*, I like women. You just remind me of someone," he said, sitting up on the bed beside her. His long legs reached across the floor as he tucked his dying erection in between his hairy, sculpted thighs.

"Who?" she asked curiously.

"My mother."

"Oh, I see," she said sympathetically. "She was in the old arts, was she?"

Dmitry nodded.

The moment was quickly over. Heated lust fizzled into nothingness.

Giving up, the woman pulled her dingy panties up on her waist, pulled her tattered dress down past her wrinkled knees and stood up beside him. She sighed, "I'd best get this dry for you then, boy. Get some rest if you can. Would you like something to eat?"

"Anything that you can manage. I'm flat broke," he said, looking up at her.

"Don't worry. Your money is no good here," she said, closing the door behind her.

Chapter Two

Ivan Medlov sat on the steps of their impoverished, over-populated apartment complex smoking a cigarette and talking to his little crew of two as he waited. He watched his watch as the dial slowly moved from one hour to the next. It was torture to wait on his big brother's arrival. Dmitry had never been late in all the time that he'd been forced to serve under him in their small gang.

Word had gotten to him that Dmitry was out, and he was to wait *right where he sat* for his arrival. However, one hour had turned to three and now frustrated, he spat on the ground and cursed.

"What is taking him so fucking long?" the young boy cursed, thumping a half-smoked cigarette at the whore only inches away working on the corner in front of him.

The older woman turned around and cursed, flipping her middle finger at the trouble maker. Ivan paid her no attention.

Their crew was anxious, talking to one another about their latest heist while they bided their precious time. They had been together for two years now, emulating the men that they had come to look up to, many whom were Vory v Zakone, the most feared and respected organized crime sect in the country.

Since they formed their small crew, a junior representation of his big brother's Medlov Crime Family, they had amassed a poor man's fortune and prided themselves on the flashy watches and cool clothes that they could not afford to purchase but had successfully stolen. Everyone in their area feared them; the police didn't bother them, and their road was set. They were on the way to being like his brother, Dmitry.

"He'll be here," Yani assured. "Calm down."

"Maybe he left without me," Ivan spoke his doubt, scratching at the back of his hairy neck and the curls that formed on it. "It would be just like him."

"He wouldn't leave you," Yani assured his friend, realizing that Ivan was still brooding over Dmitry's tardiness. He took a swig of his beer. "You're too impatient. Everything doesn't happen exactly when *you* want it to. You're not that important, you know."

"If he did leave, I'll kick his ass," Ivan promised.

"Name one time that Dmitry has left you anywhere alone?" Yani asked.

Ivan rolled his eyes. "How about the last three years"

"He's been in prison, and you've had more help since he's been in than when he was out," Gistofani chimed in.

"So, where do you think you're going now?" Yani asked as his voice cracked. He was barely 14 years old and was starting to suffer badly from growing adolescence.

"He won't tell me," Ivan answered. "But I plan to find out. When he sees what we have been up to, I'm sure that he'll take us all. We can start over somewhere nice with real weather and real pussy," he said aloud so the whore could hear him. "These cheap, nasty whores are worthless. I got crabs twice last month."

"You can't get crabs from yourself," Yani joked.

Just then, a cab pulled up, and Dmitry popped out with a small backpack hung over his broad shoulder.

All three boys jumped up. Ivan had a wide grin on his face that he normally would have repressed if he had not missed his only brother so much.

Dmitry didn't smile as he walked over. Instead, he stood face-to-face with Ivan, who was elevated by the stairwell, and looked him over. Ivan had grown a full foot since he last saw him and picked up the usual bulky Medlov weight.

Ivan had deep blue menacing eyes that were hidden under the darkest eyelashes. His perfect aquiline nose rested on his wide face, bringing out his chiseled jaw and thin lips. Even a small mustache was now above his lip making him look 25 instead of a *pipsqueak* 15.

But Ivan was thrown off by the pained look in his brother's face. *Was he already disappointed?*

Dmitry put his bag down on the step and cupped his brother's face in his hands, looking in his eyes, checking his teeth and pulling his coat down to look at the fresh tattoos.

"Those better not be forced," he warned of the markings on his little brother's neck.

"They're not," Ivan said as he snatched away. His dark black hair flipped in his face. "I earned them."

Dmitry finally stepped away. "Well, you look good."

"You look jealous," Ivan retorted, venom seeping into the veins that stuck out of his muscular neck. He wasn't used to compliments, especially from Dmitry.

"Not jealous, *brat*, pained. I've missed so much since I've been away. And for that, I guess, I'm sorry." Dmitry rubbed his hand through his brother's tousled black locks.

The words humbled Ivan. He could never read his big brother. He could never tell if his displeasure was with him or the world in general, both had grave consequences.

"We can catch up later," Ivan said with a wide grin. In his signature way, he quickly moved from one emotion to the next, hampering his sudden anger. He pointed at his friends, who watched on mesmerized by Dmitry's height and stature. *He was bigger than life.* "You remember Yani, Stepan's little brother, and this is Gistofani, my second-in- charge."

Dmitry chuckled under his breath. *What the hell did these mismatch kids know about a second-in-charge?* He started to tell them that they meant underboss but bit his tongue. *What did it matter?*

He turned and looked at Yani, a spitting image of his good friend, Stepan and his family line. Stepan was a part of his crew and had been faithful many years. He had even served time with Stepan and Yani's father and uncle while he was in prison. Yani was a good boy; he could be trusted. Then he trailed over to the olive skin boy called Gistofani and stopped.

"Gistofani, huh. Are you Italian?" Dmitry asked.

"Yeah. My father is Sicilian," Gistofani replied proudly. He stuck his chest out a little.

"What are you doing in Moscow, *Gistofani the Sicilian?*"

"My family has been here since Mussolini," he explained.

Dmitry turned to Ivan and hit him on the chest. "Get rid of him. We don't deal with Italians?"

The crew laughed thinking that Dmitry was kidding, but he was not. He turned back around with a scowl on his face at the very hesitation of his orders. He looked Ivan in the eye. "Get rid of him, Ivan. Or I will."

The small group of boys quieted.

Not looking back, Dmitry headed up the stairs to their old apartment and let the raggedy glass door rattle behind him.

"Welcome home, *dickhead*," Ivan said, turning around disgusted.

***

The stench from inside his mother's apartment building made Dmitry sick. He had seen better upkeep in prison. Every entryway was lined with urine, trash and rodents. Stepping over the small messes and passing the doors of loud arguing families, he made his way to his old apartment. He swung the door open, unsure of who was inside. Ducking into the small place, he kicked a bag of garbage out of his way and closed the door behind him. *Disgusting.*

Over the years, trapped in prison with animals, he had become accustomed to scum, but he never expected to find his old place ruined worse than the grimmest cell.

This apartment was the only thing that connected him to his mother, and because of that, he had worked very hard to keep it clean for he and his brother. Now, it too had been destroyed like everything in their lives.

Graffiti decorated the walls, beer cans and drugs covered the tables, dirty clothes and food were all over the floors, and the black and white television blasted in the corner.

Dmitry dropped his small backpack in the only clean corner he could find and immediately began to clean. *What did he expect from a 15-year-old kid left alone since he was 12?* Ivan was less than responsible. It was evident by the appearance of this apartment, but at least his brother had found a way to keep the place.

Pulling the windows up, he allowed fresh air to come rushing into the dark place and replace the repugnant odors that gagged him.   He sat on the window seal and eyed a small pile of used condoms in the corner. He shied away. *There was no way in hell he would clean that up.*

Opening a trash bag on the floor, he felt the contents in his stomach leap to his mouth. Old blood? He pulled the bag to the window to illuminate it and found a dead cat inside. How long had it been there? Closing the bag back up tightly, he looked around for a garbage can.

Ivan came through the door shortly after. He was alone now, sensing that his brother would want to talk to him private.

Ignoring the mess, he ducked into the little apartment and sat down on top of papers and bags in the chair in the corner. He looked at Dmitry, who was now bigger than before *if it were possible*, and rolled his eyes.

"Gistofani is my friend," he lamented.

Dmitry did not look up. "He's Italian. If he wants to be a part of a family, he should find his own."   He grunted as he cleaned.

"Why?   He's loyal.   Didn't you say that mattered most?" Ivan sat on the edge of his seat.

Dmitry was bent over behind the dirty couch picking up cups. He threw them in the garbage bag and looked over at his whining brother. "I was wrong. It's important, but it's not the most important thing, Ivan."

"Then what is?" Ivan's voice lowered.

"Brotherhood. Blood. *We* are most important. It doesn't work if we don't trust each other, *brat.*"

The room was silent except for Dmitry's busy hands. Ivan sat back in his seat watching his brother clean. He looked up at the stained ceiling and sighed.

"Help me clean this shit up. I don't have much time. We can talk about your little boyfriend later," Dmitry ordered. "And don't pout around me. It's irritating."

"I don't pout." Ivan rolled his eyes again. Now he was curious. "Time for what? What's going on?"

"The boss is coming over. I don't want him to see this place like this."

"The boss is coming here?" Ivan stood up. "Really?"

"*Da*. And don't go telling anyone alright...not even your little crew. He'll be here in one hour. And I don't want him to think that we are..." he looked around the apartment. "...what we are," he finally said, standing up off his knees. The garbage bag was still tucked tightly in his hand.

"You've grown a lot," Ivan said amazed. "How tall are you now?"

"The prison guard said seven feet. I think I'm a shy bit under it."

"Seven feet?"

Dmitry shook his head. "I can't find shit that fits me."

"I can't either." Ivan pointed at his pants that came way above his ankles. "No shirts, no pants, barely shoes. I stole some yesterday that give me a little more toe room," he said, wiggling his feet in his worn out boots.

"Soon, we won't have to just get by anymore." Dmitry sat down on the dirty couch across from his brother. "I put away the money I had before I got thrown in prison. I'm going to go and get it tonight. And the crew has been collecting for me since I went in, so I'll collect on that, too."

"So how much do we have?" Ivan asked intrigued. "A million dollars?" Ivan's eyes grew with anticipation. There was so much he wanted. New shoes. New underwear. A new place that didn't stink of urine and blood.

Dmitry scoffed at the idea of a million dollars, but even as he thought about it, he knew that it was only shortly out of reach. "No, not a million, Ivan." He watched his brother's shoulder's drop. "But," he put up his finger. "Very soon, if things go well, we will make our first million." Dmitry tapped Ivan on his back. "So get up off your ass, *brat*. And help me clean this place up."

They both smiled as they looked in each other's eyes. Ivan knew his brother was not a liar and had never promised more than he could deliver.

***

Dmitry looked out the window and waited for his boss to arrive. Peering down into the dirty streets, he wondered if life would have been better if he had chosen to be a regular person. He saw the men who passed his apartment building below - going from one job to the other, barely making their bills, filled with hopelessness. These were also the same men who never had to hide their faces or their hands, never had to worry about getting to close to someone or breaking the code that he so desired to live up to.

It must be easy for them, he thought to himself as he turned away from the window, *to be so weak*. He had made a choice long ago. He was either going to be a regular person or be the man he had been molded into - a young Vor with the potential to lead many. Proudly, he had chosen the Vor.

Many men would have killed to be in Dmitry's position, but only a few knew what such a title took. When he was thirteen, he was already over six feet tall and starving.

With his mother dead, the weight of raising Ivan rested heavily upon his shoulders. During that time, most of his *providing* consisted of stealing, taking charity and doing ungodly acts with older women. So, he started to work for a *John* of his mother's, who came curiously around to check on the boys after her death. The man happened to be a captain of the elite Vory v Zakone.

Kirill Derevenko was a very powerful young man - short in stature, missing a front tooth, clean-shaven head, lean and tattooed – and he had an instant appreciation for Dmitry's size. The first thing Kirill had done was offer Dmitry a job collecting money on past-due debt for him in his territory.

Once Dmitry had mastered not giving into men because they were older than he was and had suffered a few serious ass kickings for not being able to size up his opponents, he was given a more responsible job of having runners and collectors that reported to him.

By age 15, Dmitry was sleeping with a number of women, using them for their resources, and he was running the entire northeast quadrant of his boss's territory. He did so with an iron fist. His cruelty was unheard of and unnatural, which was why he had acquired the name *the butcher*. Moreover, it was why he had ended up in prison. He went from running a quadrant to assassinating drug bosses in only two years of knowing his mentor.

Now that Dmitry was out, he had been giving an even harder task. Since Dmitry had been away, Krill had made a very nasty enemy, Sacha Karpenko, who was rumored to be moving in on Kirill's territory all over Moscow.

To send a message to the outsider, Kirill had decided to send his blond butcher to visit the man in his high-rise apartment. Everyone knew that Dmitry was in jail. Everyone had heard what he and his brother had done to the last boss, Ukrainian drug lord Hamel Stegnof, but no one would be expecting what would happen tonight.

Word would get around that the blond butcher was released for the sole purpose of gruesomely killing Sacha, and he done so at the request of his boss, Kirill, who was so powerful that he could reach into jail and extract the most horrid of assassins whenever he liked. Men of his ilk only responded to that kind of brazen territorial aggression.

Ivan opened the front door of their apartment and stuck his head inside, interrupting his brother in deep thought. With a bit of a grin on his scrubby face, he looked around the now cleaned little apartment. "Kirill is downstairs. He's on his way up with his men. It's quite a few of them."

"Good. See that he gets up here without any trouble," Dmitry ordered. When the door closed, he straightened his clothes and sat down on the couch, awaiting the man who had forever changed his destiny.

A few short minutes later, the door opened and Kirill strode in with a big smile on his face wearing a pair of jeans, a turtleneck and a black leather coat. With arms opened, he motioned for Dmitry to hug him. Dmitry stood up, even taller since the last time.

"Shit, Dmitry, look at you. You grew another fucking foot," Kirill said astonished. One of his bodyguards helped him with his jacket.

"Almost a foot," Dmitry answered. "How have you been, boss?"

"Fucking wonderful," Kirill said, looking around. "Is there some place that I can sit in here that doesn't look like someone took a dump on it?" He rubbed his hands together. "It's freezing in here, *brat*. Don't you have heat?"

Dmitry looked around. The answer to both of Kirill's questions was no.

Kirill shook his head and waved. "Never mind it. I'll make this short." He stood in the center of the room on a shabby rug. "It happens tonight. Are you ready?"

"*Da*," Dmitry answered. "Ivan and I will do it as agreed."

"How you plan to get into his apartment?"

"We don't have some crazy plan. We're walking in and walking out."

Kirill sucked his teeth, then turned and grinned at his men. "*He's going to walk in and out*, eh?" he mocked. No one could tell if he was pleased or displeased by Dmitry's explanation. He looked back at Dmitry and frowned. *He pulled him out of jail for this?*

Dmitry instantly picked up on Kirill 's displeasure. Sitting back down, he placed his elbows on his knees and crossed his hands. "Tonight at ten o'clock, we go through the service elevators of his building up to his floor. No one will expect us. Since he is the only one who lives on the floor, we oozy the place down first, open the doors to his home, spray the rooms down again, then check the bodies. After that, we walk out. It's not sexy, but it works. I don't have a lot of time, and I don't have a lot of resources. If you want some elaborate plan, you'll have to give me more of both. If you want him dead tonight, then let me fucking kill him."

The room was silent except for the sounds that filtered in through the open window. The men behind Kirill looked over at each other and smirked.

With his hands still clasped, Kirill raised his brow and smiled. "Okay. Okay." He turned to his men and waved for his bodyguards to set down the large duffle bags that they held under their arms. "This is your package. Everything that you need, and..." he bent down and opened the bag to retrieve a wad of cash that he fanned in his hand, "a little more for the work."

Dmitry took the money but did not count it. "*Spasiba*."

"And you don't have any problems with killing this guy at home?"

"No."

"There might be family there."

"I don't care."

Kirill was convinced. Dmitry was a hard-core murderer now. And with him a foot taller, a lot deadlier and less respectful of his superiors, it was best to get him out of his hair. Reaching into his pants pocket, he pulled out number on a piece of paper. "Call this when it's done and shortly after, I'll have you on a plane out of Moscow headed to London."

That was all that Dmitry wanted to hear. Killing this new guy would be worth two plane tickets to London. He had plans for he and his brother, and they didn't include running Kirill's territory for the rest of his life.

Chapter Three

Dmitry had been in prison for three years, and he did not plan to spend more than one unnecessary minute locked inside of their little apartment, unless he was forced. Getting dressed in a pair of jeans that was left in the duffle bag for him by Kirill, he looked in the mirror and tried to see what his entire body looked like.

Everyone automatically thought that being nearly seven feet tall was such a wonderful thing, but he would only ask that they try living in his shoes for one day. No mirror gave him a clear view of his body. No room seemed to big enough for him to spread out in and get dressed. No chair was comfortable. And his back often hurt. Especially now, while he was bent over in the small, filthy bathroom trying to get ready.

Ivan walked to the door and stuck his head in, looking relieved that he was not the only one who shared in the torment of being big. He threw his brother a damp hand towel that was hanging on the rack as Dmitry looked around the bathroom with soap on his face.

"Where are you going?" Ivan asked.

"To see Alexandria," Dmitry answered.

"That was three years ago. Haven't you forgotten about her yet?"

"No. Should I?"

Ivan had a devious smile on his face. "Maybe you should. But if you haven't, you still might want to shave that shit off your face before you go. You look like a grizzly bear."

Dmitry wiped his face and carefully folded the towel. "I'll shave it after tonight."

"To make you more discreet?" Ivan smirked. "What is discreet about a man your size, beard or not?"

"Good point," Dmitry said, looking around the bathroom for a razor. "What do you shave with around here?"

"There is a razor in the drawer." Ivan walked over and opened the small wooden compartment. Pulling out an old razor, he passed it to Dmitry.

Dmitry took it and snarled. *Gross.* Grabbing the alcohol, he poured it over the razor and bent down into the mirror.

"Fuck you. It's the best that I could do," Ivan said offended.

Dmitry looked up in the mirror at his brother's reflection. *"Spasiba,"* he said finally.

After cleaning his face and putting on clothes that actually fit *somewhat*, Dmitry headed out into the cold night air down through the back of his apartment complex.

The snow had begun to fall again, covering his wide shoulders. He shivered a little, holding his wool coat to his chest as he made his way a few buildings down from his own.

"Dmitry is that you?" a girl asked, sitting on the step as he passed.

"Da," he answered. Turning around, he looked down to see Alexandria's sister, Angelina. She had grown up a lot. She almost looked grown. With her blond hair pulled into a ponytail and her small lips smeared with red lipstick, she stood up and hugged him.

"I didn't know that you were out," she said, looking up into his pale face.

"I just got out. I won't be here long. So, I wanted to stop and see Alexandria. Is she here?"

"No, she's over at Nicolai's house." Her face changed in shock. *Did he not know?*

"Nicolai who?" He stepped down from the door and held on to the wrought-iron banister.

"Baranski," she answered. "He's her fiancé." Angelina's face was solemn. She always liked Dmitry and would have preferred her big sister to date him instead, but they have been torn away from each other after the murders.

Dmitry gave her a clever smile. He bent down to her and moved the lonely strand of hair from her face. "Why don't you tell me where he lives, and I can go and visit them." His voice was soft, unlike his eyes that spoke venom.

Angelina swallowed hard. Everyone knew how territorial Dmitry was over Alexandria. She doubted much had changed while he was away in prison. When they were together, he had treated her sister like a queen, promised her a new life. Then he had gone away, and Alexandria had fallen apart.

"Are you going to start trouble?" she asked in a hushed voice. "Alexandria wouldn't want any trouble."

"No, I'm leaving tomorrow, *like I said*. And I just want to see her."

Angelina could feel the heat coming from his body. He was fire hot with anger, burning red in his face. She sighed and then pointed north. "He's in building 14-B, Unit 9." She instantly wished that she could have taken her words back, because without even saying goodbye, he jetted back down the stairs and into the dark night.

Dmitry walked fast. The snow beneath him hiked up under his boots as he made long, violent strides through the buildings. He reached building 14-B within minutes. Three men were sitting on the stairs sharing a bottle of vodka and laughing as he approached. They looked up stunned by his presence.

"It's the butcher," the one man whispered as Dmitry entered the apartment building. The door clanging behind him.

"I thought that he was in prison," said another.

"How can he be in prison when he is here?" the third asked as he turned to look at Dmitry's body disappear behind the doors.

Dmitry did not know what he would say, how he would come to explain why he was at this man's doorstep, but he couldn't bare not to see her.

Taking a deep breath, he balled his fist and gently tapped the door. He put his ear to the door and heard voices raised and a television playing. Hitting the door harder, he turned the doorknob. Locked.

Moments later, the door flung open and a short young man with dark brown hair appeared in a dirty brown sweatshirt and red fleece pants.

Dmitry looked him up and down and slipped his hands in his pockets to prevent himself from reaching out and choking the man.

"What do you want?" the man asked, marveling at the size of Dmitry.

"Are you Nicolai?" Dmitry smiled.

"*Da*, who wants to know?"

"I need to see *your* Alexandria for just a minute. I'm an old friend," Dmitry explained. "Is she here?"

The man's eyes narrowed. "No, she's not."

"Are you sure?" Dmitry asked. He could feel his heart rate accelerate.

"What the fuck did I say, you big bastard? She's not here."

When Dmitry first knocked on the door, he heard a woman's voice. "Are you here alone?" he asked, looking down the hallway that he had just come from.

"Yes," the man said as he stepped back to close the door. "Now, fuck off."

As the man prepared to close the door, Dmitry put his steel toe boot in the door and blocked it from closing. Then he pushed the door open and at the same time, knocked the little man down.

Curiously, he turned the corner to see a woman standing in the corner with her hand over her mouth. As Dmitry walked in the dark room, he finally crossed the path of light and it shone on his face.

"Dmitry is that you?" the woman asked.

"Alexandria?" Dmitry responded.

The woman ran her hand over the light switch and illuminated the shabby room. It was Dmitry. She put her hand over her mouth as she let out a whimper in disbelief.

Tall, muscular and stealthy, the giant before her appeared like a dark angel. Dmitry's crystal blue eyes were illuminated by the dim lights around them, causing them sparkled liked precious diamonds. His perfect nose, high cheek bones, chiseled jaw clenched tight, full lips pursed and menacing stare reminded her of what she had missed for the long years he had been away.

He didn't blink. His gaze was fixed on her. Breath slow and easy, he swallowed hard and his thick neck moved under the pressure of his tension.

Shocked that she had a black eye, Dmitry paused and turned around to look at the man who had finally stood up behind him in a daze with a bloody mouth and nose.

"Is that *your* handy work?" Dmitry asked in a deep, reverberating baritone. His shadow covering the small man as he cowered.

The man backed up in the corner. "Look, if you want our valuables, all we have is a shitty television," he said, pointing towards the small floor model in the corner.

Dmitry kept his eyes on the man. "Answer me, you little weak fuck. Is that," he pointed towards Alexandria, "*your* handy work?"

The man looked over at Alexandria. "She fell," the man lied. "She's clumsy as shit."

Dmitry spat on the floor. He reached out and picked the man up by his neck in one swoop. "I'm going to snap your neck into and piss on your remains."

"Dmitry!" Alexandria called out. "Don't!" She ran towards him.

"Who are you?" the man asked, scared to death.

"The butcher," Dmitry answered with a devious smile on his face. "Want to see *my* handy work?" He pulled a long, sharp knife from his back pocket and raised it.

The man pissed down his leg at the sight of the giant, and the urine leaked down to the floor beneath his dangling body. Shaking, he realized that the man, whom he had heard would be in jail for twenty or more years, was now in his living room with a raised weapon to him.

"Dmitry," Alexandria said, putting her hand on Dmitry's lower back.

He turned around to look at Alexandria but did not lower his weapon or the man.

"He's not worth it," she begged in a calm voice. She shook her head, gazing up at him with red, teary eyes.

"No, I'm not worth it," the weak man chimed in, holding on with both hands to Dmitry's tight grip. "Spare me, butcher. Let me live."

Dmitry was torn. He wanted to tear the man's throat out, and yet the woman whom he felt the need to avenge begged for the man's protection. He finally lowered his weapon and threw the man back in the corner.

"You're coming with me," he said, grabbing Alexandria and pulling her to the front door.

She quickly grabbed her coat from the chair and threw it on as she walked out of the door in front of him.

Abruptly, Dmitry stopped at the entrance and turned towards the man still in the corner. "And I'll be back for you later," he said smiling as he slammed the door behind him.

***

Alexandria walked through the snow silently. Still in shock, she could not believe her eyes. Dmitry Medlov had shown up at her boyfriend's apartment to save her.

She was suffering one of Nicolai's many beatings that he handed out when he was drunk. It never happened before they were engaged, but shortly after she had said *yes*, the violence flooded their relationship. He would always apologize, always try to make up for what he had done, but she inwardly knew that if she stayed around long enough, he'd end up being just like her father – a wife beater.

Shivering, even with her coat on, she felt Dmitry's arm on her shoulders. He was too tall to bend down to her, but he guarded her as they walked.

When they got back to the main street, she looked up at him.

"Where are we going?" she asked.

Dmitry raised his finger to silence her. "Be right back," he said, walking off and leaving her on the corner.

She stood confused as she waited. The gripping winds blew past her and chilled her fair skin. Wondering where he'd gone, she finally saw a truck pull up. Dmitry reached over, pulled open the door and smiled.

"Get in," he ordered.

"Is this your truck?" she asked as she stepped inside and closed the door.

Dmitry smiled. "For tonight it is."

Looking down at the steering column, she noticed that the ignition had been torn out. Typical *Dmitry*, she thought as she put her head back on the chair. Dmitry turned on the heat and turned down the radio. Sighing, he looked over at her curled up in her jacket.

"How have you been?" he asked.

"How do I look?" she turned and put her knee on the seat. "You've gotten even taller."

"*Da*, about a foot."

He turned left and avoided the police as he turned onto a dark road. He was growing tired of that being the only observation people made when they saw him. *Yes*, he was seven feet tall. *Maybe he should get a shirt that stated the obvious.* No one had noticed, however, that while he was in prison he had gained new tattoos indicating his promotion in the ranks of the Vory.

"Where are you taking me?" she asked, knowing he was contemplating something very hard.

"To a hotel."

"You are presumptuous," she scoffed.

"Should I not be?" he looked over at her. "If I recall, I was interrupted in the middle of something the last time that we were together." He looked down in between her legs.

Alexandria did not speak. Instead, she cracked a naughty little grin and turned back in her seat.

The money Kirill had given Dmitry could not have come at a better time. He got them a hotel room downtown and escorted Alexandria up the elevator. The couple that got on after them looked up at Dmitry with bright, unbelieving eyes. He could read their thoughts without trying.

"Seven feet tall," he answered the woman's bright eyes. "And no, I'm not an athlete," he said, clenching his jaw. He looked down at Alexandria and smiled. She smiled back.

The man beside his girlfriend pinched her as he gazed over at Dmitry's arm. He recognized the man's elaborate tattoos as Vory markings. It was best to leave the tall man alone before they ran into trouble. As the elevator doors opened, the man practically pulled his girlfriend off the elevator. Her eyes were still locked on Dmitry.

"Do you always have that kind of effect on women?" Alexandria asked.

"Only the straight ones," he answered.

Dmitry relaxed and pulled Alexandria in front of him. Moving her long hair out of her face, he looked into her bruised eyes. It had been three years since he had seen her. He had been snatched from her embrace in the middle of the night by cops.

To impress her one last time, he had fought hard, but it had not been hard enough for five detectives. They beat him badly, hog-tied him and drug him out of the apartment complex. Now, he had her in his arms again, and if possible, she was even more beautiful, even battered.

Alexandria didn't wear makeup for two reasons. She couldn't afford it, and she didn't need it. Bare faced, blue-eyed and angelic, she looked up at him and put her face on his lower abdomen. Just to see him was a blessing. How she had missed him. How she had wondered if he ever thought of her.

"It's been too long," she said softly. "Have you come for good?"

Dmitry ran his hand through her long, blond locks and sighed. "No."

She batted her eyes. *Did he just say no?* "I don't understand?"

"I'm leaving tonight," he said pained.

"Then why did you come and get me?" She pulled away. "Why did you even bother me?" Her voice rose. "Why?!"

The elevator opened.

Dmitry looked at the opened door and looked at her. "I missed you."

"Missed me?"

The elevator closed.

Dmitry hit the stop button on the elevator and paused it so that it would not move.

"You were up there getting your ass kicked by a man who is not big as one of my arms, and yet you argue with me because I came to collect you?" He shook his head astonished.

"*Da*, collect me for a night just to return me in the morning," she answered. "You can't just rent me out, you know." Her eyes quickly shifted from side to side.

She clenched her little jaw and breathed hard out of her small nostrils.

"You never have to go back to him," Dmitry promised. "I'm out now, Alexandria. You know that I'll take care of you, no matter where I am."

"That's not why I want you, Dmitry."

"I know."

Dmitry hit a button, and the elevator opened again on their floor. Taking her hand, he ducked out of the small contraption and led her to their room.

He didn't have much time before he had to go and take care of *that other thing*, but every moment that he had, he wanted to spend it with Alexandria.

Alexandria was three years older than Dmitry when she met him. He was fourteen, and she was seventeen. First, she had had many reservations about liking a boy so much younger than her, but he was more mature than many of the men she had met. She found it odd then that he knew so much about sex and about life in general, but she enjoyed his company and was fascinated by him.

Now, he was back and if only for one night, she thought it worth it to remember what it was like to be touched by Dmitry.

He opened the hotel room door for her and followed her in. Ducking into the room, he closed the door and leaned against it. She turned and looked up at him. She didn't even know how to make love to a man as tall as he was. *Would it even be possible?* He walked over to her and reached down to pick her up. Standing up on top of the mattress, she came to his neck. Pulling him closer, she kissed his full, warm lips, savoring the taste of a lost love. He gripped her in his needy embrace happy now that he had not slept with the old woman from the night before.

Alexandria whimpered. *More. More.* Her body begged out to him. She helped him take off his coat and then pulled at his thermal shirt.

As the shirt came up above his neck, she saw the many tattoos that covered his muscular body and the scars from the many fights in prison and before. She ran her fingers across them, astonished by the possibility of what he had done to get them.

"Is this why we can't be together?" she asked.

Dmitry looked down at his chest and arms, covered in blue ink. No one would ever know how much the markings meant to him. He looked back up at her and realized that he didn't have enough time to explain himself, so he opted not to explain at all. Instead, he pulled her coat off and pulled up her shirt. With the twist of his fingers behind her back, her bra dropped in between them.

Dmitry licked his lips. She looked at him as he slowly advanced towards the rigid, aching nipples that called out to him. His large mouth covered her little breasts, and she let out an exhilarating moan. Lapping her skin, she watched his thick, pink tongue circle her over and over until weak from ecstasy, she bent into his body.

Dmitry attacked then. He pulled down her pants and ripped her panties. There was something very sexy to him about the act. He liked to think of the tearing of the intimate garments as a sign that once he was finished with a woman, there would be no going back.

She smiled and bit her lip as she went for his pants as well. Pulling at his belt buckle, she hungrily pulled his pants down to discover that he wasn't wearing underwear. His erection prodded in her face, pink and pulsing with many thick veins.

He quickly grabbed the back of her head and pulled her into it. He wanted her to finish what the old woman had started. On her knees in the bed, Alexandria was at just the right height. She slipped the tip of his long penis in her mouth.

Dmitry closed his eyes and smiled. "Yes," he whispered. "Kiss it for me. Suck it."

Alexandria did so obediently. She took him into her mouth as far as she could, nearly choking. With both hands around his shaft, she looked up at him and giggled. "How much did you miss me?" she asked as she slipped one of her hands in between her legs.

"Enough," Dmitry said picking her up.

This was the complicated part for Dmitry. He hadn't made love at seven feet tall yet. He was curious to see how they would figure it out, but Alexandria seemed to already know. As he sat on the bed, she quickly mounted him, hovering over his towering erection as she held herself up on her feet.

"Are you on the pill?" Dmitry asked.

"No. Do you have a condom?"

"No."

Dmitry pulled her into his kiss and pushed her down on his erection. He was not about to go and get a condom. Their time was slowly dwindling down.

Alexandria gasped as she felt him inside her. Only half way in, she held herself up to try to work down his penis. But Dmitry was anxious. Placing his hands on her shoulders, he pushed her down on top of him and moaned.

It was better than sweet. His mouth watered with excitement. He pushed inside of her slowly and reached back to grab a hold of the mattress. It was then that he saw that Alexandria was nearly paralyzed. Her mouth was parted, but he couldn't tell if it was in rapture or pain.

"Are you alright?" he asked.

"Oh..." she panted. "You're so big."

He smiled. "I had a growth spurt *all over*." He pushed again. "Does it hurt?"

She moved slowly. "It hurts and it feels good."

"Should I stop?"

"No," she said, biting her lip. "Don't you dare."

Dmitry was so turned on by the naked woman and being deprived of sex until he felt a familiar apex approaching. He fought it. *Not yet*. He could feel the sweat on his forehead. *Not yet*, he chided himself. *He should have masturbated before he came to get her. How could he have forgotten?*

Alexandria was enthralled. Grabbing her aching breasts, she rotated her lips on top of him finally enjoying his over-gracious sex.

Not yet, Dmitry thought again.

She bucked on top of him, moaning with her eyes closed. The wetness from her body slid down on his thighs. She screamed out loud and bucked harder against him.

Not...not...

He tried to pull her off of him, but he was too long, and it was too quick. Instead, he pulled her closer to him and emptied himself into her. Moving slowly, he jerked and bit his lip. *Dammit*, maybe she would never know if he just kept going.

***

Ivan and his crew walked down the alleyway banging against the doors and singing. It was their friend's last night in Moscow, and they had plans to celebrate. They were going to a whorehouse not far from the apartment complex for a little sex and a lot of drugs.

"I get the heavy one," Yani said, taking a swig of his vodka.

"You can have that fat bitch," Ivan laughed. "She's as big as a house. Why do you like that, *brat*? When she sits on you, you disappear."

Yani smiled. "I know. It feels amazing."

Gistofani walked quietly. The crew was about to break up. And he would be left alone again with no one. Before he had been an outcast, but Ivan had given him something to belong to. He went from being a nerd to gangster in months.

"What's the matter?" Ivan asked Gistofani.

"Your brother doesn't think I should be here," Gistofani answered. "He'd probably kick my ass if he knew."

Ivan laughed. "He wouldn't kick your ass. He'd kick *all* of our asses." He hit the wall with his bat.

"Dmitry's weird that way. Always giving everyone orders."

"Just because I'm Italian?" Gistofani asked.

"Guess so," Ivan answered. "But fuck him for now. He's gone to see his old girlfriend, and I doubt that he'll make it back for a few hours. First, he's going to have to beat her fiancé's ass, and then he has to screw her. So, let's get laid and high in the mean time."

"Sounds good to me," Yani chimed in. "I want to see Helga."

"Ugh," Ivan shook his head. "She even has a horrible name."

"I think her name is beautiful."

"You're a *John*, dumbass. You're supposed to think everything she does is beautiful. Why else would you pay her to sit on your face?"

Yani instantly thought of Ivan's mother. Everyone knew what she had done for a living; many of their fathers had employed her. He often wondered how that affected Ivan, if that was why he was so crazy. Ivan did the oddest things. He would cut himself for no reason, kill animals, beat the crap out of people, and he never showed remorse.   Once, he had heard his brother, Stepan, say that Ivan had a mental problem, that he was a psychopath. But Yani had shrugged it off. *What did his brother know?*

Chapter Four

Alexandria slept tranquilly wrapped in the hotel bed-covers and smiling. Dmitry stood over her fully dressed and torn. He wanted to leave her money, but he knew that he would never see her again and was worried that she might misinterpret his intentions. He didn't want her to think that he thought she was a whore. But he knew that he had just torn her out of her fiancé's hands for one night of pleasure.

It became apparent what he had to do. He must get her set up as a final request to Kirill and go and take care of *two things* instead of one. Pulling on his coat, he quietly crept out of the room and headed out in the night.

The snow covered the streets by the time that he left. Driving quietly through downtown, he listened to the radio and thought of what he was leaving behind.

He wished that he could go back and get her. That he could save her somehow. But he had taken an oath. He had a code to fulfill, and no Vor would take him serious in London if he showed up with a *girlfriend*.

Plus, he had so much to do with Ivan. His immaturity was evident and if it were possible, he had some more raising the boy to do.

Pulling up to his apartment complex, he slipped on his coat and walked through the buildings until he reached *fourteen*.

The men who were sitting on the steps before were now out at an old barrel that they had lit a fire inside, drinking and talking.

"Hey butcher!" one of them screamed across the yard.

Dmitry raised his hand.

"I told you it was him," the man said to the other men around the fire.

Quietly, Dmitry made his way up to Nicolai's apartment. He looked up and down the hallways to make sure that no one was out, then pulled out his knife and pried the door lock. With a push against it, the door opened.

Nicolai stood up stunned from his couch. He never thought the man would show back up tonight. He figured he'd have at least until tomorrow to find a new place to stay.

Dmitry walked inside and took off his coat.

"Now back to what I saying," Dmitry said, sucking his teeth. "Want to see *my* handy work?"

***

Ivan looked around the small room where his friends had crashed and felt mildly annoyed. *Why was he leaving his friends again? Why was it always about Dmitry? Why did his life have to change just because Dmitry said so?* He groaned and got up from the bed where the girl beside him lay.

"Where are you going, man?" Yani asked, peering over Helga's heavy, naked body. He was still naked and uncovered.

Ivan pulled up his pants and slipped on his coat. He wasn't good with goodbyes, and Dmitry had told him that after they left, he would probably never see Yani again, unless Stepan sent him to London.

"Yeah, where are you going?" Gistofani asked.

Ivan slipped on his boots and grabbed his wallet. He walked to the door, opened it and looked back at his friends. They both sat up confused about Ivan's newest, crazy mood swing. The smell of marijuana was thick in the air.

"Fuck you faggots," he said as he slammed the door behind him.

With tears in his eyes, he walked out of the dirty apartment complex into the snowy night, headed back to his apartment. Dmitry would be home soon. He didn't have much time to waste.

***

When Ivan got to the apartment, Dmitry was in the bathroom. He walked to the door and stuck his head inside. Dmitry looked up from wiping blood from his hands and rolled his eyes at Ivan.

"Where were you?" Dmitry asked.

"Did you kill Alexandria for being a cheating bitch?" he asked without the slightest expression.

"So you knew that she was engaged?" Dmitry turned off the faucet.

"Of course, I knew." Ivan yawned. "What time do we leave?"

"I have to go over some things with you first." Dmitry pulled off his bloody shirt and threw it in the corner. "I'm going to take a shower. Change clothes, because you stink of weed and put me on some tea."

"You know, I'm not your fucking bitch, Dmitry!" Ivan exclaimed. "You can't just order me around!"

Dmitry turned to him and sighed. "I don't have time for your tantrums. Do what I told you to do, or I'll kick your ass and make you do it," he said in a low, calm voice.

"*Da*, I'd like to see that." Ivan stuck his chest out and gritted his teeth.

Dmitry pulled the knife from his pocket and put it to Ivan's throat before Ivan could speak another word. He lowered his voice more and wiped the curly strands of hair from his little brother's face. "Now's not the time to grow a pair, Ivan. Get ready so that we can go." He stepped back and motioned towards the door.

Quietly, Ivan walked away.

***

With a teacup in his hand, Dmitry sat across from his brother in their living room and went over their plan. Ivan had moved past his anger and was now focused on killing. He was happy to hear that he would have a chance to let go of some of his frustration. And he could finally show his brother what type of man he really was.

"What do we do first?" Dmitry asked.

"Service entrance. Make sure that we don't walk in front of visible cameras."

"Where do you keep your guns?"

"Under the coat."

"What do you do when we arrive on his floor?"

"Spray the walls and doors first with the oozy, then kick the door in."

"Who are we after?"

"Fat ass Sacha. Don't kill anyone that we don't have to – especially women and children."

"What do we do to Sacha?"

"Shoot him and cut his throat."

"How much time do we have?"

"Five to seven minutes."

"What do we do with the guns when we finish?"

"Drop them. They belong to another organization. They will link the murders to them."

"What do you do after you're finish?"

"Take the stairs back down. I'll be winded, but I'll be less apt to get caught."

"What do you need to have on your hands?"

"Gloves..." Ivan shook his head. "Why are we sparing women and children again?"

Dmitry sighed. "Is it not obvious?"

Ivan shook his head. "No. We shouldn't leave witnesses."

Dmitry shook his head. "We're headed to London. We're already criminals. They won't review the tapes before we get out of Moscow. Don't kill them. It's bad Karma."

"I don't believe in religion." Ivan stood and grabbed one of the guns on the table.

"Do you know how to shoot one of those things?" Dmitry asked.

"*Da da, brat,*" Ivan assured.

***

It seemed as if everything was going in slow motion when they pulled up to Sacha's high-rise condo in downtown Moscow. Guns under their coats, Dmitry and Ivan parked behind a row of dumpsters and walked right into the back of the apartment complex's entrance, which was left open for them by a soldier in the Vor who lived a few floors below Sacha.

The elevator ride was short. Every few minutes, Dmitry checked his watch and looked over to check the mood of his little brother. It had been a while since they had gone on a hit together, and he wasn't sure if his brother could handle it.

However, Ivan didn't show an ounce of nervousness. Instead, he breathed slowly as if all was right in the world.

When the doors opened, they dropped a steel pole in the door of elevator. Guns cocked, they spread apart and let the bullets fly out of their weapons.

The sound deafened them as they boomed. The rounds ripped into the walls entering into the other side. As the door of Sacha's apartment open, Dmitry was there. He shot a bodyguard in the chest and entered quickly. Ivan was right behind him with his gun pointed.

Strategically, they moved in a circle, shooting the rooms up, but Sacha was nowhere to be found. The two men who sat on the couch dead, fell over on top of each other.

Screams erupted from the back of the large white apartment. Dmitry pointed for Ivan to go to that side while he walked through the hallway leading to the master bedroom.

He dropped a cartridge and reloaded behind the wall. Then, he let the bullets fly again. He shot up each room and checked. There was no one in the bathroom, the bedroom on the side, but as he walked through the bullet-riddled hallway, he heard gurgling.

Kicking the door open, he pointed and shot the room up, hitting Sacha who lay helpless in the corner. Just as he was about to pull out his knife, he heard Ivan's gun go off several times. He hoped that his brother was still alive, but he couldn't focus on that right then. He had to finish this.

He knelt over the man, now lifeless and slit his throat with his knife as he promised Kirill he would do. Blood splattered across Dmitry's face and hands.

He stood up, breathing heavily and looked around the room. He heard a faint whimper in the other corner.

He walked over to see a woman in the corner crying, dressed in a blue silk nightgown.

Putting his gun away, he put his finger over his lips. *Shh.*

"You didn't see anything. You don't know anything. You're just glad to be alive. Say it," he ordered.

The tear-stained woman held her whimpers and looked up at the giant. "I didn't see anything. I don't know anything. I'm just glad to be alive," she repeated, curled up into a ball.

"Good," Dmitry said with his knife still dripping with blood in his hand. "Now, stand up. Do you have any guns on you?"

"No," she cried.

"Do you have any weapons?"

"No," she cried.

"Turn around and count to 100. When you finish, count again. When you finish, count again. Keep counting until the police arrive. Do you understand?"

"Yes," the woman said, turning around. "One. Two. Three...".

He turned and walked out of the room. When he arrived back into the living room, Ivan was standing by the table eating popcorn out of the bowl in front of the bodyguards.

"Who was in there?" Dmitry asked.

"Everyone's dead," Ivan said, digging his large hands back into the bowl.

"Everyone like who?" he asked.

"Everyone like *everyone.*"

Dmitry strode out of the room quickly and went into the back bedroom. He quickly emerged back out and leaned against the hallway entrance.

"You sick fuck," Dmitry gasped.

"No witnesses," Ivan said, walking to door. "We better go. The police will be here soon."

Dmitry rushed Ivan against the door and pinned him up. Picking him up off the ground, he punched him in stomach.

"There were kids in there!" Dmitry exclaimed. "Kids!"

"I didn't know until I shot the room up." Ivan's eyes were ice cold. He doubled over and spat. "Damn, they were my age. Would you have preferred for them to shoot me?"

"What the fuck is wrong with you?" Dmitry asked, looking down at his brother.

"What the fuck is wrong with you?" Ivan snatched away. "We have to go." He stood up and shook off the punch. "It's done."

Dmitry took a deep breath and pushed his brother out of the door. "Go down the stairs," he ordered, holding back vomit.

As promised less than an hour later, Kirill met Dmitry and Ivan at a restaurant on the outskirts of town, not far from the airport. He handed them two plane tickets and a duffle bag of money. They then met up with Dmitry's crew, where he collected the rest of his money. In time to catch the last red eye, the two had changed clothes and were on a plane for London.

Dmitry didn't talk to Ivan once. Instead, he sat quietly thinking about the bloody images he had seen back at Sacha's. He looked over at his brother, resting comfortably on the first-class plane ride and suddenly felt the urge to choke him.

Dmitry had done murder before. But he found that he did not have a taste for it. He tried to make it quick and painless for both he and the unfortunate souls that he had encountered.   He never killed anyone that he didn't think deserved it, and he never killed an innocent for any reason.

But Ivan was different. He had been since they were kids, even before their mother had passed. He had never once seen the boy show remorse unless it was for getting caught.

I should have killed you too, Dmitry thought to himself as he wiped his tired eyes. But the question was *would he*?

Ivan was all that he had in the world, and he knew that he would do anything to protect him no matter how sick he truly was.

Dmitry knew that without a doubt the blame rested with him. He could have taken anyone to the hit. He didn't have to take his brother. He didn't have to expose him to this life, but he did...he had for many years. Now, he had created a monster, incapable of real emotion and deadly. And not only had he created him, but now he was taking him to London. For some reason, he thought of Jack the Ripper.

Feeling for the bag nestled tightly between his legs, he thought of the task that lay before him. There was a group of Vory waiting for him in London, once they landed and a man named Davyd, who was supposed to help him learn the city.

With this money, he planned to start a completely new family, strong enough to last the decades. The only thing that could ruin everything was the 15-year old man resting beside him. He looked over at Ivan and sighed.

The End

Volume Two

Prologue

Prague, Czech Republic

Sitting in his favorite leather recliner, Dmitry Medlov watched his television in the great room and looked through his daughter's graduation pictures. Where had the time gone? It seemed that he had blinked an eye and nearly an entire century had passed him by.

Flipping through pictures of Anya and her friends at her party held at the Hotel de Arc, he stopped and held her image in his hand. Such a beautiful girl. So pure. Her resemblance to his late brother, Ivan, was almost sinful. The plains of her perfect face, the darkness of her eyebrows and lashes, the thick inky mane that reminded him of his wife, Royal, and Ivan, were all reminders of every single choice he had made in his life.

Hearing his name on the History Channel, he grabbed his remote and turned the television up. Pressing the button with his meaty fingers, he put down the picture and kicked his feet up. What new lies would the media tell about him today?

Some nameless reporter had pegged his organized crime family as the most feared and untouchable of the entire free world. The thought made his lip quiver and a smile tugged at his lips, but he quickly repressed it. He could never show his pleasure with his accomplishments for fear of what his younger sons might think.

They were growing boys. Twin angels of his size and stature but with pure hearts like their mother. They kept their heads in books, their minds on girls, their actions within reason. He imagined that he might have done the same if someone had afforded him the opportunities that he had given them.

He heard his son's name and snapped out of his thoughts back to the television. A picture of Anatoly Medlov's distinguished face flashed across the screen. They spoke of his riches, his domination and his wrath. He almost laughed again. He always thought his oldest son was much too forgiving as a Czar. Anatoly's reign was full of kindnesses afforded human demons who should have been assassinated by the very bullets that they purchased.

His wife's voice entered his mind. He could hear her admonishing him. And who are you to judge, you big ape? she would always say. You had better hope Jesus is more merciful when it's time to judge you. She was right. He had slaughtered on Biblical proportions as a young man. Not much was sacred. There was only his desire to make something out of nothing. But the History Channel would never be able to tell that story....

Chapter One

Maybe it was the fog that made Dmitry melancholy, but as he stood in the cemetery shrouded in black, he felt even darker than his macabre surroundings. It was near midnight, and he had arranged to meet with the leader of a local militant group, The Free Right, to coordinate the sale of a large shipment of USSR-made AK-47s. Only the contact was running late.

Perched against a statue of an angel, he looked across the hallowed ground and took a deep, frustrated breath. *How long was he to wait on these people?* Five minutes. Ten at the most? If they didn't show soon, he'd cancel the arrangement all together and make life a living hell for them in the future.

A few feet away, Ivan, his younger brother sat on top of a tomb drinking out of a silver flask and scanning the grounds. Dmitry nodded towards him. And Ivan quickly threw a finger sign in response, flipping his long middle finger at his brother while he wagged his elongated feet against the concrete slab.

Was it really necessary to sit atop the final resting place of a dead person? Did the boy have no respect? Inwardly, Dmitry knew the answer to both questions was no. Ivan was indiscriminately abhorrent, and there was little that could be done about that fact.

A rustle of leaves behind a copse in the far corner near the entrance of the cemetery made both of them turn. It was the petite footsteps of a redhead woman with fiery short locks dressed in green fatigues. She walked quickly over to them, hands in her pockets, her green eyes focused.

Dmitry could tell by her menacing glower that she was the contact. Most people stared at them like they were freaks of nature because of their size, but she simply strode directly to them, determined to push against the violent, cold winds that ripped through the night.

Ivan walked up beside Dmitry, only a few inches shorter than seven-feet tall, and smacked his mouth together. "A midnight snack," he said with a joker-like grin.

"Behave," Dmitry reminded his brother under his breath. "This is our contact not one of your whores."

The woman stopped a few feet from them and darted over towards the shadows. The men followed, looking around as they went to ensure that no one was watching.

Dmitry thought it odd that such a small woman would be so comfortable doing business in the middle of the night with two giants. Without so much as one hesitation in her movements, she quickly pulled a yellow envelope from her jacket and passed it to Dmitry. His large hand engulfed hers.

"Guess there's no need to ask if you're my guys," she said cleverly in an English accent. "Sorry, I'm late. Had a tail," she explained. "Some bloke in a black truck. Was it one of yours?"

"No." Dmitry took the envelope and slipped it inside of his coat. He could feel the thick bulkiness of cash inside. He nodded at Ivan as a signal to go and get the package. His brother did so obediently. Ivan never screwed up a deal, just everything else. He disappeared into the darkness, leaving them alone.

"The key will open the garage that Armand was shown earlier this week. Inside there will be a van for you filled with your shipment. We will guard the garage and the van until you pick it up. After you leave, we carry no responsibility." Dmitry's voice boomed in the silence of the night, even as he tried to speak low.

"We can take it from there," she assured. It was nearly impossible for her to look up at him. Crooking her head, she studied him carefully.

Dmitry barely blinked. Looking back for his brother, he saw Ivan approaching and turned back to the woman. "Any questions?"

"No. We'll pick up the shipment in six hours at the location," she said, reaching out to take the key from Ivan. "It's a pleasure doing business with you gents."

With that, she headed back towards the way that she had come, silently moving through the darkness back into the obscurity of the London streets. Dmitry watched her until her body disappeared then turned to his brother.

"Let's get out of here," he ordered, yawning.

As they headed towards the entrance of the cemetery, six other men - strategically hidden out of sight - came out behind him and followed him and Ivan back out to their cars.

Dmitry's crew was getting larger. It had only been a year since they had left Moscow, but already they had grown from two to ten men. His old boss, Kirill, had coordinated a few meetings that ensured him Vor soldiers from back home, who had also left the mother country to look for more opportunities. In all, the decision to flee Moscow had been a wise one. However, there were still times, like tonight, when he missed the cold, crisp air of the USSR.

Everything he had known had been replaced in the last year. London was an animal unlike anything he had ever seen before. This place was no communist society. Here, the pound spoke loudly, and people were allowed to live. Soldiers didn't monitor the streets. There was no threat of immediate danger or death on site. So polar opposite was their law enforcement until the police in London seemed more like school hall monitors to him than the filthy pigs at home.

In truth, he hardly feared prison. The only reason why he avoided it was because of his troubled little brother. He was certain that if he went back again, Ivan would get even worse. There was certainly something wrong with the boy. He was off. Touched. Troubled. Evil. *Whatever people called it.* Still, he was certain that it was his fault. Ivan had not been raised properly and probably harbored a great deal of resentment against him and his dead mother.

***

The Medlov headquarters was a dingy little ware-house in the middle of Brixton, lined with old cars and tires. The bricked building housed several abandoned apartments that the men used for business and a place to call home. Purchased through a banker with ties to the Vory in the USSR, the warehouse was given to Dmitry in exchange for a few jobs that he and his crew had done to *eliminate* the banker's competition in North London.

Dmitry was a quiet man. He enjoyed the silence of his surroundings in order to help him think, but his crew, minus an older man named Davyd, seemed to always surround themselves with chaos. Below his apartment, lined with leather bound books and piles of papers, there was a constant boom of the radio and men playing instruments. He tried desperately to drown them out, grateful that they were always at his fingertips when he needed them.   But sometimes, the noise flustered him to the point of raising his voice. He rarely did it, but when he did, there was always hell to pay.

Tonight, he chose to hold his tongue and wait. The exchange had already happened, and the pickup was scheduled for four hours from now. He looked at his watch and noted the time. It was already 2:15 a.m., and he had not slept in a day and a half. His tired eyes had dark, heavy bags under them that made him look older than nineteen.   He was due to turn twenty soon. However, considering the life that they lived, there was never a guarantee that he would see the next day.

Standing over his bathroom sink, he ran cold water over his face and grabbed a grimy, black towel from the rack. He ran the towel over the stubble of his dirty-blonde beard and looked in the mirror, trailing over his cheek with his index finger.

"Boss, you have a minute?" a deep voice screamed into his room.

Dmitry put down the towel and grabbed his gun off the counter.   *"Da,"* he answered, walking towards the doorway.

Davyd, his true underboss, came into the bedroom and closed the door. "I spoke with Carmella today. There's going to be a bid next week," he said in a hushed tone.

"Good," Dmitry said, sitting down on the tethered leather chair behind his desk. He put the gun away and grabbed a pen from the drawer.   Quickly, he scribbled something in his notebook.

Davyd watched him for a moment then continued, "Not as good as it could be. McLauren and his men are coming in as well. They have damned good connections to munitions in Ireland. We stand to lose the bid."

"Those Irish pricks can't get half the fire power that we can," Dmitry spouted off as he quickly closed his journal. He looked up and clenched his wide, square jaw. "Kirill has promised me only the best on this bid and for bottom dollar."

Davyd looked down at the ground and shook his head. "Let's hope that he comes through. Last time, you know it didn't go so well." He looked back up at Dmitry, hoping for the right response.

"So what do you suggest? We don't have any other suppliers to get the product. Plus, our allegiance is with Kirill."

"*Your* allegiance is with him. I like him alright, but there are other Vor with a hell of a lot more money. We need to diversify, Dmitry. The world is bigger than the USSR." Davyd sat down on the couch across the room and pulled out a cigar.

"Don't light that in here. It messes up the smell of the place," Dmitry said, turning around in his chair to look out the stained windows over the skyline of Brixton.

"What smell? It reeks of ink and old books in here," he said, putting the cigar away.

"I know," Dmitry answered. "I like it. It smells like knowledge. You know, I never had the chance to get an education," he lamented. "So, I try to gain as much knowledge as I can through all of these books. I read every day, all day. And I don't want my room to smell like cigars as I learn."

"You have more education than those boys in Oxford."

Dmitry frowned in thought. "I'd trade with them any day."

"Well, back to your current life. What are you going to do about your supply chain? We could crash and burn if we only depend on Kirill. No one is going to do business with us if the word gets out that we can't always deliver. We'll be pushed *out* of the London market."

The thought disturbed Dmitry. Closing his eyes, he ran through the scenarios in his head and came to one conclusion. Davyd was right.

"Fine. Find someone here, someone we can depend on with ties to the Vory or that is Vory, and I'll meet with him," Dmitry said, getting up. "I'm going to go and take a run to keep me awake. When I get back, we'll prepare for the pickup."

***

Jogging in Brixton at three in the morning was a tricky thing for most people. They stood the possibility of being mugged or killed. But Dmitry never worried about any of that. He cleared his head with every mile, with every long stride. The blackness of the night wrapped around him and even he, a seven-foot tall man, was swallowed up in its massiveness. All he could hear was his footsteps splashing through water, beating the pavement. As he ran, people moved out of his way, marveled at his height, looked on, but they never bothered him.

The sweat poured from his salty pores as he ran. Taking in the fresh air, he was no longer a killer, a murdering bastard. At that very moment, he was just a guy taking his nightly run. The wind cooled his head as he made it to the outskirts of Brixton.

Stopping at an old warehouse, he wiped the sweat from his brow and leaned against the cool bricks to catch his fleeting breath. He had gone every bit of ten miles, and his heart was pounding out of his chest.

Covering his eyes, he tried to fight the sleep that still haunted him. All he wanted to do was take a nap and rest his aching body, but he knew that if he were to lie down now, he would sleep past the pickup, *which was completely unacceptable.*

As he straightened up to run back to his place, he noticed that he was not alone. A group of men was on the other side of the building talking. When they noticed that he was near them, they stepped out from the darkness.

"Well, well. What do we have here?" one of them said in a Yorkshire accent.

Dmitry stood up and slowed his breath. Locking his eyes on them, he yawned.

"Did you get lost?" the mystery man asked Dmitry.

"No," Dmitry answered without moving. He stilled his feet, digging them down into the ground to fight.

"Well, if you're not lost, then you should know that you have to have certain *permissions* to be around here at this hour, bloke. Brixton ain't no fucking gym."

Dmitry wished for water as his throat constricted. "I don't ask anyone for permission to do shit," he said with his hands gripping the knife in his right jacket pocket.

"Sounds like he's from the USS fucking R," another man taunted. "A filthy commy."

Dmitry counted their number. All together there were four of them. Two stood in the street, one stood at the edge of the building and another stood behind the building but casted a shadow from the street light.

Dmitry didn't respond to the *commy* comment, although it pissed him off. Instead, he looked behind him, ensuring that there weren't more men on his flanks.

"I don't think you want trouble," Dmitry warned as he turned his head back to face them. "I'm just getting my nightly run in. Why don't you just go about your way?"

"Oh, he's priceless," the leader laughed, pulling out his small pistol. "How much money you got on ya' tonight, Mr. Beanstalk?"

Dmitry eyed the gun and gripped the knife tighter. "You get any closer to me and you'll find out."

They all laughed at him and began to circle around. The man hidden behind the building maintained his positioned, serving as a lookout from the other side.

"Think you can take all three of us, pretty boy?" one of the smaller men asked as he walked towards Dmitry.

"I'm sure that I could take all *four* of you," Dmitry said with a smile.

"Sure about that?" the leader asked as his face lit up under the street light.

"Positive," Dmitry assured, pulling his knife from his pocket.

With the flick of his wrist, he released the large blade from his hand and watched it fly through the air, cutting through the wind and land squarely in the leader's chest. Quietly, the man dropped to his knees, gripping the knife and gazing out at Dmitry with a startled look in his dimming eyes. He fell over on his side in the street and then rolled over onto his back.

The small gang stopped suddenly. Looking over at their leader, they all stepped back into the darkness when they saw Dmitry pull a gun from his other jacket pocket. He heard their footsteps as they turned and ran.

"I'll be here, same time, same *fucking* place tomorrow," Dmitry screamed out while they ran away.

Looking around first, Dmitry walked over to the bleeding man, who looked up at him and gurgled his last bloody breaths. Dmitry politely waited for him to finally pass. Then, he put his large foot on the man's chest, bent down and pulled the knife from his wounded chest cavity. He wiped the excess blood on the man's jeans, picked up the gun and put both weapons back into his jacket pockets.

"Told you that I could take you," Dmitry said to the lifeless body. With a chuckle, he turned and started to jog.

At least now, he was awake.

***

When Dmitry returned home, Ivan and his friends had the music blasting *again* and were poorly entertaining a group of women in the common area. He slammed the large double doors behind him and took off his jacket. Everyone looked over at him, curious as to what mood he might be in tonight.

Ivan quickly jumped up and brought him a beer. Lipstick stains covered the young boy's face, and he wore a devious grin. "Where have you been?" he asked, offering a bottle of lager.

"Running. Where do I always go at this hour?" Dmitry looked over at the small gathering and sneered. They all looked away, hoping to become invisible.

Ivan ignored his brother's irritation. "You look flushed. I was hoping that *maybe* you went and got some pussy."

Dmitry waved off the beer and covertly tucked the bloodstained knife and gun in his jacket. Yawning again, he went to the kitchen and grabbed a dirty glass off the counter.

A woman laughed loudly and then whimpered in the background. "That's not the right hole," she protested with a start.

Dmitry rolled his eyes, poured himself a glass of water and leaned against the counter as he watched a large cockroach climb the wall across from him. *Disgusting*, he thought to himself as he grabbed a black plastic bag. Carefully, he put the jacket and weapons inside.

"What are you doing?" Ivan asked, coming into the kitchen to get more beer.
He opened the old refrigerator and grabbed a six-pack.

Dmitry watched him with a grimace on his face. "You're too young to drink so much," he said, tying off the bag. "And it's none of your damned business what I'm doing."

"I'm sixteen!" Ivan exclaimed, closing the refrigerator door with a loud clang. "I'm a grown man."

"You should be in school. You're throwing your life away here."

"You couldn't run this place without me," Ivan said with a smirk on his face.

Dmitry held his tongue. He knew the reality of their existence was quite the opposite.

"I'm just saying that we have enough money now for you to go back to school, *maybe even a private school*. You could change the face of the Vory. We have to be more forward thinking. Education is the key. We can't rule from the outside without knowledge," Dmitry explained in a low, calm voice.

"Save your self-enlightenment, *brat*. I don't want to go to school, okay. I belong *here* with you. You know, you can't always depend on Davyd. He's not me," Ivan said, growing angry. He rolled his eyes. "One day, you'll realize that."

"So that's it? You think Davyd has taken your place?"

"Hasn't he?"

Dmitry threw the plastic bag in the bottom of the garbage can. "No. *But* he doesn't fill my place with whores as soon as I walk out of the door. *And* he thinks ahead. Maybe you should be more proactive, so that I can feel as though *you* can handle more responsibility."

Ivan's brow spiked. "Do you know what your problem is, Dmitry? You don't live. Those women in there aren't *technically* whores. We didn't buy them. They came here voluntarily to hang out with us and *maybe* do a little screwing."

Dmitry stared at him in wonder. "Like I said, *whores*. Discounted whores. Free whores. Paid whores. What's the difference? At the end of the night, they still are whores."

"You really need to lightened up and get laid," Ivan said, walking out of the kitchen. "You're a fucking killjoy."

"Get them out of here before five. I don't want them near the pickup," Dmitry reminded in a loud voice, sure that they could hear him.

"*Da, da*, I'll kick them out by five," Ivan answered. "But not before I screw one first."

The women laughed, adding insult to injury.

***

With the showerhead pointed as far upright as possible, Dmitry cleaned himself in their impossibly compact bathroom. The previous day's grime washed off and rushed into the rusty drain below. Hot water soothed his aches and filled a strange void that had emerged. He always welcomed this part of his day, when he could start anew. It was a reminder that he had another chance to get life right.

After a hot shower and a shave, Dmitry felt like a new man. Resting on his perfectly made, king-sized bed with three pillows under his head, he read *World Literature Since 1945* and drank a cup of herbal tea.

Under the dim lights of his room, he felt at peace for the moment learning about short-story masters like Poe and Hawthorne. *What a life they provided him.* He could sneak away from his reality and dwell in a world designed to bring constant intrigue. Licking his thumb, he turned his page and felt his eyes grow heavy.

Not yet, he reminded himself as he shifted in the bed. It was almost five, almost time for the pickup. Then, he could get some rest. As his eyes flitted, his thoughts raced back to Moscow, back to Alexandria.

He wondered what she was doing at this hour, where she was now that her fiancé was no longer in the land of the living. *He had taken care of that for her.* No man should ever beat a woman, especially one who had been with him. He had hated to leave her resting in the hotel after making love to her. He would have loved to awaken beside her the next day and talk on and on about all that he had missed while in prison. But that had never come to past for him. When he got on the plane that night one year ago to head to London, all contact with her was lost.

As his eyes finally closed, he imagined that she was there. Her petite body curled up beside him, her smooth legs brushing the side of him, her long hair splayed out over his arm. She would look up at him with her perfect, wide blue eyes and pouty mouth to receive the sweetest kiss. And she would tell him that she loved him.

"Alexandria," he said aloud as he drifted off.

Chapter Two

Before Dmitry could get into a deep sleep, his bedroom door flew open, and Ivan barged in with a bottle of beer in his hand. He flipped on the light, knowing it would irritate his big brother and sat on the end of the bed.

"Wake up," he said, nudging Dmitry's large arm. "Hey, fuckhead, get up. It's time."

The slits of Dmitry's eyes opened and gazed up at Ivan. With a growl, he sat up. "What time is it?" he asked gruffly.

"Five thirty," Ivan answered, taking a swig of his beer. "The *bitches* are gone. The boys are up and waiting. I figured that I'd let you get some rest before The Free Right got here to collect their shit."

Pulling himself off the bed, Dmitry slipped on his pants and a shirt. Even 45 minutes of rest after being up as long as he had felt wonderful. Yawning, he checked his watch and slipped on his boots. "Where's Davyd?"

"Downstairs waiting on you," Ivan answered shortly. "Look, you don't have to ask me where everyone is or what they're doing. I know my job," he said, standing up.

"You're right," Dmitry said, pacifying him. "Good job." It was too early in the morning to get into a pissing match with Ivan. All he wanted to do was ensure the pickup and get back to sleep.

Ivan looked over on the bed and saw the book. Picking it up, he flipped through the pages and shook his head. "Why do you read this shit?"

"I keep telling you," Dmitry said, tying his black, steel-toe boots. "Self-enlightenment." He quickly pulled his pants down over his boots and stood up. "Let's go. She should be here soon."

Within thirty minutes, the same woman from the cemetery the night before along with a redheaded man in his twenties and a quiet man in his thirties with a long, black ponytail showed up at the garage. Davyd opened the door on their first knock, escorted them in at gunpoint and patted them down.

The redhead woman still had a fiery look in her eyes as she glanced over at Dmitry, who sat in the corner watching. When Davyd cleared her, she walked over to him and nodded.

"You look rested," she said, wiping her own eyes.

"About 45 minutes in the last 36 hours," he answered.

"Really? I was grateful for an hour," she smiled at him.

"What's your name anyway," Dmitry asked, standing up to lead them out to the garage where their shipment waited.

"Emma...Emma Hutton."

He liked her name. It sounded as petite and feminine as she was. Looking down at her out of the corner of his eye as they walked, he noticed that while she looked like barbwire, she smiled like cherries.

"Who are your guys back there?"

She looked back and pointed. "The redhead is my baby brother, Moses, and the other fellow is one of the brothers of The Free Right, Cain." She glanced back up at him. "How does it feel to be on top of the world all the time?"

Dmitry grabbed the knob to the garage door and opened it for her. "It's awkward," he said, allowing her to pass.

She pulled out her keys and unlocked the back of the broken-down, green van to check the boxes in the back. As promised, two hundred AK-47s with a clean history were boxed up and ready. Her eyes lit up at the sight of them. Trailing her fingers over the large brown boxes, she looked back for her brothers, who quickly came to inspect the weapons themselves.

Moses pulled one of the weapons from the box and held it in his hands. "These are beautiful," he said in awe. "Just what we need to put those fucking bastards on their backs. Excuse the language, M."

"You're excused, dear brother," she grinned.

From a far, Dmitry watched on as the group talked then strode over to open the garage. The entire time, he made sure to keep his eyes on them. However, he could have cared less for the men; it was Emma who vexed him.

Barely five feet tall, the compact woman was about twenty-five years old, and even though she tried to hide it under her scruff exterior of no make-up and green fatigues, she was clearly educated and poised.

It was the way she pronounced every word, every syllable correctly. Her erect posture, her confidence, her focus made him know that she was one of those women whom he had often met from good families, harboring a very nasty beef with the entire world about the very privilege that she was afforded.

As they loaded into the van and started it, she rolled down the passenger window and called out to him. "*Spasiba*, Dmitry," she said with a glimmer in her eyes.

"No problem. Just come back and do business with me again soon." He waved.

"We will," she answered with a smile, giving a brisk nod.

The garage door lifted, and they pulled out into the foggy streets of Brixton, mingling in with the other cars that littered the road on the way to work in the early morning haze. Dmitry hit the button and the garage door closed. Alone now, his thoughts zoomed back to the bed that awaited him.

As Dmitry stepped towards the entry, Davyd stuck his head through the door and waved the phone his way. "It's Kirill," he growled. "There's a problem."

Dmitry ducked his head in frustration and made his way to Davyd. Taking the phone, he tilted his head and looked down at him. "What kind of problem?"

"See for yourself," Davyd said with a shrug of his broad shoulders.

"Hello," Dmitry answered, closing the door behind him as he went back inside of the warehouse.

"*Brat*, I've spoken with my contacts here. There's a lot of shit going down. The country is crumbling. Getting the product will be more difficult now, and the price is going to shoot up about thirty percent," his old boss Kirill explained.

Dmitry stopped in his tracks. Gripping the phone, he tried to control his growing temper. "That's ridiculous. What do you mean that the country is crumbling?"

"Haven't you been watching the news over there?"

"No," Dmitry said, eyeing his men, who sat on the shabby couches eating breakfast. "What are you talking about?"

"Do you have a television set?"

"Of course I do." *But he never watched it*. Television was meaningless to him most of the time. He walked over to it and bent down to turn it on.

"The USSR is virtually more, *brat*.   The official announcement has not been made, but military contacts are scattering fast.   We're going to have a problem getting guns now."

Dmitry shook his head in disbelief.   Changing the channels, he found a news station and sat down on the recliner across the room.   "But there is a bid coming, and I need this."   He looked at the television blankly.

"I'll call back with more information if I can get another source, but currently, the price goes up by thirty percent.   I'm sorry.   You'll have to raise the price on your buyers."

Dmitry hung up the phone and put his head back. As he looked up at the gaping ceiling, he dropped the receiver on the floor and clenched his jaw.   "Kirill is playing us.   You were right," he said to Davyd.

"I know.   I told you.   I was hoping now you would consider what we discussed earlier.   There is a guy I know, an old friend.   He's tied to the brotherhood, and he can get us what we need, probably at a better price. He has contacts."

"If we do this, you realize that we might make an enemy out of Kirill."

"If we don't do this, you realize that we stand to be pushed out," Davyd said in a matter-of-fact tone.

Dmitry contemplated his actions for a moment then sat up.   "Fine.   Make the call.   I'll deal with Kirill later."

***

A week passed quickly, and Dmitry found himself the subject of many inquiries as Davyd roamed about trying to find suitable suppliers for their munitions needs. They lost the bid with Camille and much needed clout due to their hold up.   And so far, there had been no takers after a few hard-pressed questions about the

Medlov Family operation. Everyone was leery of dealing with such a young group, even with Davyd promising that he would facilitate the buy.

When he told suppliers that Dmitry was a Vor, they complained about him being too *low level*. When they found out who his old captain was, they worried that Kirill could not be trusted. Plus, Kirill had all but ignored them since his call about the price gouging. Now, they were basically out of business unless they found a go-to guy. Yet, Davyd continuously promised Dmitry that he would find someone soon. *Just be patient*, he would grumble right before he jumped back on the phone with his small notepad in one hand and a gnawed-up pencil in the other.

Since speaking with Kirill, Dmitry had been watching the news more. Kirill had been right about one thing. The USSR was crumbling. Based on the news reporters from London, his home country was a horrid place of oppressed peoples dominated by socialism and poor spending that had led the country to bankruptcy. Everyday, he learned a new term. Often, he would write them down and study them in his room. From what he gathered of the mess back home, it wasn't so much about the fear that people lived in or the control the government had over the smallest liberties of life, it was about the mighty proverbial dollar. *And the USSR had run out of rubles.*

When Dmitry wasn't glued to the news, the rest of his day was spent roaming the city alone or with his brother. Dmitry had a strategy. After his run-in with the half-ass gang in the alleyway near the abandoned warehouse the week before, he decided that the Medlov Family should make a better name for themselves in

Brixton. They had to let people know that they were not going anywhere soon and were running the place.

Dmitry thought the best way to do that was to figure out what other criminal elements were around. *Reconnaissance for later*, he had explained to Ivan. His brother had of course returned with a snub question, "What the fuck is reconnaissance?"

When he wasn't roaming, watching television or working out a strategy with Davyd, he slept. Every time that he could steal away a moment, he made his way to his bedroom, where he hid out from the world. Buried in books, he seemed to constantly smell of ink. However, he was searching for something, and while he could not exactly articulate what it was, he knew when he ran up on it, he'd recognize it.

***

It was two o'clock in the morning when Dmitry finished reading *War and Peace*. Closing his book, he rolled over in the bed and scribbled his thoughts in his journal right under the entry he had made a few nights before on *The Art of War*.

He pulled the pillow under his aching neck and hit his pen on his leg to loosen the ink. *Two totally different concepts*, he wrote in his journal. *But I am very proud that such a great work of art was written by a fellow man from the mother country. I think I'd like to have been part of an aristocratic family. I would have liked to have been a part of any family at all. My choices would be different now, and I imagine that I would be assigned to some great station in life.*

He scratched his brow, placing pen in between his delicate lips and teeth as he flipped back in his journal to look at some other entries. The intoxication of deep sleep started to come over him in heavy waves. His eyes fluttered for a moment and then the leather bound journal fell between his thighs. Sleeping deeply, he dreamt of Tolstoy's book and even of what his mother might have looked like as a respectable woman.

As Dmitry rested, the door to his room creaked open then closed quietly. Petite footsteps slowly made their way across the hardwood floor, carrying with them the smell of cherries. Emma stood only inches away, watching him sleep. Amazed, she folded her arms in front of her as she bit her bottom lip and thought sensual thoughts that had long since *the Free Right* been forced to the back of her mind.

Dmitry's muscles were taut and defined. His body appeared to be a perfect human anatomy chart. Shirtless and only wearing boxers that were pulled down low enough on his hips to see curly, dirty-blonde hair leading from his navel down into the depths of his bulging, black underwear, Dmitry rested unaware of his new guest.

Emma found his vulnerability alluring. Had she not been pressed for time, she would have simply taken a seat and watched him sleep all night. Unfortunately, she needed him up now. Stepping forward, her cherry scent wafted up to Dmitry's nose. With somewhat of a start, his blue eyes opened, and he quickly turned towards her, pulling his arm from behind the pillow to brandish a black nine millimeter.

She stopped in her tracks. A whimper escaped through her rough exterior. Swallowing hard, hands raised, she spoke softly. "Your brother, Ivan, let me in and told me to come up," she explained. "I wouldn't have if..."

Dmitry lowered the gun. Sitting up in the bed, he clenched his jaw and gazed at her. His eyes swept over her, making a small zinger shoot through her body. He looked like raw, unadulterated sex.

"Why were you watching me sleep?" he asked, turning the alarm clock towards him to see the time.

"You looked so peaceful," she said, finally putting her hands down. "I wasn't sure that I wanted to disturb you." Her eyes would not turn from his many tattoos.

"Where you just going to stand there and spy on me all night?"

"I might have," she said in a low, soft voice.

His eyes met hers, and she quickly looked away. "I came here to place another order," she continued.

Dmitry nodded, knowing that she could have easily done that over the phone. Looking down in between his legs, he realized that his fly was open. Adjusting himself, he reached over on the floor, grabbed his jeans and stood up.

As he rose up from the bed to his seven feet of enormity, Emma's breath caught again. He was like a giant sculpture. His male scent and the heat from his body were like edible pheromones drawing her to him. Suddenly, all she wanted to do was be invited to his disheveled, book-infested bed.

"How quickly do you need this order? I imagine that it must be pretty urgent," he said with a spiked brow. His deep voice vibrated through her chest.

"One week," she answered.

He growled and pulled on a long, black flannel shirt to cover his rippling muscles. "How much product do you need?"

So much, she thought to herself.

Emma fished a list out of her pocket and passed it up to him. He looked down at her and took the list carefully. Opening it, he read it standing in front of her then walked over to the fireplace. Tossing it into the flames, he turned around and contemplated his next words. If he told her the truth – they currently were without a supplier – and turned her away, she'd just find someone else to help The Free Right. But if he asked for more time, he could possibly use the last ditch effort over the Christmas holiday to find someone willing to work a deal with him.

"Why did you just throw that away?" Emma asked confused, looking at her smoldering list as it burned in the fire. She turned her furrowed brow on him.

"I memorized it," he answered. "Relax. We don't write orders down around here." He walked past her. "But I am going to need some time. More than a week."

"How much time?" she asked, looking at the fire.

"Right after new years."

"That long?"

He walked up behind her, using the last thing he knew would change her mind. Running his hand through her hair, he lowered his voice. "It'll be worth the wait."

Instantly, her sex clenched tight. Repressing the urge to turn towards him, she nodded her head. "Alright. You have until three days after the New Year. I won't wait a minute longer," she said in a quivering voice, hoping he understood her double meaning.

"I won't disappoint," he whispered seductively.

The chill returned to Emma's spine. She could feel his words resonate deep within her, and suddenly she knew that he would not disappoint her on any front. Closing her eyes for a minute, she pulled herself together and then turned to him. He was too tall to make eye contact with face-to-face, so she focused on his rock-hard abdomen.

They stood in the silence of the room, the fireplace crackling behind them, making love in their thoughts. His sexual energy consumed her, and suddenly she was as hot as the glowing embers popping in the pit.

Why won't he just take me? she asked herself. "I should go then," she said finally.

Dmitry did not answer. Instead, he walked to the door and opened it. Lowering his head, he leaned on the wall as she passed him. Her cherry scent lingered in his nostrils. He savored her fragrant smell. Feminine. Beautiful.

As she closed the door behind her, he went back to the bed and laid down, this time fully awake. Dangerous adrenaline swiftly flowed through his body. He ached to have her, ached to have any woman. But he had to tread carefully with his money, because that was still what she was to him - a payday. Thoughts of his mother slipped into his mind. And in the moment he knew the truth. Emma was a glorified John.

Chapter Three

Even in Brixton, Christmas Eve was highly celebrated. People marked their businesses, homes and apartments with lights and signs in honor of the holiday. However, the Medlov place was gravely quiet and obscenely dark. While Ivan was out with some of the gang partying, it was just another Tuesday for Dmitry and Davyd, who sat by the television watching the news and making plans.

Out of over twenty calls, only one viable lead was being considered as a supplier. A man, who went by the name *General,* was interested in doing business with Dmitry and his crew on large orders dependent upon what happened in the next 48-72 hours in the USSR.

Dmitry thought it was a long shot, but Davyd seemed to think otherwise.

"It almost seems unreal that he'd be interested in going lower than our former rates with Kirill," Dmitry said, thumbing through his papers and eating a chicken sandwich. *How he wished for borscht this cold night and maybe even some caviar.*

"No, this is the tide of change I was telling you about, *brat.* With the Federation folding, there will be new opportunities for us. There couldn't be a better time to do what we do. He is probably a *real* general. And this is more than likely his retirement plan," Davyd explained.

Dmitry grinned. "If he's not bullshitting us, we stand to make considerable gains. And not just here, we can cover most of Europe."

"Easy, boy. Walk before you run. First, we have to find someone interested in making a very large order."

"What about Emma?"

"The Free Right may not have that type of money."

"I get the feeling that they do, and I want in. All I have to do is encourage *her* to trust me."

Davyd gave a smug grin. "You always know how to encourage women to do what you want. Now, if a man was in charge, I'd be concerned."

"I don't think Emma is in charge, but I think that she has the ear of whoever is."

"Well, let's cross our fingers and hope that the next couple of days bring good news. Then, we can move forward."

The front doors flung open and a barrage of people came barreling through, one of which was Ivan. In one hand he carried a bottle and in the other a gun. Dmitry looked up from his paperwork and eyed him as he came waltzing into the kitchen.

"What are you boring old farts up to?" Ivan asked, pulling out a vacant chair and plopping down. His gin sloshed out on his hand.

"We're working. What are you doing?" Dmitry asked, trying to control his growing agitation with Ivan's late night antics.

"I did what you said. I went and cased *all* of Brixton with my guys."

"And?" Dmitry asked, covering the papers so that Ivan could not see.

"We discovered what the community is missing." Ivan put his elbows on the table and looked around at the men with a clever grin as if he had found the Garden of Eden. "They do not have any good places to gamble." He hit the table pleased with himself.

Davyd shook his head. "They have plenty of places to gamble here, boy. It's Brixton. Hard working, underpaid men have always gambled."

"Not like I have imagined," Ivan said, turning to his brother. "What the fuck do I care about Davyd's old ass. Dmitry, I need you to hear me out on this one."

Dmitry sat back in his chair and sighed. He wasn't sure if he could take listening to one more of Ivan's hare-brained schemes.

"We can get a small place not far from here and use it as a gambling hall with a few girls and a few drugs," Ivan pitched.

"No," Dmitry said, shaking his head. "No girls. No drugs."

"Why not?" Ivan's temper flared. "What's the difference between having a few girls and having a few guns? Your shit kills people a lot faster than a little pussy and a little buzz."

"Ivan, we have spoken about this a hundred times. We are strictly in the munitions business. We're not pimps and drug dealers." Dmitry scoffed at Ivan's outrageous idea.

"No, I'll tell you what we are. We're fucking broke." Ivan took a swig out of his bottle and stood up. Kicking the table, he stormed off. "You never give me a chance to do shit around here but run your fucking errands! If you're such a big shot, why don't you find a way to get us out of this hell hole?"

Dmitry looked at Davyd and shook his head. A clang followed Ivan's infuriated voice as he knocked things and people out of his way.

Davyd disapproved. "You better rein him in, brat. He's getting out of control. You're the boss here. Remember that. Remember to keep all of your men in line, including the ones related to you. In the Vor, there is no difference between the two. There is only you and *your* last word."

"*Da, da.* I know. I just need to find something to keep him busy, out of trouble but still make him feel like he's actually an asset."

"I mean no disrespect to you, because this is your crew, Dmitry, but Ivan is no asset," Davyd said, lowering his voice. "He's going to end up getting you into a world of shit that you couldn't buy your way out of if you owned a manure factory."

Dmitry knew that Davyd was right. Ivan was getting more erratic in his behavior and more uncontrollable. He picked up his sandwich to finish the last of his late night meal, but quickly put it down. His disgust with the entire situation was more than evident. With a huff, he stood up from the table. "I'll be back," he muttered as he left the room.

The rest of the crew had convened back on the couch to watch movies with the new VCR they had stolen, but Ivan had retired upstairs to his room to pout.

Dmitry slowly made his way upstairs. The door was locked and the music blared loud enough to rattle the dirty walls and poorly hung paintings. Lately, he felt like a father instead of a brother. Tapping his knuckles against the door, he looked up only inches away at the ceiling. "Ivan it's me. Open up," he said, hitting the door again.

"What do you want?" Ivan snapped.

"Stop acting like a little girl. Now open the door before I break it down and pull you out by your hair." He knew that Ivan knew that he would do it.

The door flew open, bouncing against the doorstopper. Dmitry walked in behind his brother. Closing the door, he looked around the messy room, riddled with cans of beer and magazines. Finding a place to sit, he looked over at the radio and back at Ivan.

Ivan hated *that* look. Dmitry would bite down and clench his square jaw when he was reaching the point of pounding on him. He quickly walked over at hit the radio. *Rage Against the Machine,* Ivan's favorite band, abruptly silenced.

"What is it now? You want to tell me how stupid I am?" Ivan asked, picking up a few of the porno magazines on the floor by Dmitry's foot.

"No," Dmitry said sighing. "Look, I know you want something to do."

"That's just it," Ivan interrupted. "You promised all of these opportunities over here, and look at us." He raised his hands and turned around. "This place is a fucking dump. We aren't doing any better than we were in Moscow, and it's been a year already."

"These things take time. And we are doing better. We own this place. It's bigger than our old entire apartment building."

"But it's a dump."

"Don't you ever see the silver lining, Ivan?"

"No," Ivan shook his head. "I don't." Plopping down on the bed, he focused on his brother. "I see reality. And the reality is that we don't have *near* the respect that we did at home." His voice was strained.

"Is it that you miss your friends?"

"No. I'm not that immature. I want respect."

"You have to gain respect, Ivan."

"Don't talk to me like you're my father!"

"Then don't behave like a child," Dmitry said with a scowl on his face. The veins protruded out of his neck. "I am trying. And you have to be patient."

"But I want to help," Ivan said, backing down just a little. "And I know how to, but you don't trust me enough to let me do it."

Dmitry gritted his teeth. "You're only sixteen, Ivan. And you're telling me that you want to start a gambling hall. You're not even old enough to drink. No one would ever believe it anyway, unless they saw a birth certificate. I'm telling you, it's a good idea, *brat*. I could pull it off."

"If I give you the funds to start this *gambling hall*, you realize that it will still be under my control and my rules. I don't want you pimping young girls out of it or selling drugs."

"Fine," Ivan said, feeling his brother starting to give in.

"You say fine, now, but I'm serious. If I find out that you're fucking up, then I'll shut you down."

"I understand."

Dmitry nodded. "Alright. I know I'm going to regret this, but I'll give you the chance you keep begging for only if you work for it. I'll need to know of every gambling hall in the area, who runs it, what they run out of it, where they are, how much you suspect they are bringing in and who their major players are."

"That's a lot of work."

"That's the reconnaissance I was telling you about." Dmitry stood up and walked to the door. "You get me that information, and I'll fund your little place."

Ivan sat back on the bed with a smile on his face. "I won't disappoint you, Dmitry. Trust me. You'll see."

Dmitry didn't bother with giving his vote of confidence. Instead, he simply bent down and picked up the bottles of beer littering the doorway. Throwing them in the trashcan beside his brother's desk, he closed the door behind him and went into his room to think.

***

Exactly one day later, Dmitry could not believe his eyes or his ears. He sat with Davyd in front of the television, pen and pad on his lap as the announcement that would change their lives was made.

The leader of the Soviet Union, Mikhail Gorbachev, announced that he was stepping down from office. Broadcasting live on television, the Soviet Union became a mere page in history with the ten-minute speech that preceded what was soon to be recognized as the Commonwealth of Independent States.

"Due to the situation which has evolved as a result of the formation of the Commonwealth of Independent states I hereby discontinue my activities at the post of president of the Union of Soviet Socialist Republics," he said. "Free elections have become a reality. Free press, freedom of worship, representative legislatures and a multi-party system have all become a reality," Gorbachev said solemnly.

Dmitry looked over at Davyd and cracked a smile. They were finally in business. Flipping through his notebook, he wrote something on his pad and stood up.

"Do you know what this means for us, *brat*?" Dmitry asked excitedly.

"It means you need to find some large buyers," Davyd answered, trying to control his mounting enthusiasm through sipping on his cup of coffee.

Dmitry nodded. Davyd was right.

The phone rang, interrupting their multiplying thoughts. In dash, Dmitry ran to the phone and answered it.

"Dmitry," the deep, rough voice said.

"*Da*," Dmitry answered.

"*This is the general. Are you watching the news*?" he asked in Russian.

"*Da*."

"Good. Get your numbers together in 24 hours with your first bid. It has to be bigger than 1,000 and under 5,000 of any product to do business. Do we understand each other?"

"Perfectly," Dmitry said, signaling Davyd. "Where should we call you?"

"I'll call you," General said, hanging up the phone.

Dmitry hung up and leaned against the wall.

"Was that him?" Davyd asked, standing up.

Dmitry nodded. "I've got to get in touch with Emma tonight.

***

It only took Emma five minutes to call him back after he left the message. He sat by the phone waiting, hoping that she hadn't gone somewhere else with her order. But as she had promised, she had waited.

"That was quick," she said whispering. A barrage of voices in the background nearly drowned her out. "Hold on just a minute," she said, excusing herself from the crowded room. In silence, she returned to the phone. "You there?"

"*Da*. I can do business with you, offer you economies of scale," he said, using the word he had just learned the night before from a business management book.

"*Oookay*," Emma smiled. "You must be referring to bulk. We can order 500 AK-47s and 100 hand grenades like I told you before."

Dmitry tapped his pen against the table. "That's not going to get you anywhere, Emma, and you know it.

Now, my guy is reliable, and he's ready to get the order filled, but it has to be at least 2,000," he said, knowing as the words left his mouth that it was a hard sell.

"Are you insane?" she asked in a high-pitched voice.

"When you look at what you've been paying versus what I can offer, you'll realize that it's better to get this now, while it's at a good rate and while I'm still gracious."

Emma shook her head. "Don't try to fuck with me, Dmitry. The Free Right has been good to you."

"And I'm willing to be *very* good to you. But you need to hear me out, and you need to put me on as your primary dealer. I know that you must be getting this shit from a thousand sources. Why is beyond me. I can provide you with everything that you need at very reasonable rates, and it's all courtesy of the USSR. Or haven't you been watching the news?" He used Kirill's line.

There was silence on the other end of the phone as Emma thought. Finally, she cleared her throat. "Do you have a tuxedo?" she asked curiously.

"No," Dmitry answered suspiciously.

"Can you get one tonight?"

"I'm seven feet tall. I doubt it very seriously. Borrowing one from the neighbor would likely be out of the question."

"Well, do you have anything but jeans? I don't want you to stand out."

"I'm seven feet tall, Emma." His voice was stern.

"I suppose you're right. Fine," she said, dismissing whatever thought was on her mind. "Do you have a pen handy? I want you to meet me at this address in one hour. And bring your brother. If anyone asks, you and your brother are athletes – basketball players - in the city looking at universities."

Dmitry grabbed his pen. "Bring my brother?"

"Yes, did I stutter? You want my business, my money. Then, bring your brother and your *ass* to this address in one hour. Don't be late, or the deal is off."

Dmitry wrote down the number and hung up the phone. *What had he gotten himself into?*

Chapter Four

Dmitry pulled up to one of the many mansions of Kensington and parked down the street from the address he had been given by Emma. Kingston was one of London's top upscale neighborhoods known for its elite citizens and its exclusive parties. In short, it was no place for the likes of Dmitry and Ivan. Nevertheless, they were present and accounted for. Sighing as he eyed the crowd flooding into the home, Dmitry looked over at Ivan and checked his clothes.

"I'll do my best to make this short, but you must promise to do your best to act civilized," Dmitry lectured as he straightened Ivan's collar.

"I know how to act," Ivan said, pulling away. "And I'm not a child. I know how to dress myself. I'm here looking at colleges, remember?"

"If only that were so," Dmitry said, grabbing the door handle. "Stay close. Don't get too involved in any conversations and stay away from the alcohol."

Getting out of their banged up, black Mercedes, the pair hiked a short block up the street to the well-lit home, donning Christmas lights and decorations and checked their names at the door with the bodyguard.

A black man as wide as a wall in a black wool sweater stood with a clipboard in his hand. He took one look at Dmitry and Ivan and waved them in. "You must be the ball players," the man said, opening the door. "Lady Hutton is expecting you."

Ivan looked at Dmitry and grinned. "She's a freaking lady," Ivan muttered to Dmitry as he passed through the doors. "This chick has a title? That's awesome."

As they entered the lavish home, a woman stood behind a large, red-skirted table with gift bags. She passed them both one and wished them a Merry Christmas.

"This place is swank," Ivan observed as he walked into the large gathering with his brother.

"Let's just find Emma and get this done with," Dmitry said, envying the people who were actually supposed to be there. "And remember what I told you earlier."

"You won't let me fucking forget," Ivan said shortly.

The crowds looked up at them in total amusement. The men were baffled and mildly intimidated by their size, while the women were automatically drawn to the attractive pair – one brooding brunette with a joker-like grin and one serious blonde with a serious scowl.

"Dmitry, up here," a voice said from the top of the spiral staircase.

Dmitry looked up to see Emma dressed in a red, flowing gown. Diamonds sparkled from her ears and neck. Her red tendrils were pulled up off her face, bringing more attention to her long neck, her soft shoulders and her full bosom. She looked like Christmas morning.

"Damn," Ivan laughed. "Emma can clean up, can't she?"

Without taking her eyes off of him, she made her way quickly down the stairs to join the pair.

"On time, I see," she said, eyes sparkling.

Dmitry nodded. "Like I said, I want your business."

Emma looked around and put her index finger over her lips. "Shh... everyone around here just calls me, M. I want to introduce you to some people - one in particular that you need to speak with," she said nodding. "Come with me."

Dmitry and Ivan followed Emma down the long hall, past the beautiful paintings and gorgeous, king-like rooms to a closed door at the end of the corridor.

"Wait. What's his name?" Dmitry asked as Emma put her hand on the gold doorknob.

"Her name," Emma said narrowing her eyes at him. "The Free Right is anti-abortion group among other things." Opening the door, she led them inside the immaculate study of Lady Catherine Hutton, who was sitting with a group of women and men by the fireplace. All were dressed in formals, appearing to be more royalty than militia. They gathered around talking quietly, conspiring.

"Mom," Emma said, moving in front of them. Her skirts swooshed behind her. "I'd like you to meet the gentleman I was telling you about." She motioned toward Dmitry. "Dmitry Medlov meet Lady Catherine Hutton."

Lady Hutton turned from her group. Dressed in canary yellow, covered in yellow diamonds, draped in milky white skin, dripped in elegance, smelling of privilege, the blonde woman turned to her daughter and smiled.

There was a certain grace in her movements. Delicate hands, high cheekbones, telling eyes. Dmitry thought the older woman attractive. He put her in her late forties to early fifties, and she'd obviously been very well taken care of during her life.

She looked up at him in surprise of his startling height.

"Emma, you understated just how grand he is," she said standing. Offering her hand, she watched Dmitry glide across the room and take it.

He had read about this. Bowing his head, he took her soft hand in his own and kissed it. It hurt to bend over so far to the short woman, but if he had to woo her to get the order he needed, it was worth it.

"Well, now. From the look of you, I'd swear that you didn't have one ounce of couth," Lady Hutton said, raising her brow at Dmitry. The crowd giggled. "But your social graces are not lacking, are they young man?"

"Actually, they are," Dmitry said. His voice rumbled through the room. His crystal blue eyes sparkled through her. "This is my brother, Ivan."

"What's up," Ivan said, raising his hand towards the small gathering from the corner of the room where he looked on at the many bottles of fine liquor. He was no longer paying attention to the snobs. It was time to get drunk.

Emma laughed. She didn't know Ivan very well, but she rather appreciated how direct he often was. He looked her way and gave her a suggestive wink. Remembering herself, she turned and continued. "It seems that Dmitry has an opportunity for The Free Right."

"An opportunity? Really?" Lady Hutton turned back to Dmitry. "Is this so?"

"Yes, my lady. One that I'm sure that you'll want to consider."

Lady Hutton looked around at her small gathering, obviously loyal to the cause, and smiled. "Would you all be kind enough to follow Moses to the main hall for just a while? There is food and drink for you and plenty of people to meet. We'll convene as soon as I'm finished speaking with my new friend." Her eyes landed on Dmitry.

Moses stood in his black tuxedo from his leather wing-backed chair and escorted the small crowd out of the room. Stopping at the door, he gave a disapproving look at Dmitry. "Should I come back?" he asked his mother.

"No, that won't be necessary, dear," Lady Hutton assured. "Emma, why don't you also take-"

"Ivan with an I," Ivan said, pouring a glass of scotch.

"Right. Why don't you take Ivan with an I out to get something to eat as well. But I'd prefer, son, if you left the bottle of scotch here. When I'm done speaking with your brother, I'll make sure that he brings a couple of bottles home for you."

Ivan took a quick gulp of the fine alcohol and put the crystal goblet down. "Don't forget," he said to Dmitry, before he followed Emma out of the room.

When the door was closed, Lady Hutton walked over to it, took a key from the table and locked it. Turning around, she smiled at him and motioned at the chair where her son had sat. "Please, have a seat, Dmitry."

He did so quickly. Uncomfortable, he sat up. "This chair is obviously meant for a little person."

"Umm," Lady Hutton said, returning to her chair across from him. "So, what of this opportunity?"

"Your shipments are very small. I imagine that you must have other suppliers and many other people who are a part of your supply chain, but I have an offer that could streamline all of your munitions needs and provide you an affordable one-stop shop for everything from your AKs to hand-guided missiles and hand guns."

"From where?"

"We have a contact in the USSR military."

"Former USSR."

"Correct. He is willing to work deals with me."

"Why?"

"He is a...he has loyalties to the organization that I belong to."

The fire crackled beside him, drawing his attention. He couldn't help but to look over at it. It still reminded him of his long hike to civilization after leaving the prison over a year ago.

"How old are you, Dmitry?"

Dmitry raised his brow. "Excuse me?" He looked back over at her.

"I get the feeling that you're very young."

"I'm nearly twenty."

"Really? I thought you older than that, just younger than Emma." She searched his face with a devious grin. "I don't do business with anyone that I cannot trust."

"There is no reason not to trust me." He gazed into her eyes.

"I get this feeling from you. It's hard to describe, but I recognize it." Taking a deep breath, she looked up at the vaulted ceiling. "It's ambition." She exhaled.

"Is there something wrong with being ambitious?" He sat back in the chair. "I've come to you with an offer. 2,000 of whatever you need for thirty percent less than what you've been paying for it. I make the order tonight with you; I come in a few days to collect the money, and I have it delivered very soon. That is the nature of what I do. I'm no freedom fighter. I don't blow up clinics or save young girls from countries that would murder them for their sexual choices. I simply provide a service at a discounted price." He looked at her with an unreadable glare.

"And if there is a problem with the order," she smiled. "Are you willing to cover our losses?" Her fingers found their way to her diamond necklace.

Dmitry paused. "I don't... There won't be any problems."

"There is another type that I don't like – people who are too trusting. Naiveté is not attractive, even on a young man."

Dmitry clenched his jaw. "Can I be honest with you?" he said in a quiet voice.

"Yes," she whispered as she leaned in. "Please do." The diamonds from her ears sparkled like stars from her delicate lobes. She studied his face, listening carefully to his thick accent.

He sighed, talking with his large hands as he pleaded. "I've only just gotten this lead. I switched suppliers recently. This guy is someone who I have been told I can trust. And men of my organization do not normally work with the military. However, this guy is in the military and is also in with my organization. I guess you could say that he's an anomaly." He pulled up his sleeves revealing his tattoos. "And if you promise us something, whether we are in the Mother country or ten thousand miles away in another hell hole, you better make good on it. He knows that. So, as I was saying, you'll get your shipment."

Lady Hutton looked at the tattoos. Reaching out, she placed her fingers on his hot skin. "A Vor? You become more interesting by the moment." She sat back in her seat and crossed her legs. Her perfectly manicured toes peaked out of her delicate, sling-back shoes. "I like you," she said softly. Her eyes batted at him.

"I want you to like me," Dmitry said with a determined look on his face.

"I think I'll take you on as my new project. It's been a while since I was able to turn a man of poverty into a man of privilege. And with your...assets, both physical and otherwise, I'm sure you're going to be quite the adventure." She licked her lips.

"What does that mean?"

"It means, dear boy, I'll make an order with you. We'll see if you produce all that you promise, and we'll go from there. Only because we have done business in the past together and you've always come through before. In the meantime, I want you to stop by here twice a week. I'm going to help you on your etiquette, your dress, your speech...all the things that will get you into the door with the gentlemen whom I want you to be introduced. You see, I'm still a woman, even though I'm a lady. And there are doors, even in the 20th century, that I can't get through. However if I have you, then maybe The Free Right can gain more than just guns. We can gain power." Her eyes were bright with promise.

"You want me to be your puppet?" Dmitry asked concerned.

She lifted her finger. "No. I want to make you a global player in this game. But there are a few things that you'll need to learn first. And I am certain that I can teach you. You see, it's all about who you know, Dmitry. And I know everyone," she explained with a smug grin. "Are you interested? It's quid pro quo. I won't lie to you boy, but it's my offer. What do you say?" She waited.

"Yes," he said seriously. "I say of course. Thank you."

Lady Hutton nodded. "Thank you, dear Dmitry. Now, find Emma and tell her to proceed with The Free

Right's order. And you, I'll see tomorrow, here at noon, for your first lesson."

Dmitry narrowed his eyes on her. "Alright. Noon. Should I come through the front door or the back?"

Lady Hutton smiled. "What an odd question."

"I know how these things go. I want something from you. You want something from me. We understand each other. Like you said, quid pro quo."

Lady Hutton ran her finger over the top of her champagne glass. "Come to the back door tomorrow at Noon. I'll be waiting alone. I've given the staff the day off in celebration of the holiday." She looked up at him. "And keep this confidential."

"I wouldn't have it any other way." With that, he nodded and left her in the silence of the room.

***

Davyd could not sleep. He sat on the dusty couch with the rest of the gang, whom he referred to as the lost boys, eating a late night snack and watching the news in the darkness of the cold, lofty room. He just could not fathom it. The great and powerful USSR. His country had dissolved into nothingness in his lifetime. Baffled and amazed, he waited for Dmitry to return with news of their possible transaction with the general and The Free Right. Hopefully, the day would yield some good fruit.

Thirsty for milk, he got up from the couch, knees aching and made his way to the dingy kitchen that was painted in a horrid yellow, colored in stains and high-lighted by a very unattractive halogen light bulb some ten feet above attached to dusty rafters.

He caught a reflection of himself in the mirror hanging above the Playboy pin-up calendar and stopped. Since last week, there were more gray hairs in the top of his head. He rubbed through his healthy locks, furrowing his brow in disapproval and sighed. He was thirty-seven, still muscular, still - according to his own standards - attractive but slowly losing his sheen.

After a horrid mishap in Austria a few years back, he had been sent to London to lay low. Then out of the blue last year, he received a call from Kirill, an old friend and faithful brother of the Vor. Kirill had asked him as a favor to help young Dmitry get his start. There was no money in it except what he could make with the boy, but it did give him a rest from killing and trafficking. Plus, he'd never worked an operation from the ground up before. And something told him that Dmitry was special. He only hoped that his intuition was correct.

The front door creaked open, bringing in a sweeping, cold wind as Dmitry and Ivan entered. Putting down the gallon of milk, Davyd stepped to the opening. He nodded at the boys, seeing that both were utterly exhausted. Dmitry pulled off his coat and hung it on the rack, then went straight to the kitchen. Ivan retired to the couch with the boys, showing off his new bottle of scotch.

"Good or bad news," Davyd asked.

Dmitry looked in the old, paint-chipped cupboard and pulled out a glass. "Well," he wiped his top lip. "Very good, actually. We have our first order." Smiling, he pulled the bottle from under his arm and poured both he and Davyd a glass of scotch.

"So, Emma came through, did she?" Davyd asked with relief.

"Da, she came through. So did her mother. She's the brains behind the operation. They are some sort of women's pro-life group."

Davyd frowned. "And they need this type of fire power?"

"I know. It doesn't fit, but you know what – fuck it – it's not our problem. We are in the business of supplying, and the buck stops there. I pick up the money after we place the order and confirm the total amount of the shipment."

The tired pair clicked their cheap glasses together and sipped slowly, savoring the taste of expensive liquor for a change.

"I hear that. Then Merry Christmas to you, brat," Davyd said cheerfully. "Good job."

"I think we all did well, Davyd. Merry Christmas," Dmitry answered. He smiled. "Hopefully, Santa will bring me a little sleep."

They both laughed.

Chapter Five

At noon as promised, Dmitry entered through the back of the Hutton mansion to find Lady Hutton waiting in the kitchen alone. She looked much different in the daylight, even more graceful and unobtainable.

Dressed in a khaki skirt, a pink button down and matching cardigan, she sat pruning roses at the table and carefully placing them in a crystal vase. She looked up from her project and smiled at him. "Prompt," she said, gazing down at her Rolex watch.

"I try to be," Dmitry said, closing the door behind him.

"Good. Please have a seat," she said, motioning towards the chair beside her.

Dmitry walked over and sat down. Watching her carefully tend to the roses, he waited in silence, wondering what she had in store for today.

When she was done with her flower arrangement, she sat back and feasted her eyes on her labor. It was beautiful. With an accomplished grin, she pushed the vase to the center of the table and brushed the excess leaves and prickles into the trash can beside her.

"The first thing that I plan to teach you about is your dress." She looked down at his clothes in disgust. "Don't you have anything presentable? This is the second time that I've laid eyes on you and the second time that you have looked absolutely ...homeless."

Dmitry smirked. The long dimples in his cheeks emerged. "Are you one of those who believe that the clothes make the man?" His voice was deep and silky smooth.

"Are you one of those who believe it does not?" She tilted her head and looked at him, noticing for the first time that he had perfectly symmetrical features.

"Obviously, I am," he said, looking down at his own clothes. Did he really look that bad? he wondered.

She stood from the table and straightened her clothes. Her posture erect, her eyes focused, she turned her gloved palm and wiggled a finger. "Come with me," she directed as she headed into the main halls of the house. With care, she took her gloves off as she walked and placed them on a table near the cleaning quarters.

Their feet echoed throughout the mansion. With not a soul in the house except for them, the large place seemed even bigger to Dmitry. The night before the house had seemed gigantic with hundreds of people lurking about, but today, it seemed obscenely so. He could not believe that only one family lived there or that one family had so many expensive things. Everywhere he looked there was a priceless, precious, rare thing perfectly placed. It reminded him of a museum.

Dmitry felt like he was in school again and had been assigned to a beautiful head mistress. Lady Hutton played the part well. Not a hair was out of place. Every move was graceful. He found her unfamiliar to all notions about women he had ever had.

Nevertheless, she did give him the same curious gaze that all women, regardless of station, gave. He lit a fire in her, and no amount of grace or etiquette would hide its rearing head. If he had money, he would bet that she was wet right now, nearly soaking through her expensive lace panties, but he'd get to that later, when the time suited him.

For the time being, he wanted to get to know as much about her as possible. He and Davyd had spent the night before doing some light research and found that Lady Hutton was a widow. She was the mother of Moses and Emma Hutton and rightful owner of Hutton Enterprises. She was also royalty and from a long lineage of political figures that went as far back as the 18th century. As far as Dmitry was concerned, she was an alien, foreign to his world in every way.

When they arrived on the third floor of her lavish home, she led him to her private quarters. Opening the white, double doors, she invited him into the finest bedroom he had ever seen. Draped in expensive curtains, decorated with historic family portraits, sprinkled with gold accents and heavy woods, he felt like he had walked into a Dickens novel.

"This is where my husband and I used to retire," she explained. "It was before his death about ten years ago. He was murdered in Bosnia on business."

Dmitry put the pieces together. The Free Right obviously still had a bone to pick in that country. That was why she needed so many guns, and why her son was involved.

"I'm sorry for your loss," he said with a sorrowful grimace.

"Thank you," she said sincerely.

On the bed were boxes covered with red bows, bags with fine paper popping out of their tops and suits laid out with shirts, shoes, cuffs, socks and belts. He walked over looked at the presents. "Is all this for me?" he asked in a whisper.

"It is," she said, standing by the fireplace watching him. "I just had it brought over this morning."

He ran his hand over the clothes and smirked. "I've never been given something so nice."

"Get used to it." She folded her arms. "Go on. Try it on."

Dmitry looked at the open door hesitantly. She followed his gaze and walked over to it. Closing and locking the door behind her, she leaned against it and sighed. "You have your privacy now. You may continue." Her breaths nearly skipped at the prospect of what he must look like naked.

Dmitry pulled his coat off and laid it on the bed. He was instantly embarrassed by his dirty clothes giving great contrast to the fine linen on the bed. My things belong in the trash, he thought to himself.

With her booted foot propped up against the door, she tilted her head. "There are underpants for you as well." She licked her lips. "You can't expect to put on fine linen on top of dingy underpants."

Dmitry turned towards her and realized that she was enjoying herself. Giving her a full view, he pulled off his clothes one by one. His shirt. His tank top. His jeans. His socks. Then his briefs. Now naked, he turned to the bed and grabbed the underwear. He could hear her panting from behind him. She had walked over and placed her hands on his muscular back.

"Such magnificent artwork," she said of his tattoos. "You have to admit that your people have always been extremely creative."

Dmitry clenched his jaw. "It's been a while since I've been with a woman. If your intentions are not to be touched, I suggest that you move your hand." He stood up, still naked with the underwear in his hand.

Her voice was low. "And if it is my desire to be touched?"

"Then speak before I put on these nice clothes. A woman, even the best ones, still carries a scent after sex." He could feel her nails claw into his back.

"Then don't put them on just yet."

Turning slowly around, he looked below him at the small, petite woman. Her blonde hair smelled of the same cherry scent that her daughter's did. He found it regretful that he could not be with Emma, but her mother had decided that for the three of them with her advances.

Running his meaty fingers over her lips, he wiped her rose-colored lipstick off. Her mouth was open, awaiting a kiss, but he slipped his finger inside her orifice, feeling the fleshy velvet of her eager tongue. She sucked it hungrily. He knew what Lady Hutton desired. She wanted a pet. But he was a man, and she'd be forced to pay the price of dealing with one.

Grabbing her gently by the back of her head, he pushed her down to his steely erection. Removing his finger from her mouth, he slowly replaced it with his throbbing penis standing erect and curved upwards at her throat. His hot skin rubbed against her face. She hummed towards it, closing her eyes and smiling.

Instinctively, she grabbed his vein-covered member and impatiently kissed it, sucking his head with her warm lips. Liquid pearls beaded up to the top of his pink, bulky tip, indicating his desire for her. The thought relaxed her more. She knew then that at least a part of him was willing on a sexual level. Obediently, she licked the salty sex with the point of her tongue, then lapped him. Quietly, he guided himself in and out of her mouth, pulling her hair from its perfect bun so that he'd have something to hold on to. He ran his fingers through her hair, massaging her head as he stroked her throat.

Leaning back, he sat on the edge of her bed. She got down on her knees in front of him, placing herself firmly on the small stair below. Then she went back to her task, savoring the taste of man with every lick.

He watched in humor of how completely comfortable she was, closing his eyes occasionally as waves of pleasure swept over him. In his mind, it was Emma. And when she turned just right, he could no longer see Lady Hutton but a younger version of what she must have looked liked twenty years ago.

The enormous three-carat diamond on her ring finger sparkled as she grasped him with both hands. She tasted his sex again and then released him. Looking in his eyes, she tore off her black, lace panties, slick with cream and discarded them on the floor. Dmitry looked down and smirked. Her skirt was raised up on her supple thighs and her skin was fiery red. Reaching out, he pulled her towards him.

"Come here," he ordered in a guttural growl. He trailed his hand over her button down, tracing her nipples that hardened through the cotton. Then grabbing hold of her shirt, he ripped it off. The sound of tearing fabric colored the room.

"You don't want gentleman, do you, Lady Hutton?" he asked expressionless.

"No," she said panting. "I want a lover." She looked up into his eyes. "I haven't had a man since my husband died. I want to be dominated."

He forcefully pulled her clothes off, leaving her naked and vulnerable then laid her across his lap. He massaged her round buttocks, admiring how well she had kept herself then reached back and with a swift swing slapped her bare bottom. It turned red as she wiggled and moaned below him. Before she had time to recover, he slapped her again, this time quickly rubbing the pain away before he slipped his finger into her hot, tight spot, wet from desire and throbbing to be entered.

"Yes," she said, closing her eyes.

Feverishly burning, she laid across his lap as he played with her. In and out his firm fingers went through her body. The sound of wetness echoed through the silence. He used his other hand to brace her, massaging her back as he held her. His erect penis prodded below, nearly poking through her navel. Suddenly, she felt like a girl again. She laughed aloud. He laughed as well, turned on by her womanly prowess. He liked a woman who knew how to make love.

She finally pulled herself up and followed him into the middle of the large bed. The desire to be with him burned through her as she realized that he would give her what she wanted as long as she did the same for him in return.

He pulled her face towards him and descended with a passionate kiss. She inched up in the embrace of his solid arms and felt herself slip away into an abyss. Ahh. Young love. He kissed with the passion of a lion and yet caressed her with the care of a king. Slowly and gently, he tasted her, and then ravenously he slipped his large tongue down in the depths of her, feeding on her desire.

"How is your heart?" he asked, cupping her left breast in his hand. His fingers played with her nipples.

"My heart?" she asked curiously as he pinched her.

"Do you have any heart problems?" His look was that of true concern.

"No," she said shocked. "I'm only 49. My heart is fine. Why you ask?"

He pulled her hand towards his throbbing cock and leaned towards her blazing ear. "Because I'm not an inch shorter than a foot," he smiled. "And I don't want to kill you." He caressed her shoulders.

She laughed again with him as he laid his head back on her soft, goose-down pillows. Crawling on top of him, she avoided his mountainous member for the moment. Humor was priceless, and she rather enjoyed how sure of himself he was.

"But do you know what to do with a foot, my love?" she asked, raking her hand over his taut chest, rippling with muscles. She rested her small fingers flat on his abdomen.

He raised his head a bit and nodded, his blue eyes sparkling. "I'll fuck you within an inch of your life, my lady," he answered facetiously. "Do not let my age confuse you. I am all man." With that, he relaxed the muscles in his stomach and breathed slowly.

"That I believe."

There was silence. She sat back and shook her head. His penis stood at the crack of her bottom, reaching up from the bottom, past the top.

"But you'll never love me," she said more as a statement than a question.

"No," he said quickly. "I'll never love you, Lady Hutton. And I'll never lie to you and tell you that I will." His gaze locked on her.

"And it doesn't bother you to say that? To lie in bed and make love to me and know that you'll never have one feeling for me?"

"I never said that I wouldn't have one feeling for you. I just won't love you," he said, watching her facial expression change.

"Do you wish that I was Emma?"

He smirked. "Of course."

"Then why would you still make love to me?"

"You know why. You have more power than your daughter. You can get me what I need, and you can teach me what I need to know. You are more of an asset that she is regardless of how beautiful or young she is. At the end of the day, you are more desirable because of what you can offer."

Two things vexed Lady Hutton: his candidness and his still rock-hard penis. He was actually able to articulate such a cold statement with a straight face and remain ready to screw. She wasn't the least bit sure if she should be appalled or aroused by him.

"Then all I ask is that after you make love to me, you never touch my daughter."

With narrowed eyes, Dmitry reached down with his strong, large hands and picked her body up. Opening her legs further, he made her push her wet sex down on top of him in one aching rush.

She arched her back and screamed out in pain and pleasure.

Dmitry watched her expressionless, controlling both his physical and emotional reaction to her tight body. He gazed up at her languidly and said, "Once you have finished adjusting to the man I am below, maybe you'll look again at the man I am above. Of my own volition, I would never touch your daughter now. But since I have chosen you and you me, then I will have you as I choose from now on until we're both good and sick of each other."

Biting her lip, she shook in disbelief of his outrageous size. Nodding, she looked into his eyes. She managed after a moment to speak. Her lip quivered. "Fine, but never lie to me again."

"Lie to you?" he sat up and thrust once into her, nearly paralyzing her with his forceful blow.

"Yes," she panted. "You said a foot. You're much large than a fucking foot."

Smiling, Dmitry slowly rotated his hips, feeling her cream his thighs. "Well, I hate to over promise."

Chapter Six

Emma couldn't believe her ears. She stood at her mother's door listening to her moan and scream like a wild animal. Holding her mouth, she stepped away with tears in her eyes, sure of whom the gentleman caller was even without seeing him. Dmitry. That bastard! He used her. He betrayed her to get what he wanted. Another order. Another sale. Another contact. Shaking her head, she turned and walked away, determined to get even.

"Are you pleased yet?" Dmitry asked, wiping the sweat from his brow on Lady Hutton's white, Egyptian cotton sheets.

Out of breath and sweating, Lady Hutton rolled over on her side and gazed over at the fireplace. Her wet hair stuck to her neck. Her thighs were soaked. And she couldn't speak. Even if she wanted to, no words would slip from her dry, battered lips yet. It has been two decades since she'd erupted in such a manner. In fact, she had all but forgotten the feeling of such mesmerizing and intoxicating sex. Nodding, she closed her eyes and slowed her breathing, clenching the covers for bearing.

Pleased with himself, Dmitry laid his head back on the pillow and cocked his legs up. His semi-hard penis fell between his hairy thighs and rested on his stomach. Looking up at the canopy top above them, he yawned and closed his eyes. "Would you mind if I slept for a while?" he asked, realizing that she might have other plans and need him to take his leave soon.

There was a long, pregnant pause as she tried to pull herself together.

"You may move in if you like," she said playfully. "Yes, please. I insist. Rest a while, then shower, and you and I can talk about the finer points of dressing. Plus, I've arranged for you to go to my late husband's tailor. You have an account there. He'll dress you from now on, and money is no object. So don't be frugal."

He looked over at her and smiled. "Thank you."

"You've earned it," she said, still panting. "Also, you should go and visit our car dealer and pick out an automobile. Mercedes Benz is what I'd recommend, but it's up to you. Nothing flashy, like those damned Mazerati's. Get a black luxury sedan. I'll give you the card for Hamilton. He can be trusted and will be discreet."

Dmitry was speechless. Had he done that well?

Lady Hutton turned to him. "And call me Catherine." Her eyes were tired and red, but still bright and beautiful. Small lines formed at the sides of her lids, showing her age.

"Catherine," Dmitry repeated in reverence. "That's a beautiful name." He looked away.

She looked at him while he looked up at the ceiling. How she wanted him forever. Dmitry was such a beautiful man.

Blonde, foreboding, strikingly handsome and completely virile. He defied man's normal definition of masculine. In fact, he redefined the very thought of such a word. It was impossible for her to imagine that he was barely twenty. The thought was so obscene until she pushed it to the farthest places of her mind in order to keep from feeling like the deviant she surely was.

"Where do you live?" she finally asked, resting on her elbow. She pulled her sticky hair from her face.

"In a garage," he said without thought. "It's in Brixton. Well, actually, I live above the garage in an apartment. It's full of books. I...um...I love to read when I have time. If I could have finished school, I think I would have gone to college." He closed his eyes again.

"So you have no formal education?"

"No." His eyes were still shut.

She smiled and placed her hand on his chest. "Come three times a week, and once a week, I will teach you the art of business. It won't be like what you're used to. I will teach you the fundamentals of capitalism."

His eyes popped open. Dmitry face grew brighter than even a moment ago when she gave him a car. "That would be excellent. There is so much that I need to learn. Really, it would be an honor." He turned to her again.

"For both of us, I'm sure." She touched his face and looked over at the picture of her son on the nightstand. "How would your mother feel about this? Would she die if she were to find out that you were making love to a woman her age?" She grinned sheepishly. Her red cheeks blossomed.

Dmitry touched her hand. "My mother's dead. And she was a whore, so she'd expect no less than what we've arranged. I've never had a family. I've never been around a woman like you." He clenched his jaw. "I've never felt like this one day in my entire life." He swallowed hard. "I guess even if this didn't work, I'd still owe you for giving me a moment's rest."

Catherine listened on humbled by his delicate confession. That was the thing about young men. They didn't bottle up and keep their feelings hidden like the older ones. She could feel his honesty, and it warmed her heart to the core.

"When you've placed the order and given the quote for the cost of our shipment, then I will give you extra for yourself. You and your brother should consider a place downtown. London is very beautiful all over, but it's about location. If you need references, I'll provide the best ones in the country. No one will turn you away. Simply choose where you want to call home, and it will be arranged," she said in a matter-of-fact tone.

"Are you serious?"

"Very," she said, resting her head on his arm.

He ran his fingers through her hair. "I feel as though you've already given me too much, Catherine. At some point, you might look back at this and regret it. And I don't want that to come to pass."

"You don't know, do you?" She bit her lip.

"Know what?" His brow furrowed.

She sighed and ran her hand over her aching nipples, ready for a sixth helping. "I'm a billionaire, my love" she said, crawling over on top of him again.

"So is it possible that you already know where I live?" he asked, slipping his hard body inside of hers.

The tight stretch made her shudder. "Yes, but I wanted to see if you'd be completely honest." She rocked on his body, eager to feel him climax inside her again.

"And was I honest?"

"Yes. And as long as you continue to do that," she began to slowly ride him. "And this," she said, feeling the heat rise again in her body. "Then you can have whatever your heart desires."

***

At nearly dusk, Dmitry stood looking at his re-formed reflection in the large mirror of Lady Hutton's dressing room, marveling at how different he looked. Dressed in a black suit with 24-carat gold cuff links, a starched white button-down shirt, a leather belt and matching, black leather shoes, smelling of expensive cologne and wearing the late Lord Hutton's Presidential Rolex, he no longer recognized himself. He looked like the models he'd seen on a hundred magazine covers, only better.

Catherine sat behind him on a chaise lounge chair smiling and drinking a glass of wine. She was pleased with herself for transforming the young man into something remarkable, but Dmitry made that easy. He was remarkable already.

"So, you like it?" she asked with a clever grin.

"No. I love it," Dmitry answered.

"This is how I want to see you for the rest of our days together. I want you to remember your first lessons of today. Dress does make the man. Power is recognized through how you stand and how you present yourself. And a gentleman is always prepared at any-time for a meeting, a dinner, an engagement of any kind as long as he's in a black suit."

"Armani," Dmitry corrected.

"You'll get over that label soon. When you meet with the tailor, you'll think that suit is shabby," she grinned. As she tried to sit up, she winced. "I won't be able to see you out."

Dmitry looked back at her, and noticed that she was growing pale. "Are you still sore?"

"Yes, I need to soak. I'm afraid I'm spent now." She moved her golden locks from her face. "But I have no complaints."

"Should I come back the day after tomorrow then?" He walked over to her and knelt down.   Taking her hand in his own, he kissed it.

She ran her hand through his golden, curly locks and smiled. "We won't make love everyday. Unfortunately, my body cannot take it. However, there is so much for me to teach you in such little time until I want you to never miss an appointment with me." She looked into his eyes.

"I wouldn't dream of it," he said, standing up. He looked at his new watch. "Well, I better go."

She looked up at him, hoping he'd leave her with a kiss, but he did not. Excusing himself from her presence with a nod, she heard her bedroom door open and close shut.

***

As Dmitry pulled up to his broken down garage, he realized for the first time that he lived in a shit hole. Having spent a day in Lady Hutton's home, he was suddenly ashamed of what he thought only hours ago to be a treasure.

Stepping out of his old car, he slammed the door shut and went inside to find the place empty. The other men were gone.

Davyd had left a note on the refrigerator saying that he'd gone out for the night, and the order had already been placed with the general. He'd talk to him more about it when he returned.

Dmitry got the feeling as he read it that something was wrong. Davyd never left without them talking first. Pulling off his suit jacket, he flipped it over his shoulder and made his way upstairs.

The quiet calm of the musty building clouded his thoughts with each step he took towards his room. But as he got to his door, he noticed that his light was on.

Pulling his gun from its holster, he pushed the door open with the gun to find Ivan lying naked in his bed. Beside him lay Emma asleep and naked with Ivan's arm wrapped securely around her.

Dmitry stood beside the bed a moment looking at the both of them before he turned away. Laying his jacket on the chair, he grabbed a book and headed to the door.

"I see that you've made it back from my dear mother's," Emma said, sitting up. Her red nipples were rigid and pearled. Her short red hair seemed even more vibrant in the low lights of the room.

Dmitry looked at her and raised his brow. "Yes," he said in a low whisper to keep from waking his brother.

"And was she a good screw?" she asked angrily.

Ivan stirred.

Dmitry put his index finger to his lips. "We don't have to talk about this now. I'll leave you alone with my brother."

"I did this for you, you know." She threw Ivan's arm from around her. "I did this to hurt you."

"Well," Dmitry sighed. "You shouldn't have."

"Why? Didn't you screw my sick mother to get what you wanted?"

"Catherine's sick?" Dmitry asked.

"She's dying of ovarian cancer, you fucking asshole," she said with tears in her eyes. "Now you want to pretend that she didn't tell you?"

Dmitry pulled a handkerchief from his coat and walked over to throw it on the bed beside her. He looked her in her eyes without blinking.

"No, she didn't tell me. *Not that it would have made a bit of difference.* Look, I would have liked for it to be you in that room today, but you and I both know why it wasn't. You're not in a position to get me what I need. You can't help me help my brothers. There are men depending on me, and love, *or the thought of it*, won't pay a fucking pound. So, you'll have to excuse me if I made the wiser choice. I can assure you that it had nothing to do with feelings but everything to do with money. Your mother has it, and I'd have to wait too fucking long for you to acquire it. I had to go straight to the source. Pardon me for being honest, but I'm not a liar, and I'm not going to look you in your face and start now. It must be painful for you, but there are better things in life than being with me."

"So you're going to do it again?" she asked appalled.

"What I do is none of your business, Emma. I don't know why you thought that it was."

"You're a whore. You're a poor, stupid, worthless motherfucking whore," she cried.

Ivan's eyes popped open, and he sat up. "What the fuck did you call him?" he said her angrily. His glare was already wicked and his fist balled up.

"Don't you dare, Ivan," Dmitry ordered, raising his finger to point it at his brother. "Emma is just upset, and she has every reason to be." He looked at her sadly. It was never his intention to hurt her.

Emma turned to Ivan and touched his face. "I used you. I'm sorry."

Ivan pulled away, disgusted by her declaration of guilt. Standing up, he slid on his black shorts. "Dmitry, do you mind giving me a fucking minute with this bitch or what?"

"Don't call her a bitch," Dmitry ordered, walking to the door. "I'll be downstairs. If you need to talk to me *after you've dressed*, then I'll be willing."

"Fuck you!" Emma screamed, throwing a book.

"Yeah, fuck off," Ivan said, shaking his head at Dmitry.

With that, Dmitry left the room, closing the door completely shut to give them the privacy that they rightly deserved.

Emma grabbed her clothes angrily and began to pull them on.

Ivan watched unsure of what to say. Sitting back on the bed, he ducked his head down into his hands. "Sorry for calling you a bitch, but you sort of had it coming," he said gruffly.

She stopped dressing and walked over to his side of the bed. Taking his face in her hands, she whispered, "I don't expect you to understand this. You're much too young and... What I'm trying to say is that you're a decent kid. And you need to hear this from someone who has nothing to lose."

Ivan looked up at her. His blue eyes shined through her, open to whatever she had to confess.

"You will never be as smart as your brother. You will never be as beautiful or as powerful as he will. You'll never outrank him or out shine him. So, it's best when you can to leave and do your own thing. He's cold and calculating, Ivan. No woman will ever be able to resist him. So if you find just one who thinks more of you than him, marry her. But trust me, dear, if you stay here, bad things will happen. And more than likely, it will be by his hand."

With that, she pulled on the rest of her clothes and left him alone to think.

Ivan lay back in the bed and looked up at the dusty ceiling above. Hell, he already knew all of that himself, but if everyone else thought it – if everyone else saw it. The thought angered him. *Fuck Dmitry.*

The End

Volume Three

Prologue

The aroma of sugar cookies and chocolate cake filled the polished limestone hallways of the Medlov Chateau draped in beautiful paintings of Bohemian castles and antique busts as a violent winter storm beat on the windows outside of Dmitry's study. Taking in the scene of heavy, dark clouds whipping forceful winds about in a downpour of rain, Dmitry quietly sipped on his vodka and propped his feet up on the leather ottoman in front of him by the fireplace.

He rather liked the gloom today. It did well to remind him of how two opposite forces could be at work at one time in the same place. For at that very moment, a different type of more pleasant storm was taking place in his home. It was being overrun by the Medlov women cooking Valentine's Day treats in the kitchen and preparing the house for the family's annual grand gathering.

There was nothing more tranquil than a house full of family. His precious wife, Royal, was leading the charge, cooking with the girls and ordering about the staff in her normal fashion of graceful smiles and careful words. Emma, his nephew Gabriel's eldest daughter, and his own daughter, Anya, were making cookies while Alexandria, Anatoly's eldest daughter decorated the dining hall. His sons were surely up in their quarters looking at pictures of girls and on their phones. And he was certain that his youngest daughter, Demi, was somewhere taking a nap, in her normal lazy fashion.

Dmitry's mouth watered at the prospect of the meal to come. He hadn't had a bite since lunch, and he was near starving now.

However there was no room to grumble, because he truly loved this time of year. There was nothing that he would trade for it. It reminded him of all the wonderful years he had spent with his wife and his loving family. It reminded him of how gloomy those years were in his life before he had them. It reminded him of how hard he had fought to keep them. And the smell radiating throughout his home reminded him that they were *all* still here with him. That was a true testament to a good life.

Each year for nearly a decade his nephew, Gabriel, had come to visit on Valentine's Day. And while his eldest son was never as consistent, he also participated as much as possible, considering the constrictions of his position and his high profile in the public eye.

Still, he imagined that Anatoly would be arriving soon as well. Then tonight, they would all gather in the main dining hall to swap stories of all that they had missed in the last year. He would be caught up and revived in his youth through their many adventures – allowed to feel young again.

The thought of the word intrigued him now as an older man. Youth. The fleeting word danced through his mind like candle light in a dark room. He remembered well when he was a youth. It was a careless time for his brother, Ivan, and a time to test his own strength through fiery trials. It was as he played through the vivid thoughts of his aging mind that he decided that he wanted to see *her* face.

Getting up from his chair, Dmitry made his way, a little slowly, over behind his desk. The wind behind him continued to hit on the windows as he ran his hands over the glossy finish of his antique wooden desk. Streaks from his sweating finger tips decorated its perfect polish.

Taking a key from his jacket pocket, he unlocked the bottom drawer of his desk and pulled out a small black file with a single photo inside. He ran his hand over the image.

On the photo, Lady Catherine Hutton stood beside him in their only family portrait. She was a regal woman with the depth of the Caspian Sea in the blue of her eyes and the weight of the world on her fragile shoulders. Still, she stood - proud and triumphant even as she was dying. *His Catherine.*

Lady Hutton had been the first woman to teach him the art of being a gentleman, and she had done so painstakingly, amidst a grueling chemotherapy treatment and under the constant watchful eye of her board of directors of the former Hutton Industries.

He could still remember her smile and the clever words she always spoke even when things seemed to be completely out of control. She had been his mother in a weird sort of unthinkable way. She had been the only woman in his life to teach him something of real value before Royal. And in truth, he had given her more than he had ever expected at that time. A glimpse of love.

He remembered the day that she passed away. It was sort of like this afternoon, rife with storms of all sorts. He was a young man then, barely twenty two. There was so much that he didn't understand then, *although he thought that he knew absolutely everything.* It was only after Catherine's death that learned how ill-equipped he was for life.

It was after that Valentine's Day many years ago that Dmitry put on his full-armor, never to take it off again...

Chapter One

London, England

Valentine's Day 1994

The Hutton manor was cloaked away in the countryside nearly an hour from the busy streets of London. Wrapped in the shroud of thick trees and acres upon acres of rolling hills and lush green land, the 18th century castle was the hiding place for Lady Catherine and the pseudo-Lord Dmitry Medlov after their sudden and unexpected wedding. They had retreated to it now after Catherine had been released from the hospital for a bit of rest and for a lot of privacy.

There was not one approval among either of their families, the English royalty, the corporate community or even the Vory regarding their marriage. In fact, Catherine's daughter, Emma Hutton, upon hearing the news of her mother's engagement to a man thirty-one years her junior, disowned her, leaving Catherine completely in Dmitry's care, *which was fine by him.* And the only other rightful Hutton of noble blood, Emma's brother had been recently killed shortly after the wedding news while on a freedom operation in Kosovo with the Free Right.

On Dmitry's side of the family, Ivan Medlov was a different character altogether. He was neither shocked nor impressed. There were no foreboding words or public acts of anger. He simply requested a larger condo in the exclusive downtown area in which he lived, a larger spending account and a more respectable car.

As for the wedding itself, Ivan had missed it all together, having been arrested for a bar fight that later caused the family to hire four lawyers to get him free. In fact, for the last two years, since the night Ivan slept with Emma, he had been altogether removed, even secretive about his dealings with the Hutton family. The young man's only desire was to gain more power and to lead *the organization* further towards the Vory way of life and away from the social-norm effect that he felt the marriage was having on their grand plans of building an unstoppable crime family.

As a violent storm ripped through the countryside and rattled the priceless stain glass windows in their bedroom, Dmitry rolled over in the antique king-size bed and felt small fingers trail along his chest, shaking and cold. Grunting, his eyes fluttered open and focused on the woman beside him.

Lady Hutton was sicker than usual this morning. Trying to fight through the pain, she wiped the salty tears from her face and looked up at him with a weak smile. Her pale features were sapped of life, leaving only a shell of the woman he had met two years before. She was severely underweight and always in excruciating pain. Still, he found her beautiful.

In a cracked, weak voice, she managed to speak. "I didn't have the strength to get up and put my face on, dear," she tried to explain, rubbing her hand over her bald head. "I must look dreadful to you."

Dmitry slowly sat up in the bed, trying desperately not to disturb her fragile body too much and carefully put his muscular arm around her.

His beautiful face, full of life and bright with color was completely unreadable to her, as she had not learned him yet and doubted that she ever would.

Piercing blue eyes looked back at her under heavy lashes and arched, dirty blonde eyebrows. His high cheeks were rosy and brought even more attention to his full pink lips, wet and ready for a kiss. A blonde mop of curls danced above his head and drew attention to perfect, pale skin, unblemished and milky. She thought him to be a beautiful angel, unlike any man that she'd ever laid eyes on in all her long years. And she thought herself lucky to have him in any capacity, even more so as her husband.

Dmitry was oblivious to her private ogling. Pulling the covers over her body, he touched the crown of her head and sighed. "Would you like for me to cut my hair too? I would do it, if it would make you feel better. Maybe they can find way to make nice wig for you."

Fresh tears dotted her cheeks at his simply ridiculous and selfless statement. Shaking, she tried to pull herself up towards his hot body, but her strength had completely left her.

Dmitry stopped her from moving. With large fingers gripping her, he quickly pulled her up to cradle her in his strong embrace.

She settled in his arms, enjoying the smell of him. Sandalwood, soap and virility used to be a heady mix for her.

It killed Dmitry to see her struggle. The chemotherapy only made her weaker, and the doctor had told them that it was probably best that she simply try to enjoy her last days, instead of spending them in a hospital bed.

Ultimately, they had been given weeks, but since their arrival, Dmitry had begun to fear that it would be just days before she passed. Still, she never complained and always did everything in her power to seem less like a burden and more like the lady of the house.

Remembering himself, he took his eyes away from her aged face and the lines that showed when unmasked from behind the many layers of makeup. "Are you ready for breakfast?" he asked, wiping her tears away. "You should try to eat. You barely touched your dinner last night."

Catherine inhaled a deep breath and licked her cracked lips. "You dote over me as if I were a child," she said, touching his square jaw. "This was supposed to be a business arrangement. Remember? One that involved *me* teaching *you* how to be a gentleman, and you helping me remember what it is like to be alive again. I never said that you had to also be my bed nurse."

Dmitry clenched his jaw. "But I am still your husband. And as *your husband*, it is my responsibility to take care of your every need...even the most basic ones."

His deep voice shook the very foundation of her heart. Nodding her head, she laid back down on his chest. A few months ago, she would have been strong enough to argue her position, but now she could only submit.

"You've been a good man. You deserve every penny of what I'm leaving you," she said, giving in to him.

"Enough talk of money. It's barely seven in the morning." He laid her comfortably on the pillow and sat on the edge of the bed. His back was towards her and the many tattoos than decorated the sinewy muscle and scars called out for her attention.

Dmitry ran his hand over his curly locks and nestled his feet into the rug below. He would never admit it, but he was exhausted. He had barely slept since they had arrived. Still, he knew that he must continue as long as she did. *It was the least that he could do.*

"The maid will bring breakfast," Catherine said, reaching for him. "Why don't you lay here with me for a while?"

"No. I'm going to get your medicines and some hot food for you. When I get back, I'll bathe and dress you. Then, we can talk about what you want to do for Valentine's Day. It's today. Remember?"

"I don't deserve you," she whispered.

Dmitry looked back at her and smiled. "I know you don't," he said with a grin on his full lips. "Now, get some rest. I'll be back."

Naked, he stood up by the bed and slipped on his pajama bottoms. He could feel her eyes on his body, but he did not turn around to face her.

Even after being married for six months, she was still infatuated with his muscular build.

In a slow stroll, he made his way out of their dark master bedroom into the dimness of the stately hallway. As he closed the double doors behind him, the maid walked up with a tray of food.

He looked down at the little plump women in her black and white uniform staring up with him in amazement. She blinked quickly as she tried to speak. In her pudgy hands, she carried a silver tray with a white, porcelain bowl of cereal, a glass of juice and a flower in an antique vase.

Dmitry bent to the woman and inspected the tray. Shaking his head in disapproval, he said, "She needs warm food. How is she supposed to get better if you continue to feed her this bird seed?" Even in a whisper, his voice shook the hallway. "Here. Give to me. I'll take it downstairs and prepare something myself."

"But sir..." the woman protested in a wispy voice.

"No *buts*," Dmitry said, taking the tray from the woman. He tried to warm his tone when he saw how nervous his displeasure made her. "Look, if you want to be helpful, then have the grounds keeper bring in some fresh roses for Lady Hutton to admire or bring her up a good book and read it to her. She's wasting way in there."

"Yes, your Lordship," the maid said, bowing.

Dmitry turned from her and headed down the corridor towards the stairwell with the tray. As he did, he could still feel the woman staring at him, probably trying to cipher the tattoos that covered him. He turned quickly towards her to see her avert her gaze and turn away. He shook his head.

It would be nice to find one person on his staff that didn't gawk at him, but there was none. Their marriage was on the lips of everyone around them, regardless of station.

Plus, Ivan didn't help. Whenever he came around, *which was often*, he created even more of a buzz with his street talk, expensive dark clothes, wondering eyes and enormous mystery. Everyone was mystified by the men's youth, although no one knew their exact ages, and even more perplexed by Dmitry's maturity. He was an old wise man in a young man's body - a very attractive young man's body.

Between the two brothers, London was rife with tales of the Medlov men. Every woman who laid eyes on them desired them. Every man who met them despised them. And collective men in high places knew that soon enough, organizations would fear them.

As promised, Lady Hutton had intentionally spoiled Dmitry with obscene luxury. Only the finest clothes touched his body, flown in from around the world, tailored by only the best tailors. He drove only the best cars ordered from Germany and Italy. He only ate at the finest restaurants, drank at the finest bars, attended the best events and spoke to the most powerful people. If one was photographed with him, it was a big deal. If he accepted an invitation to your event, you were the cream of the crop, the crème de la crème. After all, he was Dmitry Medlov.

She had in two years, created a man who only knew a royal lifestyle, and she provided him such a life with intense veracity. She was always on him to inspect his lifestyle, inspect his appearance, inspect his environment, inspect his affiliations and to always when possible, control the outcome of his situation. That was the one part he had always done.

Her astute tutorship of his life had transformed him. Before he was a young man with dreams and ambitions, fighting to become someone in order to obtain a more powerful place in life. Now, he was young man with unthinkable resources and extreme power. And in return, Dmitry had been faithful – Lady Hutton's only stipulation. It wasn't even hard for him to do, although no one around him believed it.

In truth, he desired power a great deal more than being in a woman's arms. He desired to be taken seriously more than to be taken for granted, and he knew that this was the path that he must take if he wanted the last two years to count for anything. Many women over his short marriage had thrown themselves at him, but he had more than willingly thrown them back. Lady Hutton's purse was far too deep to give it up for a young woman's virtue.

***

With a bubble bath drawn, Dmitry placed Lady Hutton's delicate, fragile body into the warm water and helped her to rest her head back on the gold-plated basin. Her health had worsened since morning.

Dmitry sat on the cold marble floor beside the tub and ran the yellow sponge over her skin. Water cascaded down her back and wet the edges of her golden hair. Under heavy, tired eyes, she looked over at him and smiled, but Dmitry did not smile back. He was worried.

"Shouldn't I call the doctor?" Dmitry asked, gently rubbing her skin.

"Why? We already know what's happening," she said with a sigh. "I'm fading."

Dmitry looked down at the floor, unhappy with her answer but sure that it was so. He wasn't sure what was worse – finding his mother beaten and bloody or watching the woman he'd grown to appreciate slowly die over time. Both were cruel ends.

Lady Hutton raised her hand from the water and touched his chin. "You shouldn't be so sad. I thought that I had prepared you well for this."

"How can anyone be prepared for this?" he asked in a low, sulking voice.

"It's amazing to watch, isn't it? Life is a delicate thing. God gives it, and God takes it away," she said in aching voice.

"How can you be so calm?"

"Haven't I lived a charmed life?" she asked with a spark in her voice. "Haven't I had had more than most? Haven't I had you?"

Dmitry looked up at her with a frown. "I wouldn't say that I'm much to brag about."

"How I've tried to make you see how special you are. I've spoiled you, and yet you still feel unworthy." The water splashed around as she moved. "My only hope is that one day you will realize your own worth, Dmitry. I do not cast my pearls to swine."

Dmitry cracked a grin. He had read that once in her Bible. "This has become more than an arrangement for me, Catherine.   You have become more than a partner." His voice ached as well.

"Dare you say the words after two years?" she asked with tears in her eyes.

Dmitry sighed. Washing her skin again, he shook his head. "Dare I say the words? There are so many words to say. Why linger on a few?" He kept his gaze on her skin, intentionally looking away from her eyes.

"Before I die, if it is true, I want to hear you say them. However, if it is not, I understand. Our arrangement will still stand. I am a woman of my word."

Dmitry trailed his finger down her shoulder and made goose bumps form. He looked over at her, his bright, blue eyes beaming with sincerity. "I love you." He swallowed hard, clenching his square jaw as he waited for her response.

She looked at him with wonderment in her face. Sitting all the way up in the water despite the shooting pains, she took his beautiful face in her hands. "Do you truly mean that, my dear young husband?"

"Yes," he said sternly. "I would never say anything that I don't mean. I don't have to. You know that."

Lady Hutton rested her head back down against the basin. Looking up at the crown molding above her, she smiled. "Go into the bedroom and look inside of my desk. Bring me the paper that has been double clipped."

Dmitry thought that it was a strange response by her after saying something so intimate, but he did as she asked. Standing up, he went into the bedroom to her desk and pulled the drawer open to find a thick, legal document. Without reading it, he headed back into the bathroom.

"And bring a pen," she screamed weakly.

He turned back around and grabbed the gold Cross pen on the table. Returning back to her side with the paper in hand, he sat down on the floor beside the tub and put the document in his lap. The cold floor cooled his backside.

"Do you want me to read it to you?" he asked.

"No, I know what it says," she said, taking weak, low breaths. "Pass it to me with the pen."

Dmitry got on his knees and passed it to her. She flipped through the pages and smiled at him. "Turn around," she said, leaning over to use his back as a desk to sign her name. Scribbling her name on the dotted line, she hit his back with the pen and passed him the document. Small sprinkles of water left delicate bubbles on the document.

"What is it?" he asked, taking it.

"Your inheritance," she said, looking at the document. "It is every last cent that I own, that my family has owned since we've become what we are – English royalty, corporate giants, *lords of war.*" The last title made her grin.

Dmitry was speechless. He knew that she was going to include him in the will, but he had no idea that he was inheriting everything. Hundreds of millions of dollars. With his mouth open, he looked at the document in shock.

"What about your daughter? How will she take care of herself?" he asked.

"You are here. You have taken care of me. You will have my money." She ran her hand through the water and made waves. "Does that say I love you?"

"*Da*," Dmitry answered, putting the document on the table across from them. "It says *I love you*, and *you're insane*."

She laughed. "Ahh, humor is good for the soul. Remember that." Her weak eyes searched his.

"I will." He nodded.

"Now, help me finish bathing so that we can go back to bed and rest a while."

***

After Dmitry dressed Lady Catherine in a soft gown and placed a silk wrap on her head, he put her in their massive bed and crawled in with her. The storm outside rumbled the dark room, which was only illuminated by the candles and fireplace.

In the tranquility of their privacy, he read her favorite book to her as Carmen McRae's *Something to Live For* played on her record player in the corner of the room.

With her head on his chest as he read, she listened to his Russian brogue accent read Welsh poet Dylan Thomas' poetic work, *Death and Entrances*. With every word, she listened to his heart beat as it drummed against her, full of life, full of fight. Taking in deep breaths of his masculine scent and basking in the muscular embrace of a loving man, she drifted off with the last thoughts in her mind of his face when he said, "I love you."

When Dmitry finished reading, he placed the book down and rubbed the top of her head. Just then, the violent storm shook the windows and knocked out the power. The lights in the bathroom flickered off, pulling Dmitry's attention from the fireplace.

"It's a good thing that we have the candles out already," he said, pulling the chenille throw over her feet. "Are you cold? You feel icy?"

The silence of the room was eerie. Suddenly, Dmitry felt alone. "Catherine?" he whispered for a response. But her body was still - no faint breaths, no movement. "Catherine?" he whispered again in a strained voice.

Moving her slowly off his chest, he laid her limp body against her own pillow and looked into her hollow eyes. For a moment, he didn't know what to do. They had spoken on several occasions about what would happen when she finally passed, but somehow in his mind, he didn't exactly expect it to happen like this.

Taking her hand in his own, he bent to it and kissed her wedding ring. The warmth of his body swallowed her coldness as he hovered over her. Salty, painful tears burned the sides of his eyes as they moved down his cheeks onto her face.

His Catherine was gone. It was a devastating feeling made all the more painful because of its reminder of his mother. He tried hard to hold it, to bottle the emotions, to keep them from springing forth, but he was only a man. In his unwilling, acrimonious desperation, he began to cry. It had been the first time that he had cried in many years, and it overwhelmed him – scared him.

With his face buried into the pillow beside her, still holding her hand, he wept in his bitter dissatisfaction of all the things that he been required of him in his short life. In the darkness, he cried for his mother, for his brother, for every person he had murdered, for every family he had destroyed, for every cruel thought and every multiplied cruel action.

He cried for his wretched soul and the daunting days that lie ahead. But mostly, he cried for his Catherine. She had deserved so much more than he could give.

Chapter Two

Many miles away as the storm raged, Ivan stood looking out of the window of his penthouse apartment drinking a glass of vodka and contemplating if he would go into his club tonight or get into a little *trouble*. Lightning stuck across the night sky, illuminating it with its grand fury and suddenly reminded him of his brother. Turning from his view of downtown London, he focused his gaze on the three women quietly sleeping in his disheveled bed.

He walked over to the trio, covered in black silk sheets, drunk with vodka and high from cocaine, and touched the top of the Asian woman's head nearest the end of the bed. The slits of her eyes opened, and she stared up at him.

"What are you doing out of bed?" she asked in a distinctive English accent, trailing her finger over his leg.

Ivan smiled warmly. His perfect white teeth sparkled. "That's funny. I was just asking myself why you and your friends were still here," he said, setting down his glass on the nightstand. "Come on. Up. Up. You girls have to get out of here." He clapped his hands together creating a thunderous boom.

"Are you serious?" she asked, rising up to show her expose breasts. "It's storming outside. It's a fucking monsoon out there." The other two women began to move about in the bed because of the abrupt ruckus.

Ivan turned and looked out of the window. "Monsoon in London? Hardly. Besides, it was storming when you got here. What's the difference?" he asked, shrugging his large shoulders.

Still naked from his sexual encounter the hour before, Ivan made his way to the door of his bathroom. Running his hand over the switch, he turned and looked at the woman, who sat up looking baffled at his quick mood swing.

"By the time I get out of the shower, I do hope that you and your friends have left. I've got shit to do, and the only thing left on my agenda for you tonight is a trio human sacrifice if you stay," he said, closing the door behind him.

As the shower head pushed out hot beads of water against his body, the stench of sex wafted up to his nose before it dissipated in the steam. Ivan rested his large hands against the black tile and arched his back to let the water rush down his body. He had been up over two days, unable to sleep, uneasy for some enigmatic reason.

It was times like this when he wished that he was back in Moscow, where he could let loose some of his pent up frustration. But here, since his brother had become freaking royalty, every time that he put someone's face into a wall, he heard about it later.

A knock at his bathroom door made him forget his thoughts. He turned off the shower and grabbed a towel. "What?" he asked in a raised voice. "I thought I told you bitches to leave."

"It's me, boss," one of his soldiers answered. "Boss Dmitry is on the phone for you. He says it's urgent."

Ivan opened the door and grabbed the cordless phone. Walking out into the bedroom, he looked around. "Did they leave?" he asked as he looked down at the man.

"*Da*, just now," the man answered.

"Good." Ivan pointed towards the door. "Give me some privacy, *eh*."

Sitting on the end of the bed with the towel draping over his long hairy legs, he answered the phone. "Hello."

"Catherine passed," Dmitry said gruffly. "There are going to be things that I need to handle, and I want you here."

"Are you out at the *castle*?" he asked facetiously.

"I'm where I always am," Dmitry said shortly. "Look, I'm not asking you to come, I'm telling you. Get Davyd and meet me out here."

"What makes you think that I wouldn't come in first place? Your fucking wife just died." Hanging up the phone, Ivan laid his head back on the bed and smiled. FINALLY. He'd been waiting on that old hag to kick the bucket for two long years, so he could finally get his brother back and his organization on its feet.

Now, they could really get down to the business of being a Medlov.

***

Changing gears in his black Porsche, Ivan sped through the countryside with Davyd in the passenger seat. Music blasting, he drove quietly thinking of all the things that had been sitting on the back burner since Dmitry married Catherine.

"I imagine that he wants us to get there alive, you impatient little bastard," Davyd said, turning down the stereo.

"Stop being a pussy," Ivan answered with a smile. "If my driving makes you nervous, then why didn't you drive your own car?"

"It was oversight," Davyd said, shaking his head. "You know, your brother will need some support. So, don't go in there being...yourself." He looked over at Ivan.

"What's that supposed to mean?" Ivan asked offended. "Who else am I supposed to be?"

"Try being a loving brother for once."

Ivan rolled his eyes. "Am I the only one who remembers that this shit was supposed to happen? Dmitry never loved Catherine. He was *banging* her to get the money we need for our organization. It was business move. How is he supposed to mourn getting what he wanted?"

"This still might be difficult for him," Davyd said, irritated that he had to explain such an obvious situation. "You don't need to complicate things further with whatever on your mind is causing you to drive like idiot."

"What's on my mind is that my club is finally taking off, but I need more money, and I need women, and I need fucking drugs that Dmitry won't let me bring in. He can't be a saint and a..." Ivan couldn't think of the word.

"Sinner," Davyd answered.

"Yeah, he can't be that shit. He has to choose." He gripped the steering wheel tighter.

"Your brother is far more complicated than you, Ivan."

"That's not my fault." Ivan tugged at his suit jacket. "We all had to sacrifice for him to get where he is. He didn't do this by himself. Only, I'm the only one who reminds him of it. Everyone else just hangs on to his coattails while he drags us around the city."

"You're ungrateful, and it's pretty hard to watch while you sit in a thousand dollar suit and drive such an expensive sports car."

"I'm a fucking Medlov and a Vor. I don't have to be grateful," Ivan scowled.

"Well, you can be respectful," Davyd said, raising his brow. "Don't ask him for anything tonight. Let him get over this first."

"Let me handle my own business. You just focus on *whatever* it is that you do for him," Ivan said, pushing his foot down on the accelerator.

***

By the time that Ivan and Davyd arrived, the coroner had already taken the body to the morgue. Dmitry was alone in the study sitting by the fire and having a drink. The butler tapped on the wooden door and stepped inside.

"Your brother and your business partner have arrived, sir," the butler said, waiting for instruction.

"Bring them in here, please," Dmitry said, sitting up in the chair. He wiped his tired eyes and put down his glass.

Shortly after, Ivan and Davyd were escorted into the dark room where Dmitry sat brooding. He looked up as they entered.

Ivan was the first to note his brother's melancholy. It only took a glance to know that it was genuine. He looked like the day their mother passed. Looking around the room, Ivan sighed. "Where are the lights?"

"Leave them off," Dmitry ordered. He didn't dare want them to see that his eyes were not red from exhaustion but from crying.

"Do you still have on pajamas from this morning?" Ivan asked, walking over to the fireplace. He looked down at Dmitry and noticed his five o'clock shadow. "Shit, you *do* still have on your night clothes. Damn, you really are taking this shit to a new level."

"Ivan!" Davyd admonished.

"It's alright," Dmitry said, standing up from his chair. Rising to his full height, he walked up to his brother and stared down into his eyes. The look on his face was menacing, deadly. In an instant the man had gone from sad to quietly furious. Clenching his jaw, Dmitry narrowed his gaze and flinched. Muscles protruded from his neck and shoulders; veins lined his sinewy frame. The crackle of the fire and silence of the room made the tension even more thick.

Ivan's smirk disappeared. He swallowed hard and turned his gaze away from his brother's.

Davyd noted Dmitry's control over his brother and the fact that even amidst the finest luxuries a man could have, his young boss had not lost his ability to establish dominance in the most basic and instinctually male ways.

"I want you to have the lawyers to come out here," Dmitry said, walking away from Ivan. "There is going to be a lot to discuss, and I want them on my territory." He walked over to the bookshelf and put away the book that he had read to Catherine.

"What has happened?" Davyd asked alarmed.

Dmitry looked over at Davyd and gave a weak smile. "She gave me everything. The money in the banks. The stock in other companies. The bonds. The CDs. The land. The houses. The cars. Hutton Industries with 58 percent of the company in my possession. I now own it all, plus much, much more." His words were slow and cautious.

"The men who sit on her board are going to lose their minds. That wasn't the original agreement," Davyd said concerned. "When did this happen?"

"Today, right before she passed," Dmitry answered. "They are not going to take me seriously, Davyd. I need to make sure that I'm ready. I'm only twenty-three years old. They're going to try every move in the book. For the men who won't negotiate, we're going to need muscle." He looked over at his brother. "Ivan. That is where you come in. I need you to scout out a team of assassins we could put on payroll, but they can't be our normal guys. If we have to do something, I don't want it to be traceable back to us."

Ivan nodded and looked back into the fireplace.

"What do you know about running a multi-national corporation?" Davyd asked.

"Nothing," Dmitry said, biting his lip. "But I want you to get in touch with Khalid Sidorov. His son is at Oxford. Arrange a meeting. We'll need them. They are Vor, but they are also respected business men. Between the three of us, we should be able to figure things out."

"I'll get right on it," Davyd said, leaving the room.

As soon as the door closed, Dmitry turned to his brother. Shaking his head, he ran his hand through his hair, smelling his own musk as his arm raised. "What is bugging you, *brat*. And don't lie."

"I need money," Ivan answered shortly, turning from the fireplace to face him. "I need money for my club, but I also need a large chunk of whatever you're getting for someone else."

"*Someone* like whom?" Dmitry asked in a huff.

"I assume that if she left you everything, she left nothing for Emma," Ivan said quietly.

"That's right."

"Well, Emma has...an obligation that would be better handled if she had more money."

"An obligation?" Dmitry asked momentarily intrigued.

"A child," Ivan answered.

Dmitry was lost for words. He walked over and sat back down in the chair by the fireplace. Looking up at Ivan, he took the glass of vodka back in his hand and sipped it. "Is it yours?" he asked. His blue prisms sparkled.

Ivan didn't blink. "No. It's hers, but she deserves the money just the same."

Dmitry looked at his brother and knew that he was lying. "How old?"

"Two. Just turned two. And it's a boy before you ask," Ivan answered, shifting his weight from one foot to the other. With his hand on his hip and the other on the mantle, he shook his head. "Are you going to do it or not?"

"I've never heard you ask for money for anyone else. And you want me to believe that this child isn't yours?" he laughed. Titling his head, he looked at his brother. "Where is Emma anyway? The last word we heard was that she had left the country."

"New York," Ivan answered. "Look, it's just a bastard baby. I only know about it, because every once and a while she and I call each other and talk shit about you and your dead wife. So, considering that some of that money should have gone to Catherine's only daughter, it just seems right that you would send some to help her and the kid out. If you don't, fuck it. I don't care. But the kid isn't mine and even if it were, I wouldn't claim it, because the code doesn't bend. Or at least for me, it doesn't." He looked down at Dmitry.

Dmitry sat with his legs cocked open and his bare feet planted firmly in the 200-year old rug. Snarling, he looked up at his brother. "Don't ever in your little pathetic life *ever* remind me of the code again. I have lived by it. I have abided by it. You don't have to use guilt to get things from me. You only have to ask. I'll give Emma and her baby, *your baby, whoever's bastard kid,* the money only because it's the right thing to do. But don't push me, Ivan. No one told you to fuck that girl, in the first place." He pointed at his brother.

"It's. Not. Mine," Ivan bit out as he walked away. "I don't ever want to talk about it again. Just send the bitch the money if you want to." Crossing the room quickly, he slammed the door as he left.

Chapter Three

Three long days after the funeral, Dmitry was still numb with disbelief and discontent. Newspapers around the country were covering the sensational story of Lady Catherine's death and her unbelievable final wishes of leaving her fortune to her mysterious 23-year old husband. And because of the news, he had not left the manor. He had turned down over 50 interviews and resorted to locking off the property to ensure the paparazzi didn't get unwanted photos of his home.

Instead, he spent his time holed up in his study reading book after book on corporate law and financial investments. Evidently, he owned thirty one small businesses outside of the larger corporation. Plus, he had inherited a personal plane – not really just a plane, a jet.

Catherine had never made mention that she owned the aircraft that they often traveled on, but then again, she had also never mentioned the span of her power. It reached far beyond the shores of England into Austria, Rome, Stockholm and Prague. Many of the places where he had investments, he had never even seen with his own eyes, but he planned very soon to visit them all.

Now the phone calls were pouring in, and he had to provide answers to more than just reporters. Yes or No, would business go on as usual? The answer for at least for the time being was yes. It wasn't that he felt the least bit responsible for the people and jobs that he held in his young hands, it was just that the money was too good to simply get rid of. There would be some reorganizing, but he planned to relinquish no power in the process.

Davyd walked into the office followed by a maid who brought brunch. Setting the tray on the desk, she bowed out quietly and left the men to speak. Dmitry barely looked up from the books. Perched behind the desk, using a lamp light, he read carefully, scribbling on his notepad as he processed the information.

"You need to rest," Davyd said concerned. "Rome wasn't built in a day."

Dmitry looked up and ran his fingers over his aquiline nose. "I can't rest. I have to figure all this shit out. We have our first board of directors meeting in four days."

"I spoke with Khalid's son today. He has agreed to meet with you this afternoon, if you are available."

Dmitry smirked. "When have I not been available?" Pulling the tray of food over to him, he savored the aroma of a huge ham sandwich and cream of potato soup.

"With all your money, why don't you have them bring you something less common," Davyd asked.

"I haven't been able to eat common, *as you call it*, since Catherine came into my life. I'm trying to remember what it's like to be normal."

"You'll never be normal again, Dmitry." David cleared this throat.

Dmitry nodded in agreement as a large chunk of food caught in his own throat. He swallowed hard and felt the strain of the food breaking up. He shook off the discomfort. "Normalcy is irrelevant for the time being anyway, I guess. Has Ivan assembled a team?" He reached over and took a sip of water.

"He says that he has. He wants to bring them here to meet you tonight."

"Finally that boy does exactly as I have asked," Dmitry sighed. "It's like pulling teeth with that one."

"*Da*," Davyd agreed.

"Do you know that he has a son?" Dmitry asked, still in shock. He wiped his hands together.

"With whom or should I ask what?"

"Emma Hutton," Dmitry said, tasting the soup. "Though he says that it is not his, I don't believe him. He's lying. He has fathered a child with that woman." He shoved the rest of the sandwich in his mouth knowing that Catherine would surely disapprove.

"Are they together?" Davyd asked.

Dmitry laughed. "Ask yourself who you are talking about first. This is Ivan. He is with no woman. He called her a bitch, told me never to mention her again and stormed out."

"He's so romantic," Davyd said sarcastically. "And he wants you to take care of the child?"

"Yes," Dmitry answered.

"And will you?"

Dmitry furrowed his dirty blonde brow. "Why wouldn't I?"

"The code prevents such ties," Davyd answered. "I have no children, no wife, no obligation outside of the Vory."

"Not even a lover?" Dmitry asked.

Davyd smiled. "There is always a woman around to call, but never one to call wife."

Dmitry raised his brow. The old men were so different. "I don't consider them to be an obligation. I'm paying her to go away. It's probably safest for both she and the child. Could you imagine *him* babysitting? He'd kill the poor *rebenka* before the night was over."

"Within the hour," Davyd corrected.   He put his hands in his jacket pockets. "But what if he's being honest? What if the child isn't his?"

"Then it's not. I don't care one way or the other. I'm trying to streamline an entire empire from my dead wife's study with the education of a blind, deaf mute. I don't have time to play daddy to some woman who left her mother to die. Besides, it's not my kid. I didn't make such stupid mistake."

Davyd looked at him curiously. "Based upon your very judgmental tone, I assume that you haven't heard then."

Dmitry sat back in his chair and put down his spoon. He knew that Davyd was about to tell him something else that he didn't want to hear.   "What haven't I heard?" he asked gravely.

"There was a rumor that you had baby back in your old neighborhood in Moscow. Kirill told me that a girl named Alexandria gave birth to a boy of yours a few years ago. I believe his name was Anatoly. I assumed that you already knew."

Dmitry barely blinked. "Alexandria?"

"Yes, do you know her?" Davyd asked intrigued. Never once had he heard Dmitry mention her name.

Dmitry nodded. Pushing his food away, he put his hand over his mouth and shook his head. "Davyd, give me minute, *da*. I want to be alone to marvel at how completely fucking clueless I am."

***

At dusk, the rain finally gave way to clear, crisp skies. Dmitry stood on the balcony of his bedroom looking across the vast landscape and admired the full moon high above. However, his thoughts were not on the beauty around him but around the madness that surrounded him like an angry fog.

It had taken him the entire rest of the day to process what Davyd had told him earlier, that he was possibly a father. It had taken a few hours to process that his brother was possibly also a father. And it still had not processed that he was now such a wealthy man.

However, he did understand his brother's desperation for once. Just the thought of what could be put such a heavy weight on his chest until it made it hard for him to breathe. A child. His child. His seed.

Still, he had to compartmentalize his own emotions to prepare for the meeting that would take place in just a moment. He would think of that much later. The men with whom he was about to speak were of a different caliber than the men who sat around board room tables and discussed stakeholder interests. The men who were coming here tonight were of his ilk. They were bred for war and fed on battles.

Before now, he would have never been able to arrange such a meeting. To meet with members of the elite was only for the real players, men who had promise, who would rise to the top of the food chain – eat their way up one man at a time. Evidently, Dmitry had arrived at that level. Evidently, he was finally a prospect.

Slipping on his black suit pants, he slowly dressed himself, unable to take his eyes off the bed that his wife once slept on, where he used to make love and be loved. He found it still depressing when he truly thought about it. No one really knew that he cared deeply for her; no one could ever know how it pained him to be without her.

Instead, he would devote himself to learning his new craft. He would study on how to be a good billionaire. Funny, just days ago, he thought he was going to be a millionaire and could not fathom it. The word sounded surreal, even in his thoughts. Billionaire.

What did a billionaire do every day? How did he eat, live, play? What did he sound like? Who did he counsel, and who counseled him? He had heard that he was the one of the youngest, richest men alive now. At least, that was what the newspaper reporters wrote. He heard that he was the most sought after bachelor in the world. At least, that is what the gossip columnists wrote. He heard that his power could help reshape Europe. At least, that is what the radio and talk show hosts said. Everyone was talking about him, yet, he remained silent. No comment. No contact. He knew in his heart that eventually the standing statement would grow stale, and he would finally be forced to speak. *But what would he say?*

Fully dressed, he stared critically at himself in the custom mirror Catherine had ordered for him. He looked stately, educated – a total façade.

Running his tattooed hand over his suit jacket, he shook his head. Who was he kidding? It would be impossible to hide his marks. Anyone with eyes could see them.

Stepping closer to the mirror, he squinted as he ran his hand over his blonde locks. Could that be a gray hair in the front? *Wow.* He stood back and raised his brows in amazement. Buttoning his jacket, he slipped his hands in his pockets and walked out of his dressing room.

***

Dmitry sat behind the antique desk in his grand study, once occupied by the great and powerful Lord Hutton of a long lineage of men of notable wealth and titles of esteem and royalty - now occupied by a street kid from Moscow.

He smirked at the ironic thought as he looked around him in the quietness of the room as they all waited on Khalid's son and his men to arrive. There was much to discuss before the next board meeting, and it was imperative that Dmitry have a sound plan - one that included him losing nothing but gaining everything.

Ivan sat nearest the fire as they waited. His blue eyes sparkled as they met the quiet blaze in front of him. He was still brooding, probably over his earlier request of Dmitry and as always in a bad mood. Ivan seemed perpetually angry, unable to control his fiery temper and always eager to inflict pain.

Dmitry watched him from across the room in dismay. Ivan was only eighteen years old, and yet he carried the weight of an old man on his broad shoulders. His life was further complicated by his growing stature not only in society by his physically startling appearance. He was now six foot, nine inches and filling out more and more.

When Dmitry and Ivan were boys, they used to scrounge for food in gutters of Moscow, happy to get their hands on a steak every once in a while. Now, Ivan had a private maid and ate five times a day, worked out religiously and desired power more than regular men desired air. He breathed it in, extracting from it the explicit high that it gave him to be regarded as some important figure.

Dmitry thought that Ivan had been dealt a horrible hand in life. He was young, obviously disturbed and yet contradictable beautiful.   His pale white skin was completely unblemished; his coal, jet black, inky hair was thick and wavy; his eyes were like blue diamonds cut for the first time. Every feature on Ivan Medlov was breath taking, from the curve of his lips, to the cut of his square jaw, to the perfection of his nose to the clever smile he often gave a person right before their demise. He was muscular, animalistic, vengeful and now power-ful. Ivan Medlov was the perfect storm, only before he did not know it, and now, he relished in it.

Dmitry truly wished that his brother had not been so beautiful, for he knew that it was his attractiveness that brought people to him, that lured people into his clutches – both men and women. But he also knew that it was his brother's anger and resentment that caused senseless murders and disastrous raft.

Since his marriage to Catherine, Dmitry had not killed a soul. He had spent his time under the tutelage of his wife, learning to be more than a brut with a gun. However, Ivan had made up for his absence with his own depraved actions that according to Davyd had become unimaginable.

Dmitry knew that he needed to find Ivan a good doctor, someone who could diagnose his evil. And hopefully, he could find someone to help. He'd be willing to walk away from everything if he could just get his brother some help. Only, he couldn't tell Ivan that. He would think him too soft.

Knowing that Dmitry was looking at him, Ivan's gaze moved from the fireplace to his brother as he put his glass down on the table. Exhaling, Ivan smacked his lips and rolled his eyes. "Why are you looking at me like I've done something *else* wrong?" Ivan asked in a deep, growl of a baritone.

"Because even though I don't know about it, you probably have done something else wrong," Dmitry answered shortly.

Ivan didn't blink. "You've grown soft. I can tell. Too much gentlemen's training and not enough hunting...or pussy for that matter."

"You really think so?" Dmitry asked, titling his head. "And what would you suggest I hunt?"

"Your prey...everything beneath you."

"We are gutter rats. There is nothing beneath us," Dmitry answered, running his hand over the desk. "Don't let the clothes, money and power fool you, *brat*. We weren't born into this, and if it weren't for my ability to fuck like a wild savage animal, we still would be pulling jobs out of a park at crack of dawn and wondering where our next meal was going to come from." Dmitry looked up from his desk and raised his thick, dirty blonde brow.

Ivan countered. "We would have arrived at this point one way or another."

"I doubt it," Dmitry said, dismissing his brother. "That's what worries me about you. You pretend to be so wise, and yet you say the dumbest things."

"Fuck off," Ivan said, turning back to the fire. "I've done everything you've *ever* asked of me. I don't owe you shit. So what, you were able to get all of this stuff from that old bitch...if you hadn't done it, I would have got it through her daughter."

"Emma was using you," Dmitry said in a matter-of-fact tone. "She wanted me, but she had to settle for second best, *if* you can call yourself that."

"And that old whore you married would have settled for my back, if she couldn't have gotten yours. What's the difference? They were both pawns in our sick, twisted game. And I know the question lurking behind those unshaven, thick ass eyebrows is when would I start really caring about either one of them? Well, that's where we differ, *brat*. I would have done the same as you did, but I wouldn't have cared a bit. That is going to be your downfall. You have to stop inserting your emotions. At the end of the day, emotions are worth shit. They are worth less than shit."

Dmitry hated to admit how his brother's reference to his wife angered him. He tried hard to hide it behind his cool exterior. "The difference is that she would have never gone for you. I've seen you screw and it's unimpressive, Ivan. And as far as Catherine and her preference, I think her decision speaks louder than the words spoken by a man who lives and breathes by my generosity."

"Well, by all means, please continue to be *generous, brat*," Ivan said facetiously.

Davyd never interrupted the boys when they feuded but made an exception this time. Clearing his throat, he sat up in his chair. "The men who are coming here tonight will look for weakness within our little amateur organization. It is important that we not only appear cohesive but that we are. I trust you both can understand that."

The men did not speak but it was apparent that they understood.

Biting his lip, Ivan looked back at the fire as he felt for his gun hidden under his suit jacket. *How he wanted to kill someone right now.*

The butler interrupted the group with a tap on the door. He stepped inside, bowing towards his lordship and announced the arrival of Dmitry's guests.

Dmitry nodded and excused the butler. "You two go out and stay with his men," he said to the bodyguards in the corners, who stood quietly listening to their bosses squabble. "Ivan, do me a favor, and don't speak unless you're spoken to."

Ivan didn't respond.

The door opened with the butler re-entering and extending his arm to the three people who followed him. A bodyguard, short in stature, came in and made his way to the corner midway between Dmitry and Ivan. The notorious Vladimir Sidorov, son of the feared and powerful Khalid Sidorov, entered right behind him mirroring Dmitry in a black, tailor suit and then right behind him, walking nearly in cadence and most unexpectedly, a young black woman in a navy blue dress followed.

Davyd made sure that Vladimir and the woman were comfortably seated across the desk from Dmitry, while Ivan sat watching them all curiously. The woman had drawn his attention from the fire, but it was Vladimir who truly perplexed him. Ivan had never seen a man more sure of himself. A sense of absolute entitlement resonated deep within the young man, something that Ivan found incredibly enticing. He wanted to be like that – in that instant, he knew it.

Dmitry sat watching the two as well; only his eyes kept finding themselves landing on the coffee-colored muse in front of him. Who was she? He felt as though he would pay a king's ransom just to hear her voice.

Aware of the attention that she was causing, Vladimir looked over at her and nodded. "She does have that effect on men," he said, answering their thoughts. "Why don't you introduce yourself, love? Don't be shy."

The woman crossed her legs and nodded. "My name is Elsa." Her voice was rich and sexy, easing off her lips like silk. In a second she had captured every man in the room.

"She is here as gift from my father," Vladimir said, taking his eyes off the woman. He looked back at Dmitry proudly.

"A gift?" Dmitry asked intrigued. He sat up in his chair.

"You have acquired a great deal of wealth, Mr. Medlov. Am I to understand that you have someone who understands how to manage it?" Vladimir asked.

"No, we don't. And please call me Dmitry," he answered humbly. "We do not even understand the full scope of my estate yet."

"We thought as much," Vladimir answered with a smirk. "And are you still committed to the brother-hood?" He crossed his fingers together and rested his elbows on the arms of the leather chair.

"Of course," Dmitry said, finally taking his eyes off of Elsa. "This is why I have reached out to you. I want to use some of the money from my late wife's estate to strengthen my core businesses with the Vory, but I don't want low-level contacts. I want the best."

"You finally have the power to create a vertically integrated organization, and my father and his men understand that. We are willing to assist you in what-ever you may need. Elsa will assist you with making sure that your wishes are carried out. She is a senior at Oxford with high marks, fluent in six languages, familiar with countless cultures and one of the best business minds in the western hemisphere. She is also untracea-ble to the Vory v Zakone or any other group," Vladimir explained.

"I am happy to have her," Dmitry said, giving her one last glance. "Now, in return for your gift, what would you like of me?" he asked, turning his attention to Vladimir.

"My father would like an opportunity to speak with you about purchasing a small glass factory that you own on the outskirts of Moscow, and he would also like a seat on your board in the next three years." Vladimir waited on Dmitry's answer, but it did not come quickly.

Standing up, Dmitry went over to one of the bookshelves and pulled out a small, leather bound ledger book. Opening it, he licked his fingers and flipped through the pages until he found what he was looking for. "And how much is your father offering for this *very lucrative* glass factory that has been in my wife's family for over forty years?" he asked with his back to his guests.

"We will send over a proposal tomorrow with numbers we feel are appropriate," Vladimir said, sucking his teeth. He had underestimated Dmitry. Word was the young brut had absolutely no couth or understanding of his current situation. Evidently, the information given was wrong. Dmitry seemed extremely sure of himself, capable of handling business and formidable.

"I won't take a penny under eight," Dmitry answered, putting the book away.

"We wouldn't dream of offering a penny under eight," Vladimir said, standing. "Well, I'll leave your gift for you to make yourself more familiar. I apologize for my abruptness, but I do have other plans for the evening. I'm sure you both have a great deal to talk about."

"Leave her here?" Dmitry asked, looking at Elsa.

"As I said, *she is your gift*. I expect her to be in class tomorrow as usual. She'll need a car and a driver, a nice room, a hefty salary and a title. She is a respectable woman and her safety and well-being are expected to stay at the top of your priority list." Vladimir looked over at Ivan. "And she is expected to be kept as far away from your *men* as possible. Word has traveled around the globe and back again of your baby brother's sordid and tasteless extracurricular activities. And while I don't mind, my father does. His wishes are my own."

"I'll see to it," Dmitry said, looking at Ivan also.

"Don't worry. She's not my type," Ivan bit out with a sinister grin. "She's far too clean of a woman."

Elsa rolled her eyes and turned her back to Ivan, having already been informed of his cavalier attitude towards women.

"We'll touch base in a week. After Elsa has laid the foundation that you so desperately need then I'll arrange a meeting with my father," Vladimir said concluding their brief appointment. His bodyguard followed.

"It will be most appreciated," Dmitry said, walking behind Vladimir and his bodyguard.

Vladimir turned as he got to the door and smiled. "Congratulations, *brat*, on your arrival."

"*Spasiba*," Dmitry said nodding.

Chapter Four

The butler moved Elsa's Louis Vuitton luggage up to a guest bedroom while she and Dmitry spoke privately in his study, and Ivan and Davyd went to prepare for the next meeting, which would take place in less than thirty minutes.

Dmitry couldn't wait to have a moment alone with the woman. He found her to be complex, alluring and extremely sexy. What caught him most off guard was her height. Her legs seemed to soar on and on up into the heavens. And while she was as breathtaking as any supermodel that he'd met, she was definitely more intelligent. Her poise in a new environment was commendable. Never once did she seem nervous or unsure of herself. He liked that she knew how to control a room and was certain that it would be helpful in the near future.

However, he could also not help but wonder what she must look like against a bed, naked and in ecstasy. It was a thought that he instantly tried to repress, only being newly widowed. In the past, it was the only way that he could remain faithful.

He had to always control his thoughts when Catherine was alive, repress his imagination and desire for the feel of a youthful woman, and most importantly, never allow one opportunity for an impropriety. Such was his day-to-day life, even living at the manor. It seemed that every maid under forty was after him. Plus, Ivan never made it any easier coming around with a new woman on every visit.

Now, he was bound to nothing – no woman. The freedom hummed in his ears like a song written by angels.

Legs crossed, back straight and eyes focused on her new boss, Elsa answered each question thoroughly as though on an interview, but Dmitry knew women. He could see the curiosity hanging in the back of her dark brown eyes. It was that curiosity that he was anxious to discover, not the things that she could recite back to him.

"So where are you from, Elsa?" Dmitry asked, pouring her a glass of wine in the back of the study.

"Luanda, Angola," Elsa answered as he walked up to her with the glass. She looked up at him with a delicate smile. "Thank you," she said nodding. Her long, manicured hands took the glass from his hand.

"You're welcome," Dmitry said, looking away. Her perfume was intoxicating. "I'm from Moscow originally, although I'm sure you already know all of that. In fact, I'm sure that you know almost everything about me, *considering your source.*" He sat back down behind the desk and watched her delicate lips meet the crystal flute. Weaving his fingers together, he sat back in the chair and hid in the shadows of the dimly lit room, where he could watch her every move better.

She sipped the wine slowly as she thought about something very hard and then swallowed. "There is much about a man that cannot be adequately noted on paper," she responded.

When she looked over at him, the whites of her eyes drew Dmitry further into the depths of her. His silence only made his desire even more pronounced. He finally spoke. "Has Vladimir's father ever seen you drink wine?" Dmitry asked, running his hands over the wooden table.

"Yes," Elsa answered, confused.

"Well, now I know why he wants to buy my glass factory. I've never appreciated that wine glass until this very moment."

Elsa blushed. It would have been such a cheesy statement if she hadn't seen his eyes. From his mouth, the compliment made her melt. "He wants to buy your glass factory because of its proximity to one of the Russian armories," she answered, setting her glass down. "And I wouldn't sell it for less than 13, if I were going to sell it, Mr. Medlov."

Dmitry smiled. His voice was soft and knowing. "I am well aware that it's worth more than eight, but then Khalid will owe me more favors. If I sell it to him at market value, then there is nothing left on the table."

"Are you sure that you didn't go to Oxford," she asked intrigued. "You seem incredibly knowledgeable in comparison to the reports on you."

"It's all a front. Everything that you've heard or read about me is probably true," Dmitry joked. "So, is your family back in Angola?"

"Yes." She smiled.

"Was the scholarship a favor from Khalid?"

"No. I am not on scholarship, Mr. Medlov."

"Sorry to assume. Well, how did you come to know one of the most powerful Russian mafia bosses in the world?"

"My father knows a lot of powerful men because of his profession."

"And what is his profession?"

"He is a leader," she said with a smirk.

"Of a company?" He narrowed his brow.

"Of a country," she said, taking another sip of her wine. "The MPLA to be exact."

"Well that...," he chuckled. "That says it all, doesn't it?"

Dmitry was well aware of the MPLA. The People's Movement for the Liberation of Angola - Labour Party or in Portuguese the Movimento Popular de Libertação de Angola - Partido do Trabalho was an Angolan political party that had ruled the country since Angola's independence in 1975 and had fought against the Portuguese army in the war for nearly fifteen years against UNITA and FNLA in the civil war from 1975 to the present. If her father was who Dmitry thought he was then Elsa was the most important person in the room, not any of them.

Elsa couldn't help but laugh as well. For a man with so much to lose, he didn't seem to take himself too seriously. He was dramatically different from his counter parts, especially from Vladimir, who seemed to have been born with an air of superiority.

Looking at his presidential Rolex, Dmitry stood up and made his way around the desk to her. "Why don't I show you up to your room before my next meeting, *eh*?"

"Shouldn't I be here to assist you for your next meeting?" she asked, ready to get to work.

Dmitry nodded with a grin. His eyes sparkled at her. His full mouth curved as he bit his rose-colored lips. "No, I can handle this next one alone. Don't worry. I'll come calling for you soon enough."

Offering his hand, he helped her up from her chair and escorted her down the quiet, dimly lit corridor, past all the family photos that meant nothing to him, through the main halls with all of the priceless busts and finally up to her room. It had been Catherine's private bedroom, where she went to have complete and utter privacy. He felt that considering how important she would be to him in the near future, the least that he could do was make sure she had the best accommodations possible.

"Your castle is very impressive," she said, standing at her doorway. She looked up at him and tried to follow his changing facial expressions.

"Thank you," Dmitry answered softly. His deep voice still carried down the hall even as he tried to whisper.

"Why do you look at me the way that you do?" she asked.

Dmitry laughed a little and sucked his teeth. "I'm not used to being around a woman quite so tall. It fascinates me."

Elsa laughed. "It's ironic, don't you think, coming from a man who is seven feet tall?"

"Seven feet, one inch," he corrected. "How tall are you?"

"Six feet even without heels," she said, putting her black stiletto out. "Six, six with these on, I suppose. Is it intimidating?"

"No, it's umm...*distracting*." He looked at her legs again, then slowly ran his gaze up her thighs, passed her flat stomach, up her perky breasts to her long neck, then to her mouth and finally to her eyes. It was a long trip.

"Well, then if they are *distracting*, I'll remember to wear flats tomorrow," she said humbly.

"If you do, I'll fire you on the spot," Dmitry said, stepping back away from her. He tried to cool the growing heat burning at his collar. "Let the butler know if you need anything. His name is William, *but I call him Willie. He hates that*." He winked at her.

Elsa smiled. "Where are your bedroom quarters? Are they on a different floor?"

Dmitry nodded *no*. "I'm the big one at the end of this hall." He pointed at the double doors guarded by candle light and statues on both sides. He looked at it and then back at her.

"It looks very stately. Fits you," she said, opening her door.

"You should come and check it out sometime," Dmitry said, raising his hand. "No pressure. Just a thought. What I do *need* from you, however, is breakfast at six. I can familiarize you with my businesses before you head to school tomorrow and after you return you can get me ready for my first board meeting."

"I'll be there," she said, holding on to her door. "Good night, Mr. Medlov." Her brown eyes spoke the words that her lips would not say, but still she knew that he understood.

"Good night," Dmitry said, scratching his brow. Inwardly, he debated on if he would truly let her sleep unbothered the night through. Shaking his head, he decided to grapple with that later.

As Elsa's door closed, he turned and headed back down the stairs with a pep in his step that he had not experienced in many months, and it was all because there was a young, beautiful woman upstairs only seconds away from his bedroom. He couldn't explain it, but there was something electrifying about the idea that he had been given such a *gift* as Vladimir had called her.

Even Dmitry was shocked by his change in attitude, because even if Elsa were rich, he doubted that she was worth as much as he, and he also doubted that she would have signed over her fortune to him as Catherine had done, and yet, he felt intrigued for once, captivated by her presence and her mystery. She was the fresh breath of air that he so desperately needed, and he inhaled her happily.

As his leather-soled foot hit the bottom marble stair, he came to one conclusion about his new found emotions and over how he seemed to be healing so quickly behind Catherine's death; money simply could not buy everything.

"Down here, lover boy," Ivan said from down the hall.

Dmitry turned to his brother standing in the dimly lit corridor. Pulling his composure together, he headed towards him. The team had evidently been briefed.

"It kills you to see anyone in a good mood, doesn't it, *brat*?" Dmitry asked quietly as he walked up to him.

"Not anyone...just you," Ivan joked, pointing into the door. "They are ready for you."

Dmitry walked into the solarium to find four people waiting on him. Three men and one very sinister looking woman. Shabbily dressed in cargo pants and black t-shirts, they stood among his dead wife's flowers looking like field weeds. He smirked, remembering when he looked the exact same.

"Which of you are paramilitary?" Dmitry asked, slipping his fists into the pockets of his slacks.

"I am," the tallest and most muscular of them said. Even in his gigantic stature, he appeared petite beside Dmitry.

"And who are you?" Dmitry asked the man.

"Dorian," the man answered. "This is Mikhail, Hussein and my sister, Arie."

Dmitry's eyes stopped at Arie. She was a short woman with pitch black hair, pale white skin, fire-red lips and mossy green, Asian eyes. Her hair was cut into a perfect bob that stopped at her bejeweled ears with heavy bangs that hid her forehead but only brought more attention to her scornful glare. She was tragically beautiful in a Eurasian sort of way.

It only took a minute to know why his brother had assembled this team. It had nothing to do with their competence but everything to do with the femme fatale in front of him.

"And Arie, what is it that you do for your brother, Dorian?" Dmitry asked, looking over at Ivan.

Ivan looked back with a charged stare, unsure of how his brother would handle the woman.

"I'm into all types of wet work, but I specialize in the knives and hand-to-hand combat," she said confidently in a distinctive Eastern European accent.

"Knives?" Dmitry asked intrigued. "Do you have a record, anything on your finger prints?"

"I'm clean," she said, grinding her teeth. "I'm very critical of my work, Mr. Medlov. If I leave a fingerprint behind, then I'm not very competent."

"No, you wouldn't be," Dmitry said smiling. He turned his attention to Dorian. "And what do you specialize in?"

"IEDs, dirty bombs, syntax, other explosives..." Dorian answered. "And I too am very good at my job."

"All of their references check out," Ivan said interrupting. "They're the best."

Dmitry hardly ever went on knowledge alone. He depended on his gut, especially for important things. At that very moment, he wanted more than anything in the world to dismiss the misfits that   Ivan had assembled and start from scratch. However, his mind was battling with his heart. In the corner of his eye, he could see his brother looking at him, looking to him for approval. What would it say if he sent Dorian and his troubled gang away? Was he not supposed to trust his brother and had he not given him the task to complete?

With a quick glimpse at Davyd, who quietly shared his concern, Dmitry decided to bet on his brother. Shaking his head at Ivan, he gave fair warning. "We don't give second chances. Do exactly as you are instructed. And just for the record, my word is the last the word." His eyes landed on Ivan. "If there is a conflict in communication, your best bet is to refer to Ivan or Davyd. I don't deal in squabbles; we always make good on our promises and our debts."

Dorian stood planted in front of Dmitry with a look of seriousness and devotion. "The same applies for us. My team follows me. They are thorough, and they are professional. We will not disappoint."

"Good," Dmitry said, turning to the door. "Until this business is done, you'll stay here in the guest house. Be ready in the next couple of days to discuss the follow through on any hits that I'll need."

As he passed his brother, Dmitry stopped at his ear and spoke quietly. "Keep it in your pants, brat. At least until this is done."

"You do the same," Ivan slowly casting his own deadly gaze at his brother.

Hutton Industries board of directors as an internal director and vice president of the company for over thirty years. Most of the other board members regarded him as a permanent fixture and took his counsel as gospel.

A seasoned business man mid-way of his sixties, he was a cut throat millionaire who had made a considerable amount of money for the Hutton family and for the company that he had been trusted to oversee. And up until a week and a half ago, he felt very confident that his hard work over the years would be justly rewarded that was, however, before he heard that in Catherine's last days, she had signed a document that would jeopardize everything that he had ever done for the multinational business.

As he read through his confidential report on the twenty-three year old billionaire whom he'd only laid eyes on once, he was dumbfounded. Dmitry Medlov was nothing more than a hoodlum. Evidently, there was a debate on if he was even supposed to be out of prison. However, with the fall of the USSR and more than a dozen hands greased by Catherine Hutton to keep the Soviet prison officials quiet, his record had been blacked out and specifics had been indefinitely lost.

Outside of Dmitry's seriously shady prison stint, there were also allegations that suggested he had ties to the Vory v Zakone. On several pages, Dmitry had been referred to as not only the muscle for a local thug named Kirill in Moscow but also called specifically "the butcher." God only knew that he had done to get that name.

Closing the file, Brenneman looked up from the papers and smiled. He had enough ammo to get the young man exactly where he wanted him. Dmitry had no formal educational training outside of secondary school, which he never finished. It would be easy to suggest a reasonable buy-out and remove him from his seat as president. It was more than likely that the young thug didn't even understand what owning 58% of the Hutton Industries meant – so, as long as no one told him, by the time that Dmitry did learn of his power, it would be gone.

A quick knock on the door preceded its swift opening. "Mr. Brenneman, we'll escort you up to the board room in ten minutes," his assistant said, standing in the entrance of his executive suite. "Would you like a cup of tea while you wait, sir?"

With beady eyes and a wicked smile, the balding, fat man wrapped in a dark, blue business suit waved away his young, eager male assistant. "No," Brenneman said in a snobbish English tone. "I have everything that I need right here." Rubbing his plump hand over the manila file, he licked his thin lips. He relished in the thought of taking complete control over the business and literally getting Dmitry kicked out on his seven-foot ass.

Brenneman had in Catherine's absence over the last few months been standing in to handle most of her business requests and had gotten quite used to running things. He'd even given himself a few generous bonuses that no one was brave or bold enough to contest. His next move would be the absolutely essential to getting to where he wanted to be and a check-mate for his ascension to the top of Hutton Industries.

***

Dmitry could barely stay awake as he rode in the back of his black Bentley with Elsa from his vast, countryside manor to the bustling streets of downtown London.

Hidden behind dark shades, he closed his eyes and rested his head back on the leather headrest, allowing his thoughts to travel to mother Russia, where he was certain Alexandria still was.

He tried to picture what the boy, Anatoly, must look like, how old he would be now. Each and every time that he imagined him, his face and features were different, but the essence of the boy remained the same. He was a Medlov. The thought sent chills through his spine. If anyone of importance ever found out about him, the boy would surely be in trouble. After all of this was done, he'd have to go to Alexandria and make some sort of arrangements for the boy, if he was truly his.

"You may want to keep your eye on the ball just until your meeting is over. Then you can think about anything that you bloody-well choose," Elsa said, snatching him out of his thoughts.

Slowly rolling his head over to look at her, Dmitry swallowed hard, causing a jump in his bulging Adam's apple. "How can you tell that my mind wasn't in the game?" he asked, not denying her accurate observation.

Elsa gave a smile that Dmitry had become very familiar with in the last four days - self-assurance. She looked down at his hands, resting on his large thighs. "Your fists are balled up. You only do that when you're not thinking about work."

Dmitry looked down at his hands and chuckled. "I can't believe that I have a tell-tale," he said, looking back out of the window. "I suppose that I am human after all." The thought gave him hope. Some involuntary part of him wasn't a monster.

Elsa bit her lip. "Indeed, sir...you are all man," she said with barely any inflection in her dream-like voice.

A small smile crept across Dmitry's lips. And in return, something naughty flashed behind Elsa's eyes. This was a constant exchange between the two. Flirting. Insinuating. Waiting. Now was obviously not the time to even discuss attraction but it was there, thickening the air like a heavy cloud and choking their thoughts regularly.

For the last several days, Dmitry and Elsa had spent long hours studying his position in the company, the strategic moves it would take to keep him there, and the possible threats on the board of directors.

Elsa had identified one threat in particular. Oliver Brenneman. He had the most to lose from Dmitry taking an active role in the company and had been the most vocal in the past about leadership and the stakeholders' interests.

The only good thing that was in Dmitry's favor was the unique bylaws of the private corporation. Unlike public corporations, only 50 stockholders existed with Hutton, and in the bylaws it was stated clearly that the chairman of the board would always be a Hutton or the spouse of a Hutton, which eliminated the possibility of Brenneman taking over.

The only way that he could take over permanently would be in the event of Dmitry's death. Until then, Brenneman had only filled the position in a temporary capacity. And with Dmitry taking on his active role as chairman today, Brenneman would be forced back into his normal capacity as Vice President of Hutton Industries and a normal member of the board.

Elsa had also pointed out to Dmitry that the chairman had the power to fire the board even though he could not take away their stocks – another unique tidbit of the bylaws that was put in place during the company's inception.

Hutton Industries had managed over the years to function with this unique structure in order to protect the financial investments of the main stockholder – the Hutton family.

Because of the information that Elsa had shared with Dmitry, they had spent their time prior to this meeting reaching out to everyone who owned stock in Hutton Industries outside of the board. Elsa had assured Dmitry that it would be necessary in order to carry out his plans.

However, Dmitry had also assured Elsa that any opposition by the board would be met with quick and swift defensive tactics, none of which he was free to discuss with her. She assumed that it must not have only been clandestine in nature but also illegal - as was the nature of men of his stature.

She looked over at him now, resting back, languid with exhaustion and brimming with sexy energy that made her want to claw out her own eyes and felt a twinge of sympathy for the young billionaire. To be so fully and abruptly immersed into this lifestyle couldn't be easy, yet he took it on without even the slightest resentment.

"Why are you staring at me like that?" Dmitry asked without taking his eyes off his window.

"I just wonder if you're ready for this," she said, masking her true emotions of pure admiration.

"I can always tell when a woman is lying to me. Do you know how?"

"No," she said, turning to look out of her own window.

"It's the change in your tone, the way that you twist your words with determination."

"So what *am* I thinking about?" Elsa asked, almost hoping that he would guess.

Dmitry took a deep breath and sat up as they pulled up to the 33-floor skyscraper that he now owned. His eyes casted a jaded glare over her body before he spoke. "I'll tell you when we get out of this meeting, eh," he said, stepping out as the chauffeur opened his door.

***

As soon as the gold, revolving doors to Hutton Industries whirled Dmitry inside of the elaborate marble and glass lobby, he realized the magnitude of his position. The building was a testament to European grandeur mixed with the Hutton classic style. It was hard to swallow at first. *I own this?* he thought to himself. He tried not to look around in amazement, but Elsa could clearly see his fascination. In fact, she could not help but marvel herself.

Waiting on him was Dmitry's executive assistant, *whom he did not know that he had*, a crowd of VPs all vying for his attention with updates and reports he had never asked for and a press corps with a hard-on for a picture of the city's newest billionaire. Lights flashed his way as people screamed out his name. He felt like many of the athletes and stars he had seen on television who were often attacked by the paparazzi.

"Step back," he said, extending his arm to give himself some space.

The people stepped back in shock at the size of the giant. He cast down a serious stare, threatening people through his icy eyes.

Elsa quickly took control of the situation, informing the Hutton staff that all requests were to come through her to be filled, then ordering the doorman to get an elevator open for Mr. Medlov immediately to get him up to the board room right before she demanded to know where the on-site marketing or public relations designee was.

The reporters all pushed their microphones up as far as they could toward Dmitry asking him if he planned to sell Hutton Industries as a whole or break it up into little pieces. Elsa soon jumped from the employees to the reporters and informed them that Mr. Medlov had no comment at the moment, but a statement would be released after today's board meeting. With that, she escorted Dmitry into an empty elevator and saved him from a PR disaster.

As the doors closed, they both finally breathed.

"Thanks," Dmitry said, straightening his tie.

"It's my job," she said proudly. "I think there was even a reporter from the *Wall Street Journal* out there." Shaking her head, she wrote a note on a pad. "We need to get them in our pocket before the shit hits the fan."

"I'll leave you to all of that," he said, dismissing any thought of the dreaded *media*.

Staring at himself in the reflection of the elevator doors, he cringed at the tailored three-piece suit Elsa had picked for him to wear today. He looked like an old man – not his style at all - but she had insisted that he wear something that would make the board relate and *take him seriously.*

He looked down at the top of her head gratefully. Elsa was a hard worker and a smart woman with thick skin and a penchant for disaster-relief. And while he was still trying to figure out why she had agreed to any of this, he was happy to have her by his side now.

As the doors opened, a borage of people waited. All smiling with either eyes of wonderment at his size or eyes of deceit and conniving mischief, they greeted Dmitry and Elsa as they walked briskly down the hall, past the open doors of worrying execs and cubicles of overworked underlings to the board room where the real men of industry waited.

Elsa walked in first with her hair pulled back in a bun, a blue skirt-suit, brief case and black stiletto pumps that made her appear nearly as tall as her boss. Dmitry wanted it that way. Everything larger than life.

The board stood up and waited as Dmitry entered, towering above everyone, more beautiful than all of them and even more uncomfortable. Trying to remember not to pull at his suit, he slipped his large hands out of his pockets and shook the men's hands as they stood in a receiving line. Each of the men stared not only at his massive size but also at the many tattoos that were not able to be hidden on his hands and wrists.

Formalities, formalities, Dmitry thought to himself as he tried to remember each of the older men's names. Having been conditioned by Catherine, he amused himself with the fact that there were no women on the board of directors, no minorities and no young people. He also amused himself with the fact that that each of the men were in need of a personal trainer and diet. *Fat cats living high off the hog,* he said to himself as he unbuttoned his jacket and sat down at the head of the hand-crafted wooden board table.

"Good afternoon," Dmitry said, checking to make sure that Elsa was standing behind him. She was.

The group all greeted him in unison. They all locked their hungry stares on him, eager to take a bite out of his fortune.

"It's nice to finally meet the man instead of just see your face all over the local rags," Brenneman said, pushing his way up the table.

Dmitry looked down the table at him and smiled. He had to remember his temper, at least for the moment. "I believe in the saying, *all press is good press*. Are you familiar with the saying, Mr. Brenneman?"

The obese man looked up stunned. Either the boy had remembered his name from their brief introduction or he had done some background research on him also.

"I am familiar, Mr. Medlov. But trust me, when you've been in the business as long as I have, you can rest assured that not all press is good press." He looked around at his allies nodding in agreement. A surge of superiority rushed Dmitry's way. Most, if not all of the men there, felt as though they were much better than he. The smug grins on their faces confirmed it.

Dmitry crossed his finger as he planted his large elbows on the table. "Well, Mr. Brenneman, it's better than being obsolete, which by the end of this meeting will be a very relevant and regretfully necessary title for some of you."

The room grew still and quiet with silent chaos.

Dmitry continued with a more devious grin, sure that he had their attention now. "But before we get to that, I'd like you all to meet Elsa. She is my right hand." He raised his own right hand in demonstration of their cohesiveness and waved it at them. "All matters will go through her to me. Consider us one for the time being, gentlemen. I do not take calls, emails, letters, faxes, anything. Elsa, however, is available...within reason." His eye twitched.

It was as if the young man had just immediately added insult to injury by insisting that even they, men of this illustrious board, go through his black assistant to get to him, when they for so long had gone directly to Catherine.

The collective discomfort was obvious, but it only made Elsa smile. She stood behind Dmitry to his right side with her hands wrapped around a pound of books and papers waiting to attack on his word. She had trained for this for nearly four years. Now, she was actually getting a chance to live her dream, to be in control, to make a difference. Pinching herself quietly, she looked around the room and smiled.

"We have to decide where we are going with the company," another older man on the left side of Dmitry said, cutting through the tension. "Investors are worried that with Catherine's passing and your ascension, *for lack of a better word*, that Hutton Industries is going belly up."

Dmitry raised his brow. "Quite the opposite. I've taken the liberty to look over the various departments and their productivity. Elsa, please pass out the packets now."

Obediently, she pulled the leather bound reports from her bag and began to pass them around the table. The men took them quickly, opening them to see what departments had been possibly cut.

Dmitry watched their faces as they broke in horror. He sat quietly for a moment, wanting his expulsion of them to be as dramatic as possible.

"What are you suggesting?" asked Brenneman, "that we *actually* cut all of these departments?"

"I'm not *suggesting*," Dmitry said, pouring himself a glass of water. "As of tomorrow, they will be cut permanently."

"Do you realize the financial implications of such a thing?" the young board member, Thomas Emerson, asked horrified.

"I do realize the financial implications, but I have a different vision for Hutton Industries than my late wife did," Dmitry explained. "And I appreciate your kind flowers and note during my loss."

"It was the least that I could do," Emerson said, closing the report. "What about the jobs associated with the departments?"

"They will be cut also," Dmitry said without blinking.

Emerson was a man in his mid-forties of reasonable wealth and education. However, he seemed extremely more disturbed by the idea of hundreds of working-class people losing their jobs, rather than only he losing his. Dmitry liked that. At least there was one man who wasn't solely out for himself in the room, but there was only one.

"I'm cutting the fat to get to the meat of this business," Dmitry said, answering Emerson's frown. "We are going to invest more heavily in technology, transition the manual labor factory positions into more efficient, machine-operated facilities with less man power and more accuracy. Hutton has been losing far too much money over the last couple of years with risky investments and poor management of human and other resources. I've read the case studies. We have to turn the corner."

Elsa cracked a smile. Dmitry had only been under her tutelage for a short while, but he was a fast learner. Watching him as he commanded control over the room, she realized why Lady Hutton must have chosen him. He had a natural charisma that drew people to him and a lion-like aggression that created fear in his opponents.

"What do you think the other stockholders will have to say in the matter?" Brenneman asked, shocked that Dmitry had such a firm grip on the company in such a short time. He was growing rather uneasy with the situation. This *brut* was supposed to be an idiot not a genius.

"Well, I made a few calls after the funeral and bought a few more of the major investors out quietly. I now own more than the original 58%," Dmitry said, looking back at Elsa. "I believe that the number rightly sits at 74% now. In fact, the 26% of the business that I do not own is owned by the people in this room. Everyone else is out of the picture." He casted his glare back out over the men and swallowed hard, jolting his large Adam's apple.

"The reason that I've brought you all here today is not to bargain with you or seek your advice, but to simply offer to buy you out as well." Dmitry watched their faces. The lot of them was sick with disbelief, unhinged by their opponent. He hoped to never be in such a situation, to underestimate someone, regardless of their background.

"Buy us out?" another board member bit out.

The whispers in the room became a larger roar. Power was shifting now from the clutches of the greedy handful to one single man who obviously was hungrier than them all.

"Well, not all of you. Just as many of you who can't see the potential in what I am doing," Dmitry answered their discontent. "Those of you who can may stay. It's just that simple."

Elsa walked around for the second time passing out a completely different proposal in a red leather binder. The men were even more hesitant to open the packet than before.

Dmitry watched them all carefully, studying each man and his tell signs. None of them were ready for what had happened. He tried to hold his grin but could not. Victory was in reach. It was a big blow to elitism. How he loved Catherine for giving him this opportunity.

He cracked a smile at Elsa as she made her way back to him, glad to have someone here to witness history and to be able to recount the events later. Such a monumental thing would have been wasted on one person alone.

Dmitry continued a little more at ease now that he had stated his intentions. "Sometimes you can't teach an old dog new tricks, eh. This is why I am offering you an opportunity to simply bow out, gentlemen, through a very generous offer that would allow you to go on and pursue other dreams or business ventures without feeling obligated to Hutton Industries."

"*Hutton Industries* has been in business since 1873, and you come here and want to usurp us -men who have sat on this board for more than three generations – overnight because of a two-year *hump fest* that you've had with Catherine?" Brenneman asked. Sweat formed on his meaty, red forehead. He slammed the portfolio closed. "Tell me that you at least expect an uprising, a war? We will not take this sitting down."

"What kind of war can you wage with a man who owns everything?" Dmitry asked quietly. His eyes were focused on the fat man, but it was his heart that gave away his story. It beat like a lion against his chest, urging him to attack. If this had not been a boardroom, Dmitry would have already gutted him from his bulging belly to his double chin. He thought of doing it now even. In fact, the thought is what helped him stay calm.

Brenneman narrowed his beady, brown eyes. "You are a thug – a common rat that has managed to crawl its way out of the gutters of Moscow and bring your troubled little clan with you. Don't think that we don't already know about your sordid past – the ties to the Vory v Zakone, your old title as butcher, your stint in prison, the long money trail behind you covering up your many indiscretions. You are no match for men of industry, of name and most importantly of quality. When the world finds out what you really are, this company will go belly up and your *vision,* as you call it, will go down the tubes where it belongs with the rest of common pipe dreams from greedy little idiots who don't know how to stay in their places." He looked around in a huff as many of the men around the table silently agreed.

Dmitry could feel the heat rising under his thousand dollar shirt. Raising his arched brow, he clasped his gigantic hands together until his red, sweaty hands had turned a pale, nearly translucent white.

"Is this the consensus of the group?" Dmitry asked in a low growl.

Many of the men shook their heads.

Emerson, however, disagreed. While he had come from a good family and had a good name, he was no elitist. And he had no gripe with Dmitry Medlov about his desire to take the company in a different direction. In fact, as 74% owner, he had that right. "I do not care how you came to your position. It is not my business. However, I do not wish to be bought out either. I want to make a difference, Mr. Medlov. I wish to find a way to keep jobs for those who depend on them and see this company grow to its potential. That is why my family invested in Hutton many years ago and that is why I have stayed."

Dmitry looked past them at the sun shining brightly through the blinds of the high-rise building and stood up at the head of the table. Two different forces were at work here at the same time. Outside, the world was calm and beautiful. Inside this boardroom, there was a storm brewing. At that moment, his size was even more intimidating. His large chest stuck out, pulling at threads of his fine clothing. An animalistic desire rose in him to tear at his shirt and reveal his true identity, but he kept his fleeting composure, pulling himself into a calmer state before he spoke.

He bent and placed his hands on the table, scratching the wood with his nails and he dug into family heirloom. Looking across at them, his deep baritone voice snarled like a mad dog. "The fact that I am a rat from a gutter should only put the fear of God deep into each of you. The fact that I have in a short time arrived where you have been trying to get your entire lives with all of your money, and all of your titles and still have essentially failed, should be a testament to my superiority. And the fact that I have carried the title of butcher, the fact that I am a member of the most respected and powerful organization that you could imagine – an organization that could not be snuffed out by the government or controlled by other ethnic groups, should let you know that I am more than capable of going to war with you. And if it's war that you want, it is war that you will have. And this is how it starts. Those of you who are with this fat *suka* with his shit-eating grin and plans of controlling the universe, stand on this side." He motioned to the left wall. "Those of you who wish to either buy out and move on or simply continue with business as usual, move to this wall." He motioned towards the right wall.

"You can't be serious," Brenneman said with a chuckle. "It's a bit elementary, don't you think?"

"Oh but I am serious. There is nothing elementary about war. And I would ask that you each make your decision very quickly," Dmitry said with a grin of his own.

Emerson stood on the right wall alone with his paperwork in his hand, while the rest of the board got up and walked over to the left wall with Brenneman.

Dmitry stood still at the head of the table and watched. "Very well. Emerson, if you don't have anything else to add, get with Elsa so that we can talk later this week about the development of the new departments, but I would suggest you leave now before things get ugly."

Emerson did not say much. He nodded at Dmitry then at the group of men on the left wall and departed quietly, closing the door behind him.

When they were alone, Dmitry turned back towards the men.

"And for the rest of us?" Brenneman said, looking around at his counterparts.

"You're all fired. Everyone who works for you and reports to you is fired. I want all of your shit out of my building by five. I want all of your keys to your company cars turned over. Every perk, every fucking credit card, anything that belongs to me had better be turned over to me. If I find out that you go on spending spree tonight after you leave here, any sudden changes in my cash flow, anything usual, I come and take it out of your ass...show you why they call me the butcher." Dmitry hit his chest.

"And who is going to help you facilitate all of this?" Brenneman asked, both outraged and in awe at how quickly his world had been turned completely around. He wasn't even sure if Dmitry had the resources to pull such a coup off in such a short period of time.

"A new group of men, *my men*, will be reporting in tomorrow. These aren't the types you want to fuck with, gentlemen. They don't carry the same type of titles that you do. They actually earned theirs through blood and sweat." Dmitry laughed. "I'll leave the rest to Elsa until they arrive." He went to the doors and swung them open. "Now get the fuck out," he said, standing at the door as they passed.

Brenneman was the last one to leave. Stopping at the door, he looked up at Dmitry with a scowl on his pudgy face. "This is far from over. If it's the last thing that I do, you will be ruined, Dmitry Medlov."

Dmitry bent to the Brenneman. "Is that a threat?" His eyes gleamed with pure anger.

"Of course," Brenneman said, without blinking.

"Good," Dmitry said, standing back up. "I just wanted to make sure that we are both on the same page."

"Sleep with one eye open," Brenneman said repulsed by Dmitry's audacity. "You aren't the only one who knows unsavory characters."

"If I were you, I wouldn't sleep at all," Dmitry answered, "because I am an unsavory character you smug, little, fat oily bastard. And when I come for you, I'll be doing it myself."

Brenneman stalked off. His assistant followed behind him, carrying the paperwork that he quickly discarded on the floor.

The workers, who were witnessing the fallout, were in disbelief. Rumor was that many of them were fired, anyone who didn't work for Emerson or worked directly for any of the men on the board were now without jobs.

Dmitry stepped out of the board room last with Elsa following at his side. Smoothing his suit out, he looked around at the large group of people standing still and staring at him in the corridor. Their eyes said it all. They knew a war was coming as well. Many of them never thought they'd see the day that the board would be eliminated, but seeing them all eliminated at once was almost unthinkable.

"Can someone tell me where my office is?" he asked. His deep voice vibrated throughout the halls.

A hundred hands pointed at the large suite at the end of the hall – the office that Brenneman had thought only hours before that he would occupy. Dmitry bent to Elsa and pulled her near. His large hand wrapped around her small waist and felt her voluptuous curves. He did not try to hide his sexual attraction. Instead, he licked his lips and smiled. "Why don't you go in there and make yourself comfortable. That's your office now," he whispered into her ear.

His touch created a warm electricity throughout her body. Goosebumps formed on her skin. "My office?" Elsa asked confused. She looked up at him.

"Da. I don't work, Elsa. It's against my code. You, however, are very good at this.   Go in there and do what you do best. I trust you."

"But what are you going to do?" she asked, eager to see what great office lay behind the oak doors.

Dmitry winked. "I'm going to prepare for a war, Elsa. Were you not paying attention?"

"Yes, I was paying attention to your every word." She felt his fingers move.

"Good. Then we'll recap later," he said, hoping she understood his words. "For now, go take care of my light weight." He smiled at her and flicked her perfect little nose. "See you at home tonight. You did well."

"Yes. Thank you, sir," she said excited.

Turning from her, he headed to the golden elevators as the office women, hidden by cubicles and office doors watched him curiously pass them. Even in the middle of corporate breakdown, it truly vexed Elsa how much sexual energy radiated from the young man. Many of these same women were about to lose their jobs, yet they pined over the mysterious man, hoping for just a glimpse from his angelic eyes or a smile from his luscious lips.

However, all of Dmitry's attention was on Elsa. His carnal stare had burned through her. His eyes had said the things that his lips would not. When he turned away from her, it was like the sun stopped shining on her skin, stopped heating up her body. She was finally given a moment to rest, to feel something other than his attention as it crawled over her. Just being in his presence drove her into overload.

Chapter Six

Ivan watched Dmitry's new private team of assassins as they cleaned their weapons and went over tactical procedures in the basement of the manor home for hours. Their cohesiveness was a thing of envy to him. Even though Dorian was obviously their leader, he did not lead with an iron fist. He, instead, inquired about their suggestions and gave their opinions heavy thought.

It was a pity that Dmitry did not take a page from this black man's book. Dmitry's *word* was always the last, full of self-righteous, pseudo-omnipresent assumptions and convoluted rhetoric. He swore that the man talked just to hear his own voice sometimes. It was an irritating and often inefficient micro-management technique in Ivan's eyes. It showed that Dmitry was not nearly as confident in himself or his rule as he had others believe. A chink in the armor. The thing that would bring his brother down. Ivan didn't know why that thought made him warm and fuzzy inside but it did.

He tilted his head as he watched their leader a little closer. Was Dorian black or was he blackish? He wouldn't hold his tongue for much longer, and would soon ask when the opportunity presented itself. He simply had to know – not that it was important. However, he enjoyed the quizzical shit that no one else bothered to ponder.

Eastern Europeans were stranger than the western world in that it was not so much one's color that mattered more so than one's religion. Being Muslim, Jewish or even Christian could get you killed a lot quicker than being black. He wasn't sure which was worse. Racists or religious fanatics. He'd found that often they were one in the same.

Ivan, of course, had no religion. He found it hypocritical considering their line of work. *Why have a higher power to have to answer to upon your death when you knew that you'd show up with a bad report?* It made no sense to him. By all religious standards regardless of faith, he was hell bound.

But from what he had learned of Dorian, he was a hybrid of religions, mudded by a multi-ethnic background. Whatever his true religion, he regarded most those things that centered on honor and trust. Ivan thought the man to be a bit of Boy Scout. Then there was his half-sister, Arie. She was a completely different animal. Her exact ethnicity was unknown.

A short woman with dark-olive toned skin, jet black hair and big, almond brown eyes and full lips, Arie could have been a number of races. However, she claimed nothing. Adorned in tattoos with wild eyes and a gritty, rough disposition, she stunk of anger and hatred, quite the opposite of her balanced brother, who seemed to be in harmony with the world that he terrorized.

She was a wild card like Ivan. Rebellious down to her dead core. The stink of a thousand men was upon her. Ivan had sniffed her out in their very first meeting. But he liked that about her. There was nothing honorable about a shrewd to him. Holding out, playing hard to get, perfuming raw emotions with pretty little words all were signs of weakness to him. Arie didn't seem like that type of woman. She was his type. Complete and utterly reckless. A woman who didn't give apologies or expect them.

She watched him now as he stood across the room watching her. Her eyes started at the top of his body and slowly made their way down to his feet. Ivan's eye involuntarily flinched. He liked that – liked that she wasn't afraid to make her intentions known.

"Let me count the ways," Ivan said aloud as a dirty, lustful thought clouded his mind. His eyes told on him.

Arie cracked a smile in response. Putting down her gun, she walked over to him, past her brother, who gave her an admonishing glare.

Ivan bent down as he watched her lips curl to say something. They were red and pouty, begging to be kissed.

"I bet you wish I could give you a hand job right now," she said, making eye contact with him as her minty breath tickled his nose.

Ivan's eyes lit up. "What makes you think that you can't?" he asked quickly. "You're already eye-level with my *package.* All you have to do is open it."

Arie chuckled, happy to know that they shared the same sick humor. "The real question is can you recipro-cate?" she asked, leaning against the wall. She planted her large, steel-toe boot against the brick.

Dorian sat up from his chore of building a dirty bomb and looked across at the both of them under his make-shift glasses. "Don't you have something that you need to be doing instead of being a *sharmuta*?" he asked, gritting his teeth. His square jaw clenched down tight, revealing the small muscles in his chiseled, caramel face.

"What does *sharmuta* mean?" Ivan asked, whisper-ing into Arie's ear.

Arie rolled her eyes. "It's not a compliment," she said, nodding at her brother. Before she went back to her work, she turned to Ivan and looked up at him. "Find me later and we can finish this conversation. This place is getting old with nothing and *no one* to do."

"My thoughts exactly," Ivan said, smiling at Dorian.

He knew that her brother didn't approve, and rightly so - but what did he care? This was a Medlov compound, a Medlov operation, and if Dorian wasn't careful, his sister would be a Medlov woman.

Arie could sense Ivan's sudden territorial presence over her and used it as a shield from her over protective brother as she sauntered back over to her weapon and began cleaning it again. She kept her small, narrow back turned towards them all, certain that everyone was watching, especially Ivan, but she could feel his eyes bore through her.

They would be together if it was the last thing that they did.

***

There was nothing more pathetic than waiting for the opposing side to strike as far as Dmitry was concerned. And it was never in his nature to be second at anything.

Coming into his study, he tore out of his suit and sat behind his desk to strategize his next move. Pulling out a notepad and pen, he began to jot down notes on each of the men who had stood by Oscar Brenneman and the questions that he had about them. *Where did they live? Who were their mistresses and wives? Where did they congregate? What are their vices? Where was most of their money?*

Pulling at his tailored short, he reached to the far edge of his massive desk and grabbed a bottle of vodka and small glass. He'd have to think through this if he wanted to survive. There could be no loose ends, no fuck ups. Every part of his operation would have to be seamless.

Ivan walked to the door and knocked. Peering inside, he instantly knew that his brother was irritated. Dmitry's eyebrows spiked at the interruption until he saw who it was. Then he relaxed. Something about seeing a familiar face was soothing at that moment.

"I take it that the meeting didn't go well?" Ivan said, closing the door behind him.

"We have to crush them now," Dmitry said, looking up from his paper. He poured Ivan a glass of vodka as well and pushed it across to him.

Ivan took it and sat down in the seat in front of Dmitry's desk. "Crush them financially or kill the fuckers?" he asked with a menacing grin.

"I want you to prepare to do what you do best," Dmitry said, sitting back in his chair. The sun rays beamed across his golden hair and he slowly flapped his long eyelashes. Bright, determined eyes rested on Ivan.

"And I can do this the way that I want to do it?" Ivan asked intrigued. He never received free reign from his brother. This had to be bad.

Dmitry paused. "Yes."

Ivan let out a sigh of gratitude. "When?"

"Soon. I'll know by the end of the day after I've had a moment to calculate this all." He ran his hands over his notes.

"A blood bath will probably lead back to you," Ivan pointed out. "Should this look like an accident or a hit?"

"There is nothing accidental about a massacre," Dmitry answered. "I'm looking for a way to kill them all at once, but if we can't then pick them off one by one. Make sure that no one on the team is caught, and make sure that you are not videoed, photographed or seen. I don't want you to end up in prison before we can even get to where we want to be."

"I can handle that," Ivan assured.

"Yes, I know you can." Dmitry emptied the vodka bottle into his glass. "Well, if you'd excuse me. I've got a lot to figure out here."

"One more thing before I go," Ivan said, raising his long index finger.

Dmitry blinked.

"About the money for Emma. Have you forgotten?" Ivan waited.

Dmitry took the key from on top of a pile of paperwork beside him on the desk and opened his top drawer. He took out a check and pushed it across the table to Ivan. "I had a chance to review the previous will. This is what she was supposed to receive."

Ivan looked down at the check astonished. "Thirty-two million pounds?"

"To the penny," Dmitry answered. "See that she receives it. *All of it*. For her and *your* child."

"It's not my kid," Ivan snapped.

Dmitry raised his brow. "Whatever. I don't really care, Ivan. Just make sure that I don't lay eyes on Emma or this boy. I have too much to deal with right now, and I doubt that playing the surrogate grandfather slash uncle to my stepdaughter's illegitimate heir is going to help me find clarity."

Ivan shook his head. "Every day you sound more and more like these British aristocratic fucks and less like one of us."

Dmitry was suddenly intrigued. "And what do *we* sound like, *brat*? Please don't tell me that you're one of those self-loathing idiots who believe that we are incapable of being educated, formally trained or even elevated in society because we are Vor. If anything, it is quite the opposite. We are most ready for the challenge."

"I'll leave the social climbing to you. I'm just after cold, hard cash," Ivan sneered, rubbing his hand over the check.

Dmitry watched his brother for a moment in silent wonderment. He knew that there was a large possibility that neither Emma nor the boy would ever see a cent of the money that he had just given his brother for them.

However, the last words between Emma and he had been full of hatred and disdain, and he did not wish to return to her presence for any reason – even a good one. Plus, it was his brother's responsibility now to do right by her. He felt his hands were washed of the Hutton's completely. He owed nothing to Emma or her mother at this point.

Remembering his present issues, he cleared his throat. "Right, so why don't you go and do what I asked while I prepare to climb a different type of ladder, *da*."

"What do you have in mind for them? I'm curious."

"I'll tell you when I'm sure," Dmitry said, looking down at his notes. He needn't look up to know that Ivan was shooting him a deadly stare.

"Am I not your second-in-charge, brother?" Ivan asked. "It doesn't look like it if you layout all of your plans alone or distribute them to me like I am one of them – in front of them no less. I want to know before the team and especially before that old fart, Davyd."

Dmitry looked up, irritated that Ivan was still there and talking. "Has something changed? Did I not just give you more in your hands to trust than most men see in their entire lifetimes? If it really is about just *the cold hard cash* with you, then what does it matter how I manage things?"

Ivan opened his mouth to say something but quickly closed it shut. Nodding, he stood up and strode out of the office, slamming the door behind him.

Dmitry was a hard man for Ivan to understand. In one moment, he would entrust him with responsibilities only bestowed on heads of state and in the next he would regard with him less thought than he would give a house servant.

One day, he'd make him pay for his constant pompous attitude. One day, he'd be the boss.

***

Once Ivan was gone, Dmitry cleared his head of the thoughts that seemed to stab at him regarding his brother's growing pestilence, and he was able to refocus on the steps that he needed to take to make Hutton Industries a Medlov business.

The entire time that Dmitry had been with Catherine, he had planned to take whatever money she left him and purchase munitions from Russia in bulk. However, what he had not depended on was the amount of money that he was given or the dramatic impact it would have on his plans.

Davyd had been doing recon for him for over a year, and one thing was clear. In order to purchase munitions in bulk from Russia, one not only needed money, but he would also need the blessing of the organized crime families that ran the men who sold them. This led him right back to the men who were already filling his circle.

There were two men who were paramount to Dmitry's success. Vladimir and his father Khalid were the first men he would need to woo and form a working relationship, but the ultimate man would still be the Czar of the underworld, Boss Evgeny Smirnov. Between the two of them, Dmitry would no longer need Kirill, his old boss from Russia.

In fact, since he'd gotten married, Dmitry had all but lost contact with Kirill, especially since he'd failed him with the shipment he'd needed when he first made contact with Catherine before they began their relationship.

Khalid Sidorov and his son were part of the highest ranks and ran the second largest family that carried the exclusive name of the Vory v Zakone. With men in Russia, Ukraine, Israel, Poland, the Czech Republic and over 20 other countries across the world, the Sidorov family was a wealthy and powerful organized crime syndicate with ties to banks, industries and politicians far and wide. Khalid was also second-in-charge to the most powerful Vor in the world.

Boss Evgeny Smirnov was an institution in his own right. Admired and feared, his name was only whispered among the elite and never uttered by the underbosses of the world, *mostly because they did not know who he was*. He had a seamless operation of spies, butchers, and other powerful men throughout the ranks that reported to him and *him only*.

The only chink that Dmitry could identify in the old man's armor was that he held complete control without anyone to truly help him mediate things or provide balance. The last word came from Smirnov, without consultation of a group or the support of it.

Dmitry always thought that every man in power should have a council, and one day when he was big like Smirnov, he would have one to secure his own interests and to ensure the organization's perpetuity. But that would be for much later.

Plus, Dmitry knew that many young men from his generation were like himself. He would do anything to gain power. Rank meant nothing to him or his men when it truly came to getting what they wanted. The means was not even relevant. Only the end.

Davyd walked in and interrupted Dmitry's deep thoughts. Rubbing his large hand over his silver-patched beard, the older, muscle-bound man sat down in front of him, grunting as his bones crackled under his weight. The leather squealed a little as he sat back in the chair and huffed.

"Well, how did the meeting fair?" Davyd asked, ready for the worst.

"It went as expected. We have made formidable and permanent enemies. Obviously, I fired them all - except one. He's a good man. Emerson. Nothing like us," Dmitry said with a grin. "But I like him. The part of the business that I plan to keep I could see him and Elsa running for me on a day-to-day basis."

"Elsa?" Davyd asked with a raised brow. "You trust her so soon?"

"Oh, I don't trust her," Dmitry said, sitting up. He rocked in his chair. "I *want* her."

Davyd laughed. "Any man with eyes could have seen that the moment you laid eyes on her."

"It's been too long," Dmitry said with a nod. "Do you know how hard it is to be faithful to a woman that you're supposed to have a *business arrangement* with for two years without one hiccup?"

"I imagine it was torture," Davyd said with a sly grin.

"It was," Dmitry answered. "And I had settled in and focused, forgotten about the *need* until Elsa came breezing through here. Now, I swear that I taste her perfume."

Davyd chuckled.

"But I don't know if I should pursue her," Dmitry added before he could begin to think about her body again.

"Why not?" Davyd asked.

"She's not just a pawn in this game. Elsa is a young, brilliant, powerful woman. I don't want to scorn her. The cost could be too great."

"What does she bring to the table that is *remarkable*?"

Dmitry sat up in his chair and crossed his long finger. His blue eyes, tired with exhaustion beamed with excitement. "Her father is a very powerful leader in Angola, Africa with MPLA."

Davyd raised his brow. "Then I see your dilemma then. She's a gold mine."

"*Da*, I need to get in bed more with her father than her," Dmitry said, instantly changing his focus from sex to money. "The potential there is unlimited. All I have to do is establish a truly sound supply chain, distribution plan and transportation strategy and we can take this local show on the road." Dmitry's eyes were wide with ambition.

"I've created a monster," Davyd laughed. "*Da, da, brat*. This is good plan. Only, how do you plan to get to her father?"

"He sent her to Oxford for an education. He wants only the best for her. When I make her head of my company, he will be very proud, but he will also want to meet me...thank me. Then, when we meet, I will talk to him about his current munitions suppliers and how it would be much better to work with us." Dmitry's thick accent could barely cover his excitement.

"So, you have it all figured out, do you?" Davyd said impressed.

"No, I don't. I have two problems. The men who I just fired are going to retaliate soon. I need this team to handle them accordingly. Secondly, I need the blessing of Khalid Sidorov and Boss Smirnov to go into Russia and deal with the former generals who controlled the bases before the fall of the USSR."

Davyd's smile disappeared from his face. "The first request – the assassination of an entire board of directors *without detection* is going to be a lot easier than coordinating a meeting with Sidorov and Smirnov."

"I know," Dmitry said, nodding his head. "That is why I need you to handle that part, *brat*. Ivan can kill with the best of them, but he is no negotiator. This could make or break us for the rest of our lives."

"If we do it wrong, we could be dead for the rest of our lives, Dmitry. To even request a meeting..."

Dmitry lifted his finger. "Khalid asked to be put on the board before the end of the year. Why don't you coordinate the meeting about that with Vladimir? While I'm there, I will talk to him about Smirnov, but I need you there to help facilitate things."

"Even mentioning Evgeny Smirnov's name, even mentioning it to his right hand man without proper approval, could get you killed, Dmitry. The fact that you know who he is could get you killed. This is privileged information. It doesn't matter that you are billionaire in that circle."

"Then I guess we had better cross our fingers," Dmitry answered. "We're going after this, Davyd. The munitions black market is open right now, but the thing that people do not have is money. We can launder it through all of these businesses that I now own, and we can turn around and make our real profit through what we know best."

Davyd shook his head. "I'm with you."

Chapter Seven

Oscar Brenneman had never in his life been fired, and the thought that a lanky, uneducated rat from across the globe was able to basically destroy his five-year plan with the snap of his finger infuriated him, but the fact that he did so in front of the very men that he had once controlled forced him to the meeting with the tailor.

Pulling himself from the back of the Hutton Industries company car immediately after he left the meeting with Dmitry, he walked inside a small, bricked storefront tailor shop and took a seat by the window. His assistant stood beside him, holding his hat and coat and looking anxiously around.

"Stop fidgeting," Brenneman demanded of his assistant. "You are making me nervous for goodness sake. If you don't have the stomach for this, then go out to the car and wait." He patted his sweaty forehead with his handkerchief.

"I'll be fine, sir," his assistant assured in a low whisper.

A young man, in his mid-twenties, with a conservative hair cut that sleeked his black hair to his head and brought attention to his spikey eye-brows and dark, gloomy eyes, looked over at the pair before he took his client's inseam. Bending down, he carefully applied the tape and measured.

"I'll be with you gentlemen momentarily," he said with a straight-pen in between his stained, jagged teeth.

Brenneman looked at his assistant with a snide grin. "Do you know how to get rid of a rodent?" he asked.

"Pest control?" his assistant answered, shifting his weight from one leg to the other.

"Exactly," Brenneman said putting one large hulky hand over the other. "And this is the best exterminator in the whole of England. We'll show these Russian rats how things are really done. I told that overgrown sex toy to sleep with one eye open. Now, he'll see that I mean everything that I say."

***

The day was slowly leaving with a hundred things still on his to-do list. Up in his bedroom, Dmitry changed out of his suit and slipped on a comfortable pair of jeans and a sweater. Standing in the mirror, he looked at himself and wondered if his brother was right. Had he changed so dramatically? Leave it to Ivan to get into his head. Shaking it off, he grabbed his keys and went to his massive garage to pick out his fastest sports bike and headed back down the lane towards the city.

His thoughts moved in between what he had to do with the business and to his mysterious Elsa. There was much to be accounted for with his new pseudo-love interests. Coincidentally, he knew a private eye in the heart of the city who could give him a full report on his future CEO. Only, he wanted this done covertly.

If Vladimir got wind of him checking up on her, he might get offended and not offer him a meeting with his father, and if she found out, she might not be as pliable in his hands. Women thrived on trust. To them, it was a two way street of give and take, and even if he had to give just the perception of trust, he knew that he had to give her something. This was why he had to arrange this part of his operation himself. Plus, the PI that he had hired had some new information for him on Brenneman.

Dmitry may have been inexperienced in legitimate business, but he had thrived on Intel for many years in the Vor. It was because of his prior knowledge that he had hired someone to follow the board members, specifically Brenneman. When he made the slightest move, Dmitry would know about it and use it against him.

The feel of the wind against his skin freed Dmitry from the invisible hold of his new life. Taking deep breaths, he let his mind clear itself for the moment as he rode through the lush countryside. He needed this, needed to see the beauty of the world before he began a campaign to destroy it. Because while he could not deny who he was, he also could not deny that a part of him acknowledged that it was wrong. Still, what could he do? Walk away? *From his oath? From his code?* It would be easier to live without food or water, without air in his lungs. No one walked away from the Vory, not even a new billionaire. Therefore, if he could not run from it, he would stay and run it.

As he rode through the land that was now his, it also occurred to him truly for the first time what he had acquired. Three years ago, he did not even own a vehicle, now he was a billionaire. What did that mean, really?

What had happened that made him different from the man he was before? Was it the fact that he had six homes? Was it the fact that he owned 12 cars and three motorcycles? Was it the fact that he owned so many businesses? Did any of that change his DNA? Did any of what he inherited change who he vowed to be or what he had be forced to endure? He did not think so.

He made a promise to himself right then to never stray far from the man who was forced to walk miles in the snow to a little village after barely escaping the clutches of prison. No matter what, he would never forget who he was.

***

After meeting with his private investigator, he drove his bike down through the streets of busy London and parked in the alleyway across from Hutton Industries. Getting off the bike, he walked to the small deli. Immediately, all eyes went to the giant. The women whirled around in their seats, and the men looked on jealously in envy.

Grabbing a seat by the window, he ordered from the one-page, laminated menu and watched the building doors for Elsa to come out. There was no plan really. He just had a hunch. He wanted to know more for himself about her, and about her relationship with Vladimir, *though he was sure that the PI would not be able to get that information for him*. So, he was here at the restaurant starting that part of the investigation for himself.

When Davyd had asked him earlier that day if he trusted Elsa, he had said no, but he had avoided telling his dear friend that he wanted to trust her. However, he had learned that being trusting was a luxury that he did not have. Everyone had an ulterior motive. No one was without a price.

He sat in the window seat for a couple of hours, never taking his gaze off the windows, except to look at his food or check his surroundings. As long as he did not stand up, he went undetected with only a few stares from women who caught a glimpse of him head on. The waiting also gave him more time to think about his plans.

After a significant amount of time had passed, as the sun began to set on the horizon, through the golden doors of Hutton Industries, the tall, statuesque Elsa emerged with a pair of brown shades over her eyes and a handful of papers in her arms. Dmitry's Bentley was there to collect her, and on cue the chauffeur popped out of the car and opened the door for her to slide in the back and be carted away.

Jumping up from his seat, he dropped the money on the table and then quickly ducked out the door to the alley where his bike was. In the hectic, rush-hour traffic, he was able to tail them without being noticed. Curiously, he was led only about ten blocks away from the office to another high-rise apartment building, where the car parked out front and she briskly got out and ran inside.

Dmitry automatically assumed that Vladimir had to live in this building based upon the bodyguards who stood outside, undetectable to the untrained eye but obvious to him. He again parked and looked for a place to wait.

Grabbing a newspaper, he sat down on a wooden street bench almost a block from the building, but still in good view. This time he waited impatiently.

The idea of Elsa checking in with Vladimir caused a strain in his chest. He couldn't decide if it felt like jealousy or deceit or a mixture of the two, but he was certain that he didn't like it.

Trying to control his racing heart and his desire to go into the building after her, he finally focused on the newspaper and realized that there was a picture of him on the front page of the business section. He shook his head in disgust.

According to this reporter, *the young, blond stud was going to be the end of Hutton Industries.* What sources? Well, at least they had it half way right. He might be the end of Hutton Industries, but he'd be the beginning of Medlov Enterprises.

Half an hour later, Elsa emerged again in the same manner as before with another hand full of paperwork. After loading into the back of the car, she quickly disappeared into the busy streets, probably headed back to his home.

Dmitry waited for a minute this time, finishing the article about himself in before getting on his bike and heading back to pick a bone with his new play thing. He had to remember to remain calm and stay objective, but as the day went on it was getting nearly impossible to do.

***

As the sun set, Dorian and his team settled into the guest house behind the Medlov house for the evening. Dmitry had given them the quarters temporarily until all the jobs required had been done. It was a step up from anything the team had done before. Most of the time they stayed in old, broken-down hotels or hostels. However, Dmitry made sure that they were fed, catered to by his staff and within his grasp at all times.   Tired from hours of discussion on the best possible ways to pull off a mass hit, they all dispersed to their rooms...all except Arie.

As soon as she heard her brother's body thud against the bed next door to her own, she jumped up and snuck quietly out of the window. Lowering herself down with the rope in her backpack, she landed on the manicured lawn like a cat and hiked back in the shadows to the castle.

Opening the back door quietly, she entered in kitchen and slowly inched through the dark corridor until she heard footsteps behind her. She turned to see Ivan standing by a doorway, waiting for her.

"Took you long enough," he said with a glimmer in his majestic eyes. Even in a low tone, his voice boomed through the hallways.

She smiled. "*Impatience* is a virtue."

Anxious to get on with the night, Ivan led her up to his bedroom on the west wing of the house, far from his brother's iron grip. The entire floor was his, equipped with an office, a small workout room, an entertainment room and a two bedrooms. Dmitry had set it up so that not only would his brother not be disturbed on his visits but also Ivan would have no reason to disturb anyone else.

They walked quietly through the dimly lit halls side-by-side, much unlike Ivan. He couldn't take his eyes off her. With every step and every move, he saw the contours of her short body, perfectly sculpted into a unique masterpiece. He licked his lips as they arrived to his room, hungry to taste his prize.

With his index finger, he pushed the door open. It creaked as it hit the doorstop. "After you," he said, following her inside.

Arie looked around. "Fancy," she said, nodding in approval. "You all live like kings. It must be nice."

"Dmitry lives like a king. I just stay here when I'm summoned," he answered, closing the door behind him. The gears in his head changed. "So, my brother wants me to keep *it* in my pants until this thing is over, and I'm sure your brother would prefer you keep your legs closed until you're married. But we're both about to break the rules, eh." Crossing his arms in front of him, he guarded the door just in case she changed her mind. It was too late to turn back now, whether she liked it or not.

Arie looked up at him and smiled. There were no signs of nervousness on her face or in her body language. In fact, she looked comfortable with him. "Only if you answer my question correctly," she said, sitting on his large oak bed. Her little feet dangled a few inches from the ground as she kicked off her shoes.

"I'm listening," he said, pealing out of his shirt to reveal his taut muscles.

"Do you like it *roughhhhhh*?" she asked, biting her lip. "Because if you don't, you might want to put that shirt back on. There is no way I'm not going to tear through your flesh tonight, Vor."

Ivan could feel himself hardening with her every word. He rubbed his erection. "Oh, you have no idea how rough I like it. I'm not into love making, sweetheart. I plan to fuck you until your nose bleeds."

Arie laughed at his incredulous statement. "Don't be so sure that you're even capable of making my nose bleed or for that matter making me come. See, I've seen a million men like you. You think you're tough when everyone's looking but under fire, under pressure, undercover...all of you motherfuckers fold."

Ivan walked up to the bed, bent down gently and suddenly grabbed her by her fragile neck roughly cutting off her air supply. He could feel her heartbeat thudding through the veins right above her clavicle bone, but he did not feel her tremble, which was odd considering his grip.

Loosening his hand, he ran his finger over her red, plump lips and into her wet mouth.

She sucked it roughly, biting at his fingertips as he leaned further into her. As soon as he was in reach and eye level with her, he felt her razor sharp nails trail against his chest, cutting into his perfect skin as she attacked. He didn't bother to wince away. Instead, he pushed against her nails, into the pain, just to get closer to her.

Starring deep into the abyss of her eyes as he lay on top of her with his knees mounted into the bed, he was stunned at what he saw. His match. His equal. Finally. His mouth watered for her. "Let's dance, bitch," he whispered as he drew her into him. She wrapped her legs around his upper torso, too short to reach the rest of him and made him roll over.

With his large hands rubbing her small breasts roughly, Ivan pulled her shirt off her first, then her black satin bra. He threw her clothes on the floor and studied her bare frame. Even in the dark, he could see scars from many battles. Clutching her tiny waist, he pulled her to him as he sat his back against the headboard and slivered his long tongue around her brown areolas. Biting her nipples, he moaned feeling his breaths become more sporadic.

She closed her eyes, feeling zingers of heat shoot through her body. He sucked at her violently, like a child who had been denied his mother's breasts as a child. Fingers ran through his black inky mane and then snatched his head back. Looking into his blue eyes, she leaned in to kiss his full mouth but his hands had found her pants, stopping her. Unable to get them completely off, he threw her back on the bed and crawled over her, snatching her pants down with her panties.

Her body jerked, but she laughed, kicking him as she flayed her short, perfect legs. Her laughter was contagious. He grinned seductively as she opened wide and slipped three of her own fingers into her sex.

Ivan sat on his knees watching her while she pleasured herself, then pulled her hand away and made her taste her fingers. She sucked all but one, and then offered it to him.

"I've got something for you to suck on," Ivan growled as he moved over her. With his legs across her chest, he guided himself into her mouth as far he could fit. He heard her choke, but he only laughed. As he was about to push further down her throat, he felt her small hands squeezing his balls.

Reflexes alive, he pulled back, and she quickly pulled her body from under him. Standing on the bed, she pushed his head back and smacked him.

He laughed. "You weren't ready for that one, were you? Lesson one; don't bite off more than you can chew." His accent was lyrical. In his own way, he was making love to her, enjoying more than penetration.

She walked up to him on the bed and rubbed her hairy mound in his face. The wiry hair felt rough against his skin. "Your smell is intoxicating," he said, rubbing his large hands over her muscular thighs. "Have you showered?"

"No," she said with a grin.

"Good," he answered, opening her wide. Keeping his eyes on her, he tasted the inner folds of her body. She nearly fell into his embrace as he made her melt, until she felt from behind his large finger probing at her anus.

"Do it," she urged, bucking against him.

There was a long silence and careful calculation. Slipping one set of fingers inside of her sex and the other inside of her anus, he had her just where he wanted her.

Moaning aloud, she pinched her nipples and pushed squarely down with all of her might against him.

Ivan was becoming too aroused. Pearls of sex started to drip out of his throbbing head. He quickly removed his hand and pushed her anus down on his erection. Looking down at her, he waited for her to scream out, but she did not. Instead, little dirty Arie took all of him. Their powerful thrusts into each other made for an illicit song of pleasure down the hallways. Moans and groans were followed by cursing and slapping.

"I want you from behind," Ivan said, cupping her chin in his hand. He was dying to see her in more pleasure and pain.

Getting behind her in a swift motion, he positioned her on top of as many pillows as could balance her body and then invaded her from behind. Grabbing a hand full of her hair, he reached back with the other hand and slapped her bare behind, wet with sweat and sex.

She finally screamed out. The sound of her pleasure nearly pushed him to climax along with the freedom of raw abandon. His muscles tightened.

Reaching back again with his large, foreboding hand, he slapped her harder. The sound echoed throughout the dark room and down the hall.

She cried out in pain, but did not move. Instead, she braced herself for another.

Ivan drove deeper and harder into her anus once more before he quickly moved to her wet, open sex. He turned her over on the bed, but realized that their height difference was preventing him from going as deep as he wanted.

Picking her up, he pushed her violently against the wall and drove into her body, knocking the century old paintings to the floor and the air out of her vulnerable body. Her head hit the wall with a thud, then her body was invaded by relentless and lustful pumps. Pleasure exploded through the both of them as they finally connected.

Dazed, she held on to him as he slicked in and out of her stretched body, wet and steely, with the strength of a thousand men and the endurance of one real one. Looking down at her as he pumped into her body, he began to laugh.

"What?" she asked out of breath. "What's so fucking funny?"

"You're bleeding," he said, wiping her nose with his index finger.

Chapter Eight

Dmitry had come up to talk to Ivan about their plan of attack when he arrived back home after his long ride, but had found that his brother was currently in a compromising position. Without being detected, Dmitry slipped his hand inside of the door and locked it, then closed it shut to ensure that Dorian did not find out that his sister was being used like a rag doll.

Mentally and physically exhausted, he trudged back over to his side of the house, turning off lights as he passed them. He didn't know why he still bothered with trying to conserve electricity, but he felt compelled to never waste anything considering where he had come from as a boy.

As he arrived at the long foreboding stairwell that led up to his bedroom, he thought again about Elsa. He wondered if it would be best to let her freshen up before he confronted her or would the element of surprise be best to get the truth.

After dragging himself up the stairs that reminded him of Mount Niesen in the Swiss Alps because of their never ending climb, he finally passed her room and went down to his own to take a shower.

Patience was a virtue. Plus, at the moment, he was a bit put out.

Tonight, it seemed more aggravating than normal that Ivan was yet with another woman when he hadn't been with even one since before his arrangement with Catherine. How it was that a boy so young had such an active sex life was almost unbelievable – if he hadn't known himself.

There was also the salt on his growing wound - Elsa's possible betrayal. *What did she tell Vladimir? Why was she spying? What was she after?* This game of cat and mouse that he always found himself playing was taxing business with no possible end in sight.

Frustrated, he burst through his bedroom door and slammed it behind him. Throwing his cares to the wind, he took off his leather jacket, pulled off his jeans and sweater and threw his underwear in the hamper in the bathroom.

As he turned the brass knobs to his shower, he finally felt a little calm creeping into his hectic thoughts. *Just a moment's breather before the storm*, he muttered to himself.

Massaging his temples and thinking, while the room filled with fog and the smell of sandalwood, he knelt down into the corner of the shower and hid away from the world. The weight of his position sometimes became too much, but he could never show anyone. Instead, in moments like this, he lamented quietly without as much as a word spoken.

With the water beating against him, shooting from the jets embedded into the luxury contraption, he sat snarling like a cornered animal, looking across the shower through the water into the abyss of his thoughts. Fear. Anger. Pain. Determination. So many emotions swirled through his heart until he felt his eyes blazing, his hands trembling.

Then the moment was over. Compartmentalizing his emotions and locking them away again in the box in the back of his head, he stood up, shook it all off.

Running his face and head through the stream, he rinsed himself off and stepped out into the cool air. Blonde curly hair covered his body from ankle to waist.

He went to the sink with the large towel wrapped around his lower body and checked his chest. He had just shaved it the night before and only a little stubble had grown back.

He smirked at himself. "You still think you're going to bed her, you silly fool," he said to himself as he brushed his teeth.

After his normal grooming, he slipped on a pair of pajama bottoms and gray t-shirt and lay in his bed. Melting into the comfort of the mattress, he closed his eyes and sighed. He could hear his breathing slow into a rhythmic melody of sleep, and felt his body begging to rest. Pulling the pillow under his head, he looked up at the ceiling and thought of Catherine.

"Look what you've done to me," he said aloud. "You've handed me a mess. Now, I have to go and do this." He shook his head. Pulling himself back out of the bed, he left his bedroom and walked slowly down to Elsa's door. He stood at it for a minute debating whether or not he should knock. As he raised his hand to pound on the door, she opened it.

Peering up at him as she clutched her red kimono closed, she spoke. "Is there anything the matter, sir?" she asked innocently.

"I need to talk to you," he said, trying to avoid the smidgeon of bare flesh that peaked out of the top of her gown.

"I'll just get dressed then," she said, nodding.

As she closed the door, Dmitry caught it and sighed. "Now, Elsa. Step aside."

Walking in, he closed the door behind him. The room reeked of her sweet perfume. He took a deep breath and turned to her. She looked even more beautiful without makeup. He guessed that she too was fresh out of the shower as he noticed the wet strands of her hair dangling out of her ponytail onto her gown.

"How did you know that I was outside?" he asked, looking around her room. Papers were piled on every desk and all over her bed. She evidently had plans of working all night.

"I saw your shadow under the doorway," she answered with her arms crossed.

Dmitry looked into her doe-like eyes and smirked. "Who do you work for? Vladimir or me?"

She bucked her eyes, shocked at his question. Moving her weight from one foot to the other, she gripped her arms with her long fingers. "I don't understand your question."

"A smart *zhenshchina* like you? Of course you do."

"I work you for," she said in a matter-of-fact tone.

"Then why do you report to *him*?"

"I don't." She cleared her throat.

"Don't lie to me. You don't know me well enough to get on my bad side," he said in a low growl. He locked his eyes on her. "I try to know all of the movements around me. And *you* are around me, so I have to know what you are doing at all times."

Elsa's eyes narrowed. "I am here to help you with your business. Outside of your business, you have no right to my personal life," she snarled.

"You don't have a personal life as long as you work for me." He bent to her. "Now, what were you doing at Vladimir's apartment today after you left the office?"

"You were spying on me?" she asked in disbelief.

"I am protecting my interests," he said in a thick Russian accent. "Now, tell me this very instant what you were doing there."

Elsa breathed in through her nose, flaring her nostrils. "I left a few things behind when Vladimir moved me out. It was a sudden decision to come here, after we broke up. I was missing some of my own books for class. I went there to collect my things." Tears ran down her face. "It had nothing to do with you or your business or your interests. I have a life outside of you and outside of Vladimir." She shook her head in disgust. "I was gifted to you because he didn't want me anymore. And I was *gifted* to him by my father. But I am no object, Dmitry." She began to cry. "I *am* a person." Blinking tears, she wiped her face and turned from him.

Dmitry went to the phone and picked it up. "Call him and thank him for allowing you to pick up your things today," he said, handing her the phone. "And I'll listen. If he sounds like he knows what you are talking about, then I'll apologize. If he doesn't, then you'll leave here now with the clothes on your back and walk in the cold back to town. But I doubt you'll make it back."

Elsa grabbed the phone. Dialing Vladimir, she wiped the tears from her face.

"*Da*," Vladimir said, answering quickly.

"It's Elsa," she said, looking up at Dmitry, who bent down to her to listen onto the call.

"I know who it is. Why are you calling me?"

"I wanted to...make sure I didn't leave anything today."

"For God's sake, no. You said you left your books for class. I had the maid set them on the credenza. Nothing else is here for you. Now stop calling. You're Dmitry's problem now," he said, hanging up the phone in her face.

Elsa looked up at Dmitry and hung up. "Are you happy now?" Tears ran freely.

Dmitry took the phone and hung it up. "From the deepest parts of my heart, I apologize for offending you," he said, bowing.

Elsa wiped her face again. "Please leave," she begged.

Dmitry did not move. "Why were you gifted to a man like Vladimir?"

"You are relentless," she said, throwing her hands up.

"I really want to know." His voice was soothing now. He watched her carefully.

"My father needed money for things for his government that he could not get anywhere else but Khalid. It was untraceable, and it was a bit of an emergency." She shrugged her shoulders. "I was smart, and I was educated in the world. My father told me that part of paying off his debt was the agreement that I would come to help Vladimir while we were both in college. I was to be his assistant of sorts, but we became more than that. Then we started to have many disagreements, and when Khalid called and said that he needed Vladimir to help you to get your businesses in order, Vladimir figured that he would get rid of me and solve both of his problems at once."

Dmitry looked down at the ground. "So was this the first time that you were passed around?"

The words hurt her to her core. "Yes," she said disgusted. "I always thought that I was worth more to him than that."

Dmitry shook his head. "How often do you talk to your father?"

"When either he wants something or I need something," she answered shortly.

"How would you like to stop being passed around?"

"I don't understand."

"I'll make you a deal that doesn't involve you doing anything that you don't want to do."

"I'm listening."

"When I make you president of Hutton Industries, I want you to call your father and tell him how gracious I have been and how lucrative a relationship with someone like me could be. Then, I want you to arrange a meeting where you will encourage him to purchase all of his black market munitions from Medlov Enterprises."

Elsa looked up at him. "What is Medlov Enterprises?"

"It's the reason that I'm cutting so many jobs and so many departments. I need the capital to focus on my true business. I have obligations that I need to meet, that have been looming since before my wife's death. So, I'm going to strip the company bare-bone and use the capital to fund my own underground operation."

"Well, what I'm supposed to do with a dying company?" she asked confused.

"Build it back up.   You're coming from Oxford. You're landing a great job. You can make it what you want it to be; I don't care what you do with it after I get what I need."

She thought long and hard for a moment, and then shook her head in agreement. "Alright. If you make me president, I'll do it. But I won't owe you after that."

"No, you won't," he said, offering his hand.

Elsa looked down at his massive fingers then stuck her own delicate hand in his to shake it. As she did so, he curled his fingers around hers and pulled him to her.

Only a foot shorter than him, he bent to her waist and pulled her up to him.

"But you owe me now," he said whispering on her lips. "And I owe you. So, shall we settle up?"

Breathing against his face, she looked into his blue eyes and wrapped her long, slender fingers around him. "Yes, I thought you'd never ask."

Swooping her up in his arms, he carried her out of the bedroom. Curiously, she looked around. "Where are we going?" she asked, a little concerned.

"To my bed."

"But your wife," she protested.

"I'm not married anymore." He kicked the door open with his foot and stepped inside, then kicked it shut. "Lock that for me. It's a door meant for short people," he explained, bending down for her to reach it.

She locked it obediently with one arm around his neck and the other reaching out to the brass lock.

Carrying her to his massive bed, he laid her down gently. "I want to erase every memory of her. We start here," he said, touching the bed.

She sat up, and looked at him. "You want to erase her memory? Isn't that a bit harsh for someone who has done so much for you?"

"No," Dmitry answered angrily, reaching for her. He paused suddenly with his finger wrapped around a strand of her hair. Looking into her eyes, he frowned. "Are you on birth control of some type?"

"Yes," she answered. "But I would prefer if you used a condom anyway."

"Of course," he said smiling. "We'll get to that when it's time." Crawling into the large bed with her, he arrived back at her lips. Breathing over them, he ran his large hands over her goose-bumped shoulders. "Are you sure?"

"Yes," she said, pulling his shirt off. "Yes."

Dmitry groaned. "You're so beautiful." Kissing her lips finally, he slowly tasted her mouth, searching for every truth and every lie. Warm flesh mingled together as they slowly bonded into one. She tasted like mint leaves and smelled of rose oil. It was infused into her skin and hair, driving him mad with want. There was nothing that turned him on more than pure femininity.

Running his large hand over the soft fabric of her kimono, he found his way to her firm round breasts that had pebbled with his touch. He massaged her aching nipples carefully, savoring the feel of her body.

Spellbound by his touch, she let out a whimper. Her head rested back on the pillow that he scooped up for her and she watched as he slowly and seductively removed her gown to reveal, deep brown, perfect flesh.

He ran his hands from her hips down to her ankles, then kissed the inside arch of her foot. Closing her eyes, she felt him raise her legs and open them as he made his way to the center of her body. Heat rose from her core, greeting his welcomed arrival.

"What do you like?" Dmitry whispered as he hovered over her. His long manhood, brushed against her body.

"Do you know how long it has been since a man asked that?" she asked sincerely.

"Do you know how long it has been since I have asked a woman simply because I desired to please her?" He looked back into her eyes.

"I want to be made love to, like a queen," she said, biting her lip. "I want to be touched softly, gently." A tear ran from the corner of her eye, holding back some dark memory. "What do you want?"

Dmitry licked his lips. In a husky voice, he finally answered, "I want to make love to you all night until I cannot muster enough strength to carry on, and in the morning, I want things to go back to the way that they were before."

"You don't want love?" she asked amused.

"I don't need it," he answered. "A man in my position cannot afford love. But I need pleasure. I can give you the same measure that you give me, and I'll never feel as though either one of us belongs to the other. You won't be my possession."

She looked up at him and clenched her jaw. "Promises, promises."

"My word is all you need from me. It is the most valuable thing I own."

"Very well. Tomorrow, things will return to the way that they were," she reached out for him. "But tonight, we can pretend that we love each other, right?"

Dmitry smiled, revealing his dimples. "Tonight, we don't have to pretend."

Elsa was quiet. "So, if I scream out that I love you, it won't startle you?"

"No," Dmitry said, reaching over to the nightstand to retrieve a condom out of the drawer. "You can scream until you go hoarse. No one is going to say anything to you." He ran his hand back over her hot skin. "This AIDS epidemic is real. Have you been tested?" He looked into her eyes and waited for an answer. He wished like hell that she would give him the right answer.

"Yes, just last month. I'm negative. You?"

"Negative," he answered.

Bending down to her neck, he kissed a trail on her sweet skin from her collar bone down to her needy breasts. She arched her back as she felt his hot breath then his warm, fleshy mouth slowly suckle her. Wrapping his arms around her to protect her from the world, he tasted her skin and felt her come alive in his arms.

Her long legs wrapped around his waist and locked at the ankles. As she felt him pull her upwards into the air, she heard the sheath to the condom tear. He looked into her eyes as he slid the contraceptive on, then with great care guided her onto his pulsating shaft, giving her as much as he thought that she could take.

There was not a word for what Elsa felt. The walls of her body began to quake first and then shattered under the pressure of gigantic, erect penis. Wrapping her arms around his neck, she found herself in his warm lap and in his protective embrace. With his legs stretched out, he held her up on his thighs glistening and slick with her cream and kissed her mouth again.

"Oh, Dmitry," she whimpered as her sex muscled clenched around him.

There was nothing better than being free and tonight, she finally felt like she was with a man by choice. She felt as though she was his equal, both needing and giving something in return.

He watched her happily. With gentle strokes, he held her narrow back with his strong hands and looked into her eyes. "Say my name again," he said, pushing her body all the way down on him. Kissing her swan-like neck, he felt her quiver again, sending a shock wave down into own stomach.

"Dmitry...Medlov," she said, before he ducked in for another kiss. He loved the way her mouth formed to say his name. She said it like no other woman had, like it was something wonderful.

Laying her back on the bed, he opened her legs and slid in between them. Their bodies melted into the comforter that he used to make love to his dead wife on. He felt her body began to sweat and her scent begin to transfer on to it. He knew that he had to work harder, if he truly wanted to destroy this temple that he had built for himself.

Pulling out of her body, he took the end of the silk sheet and wiped between her legs, then slowly ducked his head between them. Cunnilingus was always something that he regarded as private. He only did such an act with a woman he was truly interested in. This time, he did it not only because he desired Elsa but because he knew it was one of the most intimate things he had done with Catherine in this very bed, at times.

Unknowing of Dmitry's thoughts, Elsa laid in rapture as he ravaged her. His pointed tongue on her clit destroyed any hopes for control. Her body convulsed as he kissed her, holding her legs in both of his arms. Pent to the bed, she cried out as she felt a wave of shocks and jolts tremor through her. The wave of sensations nearly electrified her.

"Yes!" she cried out. "Dmitry. Oh, I love you!!!"

Feeling her body erupt, he moved away from her and turned her over on her side. Her sex creamed over on him. It was just what he wanted her to do. Rubbing his hand in between her slick legs, he smeared her evidence on the sheets.

Finally, he could no longer see Catherine's face. He entered Elsa again, this time with more passion. Raising his leg, he pumped into her body with powerful, coiling strikes that made her grab the sheets for stability and to withstand the shock of his impaling shaft. The wetness continued to run over the both of them and mingle with the sweat that slicked their bodies like oil.

Dmitry loved the sensation. He loved her youth and vitality. But what he loved most was that when this was done, he would owe neither of them.

With one hand on her hip and the other wrapped in her thick, dark hair, he made her submit to his will. Growling, he pulled her to him, arching her back with his touch.

With each deafening blow, he complimented it with a softer one, creating a mind-blowing rhythm that drove her mad. For a moment, all she could do was moan, feeling her body quiver and shake then take more and more and more.

"I can't take it," she gasped, feeling her body preparing to climax again. "I can't..."

Dmitry continued, this time turning her around on her stomach, he laid her flat and rubbed his hands over her back. Massaging her small muscles, he finally lay on top of her, making sure not to drop his weight completely, then after opening her legs, he covertly slid from behind into her already quivering sex again.

"Oh, Dmitry," she said, feeling his body slap against hers.

Kissing the crown of her head, he pushed against her flesh, savoring the firmness of her backside. Digging into the bed, she arched her back just enough to make the familiar zinger run through Dmitry's body from his fingertips to his toes.

"Yes," he said, coiling his strikes and rotating his hips. "Yes." He bucked back.

She arched her back a little more to please him, loving his masculine voice.

"Turn around," Dmitry ordered, feeling himself nearing the end. "I want to see your face."

He turned her around and slipped off the condom. She looked down stunned. Opening her legs wider, she waited. This time the feeling was warmer, fleshier, better. His velvet head entered. Her sex began to clench tight as she felt his long, hard shaft pulsating inside, creating new and completely different sensations.

Kissing her lips, he slid in and out of her making her watch, until finally his toes cramped and he felt his body tense up. Pulling out, he let his seed soak her stomach. He moaned and pushed against her body, slicking both of them with cream as he finished

Elsa looked on amazed. He was absolutely beautiful.

Panting, Dmitry wiped the sweat and residue from his stone-carved abs and then took the sheet and wiped her body clean. Lying beside her, he cocked one leg up and put his arm up beside her on the pillow.

"Did you enjoy that?" he asked, looking at her.

"Yes," she said, panting.

"Good," he said, looking back at the ceiling. "Would you like some water before....we begin again?"

Elsa bit her lip in amazement. "Yes," she said, watching him as he jumped out of bed and headed to the table across the room, where the tray with beverages were.

Sitting up in bed, she took the bottle of water from him and sighed. "That was amazing."

Dmitry smiled. "It's been a long time. I'll be better in just a minute." He walked to the bathroom to wash his face. "You may want to throw those covers on the floor, eh. Unless you like sticky."

"Okay," she said, doing as he suggested. "Did we accomplish our mission to erase your Catherine?" she asked.

Dmitry looked in the bathroom mirror at his naked, sweaty, red body. "We're nearly there," he said, splashing the water in his face.

He walked back out to the bedroom and leaned against the doorway naked. "I think by morning, I'll be good."

"I think by morning, I'll be no good," Elsa said grinning.

***

Arie laid beside Ivan in the dark stillness of his bedroom and felt at peace. This man, the one she'd heard was a devil, was in actuality just an angry soul like her. He felt no obligation to the world, but a great deal of disgust with it as she did.

Trailing her fingers over his chest, she looked up at him and smiled.

Ivan didn't return the gaze. Instead, he looked up at the ceiling in deep thought.

"What's the deal with you and your brother?" Ivan asked suddenly. "He's black. You're obviously not."

"We have the same father, different mothers. His mother was African and my mother was Chechen. Our father was Ukrainian."

"Was?"

"They were all slaughtered, though not at the same time or even in the same way."

"Political bullshit or religious?"

"Both," she said, moving off his chest.

He grabbed her by her naked waist. "Where do you think that you're going?"

"Back to my room. It will be morning soon. Dorian will..."

"Fuck Dorian. You're a grown woman. You stay here with me tonight. If he has problem with that, let him come talk to me."

"Are you sure that you want to do that?" she asked amused.

Ivan lifted his head and gripped her tighter. "I'm not done with you yet."

She lowered down to his face and looked him in his eyes. "Careful, Medlov. You might trip."

"If I fall, I'm taking you with me," he said, grabbing her by the back of the head.

She fell back into his kiss, savoring the taste of the heavy alcohol on his breath and his natural male scent. Skin-to-skin, she could feel the beat of his racing heart and the warmth of his body as he embraced her in his muscular hold.

With one hand weaved into her hair and the other planted squarely on her backside, he pulled her down into a haze of lust again, drowning her with seismic pulses of adrenaline that shot through her entire body.

His long tongue moved from her mouth to her neck and the vein pumping out of it. Like a vampire, he sucked on her as his hands slid over her body, awakening the aching parts of her that he planned to ravage again.

It wasn't just his sex that drove her crazy; it was his angry demand of her, his unwillingness to yield. They were both rebels without a cause. She had never felt so at ease with any man, *and there had been many*. Only she was not certain yet, why she felt this way for him.

Ivan could feel her mind pulling her body away from him and quickly snatched her back to reality. Biting her ear, he felt her wince. "Don't go anywhere," he ordered her.

"I'm not leaving," she answered into his mouth.

"I don't mean physically," he said, letting her know that they were mentally connected for the moment. "Don't let your mind take you away right now."

Gawking at the mere mention of anything that wasn't obvious or physical, let her know that Ivan had another side. She appreciated his attentiveness, even as cave-like as it was.

"I'm here," she assured, running her hand through his coal-black hair. "I'm right here."

Chapter Nine

The Medlov manor was usually alive with movement by six in the morning, because of Dmitry's normal regiment of gym training, breakfast and then early reading of all the newspapers. However, as the sun beamed across the vast green land the morning after his escapades, at eight he was still wrapped around Elsa in his bed.

Sleeping heavily, his large chest raised her up and down with each rhythmic, deep breath as she rested upon him. Both naked and exhausted, they had ignored the chiming of the grandfather clock across the room and the brass alarm clock on the nightstand.

As the glow of the majestic room went from dark to warm and bright, they finally began to move around. Dmitry, used to Catherine sleeping on top of him, automatically pulled Elsa up on his chest and adjusted her like a baby. But she, only used to sleeping alone, finally emerged from her sleep and realized that she was tangled in a body web with her boss.

Stretching herself out, she rolled from his taut body and landed gracefully on the floor beside the bed. Feet snuggled in the plush carpet below, she found her kimono and slipped it on. There was only just under a thousand feet from his bedroom to hers. She was certain that she could go the short distance without being detected by anyone.

Checking herself in the mirror across from the bed, she saw Dmitry's reflection in the mirror. His blue prisms were watching her.

"Good morning," she whispered in a cracked voice, turning towards him.

Dmitry wiped his eyes and looked at the alarm clock. "Good morning," he said, sitting on the side of the bed. "Why are you up so early?"

"I have to fulfill my side of the bargain. Remember? Last night, you made me feel like a queen, and this morning, I need to get back to the way things were before we...made love." She twisted her hair in a long braid and tucked it away.

Dmitry raised his brow. "How can my side of the bargain be complete when you haven't eaten a thing? Come sit down. I'll have breakfast brought to you."

"You don't have to do that," she protested.

"I don't have to do anything." He waved her over. "Come...come. Sit by me."

With a lazy smile, she walked across the room and sat beside him. Even at six feet tall, she felt amazingly little beside his large frame.

Slumped over, Dmitry reached over and rubbed her back. "Thank you," he said, kissing her cheek. "I know that last night must not have been easy for you," he said in gruff voice. "But I appreciate you, and your willingness to be with me."

Elsa blushed. "Last night was the *easiest* night of my life. Being with you was mind blowing, Dmitry."

A smile tugged at Dmitry's lips. "Well, good, *da*." He turned to her. Heat rushed through his body again and raised his manhood up between his legs.

She looked down in amazement. It was even bigger in the daylight.

He did not try to hide; instead, he took her hand and softly moved it to his lap. "Maybe we can go back to the way things were tomorrow," he said with a twinkle in his eyes. "What's the rush?"

"There is no rush," she said sincerely. "I don't want there to be one, at least."

Dmitry pulled her hair out of the knot on top of her head and let it fall past her shoulders. "I just can't get over how beautiful you are," he whispered before he picked her up.

Leaning back on the headboard, Dmitry and Elsa made love again for the eighth time.

***

Dorian could barely pray. Getting up from the corner near his window, he stood up and groaned. Arie was at it again. When he had first awakened that morning, he had gone to her room to check on her and found it empty. He didn't even bother to look for her, knowing that she was with Ivan. He just didn't understand why she wouldn't take heed to his warning of these men. They were supposed to work for those who sought to upset the government and the status quo, not lay with them.

Showered and dress, Dorian and the rest of his team trekked over to main house to meet with Dmitry in his study to begin operations. The sun beamed down on them over clear blue skies and dew rested on top of the green lawn. As the birds chirped and the grounds crew worked, it seemed like a perfect way to start a good day from the outside.

From the inside of their small group, however, there was another feeling. They all walked quietly, knowing that their boss was livid over Arie. He brooded quietly, giving dark stares into each room as they made their way through the dim hallways of the castle past the workers, hoping half-heartedly to catch a glimpse of Ivan and Arie in a forbidden embrace so that he could lash out.

Both of the other men hoped that some kind of peace could be made without a full blown disagreement. They needed the money that the Medlov's were paying, and no one wanted this connection to be severed over his troubled little sister. However, none of them would dare say a word, because they knew how much Dorian loved his half-sister and how protective he was over her, despite her many indiscretions.

As they arrived at the study, Davyd was there waiting and eating breakfast while watching the news. He greeted them, completely unaware of Dorian's current state of mind. "We'll begin when Dmitry arrives," Davyd explained, offering them seats.

"Have you seen Arie?" Dorian asked, walking to the window. He looked out over the tranquil landscape blankly.

Davyd looked up from his runny eggs and put down his fork. It clanged against the expensive china. "No, I have not seen her," he said, instantly thinking of Ivan. "Maybe she ran errand," Davyd suggested.

"Or maybe she is with your boss," Dorian said, turning around.

"I doubt she would be with Dmitry," Davyd said abruptly. "But if she is, it is not my business." He sucked his teeth. "And it's not yours either."

"I'm not talking about Dmitry, but regardless of who she is with, it is my business."

"Your sister is a grown woman. Is she not?" Davyd asked.

Dorian did not answer.

Davyd continued, "Well, if she is a grown woman, then wherever she is, I am sure that she is fine. However, if you feel the need to question our employer when he arrives, feel free to do so *at your own risk*."

Dorian did not back down. "I will do just that," he said with a stone face.

Minutes later, the door opened and in walked Arie and Ivan together, talking under their breath and laughing. Arie still had on the clothes that she had worn the day before, while Ivan had obviously showered and changed. Dorian instantly took offense to the overt disrespect of his sister. It was bad enough that everyone had an idea, but now there was no question of what had happened.

"Is this how you do business?" Dorian asked, now seeing red.

Ivan with a smug smile chuckled. "What the fuck are you talking about?" He clenched his wide jaw.

"You mean to tell me that you haven't defiled her?" Dorian asked angrily.

Ivan looked at Dorian and wiped his mouth. "Quite the opposite," Ivan answered. "She defiled me." He laughed again and looked over at Davyd, who shook his head disapprovingly.

Arie snickered and looked over at her brother. "It's none of your business, Dorian," she snapped. "Stay out of it."

"Stay out of what, you being a whore?" Dorian asked, walking up to her.

"A *whore* according to you?" she asked, not backing down. "Fuck you."

No one saw Dorian's hand, but it quickly swung towards her face, knocking her down. "A whore according to our faith, to our laws, to us," he said, angrily.

Ivan stopped smiling. "Do you want me to step in? Speak now before I make up my own mind and fuck him up for good," Ivan said to Arie in a growl. He knew all too well about sibling fights regardless of how they looked from the outside. Plus, Arie was supposed to be an assassin. If she couldn't take a baby slap from her big brother then it was best that they all find out now.

Arie spit on the floor and stood up. "The next time that you raise your hand to me over my choices, I promise you, I'll cut that hand off. I swear it on my mother's grave and on my own soul," she said, foaming at the mouth.

Ivan raised his finger like a child in a school room. "I think she means it," he said, laughing and turning to Davyd. "Where's Dmitry, so we can get this show on the road?"

"He's not here yet," Davyd said, going back to eating his food.

"Well, should someone go and get him?" Ivan asked impatiently. "Shit, we don't have all day."

Davyd sighed. "You have as long as it takes for him to arrive," he said, without raising his voice or taking his eyes off the television.

Thirty minutes later, Dmitry entered the study fully dressed. In jeans and sweater, he breezed past the group to his chair and sat down. Unfolding his newspaper, he looked around at each of them and clenched his jaw.

"What has happened?" he asked.

"Nothing to worry yourself with," Davyd answered.

Dmitry looked over at his brother and knew instantly it had something to do with him. "We are not moving forward with our plans until I find out what the hell is going on in my camp. Nothing goes on without my knowledge," he said in a raised voice. The veins in his neck began to protrude. "So, I'll ask again, what *the fuck* has happened?"

Davyd spoke first, feeling an obligation as the true underboss. "Arie and Ivan were together last night. Dorian felt the act offended his family name and slapped her."

Dmitry's nostrils flared. "We don't slap women, regardless of their choices," he said, looking at Dorian. "She's a grown woman. As far as I am concerned, her sex life is her own."

"She's behaving like a whore, and I won't have it," Dorian said in a stern voice. He eyed Dmitry.

"Very well," Dmitry answered, pushing his newspaper away. "Then send her ass away. But in the meantime, don't forget who you're talking to, sister or not. I am boss. If I have to prove my title, it will be in blood."

No one was expecting that. Ivan seemed more concerned now. However, Dorian gave the idea some thought to sending his sister away.

"Don't I have a say in the matter?" Arie asked Dmitry.

"Well, of course you do." Dmitry eyed Elsa as she quietly walked in and took a seat across the room in the corner.

"Don't sit over there. Sit over here by me," Dmitry said, waving at her. His voice was softer now.

Everyone's attention soon turned to Elsa, who was dressed in a perfect black suit with her hair pulled from her long, defined face. It was her gaze that gave her away and his own on her. He seemed to forget everyone else in the room. A wave of calm swept through the study.

Elsa got up and walked past Arie and Dorian to the chair and sat down beside Davyd. Her sweet cologne filled the room again, much to Dmitry's delight. Nodding at him as she sat, she pulled out her notebook and a pen and prepared to take notes.

"You should take a note yourself, Arie," Dorian said of Elsa. "Maybe she could teach you how to have a little more respect for yourself."

"If you don't think that Dmitry hasn't fucked her six ways from Friday, you have lost your mind," Ivan said angrily.

Dmitry instantly lost his cool. His large fist hit the table. "Apologize right now, or I'll have your fucking tongue," he demanded. Standing up, he pulled the knife from his drawer.

Ivan smiled. "So, it's okay to talk about everyone else's business, but not your own. Is that about right, *brat*?"

"That's *exactly* right...*brat*," Dmitry said, holding the knife tighter with the blade extended out away from him. With his thumb pressed down on the back of the steel, he waited.

Ivan calculated his chances of getting away from his brother and finally conceded. "Forgive me for my outburst, Elsa," he said condescendingly.

Arie deflated instantly. Dmitry's harsh words and Ivan's defeat was worse than any slap to the face.

Elsa finally stopped holding her breath and turned to nod at Ivan. "All is forgiven," she said, under her breath. As she turned back to Dmitry, she caught a glimpse of the dirty stare Arie gave her.

Dmitry's chest began to fall as he exhaled. Sitting back down, he looked at Dorian. "She is your problem, not mind. I keep my house in order even with its chaotic residents. Send her away if you like. I don't care. Just make sure that you have someone trustworthy to replace her today."

Dorian looked over at Ivan in his humility and instantly felt better. "I think that she'll be fine," he said, sitting down.

"Very well. Let's get started," Dmitry said, moving forward with the meeting. "We'll get Elsa's part out of the way, and she can get to the office. Then, we can move on with the other business at hand."

Davyd chuckled under his breath at Dmitry. The boy was young, but there was never a moment that he was not in control. He looked over his shoulder to see Ivan watching him with a deadly scowl, but he was used to that. It was good as far as he was concerned that Dmitry put the young idiot and his harlot in their places.

***

Oscar Brenneman decided on a full breakfast this morning with eggs and toast, bacon and fruit and coffee and juice in celebration of silent victory. Sitting in the sun room of his mansion, he turned on the television and waited for the news to report a massacre at the Medlov manor.

The tailor would be arriving soon with a special delivery for Dmitry Medlov. If he thought that he could simply walk away from yesterday with everything, he was sorely mistaken. And he had forewarned him of what he was possible of in advance. It was the boy's fault for not taking heed to his words. It had been more than a gift to tell him to *sleep with one eye open*. Swift and just action is what he had told the tailor to provide, in the name of English wealth and English men. It would be a cold day in hell before a ratty Russian came in and had his way with the men of Hutton Industries.

All the men who had stood with him on the left side of the boardroom had pitched in for the hit. And they were using someone that they had trusted in the past. The tailor was unorthodox but highly effective. This would be over as fast as it began.

***

"One last thing to note," Davyd said before Elsa left the meeting. "Khalid has agreed on a meeting, but he's only available this afternoon at three. He will meet you at Hutton Industries. This is your chance, Dmitry. We'll need Elsa to make sure that the meeting is on the schedule and highly guarded."

"Elsa?" Dmitry asked, writing something on his trusty notepad.

"Yes, sir," she said, writing away. "I'll make sure that everything is arranged. Simply call if things should change."

Dmitry nodded. "Well, Elsa, you had better get to office. The driver is waiting for you outside." He looked up and winked at her. "Have a good day."

Elsa stood up and gathered her things then made her way out of the study with the butler following closely behind her.

Dmitry looked at Dorian. "This is where you show me why I'm paying you the kind of money that I'm paying you."

"You told us that there was a meeting still on schedule for the board members in Prague at your offices there. Is that correct?" Dorian asked, sitting in Elsa's seat.

"It is," Dmitry said curiously. "It was the one meeting that the men didn't take off the books after yesterday's meeting. I'm guessing that there is some-thing that is going to be very lucrative there."

"Well, if I were you, I wouldn't take that flight. They will be taking the company's large jet, right?"

"Yes. Elsa checked, and the pilot is still scheduled to make the run with the company's G4."

"That will be where my little creation will be planted. It will detonate two hours after takeoff at an altitude that will destroy any evidence. Not even the black box will be located." Dorian gave a small grin. "I've used it before. It's very, very effective. My team and I will make sure that it is attached an hour before takeoff. We've already secured through Davyd the company passes we need to get on the airport facility."

Dmitry looked over at Davyd. "This is how we commit a massacre without being detected," he said smiling. "What about any stragglers...people who might not get on the plane at the last minute?"

"That is what Arie is for. She is in charge of wet work. We will have eyes on all of them, between the four of us, and we will know who gets on the plane and who does not. Those who do not get on the plane will be dead by nightfall and never found again. The log will show that they boarded the plane with the rest of the men."

"All except Brenneman," Dmitry said, opening the file that he was given by the private eye on the tailor the day before. "We have to make sure that he never makes that flight. He's mine. I want him."

"Understood," Dorian said, shaking his head.

***

As Elsa arrived with the butler at the front door, a man was preparing to ring the doorbell. The butler opened the large, antique doors and escorted Elsa out to the Bentley waiting for her. "I'll be with you in just one moment, sir," he said to the stranger. "Although from now on, deliveries are made through the back door."

The stranger nodded.

"Have a good day, madam," the butler said to Elsa as the chauffeur opened her door.

"You do the same," she yelled, waving as the door closed.

The butler took his attention off Elsa as she was driven around the circular driveway and returned to the stranger with a smile. "Now, how can I help you, sir?" he asked with his hand clasped together.

"Yes, I'm here for Mr. Medlov. I was sent by Hutton Industries to suit him for the black tie gala this weekend," the man explained cheerfully. He stuck out the tuxedo bag for the butler to inspect. "We must make our new president as dashing as ever."

"I see," the butler said, noting the tuxedo that he carried with him, draped over his arms and hands. "It is on the calendar for this weekend. How I do love galas."

"This season keeps me in business. It will only take a minute, if Mr. Medlov is available. I just need a few measurements to make sure that it is perfect. I've already fitted Mr. Emerson, just this morning."

The butler was most familiar with the board after their many trips to the manor over the years, especially Mr. Emerson, who had grown up with Catherine as a child. He nodded in approval, happy to be around someone who was fondly familiar of Lady Catherine's old chums.

"Well, I am definitely overstepping my boundaries by saying this, but Mr. Medlov is normally flexible with the help. He's actually in his study in a meeting, but if you would just give me your name, I'll interrupt to find out if he can see you after," the butler said, letting his guard down.

"Certainly. I'm the tailor," the man said.

"I realize that, but I'll need your name sir," the butler replied.

"They just call me the tailor," the man said, pulling his trigger finger.

Instantly, a silenced shot was released from under the cloak of black clothing and the butler hit the marble floor, clutching his bloody stomach. The assassin walked briskly past him, dropping the tuxedo as he passed, and shooting him once more in the head.

"I should have probably asked for directions to the study first," the tailor said, throwing his backpack over his shoulder. "Pity."

With a pep in his step, the small man walked down the most logical hallway in a three-piece, black suit, black leather loafers and his hair slicked back with a gun in his hand.

As he came slowly down the hall, keeping close to the wall, a maid came out with coffee on a tray and stopped in shock.

The tailor smiled and moved a strand of black hair from his pale face. "Don't be frightened, ma'am. Can you please tell me where Dmitry Medlov's study is?"

The woman, shaking and still holding the tray, motioned a few doors down. "It's right there," she said, voice quivering.

"Thank you very kindly," he said, shooting her in the head. *No witnesses. No trouble.*

He had read the file a hundred times the night before. The Medlov manor had no cameras installed and very few bodyguards. It was a hit man's dream.

Dmitry was right in the middle of talking when he heard the tray fall on the ground. He stopped talking for a moment and frowned. Helen had never dropped a single tray in all the days that he had been here. Pulling his gun out, he put his finger over his lips.

"Gentlemen, we have company," he said, standing up.

The men turned quickly, pulling out their guns and moving away from the door.

Dmitry began to talk again. "As I was saying," he said in the same tone he had spoken before the interruption, "what we need is a united effort to drive the bastards who want me dead out into the open, but not to expose them to the public." He cocked his gun quietly. "We want to pick them off one at a time."

The doorknob slowly turned, and the men continued talking, all while positioning themselves around the room.

"Why does it have to be one at a time? Why can't it be all at one fucking time?" Ivan said, pulling out his knife.

Suddenly, the door flew open and the tailor appeared with his gun pointed. Turning the corner, he was greeted by a slice of his arm. Blood spattered across the floor. Ivan was so angry from his previous conversation with his brother that he was more than happy to handle the hit man himself. The gun dropped to the ground, and Ivan pulled the man up by his collar off the ground.

Quickly, the man kicked him and tried to get away, but Ivan had him penned down. Arie seemed to feel Ivan's frustration and quickly ran over to help him. The other's watched on for a minute, shocked at their immediate response.

With a Cross pen that she had grabbed from Dmitry's table, Arie stabbed the tailor in the eye and twisted the sharp object into his face. He screamed out, but

Ivan punched him, sending him doubled over to the ground. Arie quickly punched him also, picking up the chair and hitting him with it.

"Step aside," Dmitry said with a smirk. He walked up to the man, now blinded and sliced to the bone in his right arm. The tailor wailed out in pain.

"Who sent you?" Dmitry asked, already knowing the answer.

"Fuck you," the tailor said with a sadistic, bloody smile.

Dmitry raised his brow and shot him in his knee. The man screamed out again in agony. Dmitry hiked his pants up and knelt down beside him. He smiled and pulled the pen out of his eye socket while pushing his head up against the wall. The blood gushed out and released more pain. Wiping the pen off on the tailor's clothes, Dmitry clicked it and asked for a piece of paper. "Hand me my notebook," he said to Davyd.

Calmly, he took the paper and turned back to the tailor. "I'm going to ask you once more. If you answer me now, I'll promise to kill you by tonight. If you don't tell me this very moment, I'll torture you for two weeks. There won't be one orifice on you that won't be violated, one bone unbroken, one organ of use that isn't taken and sold." Dmitry moved the strands of lose black hair from the killer's face and sighed. "I'm listening."

The tailor tried to catch his breath. Nodding his head, he tried to speak. "Oscar Brenneman. He hired me to kill you and Emerson," he said, resting his head back on the wall.

Dmitry blinked. "Is Emerson still alive?"

The tailor was silent.

"Is he?" Dmitry asked in a raised voice.

"No," the tailor answered, holding his bloody arm. "No. I killed him this morning....him and his wife."

Dmitry stood up. "Get me the phone," he said, clearing his throat. "Did that fat fuck tell you to call him when it was done?"

"Yes," he answered in pain.

"Can you hold it together long enough to make that call. If you can, then I promise not to kill everyone you love. I'm sure someone must love you...a mother, father, grandfather, sister."

The tailor thought of his oldest sister and nodded. "I can hold it together."

"Good," Dmitry answered. "Give me the number." He dialed it quickly and warned the tailor. "No funny shit."

After the Brenneman home had been rang, Oscar answered the phone with a grin that Dmitry could hear through the phone.

"It's done," the tailor said shortly.

"Good. I'll be looking for it on the news."

"I'm sure it'll make the news," the tailor said, trying not to black out.

Dmitry hung up the phone before any cryptic messages could be sent. He and Ivan stood over the man.

"Kill him quickly, before dusk," he said, pointing at Ivan. "Harvest the organs and send them to our friends in Amsterdam to sell on the black market. Davyd head down to the office and make sure that Elsa stays safe until I get to her."

Dmitry had heard enough. This morning, he was going straight for Oscar Brenneman and anyone else that got in the way. Without changing clothes, he ran up to his personal arsenal and retrieved a chrome .44

desert eagle, black rope, duct tape, lighter fluid, and two tactical knives. Throwing them into his gym bag, he headed downstairs to the garage.

Ivan stopped him in the hall.

"You're not taking me?" he said, shocked.

"No, I want you to handle the problem in there," Dmitry said, wondering if the man was still alive after he noticed the blood stains on Ivan's clothes. "And when I get back, you and I are going to discuss this Arie situation."

"What Arie situation? There is no Arie situation. We're fucking. How is that everyone's business?"

"It's going to create a problem between us and Dorian," Dmitry whispered, not sure where Dorian was.

"It's already a none-issue," Ivan said, hunching his shoulders. "Don't ride me on this. She's mine. I'm not giving her up. Plus, I'm telling you that she can hold her own."

Dmitry knew when to concede. "Fine, but if it becomes an issue one more time, she's gone," he said, pointing at his little brother. "I'll be back later."

Chapter Ten

The sun had risen high on the horizon by the time that Dmitry arrived at Oscar Brenneman's brownstone. With no plan and deep-seeded rage, he jumped off his bike and opened the wrought-iron gate with his duffle bag thrown over his shoulder.

There would never be words invented to express the anger that was boiling deep down in his stomach. This pompous asshole actually had the gall to send a hit man to his home to kill him, not to mention that he had already had Emerson slaughtered. He really didn't want to go back to jail, although he was certain that British prison probably had nothing on a USSR hell hole, but he considered the possibility if he got caught for what he was about to do.

The door flew off the hinges under the weight and force of Dmitry's foot. Stepping onto the stained glass and wood that shattered across the oak wood floors, he already had his gun pointed.

The first person to respond in the home to the breaking and entering was the maid. Dmitry thought of his own and pointed and pulled the trigger. She hit the floor and slammed into the wall before he could even give his action any more thought.

Down the last corridor toward the back of the sprawling home, his long legs moved with much more speed than the tailor. He came quickly upon the sunroom where Oscar Brenneman was sitting with his assistant discussing the future business of Hutton Industries.

Dmitry put his ear to the door and smirked to himself. Then, he stepped back and kicked the door open.

Oscar and his assistant quickly jumped up from their seats. In a brave last act, his assistant, small in stature, stood in front of his boss to protect him.

Dmitry raised his gun and pointed. He pulled the trigger just as the man raised his hand and began to speak. Blood splattered across Oscar's face as the bullet meant for the assistant went straight through Brenneman's shoulder.

Dmitry dropped his gun and pulled out his knife. Now, it was time to work.

"I didn't mean to hit you," Dmitry said sardonically, sweeping the room with his eyes to make sure that they weren't interrupted.

"I'm sure that we can talk about this," Brenneman begged, holding his wounded arm.

"What is there to talk about?" Dmitry asked in a deep, sinister voice. "If you haven't noticed, I'm not much into talking. Plus, you have nothing to bargain with. All I want is your worthless life."

"But I do," Brenneman said with promise in his eyes. "There is a major meeting in Prague, a meeting that has nothing to do with Hutton Industries, a meeting worth millions. I can bring you, introduce you."

"I'm a billionaire," Dmitry reminded with fury in his eyes.

Blood ran down Brenneman's arm. He clutched his wound and winced. "This deal is worth many millions. The kind that makes men billionaires a few times over."

"Go on," Dmitry said, walking over to him. He towered over the coward with his knives ready to slaughter.

"Only if you promise to leave me alive."

Dmitry thought for a moment. He shook his head. "Talk first."

"We're working with scientists there to build high tech weaponry. It's nothing like the world has ever seen before. It's nuclear weaponry, Dmitry. It's the future of war."

Dmitry stopped. "I'm interested. Go on. Who is the meeting with?"

"A private-owned company called Nightstar. They want to meet with us regarding capital to help finance their operation. We have the funds. That is why Hutton Industries has not invested new money into our operations. We've been funneling it."

"And Nightstar is owned by whom?" he asked.

"Officially, it is owned by a group of land barons in the city of Prague. Unofficially, it is owned by Evgeny Smirnov." Brenneman knew the name would make Dmitry halt.

"Well, answer me one question, and I will let you live," he said, bending down. "Did you set up the hit or did Smirnov."

"He did," he said with eyes bright and sincere. "You were getting in the way with the re-organization of the company. He was the one who gave me the file and the go ahead with the hit. Trust me; I would have not done so without him."

"And somehow you think that he'll back down on this if I agree to keep things as is for now."

"I'm sure he will," Brenneman answered. "That was the only thing in his way."

The look in Brenneman's eyes made Dmitry think that the man actually believed what he was saying.

"You don't know much about us, do you?" Dmitry asked. He could hear the police sirens outside. He checked his watch and saw that it was nearly time to meet with Khalid.

"I can reassure him that it is the right move," Brenneman finally said as he pleaded.

"No need. I can do that myself." Dmitry raised his knives.

"But you promised me that I could live," Brenneman pleaded, falling backwards on the floor.

Dmitry stood over him breathing heavily and looking down on him like he was a speck of dirt. "Well you can, but it will be without the use of your feet, arms, fingers, eyes, ears or tongue." He smiled deviously as he swung his gleaming blade.

The man screamed out as he realized his fate. Worse than death...much worse.

***

As the clock struck three, Dmitry swaggered into Hutton Industries in a new suit and his duffle bag. The secretary at the front of the executive offices greeted him with a smile.

"Good afternoon, Mr. Medlov," she said with a glimmer in her eyes.

"Hello," Dmitry said, smoothing out his tie. "How are you?"

"Fine, sir. And yourself?"

"Couldn't be better," he said, headed toward his office. "Is Elsa here?"

"Yes, sir. I believe that she's waiting on you with your three o'clock."

"Excellent," he said, headed towards the board room.

He walked in the familiar meeting space to find Davyd sitting with Elsa and Khalid. Quickly passing off the bag full of evidence off to Davyd, he kissed Elsa on the cheek and embraced Khalid.

"It's an honor to have you," he said, offering Khalid a seat.

Khalid Sidorov was a pale, aging man in his late fifties with a gray hair and a large bald spot. However, there was a regal yet deadly grace about the man. In a Lagerfeld black suit, he didn't bother to hide the many unforced, high ranking tattoos of the Vory v Zakone. He was a certifiable gangster, cloaked in riches and drenched in sin.

"It's an honor to be here," Khalid said, taking his seat again.

"Have you been taken care of?" Dmitry asked, looking at Elsa.

"Yes, I have. Thank you. I was told by your Davyd that you wanted to meet with me." Khalid crossed his hands and sat back in the seat, relaxed and waiting.

"I did," Dmitry said, raising his brow. He licked his lips. "I want to make you 20 percent owner in my company for now as a peace offering of sorts, offer you a seat on this board and provide you with whatever perks I can to get you in exchange for a meeting with the boss," he said without skipping a beat.

Khalid grinned and looked over at Vladimir, who was sitting in the corner, watching with an outward cynicism.

"What *boss*?" Khalid asked, running his finger over the table.

"Smirnov," Dmitry answered, without blinking. "I need his blessing for my operations in Russia."

Khalid stopped smiling. "What operations in Russia?"

"I want to do business with some men in Russia who have access to a certain type of resource that I need." Dmitry looked at Davyd. "Also, I'm not sure that the deal in Prague is going to go through without my blessing."

"I don't know what you're talking about," Khalid said, shifting in his seat.

"The deal going down in Prague in a few days won't happen. I can assure you of that."

Khalid was drawing a blank. He looked over at his son and clenched his jaw. "Nothing happens without me knowing about it, and I don't know about anything in Prague."

Dmitry read his body language. The man was not lying. He grinned at the thought of how angry he must be right now. "Well, why would you be out of the loop? You are, after all, number two. Are you not?"

Khalid forgot the theatrics and shook his head. "I am." His face was like a stone. The age showed through the lines under his eyes.

Dmitry continued. "And if I inform you of what is going on, will you provide me the meeting and your blessing?"

"I will," Khalid agreed.

"Let's take a walk, just in case we have an infestation," Dmitry said, thinking of the possibility of bugs. He stood up at the head of the table, casting a shadow over Vladimir.

"*Da*," Khalid said, standing up also. "Let's go talk, just you and I. We will see how we can help each other, *brat*."

Vladimir tried to conceal his cringe, but it was evident for anyone who looked at him. He hated Dmitry Medlov.

***

By dusk and after long hours of deliberation, Dmitry had discovered that he was not the only one in the dark. Khalid Sidorov knew nothing about the meeting in Prague or the possibility of money to be made. This was completely unacceptable. For Khalid knew that the moment he was not a need, he too was a threat to the organization that he served.

It was because of his lack of knowledge that Khalid agreed after their long talk on coordinating a meeting between Dmitry and Smirnov and accepted the position on the board. He was a man of considerable wisdom and knew that without a doubt the young man before him would be a force to be reckoned with for many years ahead.

By the end of the meeting, both men had exactly what they wanted. Pure power.

In one day, Dmitry had eliminated his largest current threat and started an alliance that could provide what he needed to reposition himself and the Medlov family for the rest of its existence.

There was nothing more important to him than the protection of his little brother and his team that was growing in number. He knew now that there was nothing that he would not do for them, and nothing that they would not do for him. Their covenant had been sealed, and he was in it for the long haul.

As they parted, Dmitry and Khalid formed a pact to help each other. That was all Dmitry needed. The stars were aligning in his favor. And if he had anything to do with it, it would stay that way. Nothing would block him. If he had to kill half the world to get to his goal, he would do it. *Nothing was sacred. No one was safe.*

Headed back to the Medlov manor as the sun set on the horizon, Dmitry sat in the back of the Bentley with Elsa and popped his first celebratory bottle of Cristal.

"So, you have proven yourself," he said, shaking his head.

"I have," she answered.

"And are you still willing to connect me to your father?"

"It has already been arranged. He is excited about meeting you and thanking you in any way possible."

"Good." Dmitry's eye twitched. "And are you ready to become what I need in the President of Hutton Industries?"

"Everything that you need, want and more," she answered.

"To our future," he said, toasting her.

Elsa smiled back. "To our future," she said, leaning in as she kissed him. His lips tasted like success. She lingered at his mouth, sure that he would ravage her well before they reached their destination.

He grabbed her and pulled her to him. Sliding his cold hand under her skirt, he tore her lace underwear off. "You belong to no one now."

"Then finally, we are the same," she whispered.

The End

Volume Four

Prologue

So much time had passed since Dmitry was a young man. Ages. Decades. Lifetimes even. He remembered the first time that he realized that he had finally become the master of his own fate. It had also been the first time that he truly felt invincible. After that day, he had felt invincible most days, and utterly numb most others.

It was odd what dwelling on the top did to a man. He got so used to living above the clouds on a place called "nine" until when he was forced–only during occasional moments of realistic sobriety - to dwell down in the world with the rest of mankind, he felt like he was choking - suffocating even-from being too far below his station in life.

Dmitry had known many men who lived on top of the world. In fact, the only way he had truly arrived at the top was to knock one particular man off his throne. That, however, was the type of clandestine narrative that kings never spoke of. It wasn't proper to discuss the gritty business behind the image.

It was Dmitry's truest belief that one must topple an empire before he could rule it, unless he was born into it. And even then, there were certain old guards that must be moved, displaced and if really need-ed...annihilated.

The Medlov family, specifically, was a family of men who were born hungry. All of his boys had dangerous ambition coursing through their veins, but his youngest seeds seemed not as concerned about ruling the world as his oldest son, Anatoly. The *hungry* gene had skipped the twins, but as he looked at his beautiful daughter,

Anya, riding her award-winning horse through the countryside, bareback and full of life, hair flowing and form perfectly erect, he knew that she had gotten a double helping of everything good and *hungry* in him, including his raw ambition.

She would be the one that the world would be forced to bow before. He only hoped to live long enough to witness it with his own eyes.

Sipping on ginger tea and reading Hawthorne, Dmitry pulled the wool throw tighter around his broad shoulders and uncrossed his long, trouser-clad legs. Without intention, he pushed forward in his lawn chair when Anya passed below him as he sat on the elevated limestone patio.

It was a perfect view.

Green, plush, manicured grass was violently unearthed under the weight of the sturdy stallion that Anya rode violently, as if she was running from or toward something insurmountable. In sync with his master, the horse pushed mist from his flaring nostrils as the cold wind ripped through the peaceful setting and left everything frozen in time.

Like a true spectator, Dmitry marveled at Anya as she passed him going full speed, unafraid and unstoppable. In black, leather riding boots, khaki-colored riding pants, a black turtle neck and hat, she commanded the powerful beast with ease. But it was her regal nature that seemed to captivate even the staff, who stood on the side of Dmitry quietly watching in awe as the *little* lady of the house made her daily ride.

Looking at Anya, Dmitry believed that there would be few leaders that she would have to conquer against their will. Most would be happy to fall at her feet, and they would also be wise in their decision. She had grown into a cunning woman with traits of both her mother and father, but even worse...her long dead uncle, Ivan. Anya was as tough as nails, beautiful as diamonds and a true, blue predator dressed in sheep's clothing.

Barely looking her father's way as she breezed past him, holding her reigns tightly in her leather gloves, Anya kept her gaze forward towards the golden, setting sun. And then as quickly as she was there in his presence, she disappeared over the hill and then down into the countryside, but not without leaving an impression on her doting father.

Satisfied, Dmitry sat back in his chair once she was gone and began to sip his luke-warm tea again. Just a glimpse of Anya was all that he needed. She would be a ghost for the rest of the evening. Devoted to her studies, locked in her room, tending to her horses, rummaging through the study, there was always something for Anya to do.

She never allowed herself to sit idly by. The only time that she was still was when she was reading or sleeping, and even then she was thinking, figuring things out, working out problems in her mind.

Anya was so much *unlike* his other children but so much like him until it was amazing. She was thirsty for knowledge. She spoke as if she had been on the earth a hundred years, had a gaze that would imprison and destroy a man, and she had a mind that would capture and rule a country, *if not the world*.

Sounded familiar.

He guessed that it was fitting that she was now being courted by a prince.

The boy wouldn't have been *his* first choice, *prince or not*. He was far too prim and proper, interested in galas, yachts on the Riviera and such. The young man had no grit about him, but still he had stolen Anya's heart.

Dmitry could never understand the odd paring considering Anya had always been surrounded by alpha males who had been bred on grit. Dayvd, when she was younger, Gabriel, Anatoly, the council and others.

He hoped whole heartedly that she was simply sick of such a man instead of thinking that her prince was one. Besides, it was one thing to clearly avoid a certain thing than to be fooled into thinking that one had something that he or she did not. He had never been in the business of delusions...just illusions and that was only for the outside world. The family was transparent.

This *prince*, however, was not transparent, and that was what bothered Dmitry. He was a quiet man in love with his books and even at his age was still working under the auspice of peace, like such a thing really existed. Dmitry nearly chuckled at the thought. In a world like this one, the only peace that could be promised was what came in the afterlife.

A prince, a man who would soon be king, should be focused on more realistic goals like acquiring more wealth through trade and industry for his country and building up his military to protect his people.

Introduced to the prince while home from college at Oxford, Anya had met the young soon-to-be king, at a private fundraiser at the Prague Castle in the Royal Garden. The boy had taken one look at Anya, under the dancing candlelight and full moon with her long black hair flowing in a white evening gown and her blue, icy eyes that sparkled like diamonds and fell head over hills in love.

Dmitry had watched the entire thing from a far while talking to the boy's father in what felt like slow motion. Royal had stopped him from interrupting the two by insisting that he "stay put". It had been the hardest thing he had ever done, because he knew based upon the young man's face when he saw his daughter that Anya would be his most serious pursuit.

That had been a year and a half ago. Now, Dmitry was certain that as they prepared for Anya's graduation, they would soon be preparing for the wedding of the century, full of scandal and heart ache for his most precious child. Still, he had to let her live her life. And he could think of no better title for his sweet little child than princess.

The doors to the patio opened, and Royal emerged from the chateau like a breath of fresh air. Her black hair with streaks of silver was pulled into a tight bun, and she too wrapped herself in a plaid throw.

Sitting beside him at the table, she gently smiled at him, revealing soft lines in her delicate face and looked out at the vast landscape.

"Are you watching Anya ride again?" she asked, averting her gaze west to the sunset.

"I have to steal a moment with her when I can, even if the moment is literally just a glimpse," he said with a pout.

Royal chuckled. "She's a grown up now, Dmitry. You have to let her go. That's part of being a father."

He protested with a snort. "No. She's still angry at me for what I am. I know it. I can feel it," he said with conviction.

"Anya loves you. She always has," Royal answered lovingly.

"Of course, she *loves* me. I never have doubted that, but she is a woman now, an intelligent woman, and she judges me. She worries that my life and my sins will haunt her and her chance at happiness with Prince *Bookworm*."

"Anya has always known who you truly are, and she has loved you despite of it. She and I have spoken extensively about how our family might affect her relationship with Edward."

"His family might not let him propose, you know" Dmitry said with a growl. The thought of anyone thinking that they were better than his daughter made his blood boil.

"You are the wealthiest and most powerful man in Prague and nearly six other European countries. You own businesses all over the world, and the government has never been able to pin so much as a parking ticket on you. Your transgressions will be overlooked. Plus, he's not the Prince of Wales. Now, that might have been harder to pull off."

"I just don't want my life and my choices to hurt my precious daughter."

"Trust me. It won't. If anything, you'll be given a title and position in parliament, begged to consult on matters of trade and touted as a man of industry." She said so confidently as if the events had already taken place.

Dmitry huffed at her response. Royal had always been far too optimistic for his taste. Besides, it all seemed ridiculous to him. "Why couldn't she have fallen in love with a normal boy? I could have bought them a country." The statement made him think of Angola. He frowned when he realized that his old memories still haunted him.

Royal giggled. "Because Anya has never been a normal girl. Plus, her heart is her own, and she has given it to Edward in the same way that I gave my heart to you."

"I hope that she didn't give him everything that comes with her heart, if so...I'll have to put a hit out on a prince." His eyes narrowed.

Royal kept her daughter's secrets and moved the conversation along as she always did.

"We should invite the royal family to a private dinner again soon," she suggested. "You like the king, and I like Elizabeth."

"Just another reason for you to plan a grand affair." Dmitry knew a trap when he smelled one. The dinner had probably already been planned, and this was her way of telling him about it.

"It's what people do when their children reach this point in their relationship," she said as she shrugged her shoulders at the thought of throwing another party. "And it's what fathers do when they prepare to give their daughters away." Her eyes met his and for the first time Dmitry was absolutely sure that the engagement would be very, very soon.

Anya always told her mother things that she chose to keep away from him, just as he kept his boys' secrets. Only Demi, their youngest, told them both everything or nothing. *It was too early to know.*

For some reason Royal's words sent him back in time, and all that he could think of was another time in his life when the same thing applied to his own life. Only, his thoughts were full of wicked memories.

Frowning, he swallowed hard and reached over for his wife. "Come and sit on my lap, I want to tell you story," he said, extending his hand. He wiggled his long fingers at her, catching the sun's reflection in the gold band.

Royal came to him quietly with a smile on her face. Like a child, she slipped into his large embrace and looked into his vast, blue eyes.

"Did I ever tell you how I met my father?" he asked.

"Dmitry, now you know I would have never forgotten if you had told me something like that," she said in a whisper. Her hand found its way to his grayish blonde tendrils. It was amazing to her that even after so many years, she still admired every inch of him.

And Dmitry felt the exact same about her. She had only grown more beautiful over the years. Her taste had become more refined and her grace and wisdom followed.

Amazingly, his young Royal had become a queen, right before his eyes. And he had never stopped doting over her in all their years together. His gifts had only grown more extravagant, his kisses deeper, their passionate love making longer. And even as an older man now, he still felt like a lion because of her. She had chosen to make him feel powerful even though she had all the tools to humble him, humiliate him *if she wanted*.

But Royal was in the business of uplifting others and her desire to make everyone happy had led to a blissful family.

Dmitry had been *undeservingly* lucky.

Royal had noticed that as Dmitry grew older, he also seemed to share the most frightful tales with her, and what astonished her even more than his terrible truths was how much she inwardly enjoyed to listen to them, but it was only because every story ended in triumph. She knew that he didn't exaggerate his stories. He was far too honest for that. It was just in him to overcome. Some people were like that. Despite the obstacle, they found a way to get over it, to prevail in spite of...

"Go on then," she said, getting comfortable for another one of his long, amazing tales. "Tell me how you came to meet the man who made you."

Dmitry gave a troubled grin and corrected his wife. "Not just made me, but *made me* what I am," he said with a raised brow.

Chapter One

1993
Czech Republic
Prague was a place of golden statues and timeless clocks, of cobblestone streets and romantic streetlights, of thick fog and castles that made Dmitry's manor back on the hillsides of England look like an ambitious doll house.

He marveled at the city's beauty from the back of the car that escorted him to his hotel. Never in his life had he seen such opulence outside of St. Petersburg, Russia. And until this very moment, he would have sworn that no city could rival it.

Dmitry had visited St. Petersburg last year with Catherine, and it had been quite an experience for him. It was the first time in his life that he had been to the city, and he had honestly been floored by its timeless beauty.

For once, there he was not the *odd man out* like with other trips across the world, because he actually spoke the language. And the manner in which he was treated, as near royalty, was completely different from how he was treated during his last time in Russia when he was just a rogue errand boy with a mismatch group of misfits.

Before then, even though Dmitry had lived in Russia his entire life, he had had no idea that St. Petersburg used to be the capital of Russia.

Catherine had spent a great deal of time taking him around to the museums and historic sites. And she had practically given him a private tour of the Hermitage, a place he found out she visited frequently when in the city. In fact, the curator knew her personally and had informed Dmitry that the Hutton's were extremely generous contributors right before she insisted that he continue with the customary annual gift now that he was the head of the family. However, when he found out how much the customary gift was, he was floored again. The Hutton's had given more money per year to that museum than he had made in his entire life.

Now, he was feasting his eyes on another gem. Prague was a place fit for kings. And he felt strangely at home here.

The chauffeur had told him that this was the best time of the year to visit because of the snow. Dmitry had laughed when the man said it, wondering if he had heard his accent or not. Russian people were not ignorant of the snow. In fact, they were made from it with ice in their veins and a chill constantly moving up and down their spines. *Or maybe it wasn't all Russians, just him.* Regardless, he had felt the statement was lost on him.

It was too bad that this wasn't a social visit. He would have liked to *sight-see*, as people often referred to walking around and learning more about a place's culture. However, he was here presently to topple an empire.

Nasty business.

He sucked his teeth at the thought of what he had to accomplish in the two days

Over the course of the last week, he had made a considerable ally of the respected Vor, Khalid Sidorov, which had not been an easy feat.

Sidorov was an older man, who had built himself up in the ranks of the Russian mob in much of the same fashion as Dmitry. He started out in the gutters of the Soviet Union decades ago and had amassed a considerable fortune.

During his lifetime, Khalid had helped create a core of men who defied the very existence of peace, bought and sold some of the dirtiest politicians alive, taken control of entire industries, hand-picked the world's deadliest assassins, buried one son, put another son through Oxford, helped topple a country and made an underworld Czar. Such an incredible reputation would never been seen on a resume, but Dmitry had memorized Khalid's high points in his underworld life by heart.

In fact, this was all why Dmitry had chosen him. He too wanted to be a king, and in order to do so, he had to find a king-maker. Khalid was that man, because even though he had considerable power, he did not wish to be in the limelight. Khalid preferred the shadows, where he could move stealthily and only show his hand when needed. It would be the perfect marriage of power and knowledge, and it would rock the very foundations of the underworld.

But first things were still first. At the moment, he had to meet with Evgeny Smirnov, who had just been informed that the entire board of directors of Hutton Industries had gone down in a horrible plane accident – all saving Brenneman who was still unconscious after an unconscionable home invasion that had left him mangled nearly to death.

Dmitry doubted very seriously that Brenneman would recover to the point of recollection of his assault and if he did, he would be right there to remind him that although he was blind, without use of his tongue, limbless and a number of other unfortunate handicaps, there were still things that he could lose if he gave him up to the cops.

Dmitry couldn't help but smirk about that too. He rarely enjoyed mutilating a person, but Brenneman had damned near been a treat.

His mind went back to Evgeny.

Very few people in the world had ever laid eyes on Boss Smirnov and many of those people had no clue of who he actually was. In fact, this would be Dmitry's very first time laying eyes on the man, and he didn't know at all what to expect himself. Very few outside of Khalid actually knew who he was. It was said that he was a bit of an eccentric, hiring people to pretend to be him for certain meetings and events like he was some kind of a celebrity. And it was rumored that not even one picture existed of him through Interpol, Scotland Yard or even the United States FBI.

He was an elusive man very close to a figment of the underworld's imagination. He was an idea, a thought, a theory to most. But Dmitry knew that he was real, and at last their paths had crossed.

As he came to the realization of that fact, his limo quickly pulled into the iron gates of the hotel, followed by another car of bodyguards.

Before anyone could notice what he was doing, Dmitry stole a quick look at the beauty that surrounded him. Catherine had taught him early on in their relationship that *gawking* was not an option for a man in his position. So, even if he was enamored by a building, a person or an object, he had to behave as though he had seen such things over and over again.

It had been hard at first for Dmitry to get used to acting as though he had been born with a silver spoon stuffed down his throat, but lately, he had learned to simply tell his staff to give him a moment to be alone. And when he was alone, then he would study each detail, marvel at each wonderful amenity, allow himself the enjoyment of being utterly bemused by his environment.

"Boss, we're here," Davyd said as they pulled up to their destination.

"I can see that," Dmitry answered, taking his eyes off the window before Davyd could notice his intrigue.

Quickly, a doorman came running from inside the lobby of the hotel to the car as the chauffer parked. He straightened his little hat and then gracefully opened the door for the new guest that all the employees had been buzzing about.

A billionaire would be staying in one of the grand suites tonight - the infamous, young, royal widower currently being examined by all the newspapers in London.

Standing behind the door, the doorman waited as he looked straight ahead, anticipating a glance of the man of the hour.

As Dmitry stepped out of the limo into the cold, winds ripped through the air and froze his statue-like features. Still, he emerged from the black Mercedes limousine looking the part of royalty.

In a gray, double breasted suit that had been tailored for his long, lean, muscular body, a long black wool coat and a pair of black Italian loafers, Dmitry stood like a tower of elegance. He matched his opulent surroundings perfectly *outwardly*. He was as tall as he was beautiful. As perfectly put together as he was rich.

Feeling the many stares that immediately turned to him, he slipped off his shades and looked around while the other guests who were outside began to whisper.

"Who is that man?" one asked.

"Where did he come from?" another queried

"I hope he's staying here," a woman prayed.

"Isn't that the Medlov man from the papers?" a British man inquired.

Dmitry had grown accustomed to the stares and the whispers, to the women with their naughty grins and the men and their territorial frowns. He had learned to ignore it, move through it, and behave as if no one was around him. It was the only way that he kept his sanity.

A few feet below Dmitry, the short frumpy doorman in a dreadful red uniform with gold trimmings gawked in utter amazement. "Welcome to the Red Square Hotel," he said in a squeaky voice, swallowing hard. He had obviously never seen a seven-foot man up close, which made it impossible for him to take his eyes off the faultless giant.

"Thank you," Dmitry answered in a deep baritone, looking down at the man as curiously as he looked up at him. He too had never seen such an odd fellow before. The bellman was fat and awkward, lowly even for his already humble station in life.

Dmitry's eye twitched as he looked back at Davyd, who rounded the car to escort him inside. He had already grown tired of the exchange. The doors on the SUV behind him quickly popped open and a few well-dressed men in black suits came obediently to Dmitry's side, flanking around him in a protective shield that could only be recognized by military, law enforcement or any hit man that might have meant him harm. However, to the outside world, it simply appeared that the well-dressed man had a large, brooding entourage.

"What would you like to do first?" Davyd asked formally.

"We have just enough time to change clothes and get ready to meet Khalid and Smirnov," Dmitry said, looking down at his watch again. "Is Ivan already in place?"

The mere mention of the young man's name made Davyd stall. "He's at the farm with the others," he answered as he scanned his surroundings.

He didn't want to bother Dmitry at the present with the many conversations he had been forced to have with Ivan over the last day regarding his accommodations. Because while trivial to everyone else, the self-professed underboss was not happy with being exiled out of his usual lap of luxury, even for the greater good of the family. Ivan grew more pompous by the day - a regular snob.

The help from the hotel moved quickly around them, grabbing luggage and carting it inside. The bodyguards followed Dmitry obediently. However, Davyd had to look around for a moment and take it all in.

The Red Square hotel was one of many upscale boutique hotels in the heart of Prague. Topped with bright, red clay roofing, enchanting old world flavor had been masterfully mixed with new world charm and decadence, this hotel could only be appreciated and experienced by the wealthy.

The Red Square was a compilation of historic gray stone buildings with yellow stucco situated in the historical centre just minutes away from Charles Bridge.

It screamed exclusivity, just the place for a meeting of the underworld's most notorious boss and the world's most infamous billionaire.

As Dmitry entered into the main lobby of the hotel, a blonde woman in a conservative blue suit greeted him with a leather binder and a handshake.

"Good afternoon, Monsieur Medlov," the woman said with a French accent. "It is so good to have you at the Red Square." There was a pregnant pause as she made eye contact, as if she had seen him or knew him from somewhere.

"It's good to be here," Dmitry said, allowing the woman's hand to touch his own. He looked down into her eyes, certain that he had not met her before.

She lifted her brow and quietly forbade herself from stuttering even amidst her staggering surprise. "I am Manon, the general manager of the hotel. I hope you don't mind, but I wanted to escort you to your suite, ensure that you are happy with your accommodations and make sure that you don't need anything else to make your stay with us as comfortable as possible." She ended her introduction by passing Dmitry the leather bound informational packet clutched in her left arm.

Dmitry took it and quickly passed it to Davyd dismissively.

"Mademoiselle Manon?" Dmitry said, unsure if he had said her name correctly.

"Yes, sir?" she answered.

"If you could just give me my keys, then I'm sure we'll find everything in order." His eyes narrowed. There was something about her that instantly felt wrong to him.

She nodded and obediently pulled his golden keys from her the satin inner pocket of her suit jacket.

Davyd stepped in front of Dmitry and took the keys from her hands. Without his boss speaking one word, he had already picked up on the strange vibe and did his best to put some space between the two.

"Will that be all, sir?" Manon asked Davyd before averting her gaze back up to Dmitry. There was something in her eyes that said that she knew something that she was not saying.

Dmitry looked down at her again and read her face. He wanted to ask her what she was thinking, but he decided against it, knowing that like everything else, it would come out in the wash.

"*Oui*," Davyd answered, moving her out of the way. "If you need to speak with Mr. Medlov, you may contact me."

Manon nodded confused. Stepping back, she watched the small entourage head in a processional line through the lobby and disappear into several elevators, leaving only a few men behind to stay posted downstairs for the remainder of Dmitry's stay.

Chapter Two

Ivan ran his hand down the side of his AK47 and sighed. He was bored, deathly so, and could not wait for his brother to finally give them the call that they awaited.

He had arrived with the rest of the team two days before, cased the hotel and surrounding areas and finally ended up at a farm twenty miles north of the city.

Now, they were holed up in a barn the size of his garage in weather meant for polar bears, and according to Davyd *they were not supposed to be pissed.* What kind of shit was this? Wasn't he the underboss? He should be there now with his brother, but no. Instead, he was here with the outcasts, waiting like dogs on their master.

Bullshit.

Utter bullshit.

Ivan daydreamed at that very moment of cutting Davyd's throat with a rusty, dull knife and feeling his old ass bleed out on the barnyard floor. A smile tugged at his lips when he thought of hot, dark blood mingling with hay and mud and the sound of the old bastard's last curdling gurgles of blood bubbles pouring from his crooked mouth. He had played the scenario out a million times since Davyd and Dmitry had grown so close and while the place always changed, the outcome remained the same. Davyd ended up dead. Only as time had gone on, so did Dmitry.

But maybe he wouldn't have to lift a finger.

Supposedly, if Smirnov did not give Dmitry what he wanted, their plan was to take out the top man in the underworld. That would be a big order. Ivan had mixed feelings about the strategic move. When he did kill

Smirnov, he could say that he did it, not Dmitry. How many people would bow down to him then? But there were other ramifications behind the assassination, like giving his brother more of what he wanted.

Dmitry seemed interested in keeping the conversation that was going to take place today from ending in a gun fight, but Ivan had the taste of blood on the tip of his tongue. He prayed for a blood bath, a way to rid himself of the frustration he harbored for his brother's fast ascension to the top and the invisible structure that he was beginning to feel around him.

Before when they were broke, their organized crime syndicate was small, chaotic even and completely unorganized. But with more money, Dmitry became more structured. And that was the one thing that Ivan detested. He was more of a man in favor of anarchy. Anarchy ensured two things in his mind: an unstructured organization and unchecked power. And if he was ever going to move ahead of Dmitry in the Vory v Zakone, he would need both.

The words that Emma had spoken to him over two years ago still stuck in his mind. "You will never be as smart as your brother. You will never be as beautiful or as powerful as he will. You'll never outrank him or out shine him. So, it's best when you can, to leave and do your own thing. He's cold and calculating, Ivan. No woman will ever be able to resist him. So if you find just one who thinks more of you than him, marry her. But trust me, dear, if you stay here, bad things will happen. And more than likely, it will be by his hand," she had said to him only an hour after he had fucked her.

Even now as he thought of the words, he wanted to kill something.

Emma had been right, though he hated her for it, which was why he was so crazy about Arie. Elsa ate out of Dmitry's hand like a little puppy but Arie would rather be burned at the stake than kiss his ass. Ivan liked that about her. She had a backbone, unlike so many people who came into contact or did business with his brother.

"What are you mulling over?" Arie asked with a clever grin as she pushed her work to the side and made her way over to the corner where Ivan was sitting.

"I'm thinking of killing someone," he answered with a smirk.

Arie rolled her eyes and slid over on the bale of hay beside him. Dwarfed by his large body, she moved his arm and made it snake over her small frame. Looking up into his eyes, she bit her lip. "Dorian has been watching me like a snake. When are we going to get out of here and fuck? I'm horny as hell, and we haven't had two minutes together alone since we got here."

Ivan rested his head back on the exposed wooden wall of the barn and looked up into the rafters. "It's not snake." His deep voice vibrated against his own chest.

"What?" she asked, looking over at him with a frown.

"He isn't watching you like snake. He's watching you like hawk," he corrected. His icy blue eyes locked on her. Dark curly locks lined his pale, white face. "And when are you going to stop caring about what your brother thinks, eh? He knows that we're together. Yet, you behave as if he thinks that you are virgin." Ivan dipped his head lower and pressed his lip to her ear, hidden under her jet black bob haircut. "He knows that I brutally fuck you every time that I get a chance. So why do you continue to pretend, especially when you like it so much?"

Arie had to fight the desire to rip his clothes off right there. Instead, she continued on with her rant. "You don't know what it's like to have an overbearing brother," she said, growling. She shot a dirty look across the room at her brother, who at the present time was wearing headphones and listening to something or someone else, but also was reading their lips as they spoke.

"I don't know what?" Ivan asked, pulling a pack of cigarettes from his pocket. He cocked a black, Timberland boot up on the hay and rested his long arm on his knee as he lit it.

"Okay, maybe you do," Arie admitted. "But at least Dmitry doesn't try to smother your sex life."

"Eventually, your brother will give up. If you keep fucking and don't try so hard to hide it, then he'll get tired and throw you away." Ivan said so as if he knew it for a fact, which pissed Arie off even more.

"You might know your brother, but you evidently don't know mine. He never gives up. That's why his enemies always end up dead. He is relentless. As long as there is breath in his body, he never gives up."

"Then you should give up trying to hide it and let him deal with it. You're a grown woman. It's your business who you fuck. What happened to your women's lib bullshit?"

"The rules don't apply to family," she conceded.

Blowing a cloud of smoke from his mouth, Ivan looked down at Arie and moved her hair from her face. He normally detested submission, but Arie made it sexy. Plus, she was the only woman in the world that he had ever truly cared about. Only, he wasn't sure if he cared about her because she cared so little for herself, or if it was because she cared so much for him despite who and how he was. It was the most confusing relationship he had ever been in and also the *only* relationship.

With any other woman, he would have gotten rid of her already, but he enjoyed Arie. She was a sociopath like him, but she didn't try to hide that. It was a match made in heaven...or hell. Dismissing her melancholy and his attention to their present conversation, he switched the subject.

"Are you hungry?" His deep voice was sinister. He planned to feed her alright.

A smile spread across her full, red lips. She knew exactly what he meant. "Starving," she answered.

"Let's go grab something to eat," he said, standing up.

"No one leaves this barn until we get the call from your brother. If you are hungry, there is plenty of food in the cooler or in the baskets," Dorian shouted across the barn, taking off his headphones.

The other team members looked across at Arie and Ivan and knew that they were stirring up trouble again. It had become their norm.

"He really was reading our lips," Ivan said, impressed with Dorian's skill. He winked his eye at Arie's brother and chuckled under his breath. He'd have to remember that for later. For now, there was something that he needed to clear up.

"I told you that he could read lips before," Arie said, sitting back down. "I'm getting tired of being in this fucking place!" she screamed so that everyone in the barn would hear her.

Throwing an empty bottle of vodka across the barn into the wall and smashing it, she growled and pushed her head back against the wall.

Ivan smirked at Arie's fit, then turned to Dorian.

"I'm sorry...who said that we can't leave?" Ivan asked sarcastically with a growl in his gravelly voice.

"Your brother," Dorian answered, knowing that if it was just his call, Ivan would have simply dismissed it.

"*Next time*, you should *recommend* that we stay and then qualify it with the fact that it's from my brother, because I don't take orders from men that I fucking employ!" Ivan challenged. His demeanor changed to quickly for anyone in the room to process. "And the only reason that I am even considering staying now is because I need to kill something...soon. But from now on, don't read my fucking lips, and don't tell me what to do, or I'll cut your neck ear to ear, pull your head back and piss down your fucking throat."

Arie smiled, turned on by his promise of murder and mayhem.

Dorian clenched his jaw but did not respond. For now, he would simply have to swallow what was going on between his sister and Ivan. There was far too much at stake. Dmitry had already paid the team half of their fee for coming, paid for the farm, paid for guns, paid for the assassination. If he pulled out now over his whore of a sister then it would cost lives, and more than hers...his men and maybe his men's families. Frustrated, he slipped back on his headphones and continued to listen for their signal.

"There," Ivan said, turning his back to Dorian to face Arie. "Now your brother has been handled. And for the record, I'll be 12 inches deep inside of you as soon as this is done."

"You better, or else, I might explode." Arie looked up at Ivan and cupped her knees under her. "I can't wait to kill someone," she pouted. "We flew all the way over here to sit in this barn like farm animals. How much more degrading can we get?"

Ivan sauntered back over to her and sat back down. "Think of it this way. When we get Dmitry what he wants, which is evidently Smirnov's head on a stick, then he'll be so busy conquering the world that he won't notice us or how much we take for our finder's fee."

"What finder's fee?" she asked, hiding her body behind Ivan's when she saw Dorian look back her way. The last thing she wanted was him to eavesdrop on this conversation. It could very well be her key to independence, a life without her overbearing brother.

"The way that I see it, is that there is going to be a lot of money to be had when we take over Smirnov's operations. Dmitry won't be able to keep up with all of it at first. Sure he's going to inventory it, but guess who will be responsible for corralling all of his shit?"

"We will," Arie answered with eyes bright.

"Exactly. And that dream you have of setting up your own operation will be even closer to happening, because we'll be spread so thin until Dorian won't always be where you are. Before he knows it, you'll be running your own team, and he'll be across the world building bombs for Dmitry."

Arie smiled. "I'd never thought of that." However reality quickly slipped into her fantasy. "But Dorian has Dmitry's ear. And after he helps him pull this off, there is no way that Dmitry will pick me to run my own team."

"You don't know my brother as well as I do. He is always open to negotiation."

Ivan slipped the cigarette into his mouth and looked up again into the rafters with a deadly grin. "They don't know what they're asking for. All this power. All this money. They aren't going to know what to do with it. And the more they have, the more that will be ours for the taking. It's call getting in on the ground floor. We'll let them do all the work to get to the top, and then we'll just take it."

"What makes you think that your plan is going to work? Your brother is planning to take out the biggest boss in the world *or join up with him.* Either way, he wouldn't have gotten as far as he's going by trusting anyone."

"Dmitry has never *trusted* me. I don't expect him to start now. In fact, that's the way that I'm going to turn the tables around."

"I don't understand," Arie said confused.

"I'm going to use his own trust issues against him." Ivan raised his brow.

Arie smiled. "I think you hate him more than I hate Dorian."

"Based upon the look of that new shiner that Dorian gave you, I seriously doubt that. We're probably about even," Ivan said, looking down at Arie's eye. "Do you ever wonder why I don't stop your brother from hitting you?"

Arie frowned. "Sometimes. I just thought it was because it would only make bad blood between Dmitry and Dorian. And I know the only thing that matters to Dmitry is money. He would get rid of me. Send me off. And Dorian only hits me when I go against what he asks. It's not all the time."

Ivan bent down to her and made sure his voice was barely above a whisper. "I don't interrupt because a bitch that loses her bite, her anger, isn't worth anything to anyone. But if you unleash a beaten, used, angry bitch loose on the world, she'll kill everyone indiscriminately, even her master, if the opportunity presents itself."

"I'll kill anyone anyway."

Ivan smirked. "Except Dorian," he challenged with a glimmer of malice in his eyes.

Arie was quiet. She thought hard and looked back up. "Except him," she agreed.

Ivan sucked his teeth. "There will come a time whether I'm around or not when your loyalty will reach its end. Trust me. I've seen this before. It doesn't last. Anyway, Dorian really isn't your master. He's your brother, but he needs you, because you're the best person he has for wet work. I'm not your master, because even though I have some money, I don't call the shots. You're real master is Dmitry."

"You want me to *do* your brother?" she said with a frown.

Ivan took another drag of his cigarette. "When the time is right. We just have to turn everyone against each other first. Dmitry against David and so on."

"And you against Dmitry?" she added.

"Oh, I'm already against him," Ivan answered.

"Why?"

"Because he has everything and I have nothing," he snarled. "In my world, that's enough to start a war. That's enough to commit genocide."

"Didn't you say that he gave you 35 million pounds for Emma Hutton?"

"Yes."

"Well, you didn't give it to her, did you?"

Ivan rolled his eyes. "It's in an account for my son. The dumb bitch wouldn't take it." It had been the only decent, good gesture that he had ever made in his entire life, and she had turned him down flat. Emma said that she would rather eat out of a garbage can than take money from Dmitry.

Ivan wanted to kill her for her stupidity and might have if she hadn't been so far away and the only one to raise his son. Instead, he had put the money in an account for Gabriel, knowing that there would be plenty of expenses that he could pay for outright as the boy grew. Still, he could not believe Emma's blue blood, pompous, self-righteous behavior. After all of her Free Rite bullshit, she still was just a little rich girl playing pioneer. *He should have known.*

"Well, I'll take the money," Arie smirked, bringing him back to the present. "And I'll give you a son."

"I bet you would." Ivan grew quiet. "After my fucked up childhood, there is no way I'd knock up a woman *on purpose*, and the only reason that I give a damn about this one is because of who his mother is. How often do you knock up royalty?"

"So you're against children?" she asked, intrigued.

"I've never seen a use for family. My mother was whore, my father a john. If I ever got a chance to lay eyes on him, I'd kill him. It's just that simple."

"So you want your entire family dead?" Oddly enough, she understood him.

"All except my son. When I'm done, there will only be three Medlov's standing. My wife. Myself and my son."

"Wife?" This was new. She listened attentively.

"*Da, a wife.* I don't mean in the traditional sense. I hate anything traditional, but I want a wife, someone who will spend their life fucking, killing and pillaging the world with me. Someone who doesn't mind a good threesome, who doesn't get jealous when I screw other women and one who will do what I say without questioning my every word."

Arie nodded as if she saw his vision clearly. "And are you taking resume's for this upcoming position?" she asked cleverly.

"I'm actually going to be setting up some interviews really soon," he joked.

"Good. I think I might be interested in that. Just as long as it doesn't call for me being a mother. I hate kids."

Ivan smirked. "*Da, da*. Me too."

He knew even then that he'd never father another child. He wouldn't put a child through what he had gone through, and Emma would surely raise another Dmitry - a boy who thought that he was better than the world, better than his own blood. And if he had another child, one with Arie, he would just be repeating the cycle. One child would feel inferior or to his big brother. And that would be his fault. He shook it off.

"The best part of my plan is that Dmitry is worth over a billion pounds now. Can you count that high? Do you know what that kind of money means in comparison to $35 million?"

"Don't be crude." It was one thing for Ivan to call her a whore or a murderer, because she was both, but to question her intellect was crossing the line. "What of his billions?"

"It will be up for grabs when the dust settles. For now, we have to get him what he wants, and then when he has everything, we take it all."

Arie narrowed her eyes. "You know, it wasn't curiosity that killed the cat, Ivan. It was greed."

"Do I look like a pussy to you?" Ivan asked with a scowl on his face. His coal black eyebrow raised thick with menace. The gleam in his eye was deliberate, evil and terribly clear. He was out for Dmitry.

"No," she answered in a whisper.

There was something about the ice cold disposition of her new boyfriend that turned Arie on beyond control. Snaking her arm around his bulging shoulders, she leaned in and offered her blood red lips to him.

Ivan could see Dorian eyeing him from his peripheral. Tired of being cooped up in the barn, he almost wanted her big brother to say something to him. With a large hand over her aroused breast, he pulled her into his growing erection and kissed her, deep and long, lapping his large tongue through her mouth and sucking on her tongue.

Chapter Three

Dmitry allowed himself to relax as the door closed behind him to his hotel suite. Two men stood outside the double doors on post. Four bodyguards in dark black suits made their way throughout the rooms, inspecting each, checking the phones, looking out the windows, looking for anything that looked suspicious. When Davyd was comfortable with the room, he strategically placed them throughout the suite and guided Dmitry inside.

After the slaughter of the Hutton Industries board, Dmitry knew that he had to watch his every move. Retaliation was certain, but the time was unknown. They would simply have to be ready for anyone brave enough to try to finish what Brenneman had started.

Slipping out of his suit jacket, he meandered into his bedroom and lay across the bed. His long legs lazily flopped over the edge as he burrowed his head down into the pillow and let out an exasperated sigh.

No one would ever know how much this lifestyle took out of him, but he knew. On a constant basis, he felt on guard, always worried, never relaxed. Most days, he was in a constant state of quiet panic, playing over every scenario *and* he never trusted anyone...except Davyd...not even his only brother...his only relative.

Now, he had one hour before his meeting with Boss Smirnov. Over the last couple of days, he had played the scenario over in his mind a thousand times, nearly scripted his words, but yet and still he knew that things would not go as planned. He had that rotting feeling in his gut like every time before.

So much was hinging on this meeting. The Medlov Crime family was still a bunch of riff raff, but now it was well-funded riff raff. If he was ever going to arrive at the point where he was regarded in all organized crime circles as a man of true power, he would first have to win over the man who pulled all the puppet strings.

Only a handful of men had ever seen Boss Smirnov, and for all he knew the man that he was meeting today was possibly an impostor. He had thought about that a hundred times as well. Not even Brenneman had seen the man before, only spoke to him through Khalid.

Still, Dmitry knew that he had to make his presence known now or go on being invisible forever. Today, he could walk into this meeting and set himself up for life with the most powerful man in the Vory or write his own death warrant as well as the death warrants for all of his men, including his brother and Elsa.

Smirnov was known only for his reputation of being brutal. There were hundreds if not thousands of stories that were testimony to his vicious reign. But Dmitry had something that everyone wanted, money and the ability to wash it. There wasn't a crime syndicate in the world who wouldn't negotiate for that. For once, he was an asset, but he had to strike while the iron was hot.

Slowly, Dmitry's tired eyes began to flutter shut. His large chest began to hum into a blissful rhythm of sleep and his balled up fists relaxed into the warm goose-down comforter. Nuzzling his face into the pillow, he finally drifted off into a peaceful slumber.

He knew he only had moments to rest, but a power nap would at least allow him to be alert enough to handle himself, *if it came down to that today*.

At any moment for the rest of his life, he would have to be ready to die, ready to kill or unfortunately do both at the same time. He could imagine no fate worse than that. Yet, he knew that there was no backing down or turning away from his life now. He was locked in on a path of destruction.

***

Dmitry instantly recognized Davyd's tap on his bedroom door. Rolling over in the bed, he wiped his face and pulled his .45 caliber pistol from under his pillow and slipped it in its leather holster under his arm.

"It's open," Dmitry growled as he sat on the edge of the king-size bed. Looking down at his feet, he wiped his blood-shot eyes and ran his fingers through his blonde locks.

The door opened and Davyd slipped inside wearing tired eyes as well. Fully dressed in a fresh dark blue suit, guns hidden under his three-piece attire, he looked around the elegant room and stood waiting on instruction. "Would you like something to eat before you go, boss?"

Dmitry yawned. "No," he said, still a little groggy. That sounded too much like the last supper. Bad luck.

"Khalid rang down a minute ago. He's coming down to talk to you before we are escorted up to Boss Smirnov's suite."

Dmitry stood up and stretched his long arms out. Looking down at himself in the mirror on the wall across from him, he rubbed his hand over his five o'clock shadow. "Bring me my kit. I need to shave."

"*Da, da*, boss. Did you hear what I said? Khalid wants to talk to you."

"I heard you," Dmitry said, dragging into the bathroom. "Check him before he enters. Make his men wait outside. I don't want any of Smirnov's men inside of this suite," he yelled out as he ran hot water in the sink. "And bring my shaving kit."

"It's already on the mantle waiting on you," Davyd said nervously.

He tried to keep his composure, but he was just as edgy as Dmitry about the meeting. He had always been a lower level Vor, *not even a captain*, and now he was about to be in the presence of the Czar. Never in any part of his life had he imagined such a meeting.

Dmitry shaved his porcelain colored face slowly, staring at himself in a daze. The feel of the cold steel against his skin made him only think of his mortality more. It was the tempo of the meeting that was driving him crazy. Everything was going far too slow. He wanted to cut through the semantics and get to the meat of the meeting, but he knew that was not the way the game was played.

"When I'm Czar, I won't fuck people around," Dmitry said to himself in the mirror.

"Did you say something, boss?" Davyd asked from outside in the bedroom.

Dmitry hit the razor against the sink and ran it into the water stream. "*Net*," he answered.

Even to speak such a thing out loud was heresy, and he knew that, but Dmitry could not deny his inward goal. By the end of his life, he would be where Boss Smirnov was at this very moment – on top. He could feel it deep down inside, past the admiration, the fear, the nervousness and even the ambition. This was his birthright. Only, he did not know why.

When Dmitry finished freshening up, Khalid was waiting for him in the parlor. He sat looking out of the window at the setting sun and sipping on a glass of vodka, waiting patiently. As Dmitry entered, he barely looked up. The man seemed to possess a certain calm that only came from a world of knowledge.

Nothing moved Khalid to the point of losing his composure. He was a man in control of his own destiny.

"I wanted to have a word with you before your meeting with the Boss," Khalid said, gently setting his glass on the end table.

Dmitry stopped at the bar and poured himself a small glass of vodka, then joined his new acquaintance in the adjoining chair. He sat down slowly, pulling up his pants as he sat and eyed the old, graying man. "Should we go over what I am to say to him?" Dmitry asked sarcastically.

"More than that," Khalid answered. "When you meet him, you might be a bit jolted by his appearance."

Dmitry was suddenly intrigued. "How so? Is he fat, unsightly?"

A devious smile quipped at the old man's wrinkled lips. "No. He is very poised, very formidable...much like *yourself*." The gleam in his eyes spoke to something more.

Dmitry prodded. "Then what about his appearance might jolt me?"

Khalid paused, thought over something and dismissed what he was about to say. "I have found that the element of surprise works in all situations. I won't say too much. What I have said should be enough to at least allow you to be on guard when you meet him." He moved on, sitting up in his chair from his relaxed position. "You may take Davyd, no one else. He must not speak, unless spoken to and I doubt there will be a need. You get ten minutes. Boss Smirnov has somewhere to be this evening. Keep in mind that ten minutes is more than he normally gives anyone at your level. He wants definite, no maybes. He wants numbers, times, dates, and assurance that you have control over your organization. If he feels that this meeting is a waste of his time, you will be dismissed. If he feels that you have offended him in some way during the meeting, you will be killed."

Dmitry figured as much and quickly processed the information and nodded. "And if I prove to be worthy?"

"Then you'll hear from me."

"And if I prove to be a waste?"

Khalid smiled. "Let's hope for your sake that you don't. No one who lays eyes on Smirnov, knows who he is, and is considered a waste, *as you so aptly referred*, lives long enough to realize his mistake." Khalid spoke without flinching.

Dmitry took a deep breath and picked up his drink. "Well then. Let's get on with it."

***

If the Medlov crew had thought at any point that they were well organized or even well-funded when they arrived in Prague, they were sorely mistaken. Smirnov did not have a few men on guard; he had an invisible army of men who blended into the hotel like guests, but wore artillery under their coats like they were going to war. With high-tech head phones and surveillance equipment, they watched Dmitry and Davyd's every move from the time that they left their hotel room until the time that they arrived in the Presidential suite.

It was then that Davyd realized that his feeble attempts to clear Dmitry's suite downstairs earlier had been laughable. Smirnov had video surveillance everywhere and probably had tapped into the hotel's security as well. His men were well-trained, ex-military, in tip top shape and ready to kill on command. In essence, the

Medlov Organized Crime Family was way out of their depth.

They quietly and orderly entered into the suite to witness true luxury that even outshined Lady Hutton's taste. The room that Dmitry had been given a few floors down was overtly shabby in comparison to the king-like opulence of Smirnov's quarters.

The massive suite seemed to span the entire width of the hotel. Gold-gilded, antique furniture framed the rooms under large crystal chandeliers; beautiful wall-to-wall windows were decorated with fine linen curtains and the marble floors gleamed with perfection.

In the sitting area, a man sat listening to classical music and eating dates, waiting on his guests while several men with large automatic weapons stood across from him quietly on post.

Dmitry could see the man from a far and knew that it was Smirnov.

"Davyd, you wait here," Khalid said, pointing at a chair in the corner of the entryway. "Dmitry, you come with me."

Dmitry followed Khalid into the sitting room in a leisurely stroll, trying to hide his mounting nervousness that would have been evident if anyone could have heard his beating heart.

As his foot hit the bottom step that lead down into the main room, Smirnov looked up into Dmitry's eyes. A wide smile crossed the old man's perfect pink lips, and finally he stood up to receive his guest. When he rose from his chair, brandishing blonde locks with large streaks of silvery gray, peering out of crystal blue eyes and standing over seven feet tall, Dmitry stepped back in disbelief.

"Welcome, home," Smirnov said to Dmitry with a knowing grin.

Chapter Four

The room began to spin. Reaching for something to hold on to, Khalid's words finally made sense to Dmitry as he tried desperately to get his baring. Jolted, he swallowed down questions and made himself move his feet forward.

Dmitry had never seen his father. Never known him. His mother had told both he and his brother that she had fallen to the fate of two brothers, well known for their station in life but brutal in all manners of humanity.

Now, it all made sense. She had been the plaything of the Smirnov men. However, she had never uttered one word about their true identity and neither had anyone else. Maybe no one else knew, but how could they have been mistaken? Laying eyes on the man now, he knew, as must Khalid must have, that he was a son of the underworld Czar.

The questions began to multiply. Holding back the sweat that begged to push through the pours of his skin, he stilled his racing heart.

Though Smirnov was well aware of Dmitry's wide range of emotion, the man did not bat an eye of concern, excitement or even amusement. Instead, he offered a large, manicured hand, covered with tattoos and riddled with calices.

Dmitry looked down at the hand offered to him, then stuck his own inside of it. The reality that he was actually face-to-face with his father was sobering. The man's hand was cold, dead-feeling as though life had left it many moons before.

Looking at his father in his face, he studied him curiously, still with his guard very much up.

"Boss Smirnov," Dmitry said, pushing words from his diaphragm. "Thank you for giving me the opportunity to meet with you."

"You're welcome," Smirnov answered, motioning for the chair across from his own. His voice was deep and hollow. His eyes matched. "Please, have a seat." He looked down at his Presidential Rolex and nodded at Khalid. "You can leave us, Khalid. Thank you." Turning back towards his son, he placed a hand on his upper abdomen as he took a seat, crossed his long legs in his gray tweed suit and wiggled down in the comfort of his chair. With the tilt of his head, he looked Dmitry over once and smirked. "Dmitry Medlov...you've got ten minutes."

Dmitry's eye twitched. This was not his idea of a family reunion, but what did he really expect? He was the spawn of a murderer. Pushing aside any notions of warmth, he focused. Rubbing a hand over his itching nose, he leaned an elbow on the arm rest of his chair and began. "Right. Well, then I'll get to it. As you already know, I own Hutton Industries *in whole*. I control it, most of the stock in it and thus its future. The board was on its way..." Dmitry corrected himself by raising his right index finger. "Brenneman, excuse me, was on his way to diversifying Hutton's Industries core businesses through working with you on the NightStar project. Only, after a horrible mishap, he's out of the picture as well as the rest of the board."

"Yes, I heard about his unfortunate home invasion and the plane crash with the board. It seems that they can't even find the black box," Smirnov said with a smirk.

"These things happen," Dmitry said dismissively. "I'm interested in continuing the relationship between Hutton Industries and NightStar. I want to outwardly fund the scientists who are working on the cutting-edge technology along with cleaning the money that comes back to us for our black market sales. In fact, I already have someone in mind."

Smirnov looked at Dmitry, almost through him. "You have your mother's frown."

Dmitry didn't blink. "Ironically, it appears I have acquired nearly everything else from you."

"What is truly ironic is that Catherine Hutton ended up with you in her bed, not a whore who slept with half of the Vor, and then got pregnant by one."

Dmitry's interest peaked. "You knew my wife?"

Smirnov smirked again. For the boy to be so incredibly smart, he was equally as stupid. "Your wife and I had a bit of a working relationship at one point. Before I cut her off, she purchased a great deal of her arms for her work with the Free Right through me. However, we had a bit of a misunderstanding considering I was also selling to the very people who were attacking her workers."

"A serious conflict of interest," Dmitry said as he pushed more questions to the back of his mind. It was better to keep a clear head at the moment.

"Does it affect you to know that even your wife knew your father, yet she said nothing to you about it?" Smirnov asked with a devious grin. He was clearly enjoying tearing the young man's world apart.

"I'm sure that she had her reasons for keeping that information from me. Catherine had a way about her that you'd have to know to appreciate." Dmitry clenched his jaw and raised his brow. "She ended up having the last laugh, really."

"How so?"

"I'm sitting here with you, and I own everything."

He dropped his smile for the moment, pissed that Dmitry was able to keep his composure. "Don't get ahead of yourself. You don't own everything," Smirnov said with menace in his eyes. "I still own most of the world. You just own a small sampling of the scraps, my boy. It's nothing to be too proud of." Running his hand over the rim of his glass, he breathed through his nostrils. "What of your brother...my brother's son...or my son. We never had a paternity test as you could imagine. It wasn't that important to either of us, but we did have a small wager going on who belonged to whom." He watched Dmitry again, waiting for a response.

Dmitry forced himself to not care and at the same time to prohibit the images of his mother-dead and bloody, beaten by a john - to haunt his meeting. "Ivan is just as confused, I suppose, as his mother was. He's not very useful to me, but I keep him around. I guess you could say that I have an appreciation for family."

"Don't pat yourself too hard on the back. It's over-rated...having a family. Trust me. Just this last year, I had my brother decapitated for being a greasy little fuck. It's a shame that we made it through decades of our troubled youth, and I had to kill him as a older man. Life is funny."

"Sorry to hear it about your loss," Dmitry said, feeling some strange relief to know that at least one of the two Smirnov brothers was dead.

Smirnov smacked his lips and threw up his hands. "Genes are very funny. You could be my nephew or my son, *as could Ivan*. Hell, you could both be mine. You resemble both of us. But neither one of you were ever supposed to exist. Your mother was just a fertile pet. However, as you can imagine, when she dropped a litter of two worthless pups, we had to dismiss her...good bitch or not. She was eighteen when we sent her to the streets. Kirill was supposed to look after her. If I am not mistaken, he ended up having a try at her too." He cracked a devilish smile. "She was tempting like that. Your mother. Only good for one thing."

Dmitry gripped the end of the chair. His nails dug into the leather. "You said you had to get rid of her. Was she a slave?"

"No, she was a lost little tramp that your uncle and I entertained ourselves with. She was something of a supermodel. Long legs and pouty mouth, big blue eyes and a voluptuous body. No one would have ever thought that she was fourteen when we found her eating scraps out of a garbage can outside of our club. We kept her as long as we could, but with two starving, whining boys, she simply had to go." He said so in a matter-of-fact tone with no sympathy or concern.

"It's unimportant. Water under the bridge. What I want to know is will you consider a new partner with the NightStar project? Even though I have a small scrap of the world to offer, it's still more than what you have without Hutton Industries." Dmitry pushed toward the end of his seat and looked at his watch. He only had a few minutes left and there was still plenty of convincing to do. He doubted very seriously that his father gave a damn about their blood link. There had to be a financial payout for him to listen.

Smirnov lit up as he began to talk. "NightStar is my baby. I thought of it. I arranged it. And up until this point, I have funded it. You see, this is the new wave of weaponry, and it's all about harnessing the power of mass destruction into assault rifles. A scientist from the USSR began the work before the fall of the country, but could not find funding after. I scooped him up and gave him a little incentive to continue, i.e. a life of luxury. Now that he's here in Prague, the advancements in his work have exponentially progressed. So, it's time to focus on moving from the baby stages of prototypes and plans on paper to tangible products ready for manufacturing and distributing *to the highest bidders*. So you see, Brenneman was never going to be a partner. He's not a Vor, not a Russian and not even a real criminal." Smirnov laughed. "He was merely a means to an end. He would have found the same demise that *you* provided him even if he had come to Prague. But I must admit that based upon the reports you were *very* original in your choice of torture. Still alive but barely and *in such a brutal way*. It reminds me of when I was a boy... the things that Khalid and I did were the stuff of nightmares." He laughed as he reminisced.

Dmitry returned an admiring nod, holding back his disgust by thinking of just how slowly to kill the old man when the time was right. "Great minds think alike then," he said as he exhaled. "Just one question. You wouldn't have killed him until he provided something. What was it that he was going to give you?" His eyes narrowed.

"You are smarter than you look. I'm impressed. No formal education, yet advanced deductive reasoning." Smirnov winked at Dmitry. "After he appointed me to the Hutton Board as I requested, I plan to have him killed."

Dmitry smiled. "Brenneman was a puppet. I, on the other hand, can offer you more than a seat on my board."

Smirnov liked the sound of that. He smiled. "Yes, you can, but the question is *will you*, my little bastard child?"

"You said that NightStar is your project, and you have no partners. Well, I don't want to be an equal partner, just a silent one. This will give us an opportunity to get to know each other better and build a foundation for other deals in the future, if you don't mind me being a tad bit hopeful."

Smirnov was a true opportunist. His interest spiked immediately. "What could you possibly offer me that I don't already have outside of a seat at Hutton?"

"How about the MPLA for starters?"

Big words for a young man, everyone in the room knew that. The MPLA had been splashed across world news for years now. There money was long. Their connections longer. To get in with them was any organized crime syndicate's dream, but the leadership was picky and their customs dramatically different from any others. One had to know someone on the inside and not just anyone, someone high up in the organization.

Smirnov's interest in Dmitry's African connection drew him in to the point where he had forgotten his ten minute cutoff. Quietly, he studied the young man in all of his movements, reading his tale signs, watching all of his ticks.

However, Dmitry didn't give much away. He could not tell if the boy was angry or serious. In fact, Dmitry had all but gone numb.

From the beginning of the conversation, when he was certain that he had gotten under his skin, Dmitry's eyes had gone from a desperate red pool of anger to a muted blue sea of nothingness.

"It is true. I do not have my hands on the MPLA...yet," Smirnov said, sitting back in his chair. "But I would be interested. They are having quite the revolt over in Angola right now. There is a great deal of money to be made."

"Like I said, it's all about building relationships," Dmitry responded.

"Maybe I won't kill you tonight after all."

"Well, *father*, that's the nicest thing that you've ever done for me," Dmitry said sarcastically.

"Careful. Don't tempt me, boy."

Dmitry smirked, but he knew his father was serious. He had tried to kill him already once with the tailor back in London. Only he didn't lead on that he knew that it was Smirnov who had put out the hit. So, he wasn't surprised that his father had plans to kill him now.

Dmitry channeled his rage into persuasion, trying desperately to prove to his father that he had something to offer.

Smirnov looked at his watch and clasped his hand together. "Your ten minutes are up."

"So they are," Dmitry said quickly.

Smirnov stood up and walked over to the window overlooking a clear, crisp, Prague night. "Khalid will call you tomorrow with the time and place to meet me along with any directions that I feel are necessary." He looked over at his son who still sat poised in his chair. "*But if you try to bite my hand, I'll rip out your tongue and serve it up to your brother for dinner.*"

Dmitry's beautiful face was like stone, stripped of emotion. "If you knew my brother, you would know that he's always one step from doing that himself. He's a fucking sociopath."

"Sounds like he really could be my son." Smirnov wouldn't admit it, but he had an urge to see the boy. Boss or not, he was not without a father's curiosity.

"I can see a few similarities," Dmitry said, standing up to his full height. He pulled down his suit jacket and looked over at the bodyguard watching his every move from the corner of the room in the shadows. He rolled his eyes at the automatic weapon hanging from the man's shoulder.

Dmitry was certain that he could have taken the man with just the knife he had managed to smuggle inside his pants. Russian men were too homophobic to check the inner thigh well. It was far too close to a man's penis.

Looking at the back of his father's head, he put all of his chaotic emotions in check. "I'll be waiting on further instruction from my hotel room. In the meantime, thank you again for the opportunity to finally meet you."

Smirnov turned his eyes to the street lights below. "Have you ever been to Prague before today?"

"No."

"You should get out and explore the city instead of waiting for my decision. When I want to get in touch with you, I will, no matter where you are or who you are with. I have eyes everywhere." He turned and looked at his son, who was an exact replica of him as a young man.

Dmitry slipped his hands into his pockets. "I'll take your advice then. Maybe I'll order up a woman or two and have a bite to eat."

"Manon, the little manager/whore from downstairs, can help you find something to your liking in Prague.

She's good at that and at giving good head. I would recommend her for both."

"I'll keep that in mind," Dmitry said, excusing himself. As he walked up the stairs to head back to Davyd, he stopped and turned back towards his father. There was a long pause before he spoke.

"Was I what you expected?" Dmitry asked, unable to help himself.

Smirnov sucked his teeth again. "That's the thing...I didn't care enough to expect anything from you, Dmitry. Whether you're my blood or not, it is not relevant...only money is relevant. If you did not have any to offer, you'd be dead. Know that and remember it. You'll live a hell of a lot longer if you do. I'm not interested in a family reunion or developing familial relationships. That's why I'm boss. I could care less about you or your brother. I just want to get paid, and you *just happen* to be the one with the check. Count your lucking fucking stars."

"Do you have any more questions?" Smirnov asked, frustrated that the man was still in his presence.

"No," Dmitry said, sucking down his pride.

"Well then go," Smirnov said, dismissing him.

Dmitry was again lost for words. Turning back around, he walked past the bodyguards standing at the entrance of the doorway and headed back towards Davyd. He could feel his own blood boiling and the heat around his collar rising. Yet, he had to maintain for more than just himself. Too many people where counting on him; so to do something stupid like losing his cool simply because his feelings were hurt was not an option.

Davyd stood when he heard his boss's long stride down the marble hallway. Looking up at him, he frowned as Dmitry barreled into the room.

"Is everything alright?" Davyd asked concerned. He followed him quickly, looking back down the empty corridor to make sure that no one was following them.

"No," Dmitry answered quickly, looking forward with a scowl on his face. "Just get me back to my fucking hotel room *now*."

***

Khalid waited in the next room quietly listening to the exchange between his longtime friend and his new ally. The gut-wrenching first reunion brought even a foul taste to his mouth, and he was a man made from very foul things.

As a father and faithful Vor, Khalid was ashamed at that moment of how thoughtless Evgeny had been towards his own blood. There were a hundred other ways that he could have handled things, instead he purposefully was inciting a war, and for what?

Smirnov had more power alone than any other single organized crime syndicate in the world. He had more money than many small countries. And yet, he fought for every inch as though losing even an inkling of amassed wealth would cause the demise of his life. This was why they were now mere shadows of themselves. The power that they had originally sought to balance the wealth and control between the government that oppressed them and the men who were considered less than human had turned him, soured him, devoured him whole and left him a shell of himself. He was now only concerned with feeding his face, spending his money, controlling everything around him and screwing young women.

Khalid had lived many long hard years and witnessed many hard things. Yet, over time he had learned a true and apt appreciation for alliances. He knew that in order to make a king, he must have true followers, men willing to die for him. Smirnov had that once, but not anymore. Now he made secret meetings to develop secret things even from his closest of men. In fact, the only way that he had found out about NightStar was through the fumbling of Dmitry. What else did he not know about? And was it not his place to know every-thing?

Smirnov rounded the corner, glass-in-hand, eyes hollow and voice growling with seedy mischief.

"I should have pulled him from his mother's belly and skewered him on paring knife," Smirnov said, passing Khalid to make his way to the bar.

"Is the boy really so bad?" Khalid asked as he turned to look up at his withering liege.

"He's not a boy. He's an ambitious man, twice our youth and full of ideas. He's the most dangerous type of thing."

"And what do you propose that we do? Kill him?"

Smirnov smiled. "Is there any other choice?"

"There are many," Khalid countered. "Though I would be better able to counsel you, if you tell me your vision of this NightStar project."

Smirnov poured a drink and slammed the bottle against the granite top bar. "What I do is still my business. NightStar is *my* project." He seethed with anger. "I am boss! And I won't have it taken from me by some snot-nosed cum stain that I forgot to dispose of twenty-three years ago."

"I meant no disrespect. You are still my boss. I am here to serve you," Khalid said with a façade of humility. He lowered his head and waited for Smirnov to come to his senses.

It didn't' take long. "Then act like it, Khalid. Focus on tomorrow's meeting and for now send that bitch of mine in here to get me ready for this party tonight. I don't want to be late."

"Yes, sir," Khalid said, excusing himself from the room.

Ten years ago, Evgeny Smirnov would not have kept one secret for Khalid. But with his age, he had become more paranoid, less trusting. That was the thing about being a giant for an entire lifetime. When a man had been the biggest, tallest, toughest man in the room since he could remember and then grown old and suddenly was no longer a physical threat, he became angry, even more cruel, always out to prove himself. And Smirnov had reached that point.

Walking into Smirnov's master bedroom, Khalid snapped his fingers at the young blonde laying on the bed flipping through a fashion magazine.

"Smirnov is ready for you," he said absently.

The young woman obediently closed her magazine with a huff and pushed herself off the bed. "He told me that we were going shopping tonight before this thing," she said, whisking past him in a pink negligee.

"Well, your plans have changed," Khalid said disgusted by her lack of humility.

"They weren't *my* plans in the first place. I would never purposefully go and rub elbows with these twits. I don't know why he does it."

"It's not for you to know," Khalid snapped. "Do yourself a favor. Quiet your mouth tonight and do what your boss says. Otherwise, he might decide that you and your barely-legal womb are unneeded."

The threat of losing her ability to spend reckless amounts of money and be carted around by large bodyguards and put up in the best of hotels quickly numbed her irritation. Grabbing Smirnov's tuxedo off the chaise lounge chair, she stormed pass Khalid and left him alone in the room.

"What have we become?" Khalid asked himself as he looked around the suite. "By now, we were supposed to be done with the rat race." Closing the bedroom door, he walked quietly down the dark hall to his bedroom to get ready for the party himself.

In his silence, however, he was haunted. How did a man regain his soul when he lost it? How did he regain his independence from such a volatile tyrant?

Chapter Five

Davyd felt the rancid anger dripping off of Dmitry as they rode in the elevator down to their floor. Every few seconds, he would look out of the corner of his eye up to his boss and check his disposition.

Things didn't look good for them based upon Dmitry's reaction to the meeting, though he wasn't sure how to broach the subject to find out exactly what had been said.

He had never suspected the meeting would go well. In fact, he had come to the conclusion beforehand that they could end up dead by the end of their ten-minute meeting, but somewhere under the negativity, he had held a bit of hope that maybe, just maybe things would go well.

So much for wishful thinking.

In the corner with his head pushed against the top of the small compartment, Dmitry stood stone-faced, looking forward and brooding. The quiet chaos was almost too much for Davyd as he waited for Dmitry to utter one word.... something... anything would do. But Dmitry stayed tight-lipped with his hands pushed down in the pockets of his tailored pants. Barely blinking, he pursed his lips together and breathed through his flared nostrils.

As the bell chimed and the golden doors swung open, Dmitry's men stood at the suite door on post awaiting his return. He stormed past them, pushing the double doors to the suite open with Davyd in tow.

"Tell me what happened, Dmitry," Davyd finally demanded as he watched the young man walk over to the bar.

"Call my brother. Tell him to come here *alone*," Dmitry ordered, pouring himself a shot of vodka. "I don't want that bitch of his with him eavesdropping." He stopped, shoulders squared and looked down at the glass in his hands and pushed it off the table. With the neck of the bottle in his hand, he lifted the spirit up and guzzled it down in large gulps. Wiping his mouth, he looked over at Davyd and scowled. "Smirnov is my fucking father. Did you know that?"

Davyd frowned. "No."

"Did you fucking know that!?" Dmitry screamed, kicking the bar stool in front of him across the room.

"How would I know that he was your father? I've never laid eyes on him. Not many people have. He's the Czar," Davyd said confused.

"Everyone else knew. My *wife* knew. My mother knew. Kirill knew. God only knows who else knew and quietly laughed at me all this time, but not anymore. No one will ever laugh at me again!"

"I would never laugh at you, and I didn't know," Davyd digressed.

The bodyguards looked around confused, gripping their guns and watching the interaction.

Dmitry tried to control his ramping anger. Clenching the bottle tighter, he leaned against the wall, propping his foot up behind him. Taking another gulp and looked up at the ceiling, he growled, "Just get my fucking little *brat* here now."

A pain deeper than Davyd had ever seen before was evident on the young man's face. He couldn't tell if he had been defeated by the conversation or pushed to move beyond it. Only time would tell. A short time. Dmitry hardly ever called for his brother, unless someone needed to die a painful death.

"*Da, da.* I'll get him here right now," Davyd said, walking over to the table to use the phone.

"The phones are probably tapped. This room is probably tapped. Go across the street and use a phone at one of the stores over there," Dmitry said, walking over to the window. He pushed the curtains out of the way. "They are watching our every move, Davyd. They know that we're a threat."

"I take it that he won't allow us in on the NightStar deal."

Dmitry didn't answer. He glared across the room at Davyd and raised his brow.

"I'll go make the call," Davyd said, turning on his heels with his men behind him.

Left alone in the room, Dmitry was consumed by the silence. Suddenly, he stood up from his perched position by the window and threw the bottle in his hand with all of his might. It landed against the twenty-thousand dollar painting across the room and splattered. Shards of glass flew in every direction, and the vodka quickly changed the color of the painting and ran down the wall.

Pulling off his suit jacket, Dmitry closed his eyes. He held his head as his thoughts assailed him. Grunting, he shook his head.

Was he having a breakdown? Was he going crazy?

"No," he said as the room began to spin. "No!" his deep voice carried throughout the suite.

One of the bodyguards quickly stepped in. "Did you say something boss?" he asked, opening the front door.

"Get the fuck out of here!" Dmitry yelled, picking up the end table and throwing it. It slammed against the floor hard and cracked apart. Splinters of wood and glass exploded against the marble.

The man quickly closed the door.

Dmitry caught a glimpse of himself in the mirror across the room. He walked up to it and looked at his face, then down at his clothes.

All of the fighting, all of the killing was for this? To arrive at the same point as his father? To realize that he was a mockery?

Pulling his shirt off his body, ripping it and pulling the buttons as his tore the fine cotton, he then snatched off his undershirt. His hand ran down to the buckle of his belt. He quickly unclasped it and pulled off his pants, his shoes and socks.

Why bothering looking civilized when he was anything but? They wanted an animal; he would give them a fucking animal.

He probably was a rape child. His mother more than likely hated him for what he was and hated him for who he reminded her of. Evgeny Smirnov.

The bastard of bastards.

Fury encapsulated him. Grabbing another bottle of vodka from the bar, he quickly uncorked it and down the contents.

Normally he was against drinking heavily, but today...

Fuck it.

Fuck Smirnov.

Fuck the world.

The front door opened and closed again. Davyd looked around the room confused and then at Dmitry who was nearly naked except for his boxer shorts.

"I need some jeans, a hoodie, some boots and a gun," Dmitry ordered. His eyes were hooded. "Is Ivan on the way or what?"

"He said that he'd be here in thirty minutes."

"Good," Dmitry said, looking at his bodyguard. "Should I get in the habit of repeating my own fucking orders now?"

The man standing beside Davyd quickly shook his head. "No, boss. I heard you." He left the room, headed to the concierge to get Dmitry a new wardrobe without another word.

Davyd reached under his coat and passed Dmitry his side arm.

"Will this do?" Davyd asked, passing him a .45 caliber, black, unmarked pistol.

Dmitry took the gun and inspected it. "For now, but I'm going to need something a lot bigger. We're arms dealers. So find me a real fucking gun...something that kills in double digits."

Davyd nodded. "Do you want to talk?"

"Not until he arrives," Dmitry said, looking around his room.

***

It took less than twenty minutes for Ivan to get to the hotel and even then he felt that he was moving in slow motion. Racing through the city in a silver Lamborghini under the fall of night, he sped from the farm to his brother without knowing what urgent matter had him pulled from obscurity into life-or-death need. However, unlike others, he didn't need a reason. When Davyd called, he dropped everything and headed out.

While he drove, he wondered if the meeting with Smirnov had gone awry. Or in Dmitry's normal way, had he managed to charm even the head of the Vory? He wondered a million things, but for once, even after planning his brother's demise, he prayed that nothing had harmed him.

At that moment, in the dark, he wanted to take back the words he had spoken to Arie. In theory, the plan sounded flawless, but in reality, the idea of Dmitry being in peril made him sick to his stomach. After all, Dmitry was all that he had, and even though he hadn't been much of a brother or a father for that matter, he had still been there for him his entire life, which was more than anyone else had ever done.

Frantic inside, Ivan pulled up to the front of the hotel, hopped out of his car and threw his keys at the valet, who barely caught them, as he looked at Ivan's unbelievable size or the weapons that he didn't bother to hide.

Like an angry tyrant, he came barreling through the lobby in dark denim pants and a black button down with the nickel plated guns under his arms in their brown leather holsters brandished for all to see.

People looked on at the towering monster as he passed by them tattooed from the top of his neck to the tips of his fingers. Women moved out of his way. The help stood to the side.

But one unfortunate businessman who stood with his back to Ivan, in the middle of the hallway reading a newspaper was pushed by his head out of Ivan's way and onto the ground as he headed towards the elevators.

"Move the fuck out of the way, you pussy," Ivan barked as the man's body violently hit the floor.

Dazed, the man looked around the floor for his glasses and tried to figure out what had just happened to him.

Ivan stepped over him, crushing his glasses under his boot and went into the elevator where a couple quickly stepped back out and let him go up alone.

For once, Ivan had done as his brother instructed and came alone. Carrying a duffle bag with him and smoking a cigarette, he arrived at the fourth floor to be greeted by the bodyguards standing post at the door.

"Where the fuck is my *brat*?" Ivan asked as they opened the doors of the suite for him.

"Inside," one of them said, moving out of the way.

"Close the doors. Kill anyone who tries to come inside," Ivan said, looking around the disheveled hotel room.

Davyd rounded the corner with a drink in his right hand. He looked up at Ivan and raised his brow. "He's in his bedroom. He wants to talk to you alone."

"Who did this?" Ivan asked, knowing that Dmitry hated for anything to be out of order.

"He did." Davyd answered. "He won't talk to anyone. Says that he waiting on you."

Ivan put out his cigarette on the end table beside him and sucked his teeth. "Where's his room?"

"Down the hall to your right," Davyd said, walking to the bar. He sat at the only bar stool that hadn't been knocked over by Dmitry and took a deep breath. "He is undone," he said gloomily.

"Good," Ivan said without a second thought as he disappeared out of the room.

***

Dmitry sat on the edge of his bed in the dark looking out of the window with a blank stare on his face. The curtains had been pulled so that he could see the full moon and in his hand, he clenched a glass of vodka. Beside him on the bed sat two chrome Glocks.

Ivan walked into the room and looked around. It too had been destroyed. Ivan had only seen his brother ransack a room once before. The night their mother had been killed. His brother was the quiet, calm type. He wasn't one for theatrics. He didn't think well in disorganization. It irritated him.

"I take it that the meeting didn't go well," Ivan said, walking over to the chair in the corner across from Dmitry. He sat down and grabbed the empty bottle on the nightstand and looked at it.

"The meeting went fine," Dmitry answered, putting his fingers over his lips. He pointed out to the balcony and stood up. Ivan followed, dropping the duffle bag at the edge of the bed. Once they were outside, Dmitry closed the balcony doors behind him and then pushed a chair up against the handles. Running his hands around the edges of the door, he felt around for bugs. Pulling a small black gadget from behind the light above them, he dropped it on the ground and crushed it under his boot.

Ivan knew exactly what he was doing and picked up the flower pots and threw them over the edge, watching them fall several stories before they splattered on the concrete below.

"I hate bugs," Ivan said with a smirk.

"*Da, da.* This place is infested," Dmitry answered warily.

"Am I free to talk?" Ivan asked, looking around the small patio space.

"Yeah," Dmitry said, resting his hands on the black, wrought-iron railing. He looked over the city with new eyes.

Ivan stood beside his brother and placed his hands on the cold railing and gripped the metal. "What is really going on around here? This place is a fucking mess. Did you get into something with Smirnov's people?"

"Not yet."

"So, are we picking a fight?" Ivan asked, sucking his teeth.

"Do you ever think about our mother?" Dmitry asked, taking his eyes off the scenery.

Ivan was taken aback. "Of course I think about her." He looked into his brother's tired eyes.

"If there was some way to avenge her, would you?"

"What is this about? You haven't brought up our *mat* in years."

"Only because it was too painful to discuss."

"Why do you look like shit all of a sudden? You're in jeans and a t-shirt. What the fuck? I haven't seen you out of a suit since this shit went down." Ivan squinted. "What happened?"

Dmitry let go a deep sigh. "Smirnov *happened*. I went up to meet with him, and I had this bad feeling the entire time, because of the way the little hotel manager girl looked at me earlier...like she knew something."

"Was it an ambush?"

Dmitry smirked. "He's our father, Ivan."

"What?"

Dmitry shook his head. "Boss Evgeny Smirnov is either my father or yours and his brother is either my father or yours or some variation of that fucked up combination. And our mother...our mother was their whore."

Ivan was lost for words. He clenched his wide, square jaw.

The space was too small to move too far. Stepping back just a few inches, he tilted his head and looked at his brother again. *Did he just hear him right?*

"He didn't care, Ivan. He..." Dmitry swallowed hard and looked away from his brother, who was now fighting a million emotions. "Our *mat* was just one of his whores, a play thing. We were a mistake. *Two fucking mistakes*. He all but called her a dumb cunt. He said Kirill knew, too. Catherine knew. God only knows who else. We were a joke. Up until this very moment. If you ask me, he never thought that we'd make it this far. But Catherine put us in a position to really get even. She had done business with Smirnov before but he double-crossed her, and evidently she was too powerful to just kill. So, she did the only thing she could do to get back at him. She gave me everything."

Ivan cleared his throat and cocked a brow. Running his sweaty hands down his pants, he adjusted to the news. "What are we going to do about it?" he asked in a low voice.

"This isn't about business anymore," Dmitry answered. He walked over to his brother and held his pale face in his hands. Looking into his eyes, he whispered. "Our whole life we said that if we ever got a chance we would do something about what happened to our mother. And now we have that chance, but in order to do it, we're going to have to put everything and everyone on the line. Is it worth it to you?"

Ivan frowned. "How can you ask me that?"

"I *have* to ask you. It's your life, too. I know that I've been a shitty father and even shittier brother, but you're still my blood. And I love you."

Ivan became uncomfortable at the acknowledgement of his brother's true feelings. True, it had always been understood but to verbalize it now was disconcerting. He tried to pull away, but Dmitry held him.

"Tell me that you'll stand with me, *brat*. I need you," Dmitry pleaded. "We're about to wage war...serious war."

"Why do you think that you have to ask?" Ivan answered, looking into his brother's eyes with a stone glare.

Wrapping his arms around Ivan, Dmitry hugged him sincerely. "We're going to take everything from him...everything. And we're going to kill anyone who isn't with us...or we're going to die trying. I'm going to make him pay for what he did to you and *mat*."

"It's worth it...isn't it?" Ivan wiped his face and pulled together his fleeting composure. Shaking off his sudden melancholy, he bottled up his emotions, just as he had done a hundred times before.

"It's the only thing that is worth this," Dmitry said, convinced that this was the only path to take.

They both turned and took one last look at the beautiful lights of the city and the bustling night life.

"Prague will never be the same after this," Ivan said with a grin.

"Neither will we," Dmitry lamented.

Chapter Six

A few hours after his meeting, Ivan pulled up to the dark barn where his team waited and parked his car near a large, overgrown oak tree. House music played, low and unnoticed on his radio. He turned off the lights that shined bright across a baron field and rested his head back against the leather seat.

Staring out of the window with his hands clasping the steering wheel, he gazed into nothingness, dwelling on the news that had just been thrown on him like hot, scalding grease.

His father was a boss who had pimped his mother. And he was a byproduct of a sex session that meant less than nothing. He was not born out of love or even admiration but pure unadulterated lust.

More than likely, he had been conceived during a tasteless act that had included more than one man. His father's swimmers were just faster and more triumphant than the others, *nothing to brag about or be the least bit proud of.* He was trick baby.

In his mind, Ivan had always imagined that his father was some powerful man who had fallen in love with his mother but lost contact with her because of some ill-gotten fate.

Often, he had daydreamed about a stranger searching the earth, looking for his mother and finally finding him, taking care of him, loving him. However, it had never occurred to him that he was really just a mistake. *Kids didn't like to think like that.*

But now he was a grown man and he knew the truth finally. It only drew his fire deeper down into his soul, made him angrier, darker and more determined to destroy anything that got in his path.

This news also made him look at his brother in a different light. Sure, Dmitry had mourned Catherine's old ass. In fact, Dmitry had shed a tear, but it was only because she had been the first woman who had actually been kind to him.

She had been the mother that Dmitry had never had. Ivan envied that relationship in truth. He wanted Catherine for himself or *someone like her*. He wanted a woman to dote over him, shower him with gifts and attention, give him a fortune and then die so that he could get on with his life. She had been kind enough to at least do that. And when she couldn't fight Evgeny herself, so she put his son in place to do it for her *after her death*.

"Smart bitch," he said aloud.

It had killed Dmitry to know that he was the only one who wasn't in on the joke, but like a Medlov always did, they would get the last laugh.

A tap on the window made Ivan look up.

Arie.

She bit her fiery red lips and pushed her small exposed breasts against the cold glass in an attempt to draw him out.

It worked.

Pushed to by the depths of his anger, he turned off the car and stepped out. Towering over both her and the car, he looked down at her with gleaming blue eyes in the darkness and grabbed her with one hand by her small neck.

The beat of her heart pulsed in his fingers. Yanking her up to him, nearly cutting off her air supply as he pulled up over two feet in the air, he felt her legs clasp around his upper torso.

"What took you so long?" she asked, hissing a kiss to his cold mouth.

He didn't answer. Instead, he allowed his hands to pull at her black cargo pants until they were just low enough for him to stick his icy hands down into the heat of her bottom.

The contact made her cream. Having waited for too long, she undulated her hips back and forth, urging him to stick a greedy digit into her slick womb. He did so quickly, biting her neck as he pressed his body up against the car for balance.

Her black hair, ripe with the odor from the dank barn, brushed against him as she cradled his chiseled face in her hands. Kissing him deeply on his wide, heart-shaped mouth, she tasted the vodka that lingered on his long tongue. It snaked into her mouth and lapped against her flesh while the jingle of his belt being unclasped interrupted the quiet of the night.

As soon as his pants were down to his knees, Ivan slid lower in a crouching position, muscles rigid and bulging in both his legs and arms.

Like sitting on a chair, she managed to first crawl up him to finishing undressing her lower body and then lower herself onto his exposed, pulsing manhood.

A long moan escaped her mouth. "Ahh," she exclaimed.

Rock hard, he pumped one jolting push through her sensitive flesh, pushing her down its length with his strong hand on her back. He grunted, saying something under his breath.

She winced at first, taking all twelve inches into her little body, but then grinded hard and fast against the pressure of his shaft, mouth open, moans leaping from her diaphragm.

Ivan was like a drug to her. Devastating from head to toe, stronger than any man she had ever seen, Arie enjoyed the pleasure pain that he gave her each and every time that screwed like wild animals. She could always count on him to be unforgiving in his methods, bruising her body every time that they connected, but that was what she enjoyed. Pure unadulterated sex.

Only, Ivan did not have it in him to treat her as vile as he wanted. Normally, he would have slapped her, pulled her in angry positions, fucked her like a dirty whore.

But flashes of his mother continued to torture his mind and wound his libido.

Consumed by his thoughts, his hard pumps became slow and sensual, a feeling she had not experienced with him before.

Looking up into his eyes, she was confused. But he would not give her an explanation. It was simply not in Ivan to do. Instead, he slid down to the cold ground, ignoring the discomfort, and let her ride him.

His strong hand grabbed a hold of her boney waist. Lips pursed, eyes hooded, he stared at her like he was seeing her for the first time. Her body pushed against his hard, hot chest, connecting them and creating more heat. His hand raced over her, touching her, exploring her, but he no longer was brutal.

Suddenly, she was afraid. She had never had this Ivan before. He was far more intimate, more real.

Kissing her again, he suddenly pushed his face away from her, hoping his tears would not fall against her bare skin. Hiding in the darkness, he bit back his pain, although it was hard to do. But Arie had already smelled it in the air.

Need.

She cradled him in her small arms, holding him as best she could. His vulnerability made her fearful, an emotion she seldom experienced. She nuzzled her head into his neck to hide herself from view, knowing that he did not want to be looked at in such a foul state.

Still, he slowly moved inside of her, creating a sensation different and more exhilarating that she had ever known. The thought made her body began to tingle all over and finally the muscles of her womb tightened around his sex and hummed.

The warmth of being in his lap, the feel of being slowly rocked back and forth by his body, the sensation of his cold hands searching over her body and his long tongue slowly searching her mouth, the rock-hard shaft that nearly impaled her was enough to make her climax hard. However, trying to hold it at bay just to keep him going was even harder.

It was then that she realized that in the bitter cold darkness of the forest Ivan Medlov was making love to her for the first time, and it was amazing.

***

When the sun rose, while the rest of the world was waking up, Dmitry Medlov was moving to his second day with no sleep. Sitting at the dining room table of his suite still dressed in jeans and a dirty t-shirt, he ate a full breakfast and went over his strategy in his mind again for the fifth time.

He was waiting on one thing.

The word from the Smirnov camp.

He knew that he had something that Evgeny wanted and was not at all worried about an ambush, but it was what was looming after that he had to prepare for.

Davyd had been ordered to rest, *albeit against his better judgment*. He had tried to stay near his boss the remainder of the night, but Dmitry had told him to take a breather.

"You'll need your sleep, old man," Dmitry had warned before he patted him on the back and sent him to the adjoining bedroom to finally get some much deserved rest.

Davyd wasn't happy about it, but his tired eyes and slumping body showed that pretty soon, he would be no use at all if he didn't sleep.

The bodyguards, however, had stayed on post all night. They were much younger and able to handle more brutality to their bodies.

Scruffy, blonde stubble had formed on Dmitry's face overnight and his curly hair no longer looked immaculately groomed. Instead, he was taking on the look of a gutter rat, like when he first had come out of prison only a few years prior. It felt fitting for the situation.

Last night had changed Dmitry forever. All the suits and grooming in the world would not hide what he was until he changed who he was. And until that time came, he would no longer pretend. He would eat and sleep only to focus on his goal. Evgeny Smirnov.

The large grandfather clock in the corner of the room finally chimed seven o'clock as Dmitry pushed away from his empty plate and stood up. Stretching, he walked slowly to the living room and sat waiting for the call on the phone or the knock on the door.

He was not disappointed.

At eight thirty, the door bell rang and Khalid walked in with a proposition, just as Dmitry had forecasted.

Khalid took one look at Dmitry and knew that the boy had gone rabid. Taking a seat across from him, he dismissed his bodyguards and out of respect, Dmitry did the same.

"You look...*different*," Khalid said, turning up his lip.

"I feel different," Dmitry answered. He shrugged his large, square shoulders. "What of my family? Has he made a decision?" His voice was deep and ominous. His eyes were colder than the Siberian winter.

"He has come to a decision. He will accept your proposition to take a seat on your board for ten percent ownership on the NightStar project with an investment of fifteen million dollars due today by three," Khalid said in a soft tone.

"Done," Dmitry answered quickly. "Cash or check?"

"Transfer the funds to this account," Khalid answered, taking out a white card with numbers written in red ink.

Dmitry reached over the coffee table and took the card without looking at it and slipped it into his jean pocket.

The two men looked at each other for a moment without words, and then Dmitry sat back on the sofa and crossed his legs.

"We will meet this evening no later than six o'clock but no earlier than five at the facility with the scientists. It's about fifteen minutes northeast of the city in a vacant limestone plant owned by *your* company, ironically. Brenneman set it up prior to his little accident. One of our cars will drive you out there. None of your men will be allowed at the meeting *for security purposes*. We can't allow for an ambush or for that matter for you to know where we're going," Khalid said, standing up. "You will have your chance to see your father again there if you can come up with the deposit. I do hope that you'll be ready."

Dmitry stood up and offered his hand. "*Spasiba, brat*," he said sincerely.

Khalid shook his hand graciously and excused himself from the room.

Before the door could close behind Dmitry's guest, Davyd peaked out of the door. "Is he gone, boss?"

"*Da, da,*" Dmitry said, standing up. "Get Elsa on the line, and get the car out front. We're going to the bank."

"Like that?" Davyd asked, looking at Dmitry's clothes.

"*Like this,*" Dmitry answered. "Money speaks louder than clothes."

***

Every news outlet in England, all the major outlets in the U.S. and several other major countries were following the tragic yet suspicious deaths of the Hutton Industries board, and Elsa was the lead on all communication. Her face was plastered on every television station and her words printed in every magazine. Overnight, she had become a household name, just as Dmitry had promised.

Swamped in her executive suite with two assistants, she sat on the phone giving yet another interview and awaiting a call from Dmitry, who had gone AWOL.

The hard hitting questions, she could handle but the absence of Dmitry's touch was nearly driving her mad. The night before he had left, he had made sweet, gentle love to her in his chambers, exhausting her body to the point where she could barely move. And in her ear, he had whispered promises of handing her the world, yet in the morning, when she had awakened, he was gone. No sign of him anywhere.

Since that morning, when the sun gleamed through the windows and kissed her skin, she had been alone and unable to think about anything but him...and her father.

As promised, she had made a call to the general of the MPLA and made him Dmitry's offer. He liked what he heard and was offering a meeting in the next four days in Angola, on his turf with his men.

However, she worried now. With no word on where Dmitry was or what he was doing, the meeting and her father's trust could be ruined.

The consequences could be great - at least for her. While the general was her father, he put nothing and no one in front of his precious resistance. It was a fact that had made her grow bitter over the years along with being well aware of her position in his life.

As Elsa's fingers trailed over her keyboard, the phone rang for the hundredth time that morning. She ignored it as she prepared to write her thoughts down for a much-needed inter-office memo that needed to go out regarding the death of the board. Her assistant quickly picked it up and answered. After a few short words, she picked up the phone and walked it over to Elsa.

"It's Mr. Medlov, ma'am," her assistant said, passing her the phone.

Elsa took it quickly and pointed towards the door. "Ladies, give me a moment, please." Her heart skipped a beat as she held it tightly in her hands.

"Elsa," Dmitry said into the phone.

"Hello," Elsa said coolly. She exhaled a deep breath at just the thought that he was okay.

"*Privet,*" Dmitry answered *hello* in Russian. He could hear her voice restrict at the sound of his. Suddenly, he could smell her perfume on his tongue. He swallowed hard and continued, fighting the thought of her lying in his bed naked. "How are things there?"

"Insane," she answered, getting up from her desk. She walked over to her door and locked it.

"Has Scotland Yard come calling yet?" he asked.

"Every day they have questions. I told them that once they cleared you as a suspect in the Brenneman case and you were free to leave the country that you had a hundred meetings to attend."

"And you weren't lying." He looked at his watch and realized that he had to hurry the conversation along, even though he didn't want to. "I need you to transfer $15 million to my account in Prague for an upcoming business transaction."

"When would you like me to do it?"

"Now." He slipped on his coat and nodded at Davyd. "Can you do that?"

Elsa was already at her computer typing away. "It will be done in the next five minutes. Is there anything else that I can do for you?"

"Not at the moment. Stay by the phone though, *da.*"

"I have my mobile." Elsa knew now might be the only opportunity that she would get to share the news of her father. "One other thing before you go...I have successfully coordinated a meeting with my father regarding your proposal."

"Good. When?"

"Four days from today."

Dmitry was proud that she was able to come through for him yet again. He realized also that he would need to be very specific about what he could offer and when he could meet. Men like her father were always being presented with business opportunities. But Dmitry needed him to take his seriously.

"He wants us to come to Angola, Africa. Will that be a problem?" she asked.

"No. Charter a jet and get to Prague in the next day. You can brief me when you get here, and we can fly out together."

"Why don't I just fly in on one of yours?" she asked confused.

"After the board went down in a plume of smoke, do you really want to chance it?"

Elsa hadn't thought of that. "Maybe you're right."

"Speaking of which, sell all of my planes and get new ones...just in case." Dmitry didn't trust anyone any-more...even the men he had hired to work for him.

"I'll work on both things today." She paused, heart racing in her ears. "I've missed you." Nervousness crept in.

Dmitry hadn't exactly been a romantic over the last few weeks, yet she found herself drawing nearer to him. The only problem was that she still recalled his wish-es...*to keep things simple.* Only, everything was becom-ing very complicated for her.

He heard the quiver in her soft voice, but he was un-able to reciprocate. There were too many variables right now...even the notion in the back of his mind that she too was untrustworthy. Still, he did miss her or the idea of her.

The pause had been too long. He cleared his throat.

"When you get here, we can spend some time to-gether," he said, avoiding telling her that he missed her as well.

Elsa sighed quietly away from the mouth of the phone. Still, no sign of true emotion from him. "That would be nice," she conceded.

"Tomorrow it is then," he said, biting his lip. He could tell that she wanted more. But he could not give it. Catherine was barely cold in the grave and he was planning a full-on war. Love was not an option.

Elsa wrapped the chord around her long fingers and curled her face into the phone. "At what hotel should I make arrangements in Prague once I arrive tomorrow?"

She was certain based upon his response that he wouldn't want her curled under him in his hotel room. Plus, the space might make things easier on her. Just being around him drove her mad. His look. His cologne. His deep voice. Even over the phone, he stirred some twisted lust inside of her that was barely controllable.

Dmitry looked at his watch as he held the phone. He had been on the call longer than expected. He had to cut things short. "Come to the Red Square. Tell the front desk you're my guest, and they'll bring you up to my room," Dmitry said, standing up from the chair. "Look, I had better go." He scratched his stubby, blonde beard.

"Take care of yourself, Dmitry," she said quickly. Sitting up in her chair, she held her breath.

"*Da, da.* You too," Dmitry said, hanging up.

He hung the phone up carefully, knowing that she had not yet hung up herself. She was waiting on him. And the thought bothered him. While he genuinely liked Elsa, he knew that there was no place in his life for love, and *she* was falling head over heels for him. It was a doubled-edged sword for Dmitry.

Having her eating out of his hand would prevent her from being a complete threat, but it also put her in danger. He couldn't decide which was worse.

There was no doubt that he was attracted to her. There was no doubt that she was educated, sensible and probably the perfect person for him. If he did make it out of this current ordeal, they would be a serious power couple, able to conquer the world together.

But long term, Dmitry knew that he was not interested in a serious relationship. He never wanted a wife or children. He was too fucked up inside for that. He would just end up ruining them, the way that his mother had ruined him and his brother. And if he knew that he had nothing more to offer than money, then why would he ever get into a situation like that?

"I don't have time for this," he said aloud, admonishing himself for thinking of marriage and children when he needed to be worried about if he would even be alive by the end of the night.

Right now, he had a family member to kill.

Chapter Seven

As a light snow began to fall, less than 300 meters from the limestone plant and hidden under the dark of night, Ivan and his team sat anxiously awaiting a signal from Dmitry. Ivan had never gone completely blind into a situation before tonight. Dmitry always gave some kind of direction, but at the present, they were without any real etched-in-stone attack plans, even though they were in definite need of one.

The word from Dmitry before Ivan left the hotel the night before was simply to *come with the full team, guns blazing and a few dirty bombs ready.* "Make them prove to me why I pay them at all," Dmitry told Ivan in his ear. "Bring your worst, *brat.*"

Ivan felt as though he had been given a carte blanche – for once in his life with his brother – and he was prepared to destroy everything in his path. However, for extra measure he had brought along Arie for wet work, Dorian for a few more explosive fireworks and a BS-1 30 mm grenade launcher, and two Siberian twins who were surgical with their Russian-made automatic weapons.

Ivan's specialty was of course his trusty knives, his Glock, Desert Eagle and his bare hands. He had found over time that those whom he could not shoot, he could always catch and choke out, crack their necks, cave-in their chests with his boots or simply break their spines. It didn't matter to him how he killed them tonight. The point was that he was going to kill them...each of them, saving his long, lost papa for last.

Ivan stood like a statue, almost disappearing into the night. As tall as the oak he leaned against with his eyes focused on the building in the distance. The only thing that could have possibly given him away was the cigarette that he slowly inhaled. He tasted blood in his mouth as he bit down on his lip. Sucking the hot fluid from his bleeding mouth, he controlled his breathing and waited.

The wind ripped through the small group, occasionally causing them to grunt in discomfort at the feel of the bone-cutting chill that accompanied their deadly field trip.

The wintry air had Arie huddling her in coat by the tree with her eyes covered by snow goggles and looking through the scope of her Draganov sniper rifle. She had been the only person that Ivan had divulged the truth to. Everyone else simply knew that they were attacking an enemy...auditioning for the "big show." But she knew that this was as personal as it could get. Tonight was about Ivan's dead mother. And to her that was far more respectable than killing for money. Hell, she would have done this one for free, if it were not for her money-hungry brother.

Looking over at Ivan, she felt her thighs steam even in the cold. He looked unbeatable and undeniable in his black steel-toe boots, black cargo pants, black turtleneck and overcoat, guns holstered, eyes gleaming. He was definitely her type of monster. Devilish in the bed and with a weapon, Ivan Medlov was the ultimate alpha male.

As she looked at him, she realized that for Ivan, she would do just about anything. All he had to do was ask.

***

After the money was transferred to Smirnov by Dmitry's people, the phone call from Smirnov's camp came. The boss wanted to meet. He was feeding right into Dmitry's hands and Dmitry right into his. The evening had an ominous feeling to it, even despite its dazzling beauty.

As Dmitry emerged from the hotel escorted by Smirnov's men, he felt both vulnerable and empowered. Flanked by five brooding mafia types in dark suits and dark shades at least a foot shorter than he, Dmitry allowed them to place him in the back of a white Land Rover in front of the hotel.

Even though they were supposed to be intimidating with their barely-hidden weapons, it was Dmitry that caused the unease.

Filthy, unshaved and in a dirty pair of jeans and a hoodie, he looked like more like the man who had recently walked out of a prison and committed a mass homicide than a billionaire.

Deafly quiet and watching everyone, he slipped inside the car and widened his stance, making one man have to ride in the car behind them.

Square-shouldered and stealthy, he sat with his legs open and his hands comfortably in front of him.

The men could not help but stare at him, marveling at the remarkable likeness that the stranger shared with the boss. They had the same eyes, the same hair, the same height and the same killer stare that nearly always preceded mayhem.

However, Dmitry had no interest in impressing Smirnov with suits and swagger tonight. And he knew that by the time that he laid eyes on him again, he would already know what was about to happen.

Total anarchy.

Prior to the car pulling up to pick him up, Dmitry had already instructed Davyd to stay put there and keep things looking as though everything was normal until just the right time. That had made Davyd even more uncomfortable. He went everywhere with his liege, even into the depths of hell. It was his job to protect him, to ensure his safety even over his own life. But Dmitry would not allow it today.

"The time will come for you to prove yourself, *brat*. Right now, I need you here," Dmitry had said to Davyd, patting his dear old friend on the back.

"Who will protect you?" Davyd asked.

"God, *if he is willing*," Dmitry had answered with a smile. "And if he won't then, there is nothing you can do anyway."

He had left Davyd up in the suite with his men, forced to wait it out-a horrid torture. But Dmitry knew that this was one time that he had to leave his men behind and go into the darkness alone.

However, one thing that Smirnov did not anticipate was that Dmitry knew exactly where he was going. Khalid had purposefully informed him of their exact location, even though he knew what the boy would do. An ambush was more than likely, it was fore surely coming. Though Dmitry was not sure why his new ally had given rise to the change of the guard. Maybe it was because the old man had a son as well, and he knew if Smirnov had no regard for his own children, then he would definitely have no regard for Vladimir. Maybe Khalid wanted more of the action or maybe the old man was simply tired of the unneeded blood baths and continued reign of terror. Whatever had provoked him to give him the information, Dmitry was grateful to

Khalid and would remember the favor when the time came.

"You have to put on this," a man sitting in the passenger seat of the Land Rover said, passing Dmitry a black bag for his head.

"I'm not putting that on," Dmitry said, looking at the bag.

"This is not option," the man pushed.

"I know it is *not an option*," Dmitry snapped. "I'm not putting a fucking bag over my head. "Fuck off," Dmitry said, sitting his head back.

"You put bag on or we put it on for you," the man answered, turning around in his seat. He swallowed hard at the sight of Dmitry, clenching his wide jaw and glaring at him like he was ready to bite his head off.

"Try," Dmitry said with a smile. "And I'll snap your neck and turn this truck over. I'm no *suka*. You can try, *little errand boy*, but you will not succeed. And your boss will be very angry if the deal does not go down. Your choice. Your fucking funeral," Dmitry said, locking his eyes on the man.

The man knew Dmitry was serious. He looked over at the man driving the car. "*Chto vy dumaete ?*" he asked his colleague. *(What do you think?)*

"It doesn't matter what he thinks," Dmitry answered. "I'm not doing it."

"*Kakaya raznitsa, sdelat' inache?*" the driver said, hunching his shoulders. *(What difference does it make?)*

The man looked at Dmitry one last time and turned around, knowing that he had been punked out, but he also knew that he had come within an inch of defending his own life. The bodyguard smiled as he turned his head, knowing that in time he would get the chance to kill the rich bastard, maybe even tonight. So his friend was right. What difference did it make? They had patted him down for guns, trackers or phones. Dmitry was alone, unarmed and unprotected. Plus, he didn't know where he was going. He could look out the window all he wanted. His ass would still be his at the end of all of this.

The drive was short and before Dmitry knew it, they were pulling up exactly where Khalid had said. The limestone plant appeared to be empty and dark from the outside, but from the inside, it was guarded by several men carrying automatic weapons.

Entering the gate, they drove to the loading dock of the dilapidated factory and got out.

"I see him," Arie said as he looked through her scope.

Dmitry stepped out and looked south into the darkness. He could not see his men, but he knew that Ivan was there watching.

"This way," the bodyguard who was itching to kill Dmitry said, pointing with his gun up the staircase to the only door.

"Do you have a cigarette?" Dmitry asked as he walked up the stairs in front of the men.

"*Da*," one of them answered, reaching into his pocket.

"I want one smoke before I go in," Dmitry said, standing at the top of the staircase. He ran his hand through his blonde locks.

"One cigarette and then you go in with boss," the man said, passing Dmitry a cigarette and a light.

Dmitry hated cigarettes, but slipped it in between his lips and lit it. Taking a puff on it, he clasped it in between his index finger and his thumb and raised his other three fingers. Then stretched his left hand out.

Ivan was already looking through the scope by then and shook his head.

"Eight minutes," Ivan said aloud to his team. "Let's move closer for the take. We don't have much time."

Finishing his cigarette, Dmitry threw down the butt on the ground and stepped on it. "Ready," he said with a smile.

One of the bodyguards opened the door and allowed the rest of the men, including Dmitry to go inside.

Chapter Eight

The limestone plant had be retrofitted inside and transformed into a germ-free white lab. The entire place was lit up inside by large halogen lights hanging down on the sterile surroundings to illuminate the various workstations and divided by transparent glass partitions for the scientists who were working on the NightStar project.

Bodyguards stood post high above on a suspended walkway, where they were able to look down on the workers and in the bottom far corner was a control center where security watched on several monitors all of the movements both on the inside and outside of the building.

Dmitry was brought inside by the bodyguards with him and walked through the main entrance into the center of the building, where a make-shift board room had been set up.

As Dmitry made his way to the room, he saw Smirnov and Khalid waiting for him, sitting and talking to one another. They both looked up when the door opened and Dmitry was escorted inside. Smirnov had a smirky smile, but Khalid had a death stare.

"Gentlemen," Dmitry said, taking a seat before instructed.

"Glad you could make it," Smirnov said, narrowing his stare on his son. He picked up his cup of coffee and sipped it slowly, looking down at the table, obviously in thought, then sat the cup back down and smacked his lips. "Well now, since we're all here, why don't we begin," Smirnov said, looking over at Khalid, who said nothing but did raise his brow.

"First thing first, thank you for your investment into the NightStar project," Smirnov said, pushing up to the table. He placed his large, cold hands on the shiny wood and looked over Dmitry. "I hope that you also have the papers appointing me to the Hutton Industries board."

"I do," Dmitry said, pulling the papers from the inside of his gray hoodie. But before he pushed them across the table to Smirnov he stopped.

"How do I know that when I pass these over to you and you sign them, that you won't kill me?"

Smirnov laughed aloud. "Where's your trust, my boy? Don't forget that you are my blood."

"I wasn't aware that that counted for much," Dmitry said, raising his brow and placing the paper in front of him.

Smirnov looked at the paper and then back at Dmitry. He chuckled deviously under his breath. "That paper may be the only thing that keeps you alive."

"Well, that doesn't exactly evoke trust," Dmitry said, putting his hand on the paper.

"Did you really come all this way to ask questions, or did you come here to make a deal, boy?" Smirnov asked.

Dmitry twisted up his lips. "I just have a couple of questions first, and then I'll be better able to answer that question."

"Alright," Smirnov said, entertaining Dmitry for the moment.

"NightStar is nuclear, correct?"

"*Da*," Smirnov answered snidely.

"And unsanctioned?"

"*Da*."

"And untraceable?"

"That's the whole point."

"To go to the largest bidder, who could even be Russian enemies, English enemies?"

"They could be fucking American enemies for all I care. This is about supreme profit and power. No one is doing what we are doing. I've hired the best and brightest scientists in the world. When they are done, NightStar could very well insight World War III or save the world entirely. I don't really give two shits as long as I get paid."

Dmitry looked at Khalid and suddenly understood why he had chosen to turn on his old friend. The man had gone mad.

"So, this project is about the highest bidder."

"Exactly." Smirnov frowned. "You behave as if it bothers you. What do you care? You're a rat from the gutters with no political ties. I'm surprised that you can even read with the limited education that you've received. This is high as you can go, my boy. I'm the pinnacle for you."

Dmitry shook his head. "You're right about that."

"So, what are these questions about then? What difference does it make? You're not wealthy enough to lead this, you're just wealthy enough to become an investor. Hutton is just the tip of the iceberg. Once we move into the second phase of the project, then we'll have everyone from the middle east to Africa involved. Don't think too highly of yourself. Be glad that I'm letting you in on this at all."

"Well, why do you need Hutton Industries?"

"Because it's quite difficult to buy legitimacy. You should know. You had to fuck a cancerous dinosaur to get your bones." Smirnov laughed. "You are smart. I'll give you that. I just don't know how you managed it. I've never fucked at thing older than twenty-two."

Dmitry bit down his anger. "I did what I had to do," he said without emotion. "So you're at the beginning stages now. There really has been no major motions."

"I have the scientists. They are willing to work for me. They are doctors of fortune. They understand that working for the government will only get them locked up in a lab, maybe even killed afterward. There would be no recognition and absolutely no riches. *But* working for me, they get the high life." He said with an exaggerated smile.

"And a *heads-up* of where the NightStar won't be when it detonates," Dmitry added.

Smirnov shook his head and pursed his lips together. "Do you know what happens to a star when it dies?"

"An explosion, I imagine."

"Not just an explosion. Stars that are greater than eight solar masses when they are born usually end their lives in a gigantic supernova, one of the brightest events in the universe. After this violent and dramatic death, they leave behind a neutron star or black hole and that's just what this little project is going to leave on the poor bastards that it's detonated on. The NightStar project is actually named for my lead scientist, Dr. Hamilton McKnight. It's his research and his desire to explore or add on if you will to Einstein's Atom Bomb, along with his desire to be filthy rich that has led us to this point. Thank the heavens that he's more interested in hot young women and cocaine that he ever was with the Nobel Prize."

"Is he here now?"

"Why? Would you like to meet him?"

"Of course. He sounds like a genius and he's going to make me a very rich man."

Smirnov twisted up his lips into another evil grin. "McKnight is always here, under lock and key with the rest of the team. I'll introduce him to you after our meeting. Now, back to the appointment to the board."

Dmitry smiled and pushed the paper towards him. "Here it is. Everything that I promised." His eyes locked on his father.

Smirnov's long hand reached across the table and took the black linen folder, carefully opened it and read it quietly. The sides of his weathered, tan mouth slowly pulled into a grin. Nearly in slow motion, he looked up from the paper at Dmitry in approval.

"So it is," Smirnov said, passing the folder to Khalid. "Put this away for later," he said to his old friend.

Dmitry looked down at his watch. Eight minutes on the dot.

Smirnov instantly picked up on it. "Do you have somewhere to be?" he asked, dropping his smug grin.

"No," Dmitry said slowly. He grinned back.

Just then the quietness of the meeting was sorely interrupted. A loud, deafening boom followed by a powerful eruption exploded at the dock door, knocking the men who stood at guarding the area back several feet into the wall.

"What the fuck?" Smirnov said, pulling his gun. He pointed it at Dmitry but heard the distinctive click of another gun beside him. He looked over stunned as Khalid stood up with his pistol pointed at him.

"You can't be serious," Smirnov said to Khalid.

"Can't I?" Khalid said, pointing waving his gun for Smirnov to move.

"It's over," Dmitry said, standing up. He took his father's gun quickly and pointed it at the man who came rushing through the door unexpectedly to retrieve his boss.

When the man saw Dmitry he raised his uzi but was too late. Without thought, Dmitry shot him in his head. The bodyguard fell to the ground as blood spattered across the acrylic wall. Quickly, Dmitry turned the gun back to his father.

"You won't get away with this," Smirnov sneered.

"I beg to differ," Dmitry said, nodding at Khalid. "It's good to have you on board."

"It's good to be done with this shit for brains," Khalid said with his nose turned up at Smirnov. "All the years that I followed you, I never thought I'd see the day when you would blatantly cut me out of a deal or at least not consult me. *NightStar?* Are you serious? This is fucking psychotic. It's the worse idea that I've ever heard about. And you're basically inciting a world war for profit, and what do you expect to happen? Do you think that our families or our men will survive it? Just so you can get richer? How much does one man need?"

"Stop being a pussy, you ignorant fuck. What is really the issue here, *eh*? Is it my project or the fact that I cut you out of it? You're a flunky for God's sake, not my equal. You should be glad that I carried you for as long as I did. The only thing you have ever been good for is delivering my messages and running my errands. You're a glorified bitch. Hell, I should have killed you the moment you wanted to have a family with that cunt of a wife of yours. You were the one who begged to *bend the code* just so you could have your little fucked up family. And *I* let it happen like a fool. Look at you. You've become weak and complacent just like all the others," Smirnov said with his hands still up.

"By others do you mean your own brother?" Khalid snapped. "You have no loyalty. You murdered him because he didn't need you anymore."

"I did the world a favor," Smirnov said with a chuckle. "Are you seriously seeking revenge for that fuck up? I bet you didn't know that he fucked your wife." Smirnov laughed. "All this for him?"

"No, Evgeny, all this for all of us. We're tired of you, Smirnov. We're tired of you getting rich off of us and treating us like shit when you can't do anything without us."

"Who is *us*?"

"You think I'm the only one who knew about this...who is okay with this? The council wants you out."

"The council? Fuck the council. You're expendable, you're fucking replaceable. Is that my fault...that you've never amounted to shit if you weren't huddled together to try to complete a thought?"

Dmitry watched on quietly. It amazed him that even though his father was clearly outnumbered and about to be killed, he showed no fear and still exerted as much power as he did moments before.

Khalid gripped the gun. "When we first started out, this was about balancing the scales, giving our men something that the government would not. We are not terrorists. And I made you who you are. You didn't have a brain in your head when we started this, just the ability to kill and the body to intimidate. Everything else was built on my knowledge."

Smirnov shook his head. "You're a funny man. Don't you realize that without me, you would have been nothing? You owe everything to me, including your worthless life...you and all your offspring. I tell you what, you had better kill me, because if I get just a small chance, I'm going to slaughter your wheezily little shit of a son, I'm going to fuck your teenage daughter to death and I'm going to peel the skin off your wife. And you know what I'm going to make you watch, Khalid." Smirnov did not bat an eye. His murderous rage was only vaguely reduced by his old age.

"That's enough," Dmitry said, disgusted by his father's rant.

"You don't get to tell me when enough is enough, you fucking gutter rat!" Smirnov shouted. "In fact, you don't get to address me at all."

Dmitry walked up to his father face-to-face and smiled. "Before you die, I'm going to make you beg for it."

"You could cut me open and pull out my entrails, and you still couldn't make me *beg for it*. You're not man enough. You're just a little boy with a big gun." Smirnov growled. "I'm a fucking Vor. Don't you ever forget that! If I don't kill you, one of my soldiers will."

"Let them try," Dmitry growled back. "You have no idea what I'm capable of."

"Do I look scared?" Smirnov asked.

"You should be," Ivan said, walking into the small room. He locked eyes with his father and felt a since of utter satisfaction. "This place is secure, *brat*. Those pussy guards are all dead. The others are lined up out front for you to do what you want with."

"Good," Dmitry said, pushing his father towards the door. "Move, old man." He knew that wounded Smirnov's ego more than anything else.

Khalid and Ivan followed Dmitry and his father who walked at gunpoint into the main foyer where they found the scientists on their knees with their hands behind their backs.

Dmitry looked over at his team who stood proudly bearing the fruit of their hard work and hoping for their boss's approval.

They had it.

"Which one of you is McKnight?" Dmitry asked.

Near the far end of the line of scientists was a small framed man with dark curly hair and glasses. He had evidently been working when the attacked happened, because he was still in his white smock. He raised his shaky hand and looked up at Dmitry for mercy.

"Are you the only ones who can complete this NightStar project?" Dmitry asked in an eager voice.

"We are," the man said, hoping that their knowledge would save their lives.

Dmitry stood quietly thinking then raised his gun and shot the man quickly. It hurt him to his core with every bullet, but he knew that it had to be done. This man was capable of the mass destruction an entire nation and would do it all for profit.

While Dmitry was no saint, he knew that this was now his responsibility. In quick chaos as the man was riddled with bullets, it made him wonder what was so different about him selling a few guns at a time to people who were going to use them to kill versus his father who going to do it all at once. It was then that he realized that he was a hypocrite.

Dmitry finally stopped shooting just a few bullets shy of emptying his clip and looked down at the gun in his trembling hand. His team looked on confused at their boss's surge of emotion but did not speak.

Smirnov looked on pissed off. "Do you know how much money I have paid him?" he asked his son in disgust. "It's all been wasted and for what?"

"If but for nothing more than to destroy you, then it's worth it," Dmitry answered in a lie.

"You used that thing like it was your first time. Who do you normally get to do your dirty work...him?" Smirnov asked, looking over at Ivan. He smiled at his son. "What do you think he's going to do for *you* when the time comes?"

"Let me worry about that, you old fuck," Ivan said, spitting on the cold floor.

Dmitry knew he had gone too far to turn back now. He had to see it all through. Looking over at Ivan, he clenched his wide jaw. "Do the rest of them, find the prototype, and burn the place down. Get rid of the bodies."

Ivan saw Smirnov smirk at Dmitry's orders as if to say *I told you so*. He turned his back to him. "What are you going to do with Smirnov?" Ivan asked. "You can't take him back to the hotel. And you can't *do him* without me."

"He owns a chateau not far from here. There are on- ly a few men there. It won't be hard to take it over and use it to complete the job," Khalid interrupted.

Dmitry knew that it could be a trap, but he had a gut feeling that he could trust Khalid. He was as in as far as he was.

"Fine. Let's go there," Dmitry said, pushing his father out the door.

"Wait," Ivan said, looking over at Khalid. "Who is this guy?"

"Vladimir's father," Dmitry explained.

"Oh, shit," Ivan chuckled. "Talk about being stabbed in the back." He looked over at his father. "Tonight is not your night. Is it?"

"Everyone has their night. Yours will come soon enough, my boy. Mark my words," Smirnov vowed.

"Promises, promises," Ivan said, rolling his eyes. "Give me twenty minutes and this place will be a memory."

Chapter Nine

Loading up into one of the trucks that were used to escort him to the factory only a few minutes before, Dmitry, Khalid and Smirnov pulled off into the dark, cold night headed for Smirnov's hideaway out in the countryside.

It was a quiet drive for the men. Smirnov looked out of the window with Dmitry still pointing the gun at him from the other passenger seat. Khalid drove, while continuously looking out of his rearview mirror for any straggler bodyguards who may have had a superhero itch.

Dmitry couldn't help but look at his father. He never thought in a million years that he would have his family reunion like this. But as things often went in his life, he was forced to suffer yet another disappointment.

The eerie quietness forced him to question his own motives. Whether he liked it or not, he was very similar to the man that he would not doubt, before the end of the night, murder. They both were unnaturally ambitious with cold blood that allowed them the ability to murder at will. They both had been cursed with a formidable build and the ability to sway others to do their deeds. Yet, Dmitry couldn't force himself to ever believe that he would be capable of killing his own brother, that he would grow rich off the back of others or exploit young women.

No. He was much different from this man.

"If you're having second thoughts about signing your own death warrant, now is the time to reconsider," Smirnov finally said, taking his eyes off the window.

He looked over at his son with the same piercing blue eyes.

Dmitry swallowed hard and tried to show no emotion. He sat back in his seat and rested his head, still keeping his gun pointed towards his father.

"I've made my decision," Dmitry finally said.

"Based upon what?" Smirnov asked. "The word of a traitor?" He looked at the back of Khalid's head.

"Based upon your own decision to have me murdered earlier by the tailor," Dmitry replied pointedly.

"Oh...that." Smirnov shifted in his seat a little. "Well, you can't blame a man for trying to knock out the competition."

"How was I competition?" Dmitry asked.

"You want to own the world, boy. I can see it in your face. Hiding behind those angelic features lies a greedy demon. If I had allowed you in, the moment that I let my guard down, you would have done exactly what you are doing now."

Dmitry shook his head. "You don't know me at all."

"Don't I?" Smirnov asked. "There is nothing that I can do to change how you feel about me." He narrowed his eyes. "This is personal. It's not about business for you, but for me...there is nothing personal about it."

"You're referring to my mother."

"I am."

"Why did you cast her away like that?"

"She was a whore. That is what you do with whores. You cast them away."

"She was not a whore. She was a confused young woman who you took advantage of."

"Aren't all whores." Smirnov laughed. "You have a lot to learn about women."

"She was barely a woman. She was a child."

"Depending on what part of the world you were raised in. In my mind, she was a woman."

"What about us?"

"*What about you*? You and your brother were a mistake. It happens. She had the chance to get an abortion. I had her in my home. She was well kept...well decent enough. When you came, I warned her and then three years later, the same shit again. I had no choice but to put her out."

"Do you have any more children?"

"Why would I tell you?"

"Khalid?" Dmitry asked.

"Not that I know of, but he has many secrets," Khalid answered.

"That's right," Smirnov smiled. "Dead or alive, I have many secrets, and you couldn't unravel all of them in a lifetime." After taking another look at Dmitry's gun, he rested his head back. "Even if you accomplish everything you have set out to, answer me this...what will you have gained."

"I'll be able to sleep at night knowing that the man who tortured my mother is dead."

"I didn't torture her. I didn't kill her."

"Who did?"

"How the hell am I supposed to know? Some john, I suppose. Your mother had options. She was a beautiful girl. She could have stopped selling her body. When you were born, she was barely seventeen. When you died, she was barely in her thirties. All that time in between and the only thing she could find to do was sell pussy, and you think that I'm the bad guy."

"Don't let him get into your head, Dmitry. He knows that he's outnumbered. So now, he wants to try to outsmart you," Khalid warned.

"Do me a favor. If you're going to allow this *suka* to continue to talk to me, then just shoot me now and save me a little sanity, *eh*," Smirnov said repulsed.

Dmitry felt himself drowning in his thoughts. "You had a chance to help her," he argued.

"Who says that I didn't? Your mother had a little drug problem to go along with her profession. Any money that I gave her went straight into her veins."

"She wasn't on heroin."

"Really?" Smirnov frowned. "Funny, I don't recall that being the case." He winked at Dmitry. "Maybe you were better off without both of us. Did you ever think of that?"

"Maybe the world will be better off without the both of you. I have thought of that," Dmitry answered.

Smirnov didn't like that he couldn't break Dmitry. He kept looking for a chink in his armor, but as far as he could see, the young boy didn't have any. *Pity for him.* He never thought that he'd go out at the hand of his bitch boy and a bastard son.

"Life is ironic," Smirnov said aloud.

"Tell me about it," Dmitry said with a huff.

"So, what are your plans for me? I'm curious to know," Smirnov said, changing the subject.

"What do you think I have planned for you?"

"A quick death. Maybe one to the back of the head," Smirnov said, rubbing the back of his skull.

"My mother didn't have a quick death. She choked on her own blood. Her face was smashed in to the point that she couldn't see out of her own eyes. She died a painful death unable to see her sons even in her last moments." Dmitry fought hard to keep the images of her out of his mind. He had to focus now.

"So you plan to beat me and then rape me?" Smirnov smacked his lips. "That's a bit much."

"I plan to rape a part of you that is far more important than your body," Dmitry growled. "I'm going to take everything, and you're going to give it to me, or you're going to meet the other side of your *other* son. Ivan is known for his craftsmanship with a knife. I'll have him carve you like a roasted duck if you don't do everything that I say when I say it."

"Money." Smirnov smiled. "You are just like me."

"Does that scare you?" Dmitry asked.

"No. It makes me proud, actually. If I had been taken over by Khalid, then I would be devastated, but in the *Smirnov way*, you are simply taking over the change of the guard. I'll give you what you want, because in your own way and as much as it kills you, you're giving me what I want."

"And what is that?"

"A legacy." Smirnov laughed. "Word will get around that my son has taken over. You look just like me; you think like me. It will only make me more notorious."

"And what makes you think that word will get around?" Dmitry asked.

"Look in the mirror. You can't hide it."

The thought infuriated Dmitry. Rolling his eyes, he looked out the window as they pulled towards the gate of a large chateau lit up in the distance.

"You make a noise, and I'll shoot you in the neck," Dmitry said to Smirnov. "It's one of the most painful ways to go."

"I know that," Smirnov answered, frustrated that the boy was talking to him like an idiot. He sat back in his seat quietly.

Dmitry rolled down his window before the guard could walk out and raised his gun.

The guard stepped out of his shack and flipped on his flashlight. Walking up to the Land Rover with his dog, he took one look at Khalid and stepped back.

"Hello, sir," he said robotically. "I'm sorry. I didn't recognize you at first." He looked in the back of the truck quickly and saw a strange man bearing close resemblance to boss Smirnov and knew that it must be his son. He nodded quickly and stepped back to hit the button to open the gate.

As he did so, Dmitry opened the door and pointed the gun. Two shots and the man was in a pool of his own blood, half in the shack and half out of it.

Smirnov saw a glimmer of an opportunity to wrestle the gun out of Dmitry's hand but remembered Khalid was already turned towards him with the gun pointed.

"Don't try anything," Khalid said with a sinister glare on his face.

"I bet you're enjoying every minute of this, aren't you?" Smirnov said, sitting back.

"Like you wouldn't believe," Khalid answered.

Dmitry jumped out of the truck and went to the shack. Picking the man up, he threw him over his shoulder, took his gun. The dog didn't bark or move, obviously aware that Dmitry was not afraid of him.

"I don't like shooting dogs. So be good for me," Dmitry said, turning his back to the animal.

Khalid popped the trunk and Dmitry threw the dead body in the back. Within seconds, they were headed quietly down the mile-long drive to the house.

"Nice place," Dmitry said, wiping the blood off his hands.

"Thank you. I bought it a few years ago," Smirnov said, unmoved by the gun down he had just witnessed.

"The deed for it is locked in the safe," Khalid informed Dmitry.

"Good," Dmitry said with a grin. "Then I'll have an excellent summer home for the holidays."

Smirnov cut his eyes at Dmitry. "Only a gutter rat would come here in the summer. This place is designed for the beauty of the snow."

"I'll make a note of that," Dmitry chuckled. "How many men are normally here when he's away?"

"Five," Khalid answered.

"Why didn't he stay out here instead of at the hotel?" Dmitry looked over at his father for an explanation but he didn't receive one.

"He owns the hotel," Khalid answered again. "And there are no silent partners. He owns it all himself."

"Can you get your hands on that deed, too?" Dmitry asked Khalid.

"Of course, I can. I can get you every deed that he owns."

"Good," Dmitry said with the same smug grin that Smirnov had given him earlier that evening. "Looks like you and I have some work to do."

***

Raging yellow flames and plumes of gray smoke billowed up into the night sky hiding the beautiful, tranquil scene of brilliant stars as the limestone plant burned to the ground. The crackle of wood and cement crashing to the ground interrupted what was once a peaceful night. And in the distance, a few kilometers south, the sound of a fire trucks could be heard blaring their sirens as they made their way to the call from locals who had seen the sight from their homes near the city. There was no doubt this was their cue to depart.

Covered in blood and smelling like burning chemicals, Ivan and his team loaded up in their cars and headed out onto the dark road about a half hour after Dmitry left with Khalid and Smirnov. As instructed the deed had been done and no evidence left. Ivan had personally seen to the execution of the other scientists, a task that he had not assigned to anyone else. He wasn't sure what these people had to do with his brother or his father, but he knew that if Dmitry taken the time to kill one, then it was not a waste of his time to do the others.

When everyone else loaded into a rusty van they had used to transport their weaponry out to the factory, Arie instead had followed Ivan into his red Lamborghini. She jumped in the passenger seat and gave an excited yelp of achievement before he demonstrated a perfect donut on the dusty road and sped off. At that moment, they were the perfect Bonnie and Clyde team, fueled by violence and aching to release through sexual pleasure.

Even amidst a massacre, however, Ivan could feel the disapproval of Dorian and the relationship he had with Arie. There was a power struggle between the men concerning who actually owned her. Dorian felt as her brother and protector, he had final say of all of her actions, regardless of how futile his opinion was. And Ivan felt that because he was sleeping with her, regardless of that fact that there were many other women, that he had the final say.

But in fact, it was Arie who had managed total control. She willingly played the two against each other in order to keep herself protected from both. Dorian was still caught up in their old ways developed from long centuries of religion passed down to them from their family. Ivan was infatuated with her sexual prowess and her detachment from society's idea of a relationship.

During the last few weeks that they had been together, she had taken part in several three-way sexual adventures with Ivan where she was not always the star, but had a leading role. She enjoyed the spontaneity of dating a sociopath and the relaxation that came with having a partner with no conscience. It was refreshing to her not to be the only monster in the room, and their common link was their overbearing siblings, which gave them plenty of things to talk about after their sexual conquests.

There was also the idea that for the first time in her life, through Ivan, she was able to enjoy a freedom that had once been a mere dream.

With the money that Dmitry was funneling into her brother's operation and the attention that Ivan continued to lavish her with, she had gone from sleeping in a van during cold winter months to sharing a guest house on a manor and being served by maids and butlers.

Even as she looked at him now, driving wildly through the countryside, she felt a surge of heat in between her thighs. Reaching over, she ran her small hand over his large bulge and licked her lips.

"I want you in my mouth right now," she said with a devilish grin. Her eyes pleaded with his mind, knowing that it was somewhere dark at the moment. She willed him to forget his woes and give her his attention.

Ivan quickly responded. With a cigarette in his mouth, he squinted his smoke-filled eyes as he held on to the steering wheel with one hand and unbuckled his pants with the other. Pulling out a firm, thick, erect penis and massaging it with long strokes with his right hand, he guided her head down.

"You never have to ask me twice," he said, feeling her warm mouth take the tip of him inside of her fleshy orifice. He wanted to close his eyes and enjoy the ride but he had to keep control of his vehicle as it raced down the road at nearly eighty miles an hour.

Still, he needed what she was offering at the moment. The high tempo attack on Smirnov's place had nearly unnerved him and not because of the killing. It was his father that had done it. Laying eyes on him for the first time, seeing how much he looked like his brother, hearing his voice and being in his presence was the most surreal experience that he had ever had.

The slurp of Arie's mouth pulled him out of his thought for a moment. "Focus on me," she demanded as her small hand surrounded his manhood.

He glanced down at her bobbing head and pushed his hips forward.

"Suck it harder," he growled. "Suck it until I come." Taking the cigarette out of his mouth to ash it out of the window, he pushed his foot down harder on the accelerator and looked out his rearview mirror.

Dorian was barely keeping up, but he was sure from his elevated position, he could see what his sister was doing at the moment. Giving him head.

Ivan bit his lip and laughed. "Watch your teeth," he groaned.

"Don't tell me how to give head," she said, raising her head.

Ivan caught her before she could get up and pushed her back down. "Take it all," he said, breathing hard. "And swallow every drop."

No matter how tasteless he chose to talk to Arie, deep inside his cold heart he was grateful for her actions. Only Arie knew how to hold his attention. Only she knew how to talk to him. Only she knew when he was troubled, even more so than his own blood. Arie paid attention to him, understood him and even nurtured him in her own sick way.

Like right now, she got that after killing someone, the only thing he wanted to do was fuck someone else. He didn't have to explain it to her, she just knew. But it was also strange to him, how he never tired of her or her simple body. While she was very attractive and her athletic build very stimulating, there was something else holding him captive.

Her mind controlled his libido. Her thoughts assailed him every time she spoke about her dreams and her desires, because they were very much like his own. And other people, if they were privy to their conversations, would be outright repulsed.

She was the only woman who could do it for him more than once. And whether he admitted it or not, he had feelings for her. In fact, she was the only woman that he'd actually kill for.

The new emotion was alien to him, but he was slowly coming to grips with it.

Easing his foot off the break, he could feel another familiar feeling approaching. The apex of her circular suction on his rock hard cock was approaching fast. Moving his hips around, he let his hand run down her short back and slip into the back of her pants. He slipped one long, cold digit in between her legs and dipped into her hot womb.

She was soaking wet.

As she squeezed her womb tight around his fingers, he came. And obediently, she sucked him dry.

"Umm, thank you," he moaned as she sat back up.

Wiping her mouth, she rested her head back on the seat. "You're welcome," she said as if the entire thing had been nothing at all. To her, it had not been.

But as soon as his orgasmic experience had ended, his father was right back in his head. Ivan pushed his foot down on the accelerator and moved faster. He had to get to the chateau and kill this man to get him out of his mind for good before the old bastard drove him crazy.

***

Smirnov was amazed at how much he and his son were actually alike. Besides their physical appearance, they also shared the innate ability to unleash unbridled brutality with remarkable precision. It had only taken Dmitry ten minutes to fully compromise Smirnov's entire team, and secure the chateau. And he did it alone with such stealth-like, quiet movements until one would have sworn that more than just one man had done it all.

When Dmitry was finished, he met Khalid in his father's study. Walking into the door, he cleaned the large serrated-edged, knife with the end of his jacket and looked over at his father. "You're next," he said menacingly.

"Well, get it over with then," Smirnov said, raising his brow. "I'm tired of the theatrics. In my day, it was always thought to be rude to toy with your food."

Inwardly Dmitry agreed that this was dragging on, but he didn't want to admit that there was something so intriguing about the man until he did not want to particularly kill him quickly. Plus, there were many things to sign over.

Khalid was already working hard on the computer, typing in account numbers, transferring money, and printing documents.

Smirnov sat tied and bound to a chair looking away from Khalid at the door. He still didn't appear too shaken, even as his empire fell around him. However, he did seem to be curious.

"Most of the major accounts been drained," Khalid informed Dmitry without looking up from the computer.

"And how are you not sure that he's draining all of my accounts into his own?" Smirnov asked Dmitry. "Do you already trust him so much? Are you that naïve?"

Dmitry closed the door behind him and locked it. "He can take what he wants. A man deserves something for his allegiance. Nothing comes for free. Besides, you and I both know that you have plenty to go around."

"To the victor goes the spoils," Smirnov taunted. "As I said before, you are very much like me."

"I am nothing like you," Dmitry challenged.

"We'll need his signatures for the deeds," Khalid said, stacking the papers that quickly printed from the printer. "I can have a friend notarize them and vouch for their legitimacy."

"How will you explain my sudden departure?" Smirnov asked.

"As elusive as you are to the general public and even to most governments, I doubt that they will even notice your absence *for a while*. That will give me ample time to figure out how to explain your passing." Dmitry had already thought of that and knew from experience that the easy part of any murder was the cover-up. The hard part was what was in front of him.

A knock at the door interrupted the conversation and Dmitry only slightly took his eyes off his father to find out who it was.

"*Da*," he said without opening the door.

"It's me," Ivan growled. "Let me in. I want to see the fucker."

Dmitry quickly opened the door and looked behind him. Arie and a few others had already posted up around the perimeter.

"Ivan the horrid," Smirnov said. "I'm willing to bet that you were my brother's son."

Ivan sucked his teeth. "And what led you to that conclusion?"

"You're the least of the two," Smirnov said with a chuckle as he looked between Ivan and Dmitry. "How could you be anything but...and with that dark hair, just like my dearly departed brother? It's definitely comical. It's like God spent all of his time creating myself and your brother and only spent a second on you and your father. Pity. We got the looks and the brains and the money and the women...no doubt." He took a deep breath as he slowed his laugh. "God is funny some-times."

"I don't believe in God," Ivan confessed as if he had one up on his self-professed uncle.

"Well you're more idiotic than you look," Smirnov said, trying to cross his legs. He evidently had shortly forgotten that he was tied up. Giving up on the attempt, he sighed. "There is a God, a heaven for people unlike us and a hell for people just like us." He clenched his jaw. "Why do you think that I'm not bothering to fight you? My time is up. The contract is due. But don't worry. Infamy does not come cheap. It'll be time for you to pay before long."

Smirnov words shook Dmitry to the core, but Ivan was on the other hand was completely unmoved. Ivan snarled. "Hocus pocus from an old scared man. I liked you a lot more before you started spouting off all of that religious nonsense." He looked at his brother and shook his head. Why wasn't he surprised that his brother believed every word. "And you've scared this one shitless. You both are a couple of superstitious idiots."

"Well, Dmitry," Smirnov said, realizing he had tapped into the boy's head. "Do you believe that I'm lying, or do you know what I'm saying to be true? Is this how you will start your contract off...slaughtering your father, taking his riches and enjoying his life? Just remember that the time will come for your seed to do the same."

"The Vor doesn't allow for family. So, I won't bother making one whether on purpose or otherwise. I doubt I'll have to worry," Dmitry answered, unwilling to share that he knew about a boy in Moscow who could possibly share his blood. "And it doesn't matter what I believe...tonight, you die."

Smirnov raised his brow but did not say a word.

Things had suddenly become far too tense. And even bound to a chair, Smirnov seemed to have far too much control of the situation. Dmitry needed a breath of fresh air. Hitting his brother on the shoulder, he put his hand on the doorknob. "Watch him. If he does anything, shoot him in his knees."

"With pleasure," Ivan said, licking his lips.

***

Dmitry felt dizzy. He had started this thing feeling vindicated and knowing that the revenge that he had taken for his mother was the right thing to do. But now, hearing his father's words, regardless of the fact that they were only to spare his life, made it hard for him to carry the act out. However, if he didn't kill him and kill him soon, then all of their lives would be endanger. There was no other answer. He had to follow through.

He walked down the dark halls of the chateau, past the priceless artwork hanging on the walls and the antique vases and busts on the columns into the oblivion of his disheveled mind. He was breaking the code by killing his father. There would surely be men who wanted his head. But Khalid had said that the council was tired of him, sick of protecting him, angered by his growing antics. Then there was the NightStar project, reason enough for the man to be killed. And yet, the idea of killing his father was as grotesque as the thought of killing his brother. Perhaps he was just a gutter rat? Sure, he had always thought himself to be more than that, but what about his actions, they weren't noble in the least bit.

People had put him here because they knew what he was, even if he wanted to deny it...Catherine, Khalid... even his own mother had a part to play. But regardless of who had led him to this point, he was a man and the decision would ultimately be his.

And so would the consequences.

Feeling the pull of his obligations directing him back to his father's study, he stopped in his tracks and turned out of the darkness and began to walk towards the light. He hoped that was a sign. God in Heaven knew that he sure needed one at the moment.

***

Ivan was happy to have a moment with the old man by himself. He bent down, holding his hands on his knees and looked him in his eyes. "What are you thinking right now?" Ivan asked curiously.

"I'm thinking that you won't be around long enough to enjoy the empire that your brother is taking over. I'm thinking that's a waste."

Khalid stopped typing and looked over at Ivan with a warning look. "Better stop him from talking now. He's got a slippery tongue."

"Are you a snake?" Ivan taunted.

"No more than anyone else...I just call it like I see it. And you want to know what I see in you?"

"Da, I guess I do," Ivan answered.

"Enormous potential wasted on a brother that will never see you as his equal."

Ivan's eyes narrowed.

"Oh, so you've heard this before," Smirnov said with a smirk. "How many times have your gifts been underplayed because of your big brother? How many times have you been over looked?"

Ivan thought of Davyd and instantly became infuriated. "What do you know?"

"Much more than you think," Smirnov said with a devious glare. "What do I have to lose by telling you the truth? I'm about to die...remember?"

"I would stop him now," Khalid finally said.

"Hey, you...shut your mouth and type or...whatever," Ivan snapped at Khalid. He looked back at Smirnov. "Go on."

"He's taking everything, and I don't recall your name coming up once. He's even giving a little to..." Smirnov nodded Khalid's way, "to the little *suka* over there who stabbed me in the back. Imagine if one of your men did that. Would they be rewarded with billions?"

"Dmitry will give me mine. That I can guarantee," Ivan said enraged. He looked over at Khalid. "So, why did you kill my father?"

"Because dear boy, he was like you, an easy target, a push over... but unlike you, he wasn't smart enough to see it. You can still do something about it?"

"Like what?" Ivan asked. His eye twitched.

Smirnov shrugged his shoulders. "Well, I'm currently in the market for a new underboss." He smiled at Ivan. "No what I mean?" He looked at his bound hands.

Ivan sucked his teeth again.

Khalid slowly and undetected felt for his gun, velcroed under the desk.

"And what about my mother, what job would you have for her?" Ivan asked.

Khalid quickly let go of the gun as he realized where the conversation was going.

"As I said before..."

Ivan cut Smirnov off. "There is no more to say, old man. Make peace with your God."

The door opened again and Dmitry walked inside. He looked over at his brother and realized that a heated discussion had been taking place.

"Stop talking to him, *brat*. He's a snake," Dmitry said, closing the door.

"So, I've learned," Ivan said, feeling the sweat on his brow. *Snake or not, the man had gotten into his head.*

"You know," Khalid interrupted. "I have his signature down to a science. We don't need him anymore and we had better change venues before too long. There are a few in the city who still know that he's associated with that factory."

Dmitry nodded and looked at his father. "Well, you take the paperwork and go and stay with Dorian and his team. We'll finish up in here." He took a deep breath.

Ivan looked over at his brother and back at Smirnov with an uncomfortable look.

Dmitry could identify.

Neither wanted to be the one who ended this man's life.

Khalid grabbed the papers and walked toward the door.

"Aren't you going to bid an old friend goodbye, Khalid? Don't I at least deserve that?" Smirnov said sincerely.

Khalid turned on his heels and looked at Smirnov. With slumping shoulders, he nodded his head. "I hate that things had to end this way. But you have to know that this stems from your total destruction of everything in your path. I am sorry, brat. I wish you well on your journey."

"How long have we been friends?"

"Five decades."

"And how many times have we seen these things go full circle?" Smirnov asked.

"Always."

"So you know what's coming for you as well, *brat*?"

"When the time comes, I only hope to leave as gracefully as you will do...even if it is by my son's hand," Khalid said with a chill of finality. "God's speed." With that, he left the room quickly, closing the door behind him.

As soon as they were alone, Ivan pulled his gun from his holster, but Dmitry stopped him.

"What now?" Ivan asked exasperated.

"Step outside for a minute," Dmitry said to Ivan under his breath.

"I thought you weren't supposed to leave him unattended?" Ivan said with a huff.

"He can't go anywhere. Just step out here for a minute," Dmitry said, rolling his eyes.

"Fine," Ivan said, pushing Dmitry out of the way. He looked back at Smirnov. "Now would be time to do that praying you and I were talking about."

"I'll keep that in mind," Smirnov replied nonchalantly.

They walked quickly down into the darkness of the corridor away from the men and Arie to talk. As soon as they stopped, Ivan turned and pushed his brother and growled. "Why are we stalling?"

"I...I don't want you to take any part in what is about to happen."

"Why?"

"Because I don't know if he's your father or your uncle. And what if he is your father, Ivan. Then you've slaughtered him."

"Yeah, so?"

Dmitry sighed. "It's a bad omen."

"Please don't tell me that you're actually having second thoughts about killing him."

"What we are about to do will have long term effect that you might not understand, Ivan."

"Are you talking about that religious shit? Murder is murder. We've done it a hundred times."

"He's the father to one of us and we are brothers. It is much deeper."

"So you want to let him live?"

"No. I'm not stupid. I know that can't happen, but I don't want the blood on your hands."

Ivan wasn't sure if he really wanted to do it before but just the restriction by his brother was slowly changing his mind.

In earshot, Arie could hear everything. The Medlov men were having serious second thoughts. While they wanted their father dead, they were afraid to do it themselves. She knew that when it came down to it, it would be Dmitry who would pull the trigger, simply because of his overprotective nature over Ivan, but that would not benefit her at all.

She looked down the opposite corridor at her brother talking to Khalid and realized that this might be her only opportunity to get from under his stifling control. Feeling her side for her gun attached to her leg, she quietly slipped into his study where Smirnov was being held and closed the door behind her.

Smirnov looked up surprised.

"They sent a *suka* to do a man's job," he said disappointed.

Arie pulled her gun out and pulled back the lever. "This isn't about your sons. This is about my brother," she said, pulling back the trigger.

The silencer made the six bullets that she emptied into his body from his head down into the chest nearly inaudible. But the loud thump of a huge body falling to the ground caught everyone's attention.

The door opened and Dmitry and Ivan came barreling through first, then Dorian and Khalid. They all looked over at her in confusion.

"No one should have to kill their own father," Arie said in a matter of fact tone. She looked over at her brother. "Consider it a favor."

Dmitry looked down at his lifeless father and clenched his jaw. "Khalid...Dorian...leave me alone with your sister for a minute."

"She will be harshly punished for this," Dorian said, not taking his eyes off of Arie. "I promise you this, Dmitry. All I ask is that you do her no harm by your own hand. She is my sister. I should be the one to carry out her punishment."

"You will keep your fucking hands off of her," Ivan snarled.

Dmitry turned around and looked over at Dorian. "Leave us. Don't worry. I won't bring any harm to her."

Dorian bowed his head respectfully and left with Khalid. As the door closed, Dmitry walked over to his father and picked him up off the floor, re-erecting his chair and wiping the blood from his face with the napkin in his suit jacket.

"I've found that nothing comes free," Dmitry said, looking at his father's face. "What do you want for this *kindness*?"

Arie looked over at Ivan. "I want...I want my freedom. I want to run this team, because I know what's best and because it's my turn now."

Dmitry looked over at Ivan. "Is she ready?"

"She is," Ivan vouched. "No one else ran in here to take care of our problems. She stuck her head out and got it done, like she always does. I've seen her in action. She's ready, *brat*."

Dmitry nodded. "And who is going to tell Dorian that he's no longer in charge of his own team?"

"Leave it to me. They are my team," Ivan said, knowing that it would create a riff between he and his friend. Still, he loved Arie and her wants were far more important than Dorian's need to feel superior to his own blood.

"Any other requests," Dmitry asked.

"With your new acquisitions would it be too much to ask for more money?" she asked with her hand on her hip.

"That's reasonable," Dmitry answered softly. "Anything else?"

"No. I'm a very simple woman," she answered.

"Fine. Ivan, tell Dorian after we get this all taken care of that his sister is now in charge. And get her some cash to start. For now, just make sure that he keeps his hands off of her," Dmitry ordered. He looked at Arie one last time. "Thank you."

Arie nodded graciously and walked out of the room with Ivan.

Dmitry looked one last time at the bloody, lifeless corpse in front of him and looked at his watch. Out of respect, he stopped the dial and slipped the watch off his wrist and put it in his pocket. It would be the only reminder that tonight actually happened besides the new wealth he had acquired from his father.

It was ironic. He had married Catherine for her wealth, and she had married him for his body, contacts and the fact that she wanted the last laugh on his father. But the last laugh had not only brought Catherine revenge, it has also brought his mother her revenge, and he and his brother to the top of the Vor with billions of dollars at his fingertips.

And what had he done to acquire it? Everything no one else in the world would ever want to do. Maybe he was a gutter rat, but he was the most eager one to ever emerge from Mother Russia. And eventually, he just have to come to grips with that fact if he was ever going to survive the uphill battle that he was about to embark upon, starting with Elsa's father.

Chapter Ten

The sun was beginning to rise on the horizon by the time that Dmitry arrived back into the city of Prague. Stained in dried blood, he had changed into some of his father's clothes back at his chateau, showered in his father's bathroom and shaved with his father's gold-platted kit.

Now, he looked nothing like the man who had just slaughtered a team of unsuspecting bodyguards and scientists, had his father murdered by a psychotic teenage girl and taken over a thirty-year, billion dollar empire.

And ironically, his father's suits had fit perfectly. That had never happened before. For that matter, none of last night's events had ever happened before.

At seven feet tall and ripped with 3D muscle, Dmitry had never been able to borrow anyone's clothes outside of Ivan, and even his things ran short.

Dmitry bit his lipped. Borrowed was probably not the best word to use.

Taken.

He had taken his father's clothes, taken his life, and ultimately he had taken over Smirnov's vast empire. Taken was a word that deserved to be tattooed across Dmitry's forehead along with a few other choice words. But he had to get over that now. What was done was done. There was no turning back.

In just a few short hours, Khalid had arranged for him to sign over a hundred different forged documents signing over everything from the chateau to businesses to even the hotel that he presently pulled up in front of.

He rolled down the window and looked up at it again. For the first time, it seemed ornate...just like everything else he owned.

Stepping out, the glass doors automatically opened for him as he buttoned the top of his new suit jacket and proceeded inside the hotel, he looked around. People were busy bustling about. They all were clueless that he was now the owner of this fine establishment. A since of pride overwhelmed him unexpectedly. This place was his, just like Hutton, just like so many.

He smirked as he made his way to the front desk. The women behind the desk saw him approaching and quickly moved in front of their computers to help him.

Dmitry looked down at them, reacting as all women did to his deceiving face and gave a charming smile.

"Hello, ladies," he said in a deep sultry baritone.

"Hello, Mr. Medlov," they said in unison.

"I'll be taking over Smirnov's suite from now on," he said, knowing that they would be confused.

The two desk clerks looked at each other then back up at him for more of an explanation.

Dmitry pulled the deed to the hotel out of his jacket pocket and put it on the desk in front of them. They looked down at it confused.

"There's been a change in management, girls. Now, I'll need my key," he said, putting the deed away.

"Yes, sir," the smaller brunette said, clicking on her computer quickly. "Will you be keeping the same employees?" There was worry in her voice.

"Do you have a family to take care of?" Dmitry asked.

"A little girl," she answered.

Dmitry nodded. "Most things will be kept the same. You don't have to worry about your job."

The woman's shoulders eased of their tension. Pulling the keys from the top desk, she handed them to Dmitry. "I'm not sure if Mr. Smirnov's belongings are still up there. I'll have someone run and check."

"No need. Mr. Smirnov as you refer to him is my father. I purchased it from him. I'll have whatever he left taken out to the chateau," Dmitry answered.

The woman breathed through her nostrils and passed him the key. Her small hand rested in his.

"If there is anything that I can do for you, please let me know."

"Thank you," Dmitry said, reading between the lines. As he was about to turn around, he stopped. "As a matter of fact, there is something you can do for me. There is a very special woman coming this morning. Her name is Elsa. She's a six foot two black woman...looks like a supermodel. See her up to my suite as soon as she arrives. I don't want her to wait for one second."

"No sir, I won't make her wait."

"Great," Dmitry said, nodding. "You ladies have a great day."

He could feel them watching him as he walked away. He imagined that their questions multiplied with each step. But for every question anyone might have, he had an answer as long as he had Khalid. And his father was still at his fingertips, boxed up in a freezer in the cellar under his new chateau. And when the time came, he'd unthaw him and blow him to high hell on one of his planes, but for now, he needed his fingertips just in case they had other things that had to be validated. That had been Ivan's clever idea. The boy was evidently good for several things.

***

When Davyd got the call from Dmitry, he ran as quickly as he could up to the suite. Walking inside with his men, holding on to his gun, he called out for his boss, unsure if he was walking into a trap. Dmitry called out from the same room that he had met his father and sat in the same seat that his father had sat.

Davyd walked into the room quietly and looked down the steps at Dmitry in his suit, eyes focused, legs crossed and felt suddenly out of the loop.

"I take it that you got what you came for," Davyd said, putting away his gun.

"I did," Dmitry said, standing up. He walked over to Davyd and looked down at the man who had become something of a father to him.

"Did you kill him?" Davyd asked on baited breath.

Dmitry nodded but did not utter a word.

Davyd nodded back, clenching his jaw. He knew that the war was far from over, but he also knew that this had been a uncompromising success.

"You look worried," Dmitry said, hitting Davyd on the shoulder. "Did you doubt me, old friend?"

"In the last few hours, I have doubted everything and everyone, including myself," Davyd answered sincerely.

Dmitry turned and offered Davyd a seat. "We've gotten off on the wrong foot this morning, already. Look, I don't want you to worry, Davyd. We are friends...brothers even. I called you up here to have breakfast with me. After such a long night, I'm afraid that I don't want to eat alone. I'll fill you in on everything that you missed."

"I should have been there," Davyd lamented gruffly. Taking a seat at the chair nearest the window overlooking the city, he pushed himself up to the table.

Dmitry sat down across from him and waved at his bodyguard. "Have the butler come in now. We're ready for breakfast. Have you eaten?" he asked Davyd.

"No," Davyd nodded. "Not a bite."

"I didn't mean to worry you, but you understand that I couldn't just call."

"I understand." Davyd calmed himself with each slowed breath. He was not a young man anymore and could feel it in the strain in his chest. Looking around the elegant dayroom, it suddenly hit him. Dmitry was now Czar. Such a young man was now the most power-ful mob boss in the entire eastern hemisphere and the world did not yet even know.

Dmitry pulled off his jacket and placed it behind his chair. Placing his large elbows on the table, he let out a deep breath before he smiled. "It's done, Davyd. We own everything."

"You own everything," Davyd corrected. "I didn't do all of this." He looked around the room again. It was starting to sink in slowly. "You've pulled yourself from the depths of obscurity to underground royalty to riches beyond my imagination."

"I have you to thank for it," Dmitry said humbly.

As the butler came in, dressed in a simple black suit, he bowed and then popped up into his an erect, almost rigid stance. "Good morning, sirs. What may I order up for breakfast today?" he said with a British accent.

"Eggs, bacon, steak, orange juice, fruit and..." Dmitry looked at Davyd. "Vodka."

Davyd smiled. "Especially vodka."

For the next hour among a table full of food and drinks, the men sat near the sunlight recounting the previous night's events. Dmitry did not miss one detail. Forgetting his elevated position, he reverted back to the boy that Davyd had known before he'd ever laid eyes on the Hutton family and with the enthusiasm of a young child, he told his story.

Davyd listened on amazed at what he had missed, regretful that he had been ordered to stay. Only, he knew that this was something that his boss had to do alone. He had faced his deepest, darkest dread with his brother at his side. As he watched Dmitry talk, he wondered if finally Ivan's lust for power had been sated, wondered if he finally felt a part of the family that he had helped built. He wanted desperately to even as Dmitry but was afraid to drown his uncharacteristic happiness with the cold reality that he had in his camp, his greatest obstacle still.

When they were done, Dmitry stood and hugged him tightly, thanking him again for his support and promising that this new unchartered journey would benefit them all.

"Go to my suite. It's yours now. Get some rest and then head back to London. We have loads to do. When I get back from Angola, I'll meet you at the castle," Dmitry said, patting Davyd on the back as they walked down the marble hallway to the golden elevators with the bodyguards in front of them and behind them.

"Don't you think I should go with you?"

"No, I'll take a few men, but I need eyes and ears in London. I need someone I can trust to tell me what's really being said and done while I'm gone. I can't be at two places at one time. I'll need you to watch my back, run the men," Dmitry said, wiping his tired, red eyes. He yawned. "I'll get a few hours of rest and then head out once Elsa gets here."

"Can you trust her?" Davyd asked directly.

Dmitry shrugged his shoulders. "Time will tell. For now, she seems very useful."

"Just do me a favor, boy?" Davyd asked as he hit the button on the elevator to go down.

"Anything."

"Don't start thinking with your cock. You're not like most young men, and I know that. But I just don't want to see you deceived."

"You don't have to worry about that," Dmitry said with a chuckle.

As he assured Davyd the doors to the elevator opened and there stood Elsa. In a simple gray wool dress that stopped right above her knees and in red stilettos that made her even taller than Davyd, she clutched an arm full of papers. Her long black hair was pulled into a bun and her face was flawlessly colored with deep, red lips and bright brown eyes. Chanel perfume wafted up to their noses, tickling their senses as only a woman could.

Dmitry was awestruck. Pure, illogical lust imploded in his body.

Davyd's point was made. With a quiet nod, he stepped past Elsa on to the elevator and nodded at Dmitry. "Remember what I said, *brat*," he said as the doors closed.

Elsa heart skipped at beat at the sight of Dmitry. He stood like a king in the hallway, dressed like a lord in the early morn, his golden hair and blue eyes sparkled in the sunlight. Biting her lip, she smiled at him.

Dmitry stepped forward without a word and bent to her lips.

She lifted her chin and received a single, sweet kiss. His tongue brushing lightly on her own, tasting of orange juice and mint.

"It's good to see you," she whispered, clutching her papers tighter.

Dmitry growled, sweeping her body with one devastating look. "But I haven't seen you yet," he said, wrapping his arm around her thin shoulders.

They walked quietly back down the hallway. The clink of her heels on the floor echoed around them.

Dmitry's bodyguards quietly moved to the side, knowing that Elsa would not have the same greeting as Davyd.

The strain of exhaustion quickly left Dmitry. With a guided hand, he led her to the master bedroom.

"You have a very nice suite," she noted.

"I recently acquired the hotel," Dmitry confessed.

"More acquisitions?" she said with a raised brow.

"It's a long story. How is everything at Hutton? I trust all is running smoothly."

"As smoothly as it can be," she answered with a huff. "Scotland Yard called again this morning with more questions. We submitted a statement about the plane accident, but you really should consider attending the funerals of your board members."

Dmitry ignored her advice. "I'll think about it," he said under his breath.

Opening the door to the bedroom, he stepped aside and let her examine the room.

She stepped inside and looked around. It was an enormous room adorned with dark drapes, a king-sized bed and a large oak desk. She placed her papers the desk and turned to him.

He looked back at his bodyguards who took their posts at the bedroom door, quietly aware of what was about to happen. Closing the door behind him, he leaned against it and watched her.

"And so here we are," she said in a playful voice.

"Finally." Dmitry walked over to her and placed his hands on her shoulders. Looking down at her, he pushed closer to her body until they were nearly one.

His heat felt like the sun radiating down on her body. She relished in it...missed it. "Dmitry," she said, feeling herself lose all composure.

"Hmm," he answered as he unzipped her wool dress. His cold hands touched her bare skin and sent a zinger up her spine.

Nervousness made her voice tremble. "I think that I'm falling in love with you." She looked up at him for approval. Her brown eyes sparkled with innocence and despair.

Dmitry pulled the dress from her shoulders and pushed it down past her wide hips until it pooled around her heels. He clenched his square jaw tight as he looked at her, holding back words that he knew might hurt her. She shielded her eyes when he did not respond to hide her disappointment, but Dmitry quickly pulled her chin up.

His own confession was looming. "I do not think that I'm capable of love, but I..." he frowned. "I can show you tremendous favor, Elsa."

Favor?

Elsa was sure that of all the responses in the entire world *that* response had been a first. She was confused about what to say. A sensible woman would have told him to go and fuck himself before she stormed out, but she was not a sensible woman. Thinking about Vladimir only confirmed that fact.

Swallowing hard, she shook her head. "I've always moved to fast," she explained, thinking of her last bad relationship – one that had ended in her being traded off like livestock. It was amazing that she had any self-esteem left between her father and the men who had sworn to love her. Life was strange that way, always full of winding roads and deep valleys. It was just sad that she had to learn that through the people that she had chosen to trust the most.

"Don't beat yourself up about it," Dmitry said, unsnapping her bra. "I married a woman, because she promised to teach me good manners," he joked.

Elsa couldn't help but laugh. It dramatically changed the mood. She liked that he was candid and always as hard on himself as she was on herself. It made them a perfect pair.

Pulling the black undergarment from her chocolate skin, he watched her nipples pebble before him. His mouth watered. Her form was perfect and the deep, dark color of her areoles.

Trailing his finger down her collar bone down to her breasts, he massaged the inviting globes slowly, watching her fall under his spell. "I need you, Elsa. That might not be love, but it's the closest thing that I can offer to it." His deep voice rumbled near her throat as he growled a kiss to her neck.

Instinctively, she closed her eyes and felt goose bumps form. Like an avalanche they ran down from the peaks of her breasts down to her ankles. Breathing deeply, she raked her nails over his back as he kissed her skin.

"I'll take it. Your favor," she said in a strange English accent as he picked her up. She loved the way he cradled her, like a baby. She had never felt so safe in a man's arms before. And she doubted that she would ever feel this safe again.

Carrying her to the bed, Dmitry laid her down in the middle of the bed and pulled her lace panties from her body. Parting her legs with eager hands, he slipped a finger in between her steamy thighs and into the wetness of her womanhood. He wiggled it around, making her come alive and shed her protective wall, invisibly keeping her from responding to his every will.

Dmitry knew that sex with a real woman was never about the act, but about the underlying promises made before, during and after. She needed to know that there was always more between them than just making love. That was why it was so hard to be with a real woman.

Arching her back, she looked up at him, watching his every move. In her mind, she wondered what it would take to turn the lust she saw in his dreamy eyes into love. She wondered if he knew that she would do anything to have that transformation in him.

Dmitry, however, was on another wave length. The anger that he had felt for his father, the rage that he had unleashed on all those people had quickly dissolved into a raging need that only she could satisfy. He truly did need her right now. He needed her to put out the fire, to sate the dragon lurking deep down in his soul.

Pulling off his shirt and tie, finally his undershirt and pants, he stood in front of her naked, ripped with muscles, breathing hard, and colored in tattoos that served as testimony to elevated position in the Vor. Just the sight of him was overwhelming. Dmitry Medlov was force to be reckoned with.

One strong hand stroked his eager penis and the other reached out for her.

She responded by reaching out her hand to him. As soon as she did, he grabbed her and pulled her to the end of the large bed. The friction heated her back as she slid down the gold satin down comforter to his prison-like embrace.

Glancing down at the dark curly hair trimmed against her panty line, he kneeled on his knees before her like he was feasting on a meal. His hands rested on her inner thighs. Only inches away, she felt his warm breath hissing on her skin.

"Favor," he said seductively before pummeling mercilessly into her.

Grabbing his blonde locks, she coiled her long legs around him as he tasted her. His kiss was so deep until she could feel his skillful tongue slithering deep inside her.

"Yes," she gasped. "Yes." Her voice sounded like a caged bird finally being set free.

Dmitry's hands clenched her thighs, holding her down to the bed in position. Sucking her body and lapping up the scent of arousal, he felt her sex clench tight.

"Dmitry," she moaned. Her eyes averted to the top of the canopy. "I love you," she confessed again in a near whisper. Tears ran down the sides of her cheeks, burning her beautiful brown eyes. And although she could not contain them, she hoped desperately that he would not see them.

He did, however, only he chose to ignore them.

How Dmitry wished the words would fill the emptiness that hollowed him from the inside out. How he wished that she could take away his pain. But he knew that while he enjoyed the feel of her, he was void of what she needed. A man incomplete could never provide any absolution for a woman - only pain. And one thing he was certain of is that he was overflowing with pain. It burdened him even now, flanked over him like large, black crow. Death was on his scent and he knew death was in his future.

Flashes of his father's pale, dead face entered his racing mind as he licked her. He tried to push it away, but the enclosure of her legs suddenly felt suffocating like the box his father was currently housed in. He emerged with a deep breath, head up, eyes closed.

Elsa felt his surge of emotion. She looked up at him just in time to see his eyes open and pain flash in them. It was then that she knew that in her own thoughts, she hadn't taken time to notice. Something bad had happened over the last day ... something tragic even.

Standing up, Dmitry reached for her narrow hips and in one sweeping motion, rolled her over in the bed on to her belly. Her long legs adjusted to sink her knees into the mattress. She felt him pull her shoes off and heard them as they hit the floor beside them, followed by her silk stockings. Then there was a long pause.

Looking back at him, she saw Dmitry slip a condom on to his long shaft. He focused attentively on the latex, rolling it over his exposed flesh with care. Looking up at her, he winked.

"This will only take a minute," he said in a deep, Russian accent that sent chills down her spine.

"Hurry," she said eager to feel him.

Nearly a foot away from her, he stealthily moved forward, planting one tattooed knee up on the bed. And then, she felt a familiar stab. Flesh entering flesh. A warmness sucked into her body, invading her sanity.

"Ahh," she cried out, eyes focusing back on the ornate oak headboard.

His hands found their way to her hips as he guided himself in and out slowly, never fully entering until she was perfectly ready.

Tight and starting to sweat, she reached a hand back to put on his. A pain stretched through her from her toes to her neck.

"Are you ready?" he asked calmly.

"Yes," she panted, nodding at the same time that she fought to breathe.

He stroked her slowly. "Are you sure?" he stroked her again. His voice was deeper. His eyes never left the single bead of sweat that had fallen from his face onto the small of her slim back.

"Please," she begged, gripping the covers. Her red nails snagged the fabric. "Make love to me." Just then, her long black hair fanned over her shoulder.

There was something feminine and beautiful about her feline movements. He found her completely different from Catherine. She was more agile, more generous, more enjoyable, and if possible more beautiful.

Dmitry slowed to a stop. Pausing as he watched her move her hips around, he ran his hand down her back. "You're so beautiful, Elsa." He said it as if it was the first time that he had noticed.

The small acknowledgment only turned her on more. "Do it," she growled. "Give me *all* of you."

He wanted to do just that. In fact, he had thought about making love to her every single night since he had been away from her. Still he had to remember not to indulge too much in her treasures, less he fall into an abyss of emotional confusion the way many men of power had done before him. And the result had always been the same.

Despair.

Deceit.

Destruction.

No.

He could not afford such a tragedy and neither could she. Yet, he longed to know what love felt like, what even she must have been feeling at that very moment.

The least that he could do was give her pleasure beyond her wildest dreams, the favor of an exciting life and finally the choice to move on when she found someone who could provide her with what he surely could not. A man in his position was required to do at least that for a woman who had given so much and asked nothing in return.

Moving back into the present reality, he finally did as she begged, he felt her buck her firm backside against his shaft and arch her back. Pulling away from her slick womb, he held her tiny hips up and thrust into her ripe body until she exploded. The connection was unmistakable.

Dmitry's head flung back as he invaded her. She swallowed him greedily, moving against his force with immense power of her own. He gave to her as much as he knew that she could take, each pump into her body making her voice raise an octave. He could see that he was paralyzing her, still she begged for more.

Bending down to make sure that his chest lay on her back, he kissed the side of her neck. She purred like a cat when she felt his lips on her clavicle.

Moving inside of her was like a dream. He floated somewhere between reality and bliss. The delicious feeling of her flower opening up and blooming around him made him forget the festering images quietly hunting him.

In a beautiful synchronic dance, she moved with him, holding him close, riding him hard, bearing down on his body and closing in on his evanescent thoughts.

They fought against each other quietly until he finally needed to see her face. Pulling her off of him like a sheath, he turned her to her side and held her long legs like scissors. In between them, he pushed into her body slowly, exacting his thrust until he felt her body began to clench tighter.

Her weak pants became long moans and then finally screams of ecstasy. Gripping her tightly, he moved quicker inside her body, pushing harder through the layers of her wet, velvety skin. Her heavy breasts swayed in the air, begging to be kissed. He met her rigid nipples with his mouth and sucked her wildly, lapping at her skin like a starving dog.

"I love you, Dmitry," she said again, this time with more passion.

He drowned out her words and pumped her harder. Picking her up off the bed in his arms, he pulled her hips on his lap and laid her back on the bed.

Sweat transferred between their locked bodies as he moved her up and down on him. Needing to adjust, she pulled herself into his embrace, wrapping her legs around his hips and sitting fully on his lap. He held her up without effort with one hand on her back and the other on her face. He made her watch him as he kissed her and pumped into her, harder and harder.

The sound of skin slapping skin and moans drifted into the hallway where the bodyguards quietly listened.

She screamed aloud, bound by his large hands.

Then suddenly even though she tried to fight it, she imploded. Her body vibrated from the inside out, tightening around the base of his shaft.

Dmitry watched her face strain with a thousand expressions as she arrived at her climax and finally he felt her body relax. It was then that he finished, slowly, while she watched. He kept his beautiful, blue eyes on her. His growl was virile and masculine. Veins protruded from his neck and the line down his forehead. She felt his hands grip her, and the muscles in his chest constrict.

Pushing her hips down as hard as she could against the latex, she felt the surge of hot seed pulsing out of his body into hers only protected by the covering. It was strange, but she wished it was not there at the moment.

Breathing hard and fast into each others mouths, they kissed as they collapsed onto the bed. With a smile on her face, she raked her hands through his blonde tendrils and felt him bite her bottom lip.

"*Spasiba*," he said, wiping his brow.

"You're welcome," she answered in a cracked voice.

Exhausted, he moved her over under his arm and laid his head back on the pillow. Looking up at the ceiling, he felt his body finally start to relax and much-needed sleep begin to set in.

"I haven't slept since night before last," he said in realization. "I think I need to take a nap." Rubbing his hand over his chest, he looked over at her and smiled.

"Sleep then, my love," she whispered, touching his face.

Her voice soothed him. Closing his eyes, he cocked a long, hairy leg up and slipped his arm behind her so that she could sleep under him. Snuggling under him and sucking up the heat of his body, she closed her own eyes, happy to finally be joined with him.

Dmitry was surprised how at peace he felt, and how much of an effect she had on him.

Her words entered back into his mind. "I love you."

He knew that she did love him. Only, he knew what a serious problem that would be for her later. Still, he truly appreciated her honesty. And he could see how it would be easy to love him. He had saved her, but she had saved him too. There was no way he could have handled the acquisition of Hutton Industries alone. But she had done it and with a certain amount of ease that only a true businesswoman could have pulled off. It spoke to her intelligence and her education at the finest school of the land. After this, he just might make a serious contribution to Oxford.

Opening his eyes, he put a careful hand on her exposed, brown shoulder and rubbed her silky skin.

"I know that I'm not what you deserve, Elsa, but I want you to know that I *appreciate* you." His deep voice was sincere.

Elsa looked up at him under heavy dark lashes and smiled. "I love you just the way you are, Dmitry. And I know that you appreciate me. That's why I work so hard."

Dmitry raised his brow. "I'll make it worth your while. I don't exactly know how yet, but my word is my bond."

"I know," she said, pushing her body closer to him to smell the musk of sandalwood coming from his skin.

"Now, get some rest. When we wake up, we head to Angola."

Elsa smiled. "My home country is a mess right now, but I'm so happy to be going back. I haven't set foot in the country in over three years." Her eyes lit up at the thought of seeing her mother again. "It's beautiful there. The coast is like a dream, more beautiful than any island."

Dmitry smirked. "If I like it enough, I just might buy it."

Elsa laughed at his humor. It was good to see him coming back into himself. "I wish you could. It might be better off." She refused to speak more about politics and her war-torn country. This moment needn't be spoiled by all of that. "Good night," she said happily.

"Hmm," Dmitry responded.

With that, they drifted off as the sunlight from the windows kissed their skin. Naked and wrapped in a warm embrace, they slept peacefully.

***

As Ivan's team packed up and prepared to head back to London, he stood outside in the sunlight facing towards the mountains, looking at the beautiful landscapes and plotting. A cigarette burned at the end of his lips, and occasionally, he took a drag, but his mind had him enslaved.

Last night, he had seen a side of his brother that he thought had long died. The warrior that he once looked up to had re-emerged, and it had made him proud, so proud until he wondered if his previous plans of toppling his brother's empire once he acquired almost seemed foolish.

If word of Dmitry's newest defeat reached the streets, then he would be unstoppable. Not many would have the balls to face the Medlov family, and not many would stand against him.

He knew how these things worked. Smirnov was an unmovable force who had put fear into so many until people barely spoke his name. Now, his brother was Czar. Such a thing could prove to be very valuable to a man like Ivan.

Dmitry had already promised him his father's clubs in Prague and London. Khalid had already given him the deeds. He had them now in his coat pocket ready to throw down on the desks of those who would bow before him once he arrived back. Plus, his brother had transferred a hefty bounty to him right before they left his father's house.

Ivan wondered now what need there might be in fighting his brother. Still, there was another little voice in the back of his head. Smirnov's voice to be exact.

The old man had warned him just like Emma had that in the grand scheme of things, he would be pushed out by his big brother...made of fool of by him. While he didn't want to believe it, he had to pay attention to the signs.

Would more power change his brother even more? Would more money tear apart their familial bond?

"If it does, I'll kill him myself," Ivan said aloud as he heard the cold ground behind him crunch under the foot of an intruder.

He turned quickly to find Arie spying on him.

The wind ripped through her hair and iced her pale face. Red lips smiled deviously at him as she stuck her small hands in the pockets of her leather coat and made her way from the back of the barn towards him.

"You're up," Ivan said, turning back around.

She joined him, popped a cigarette in her mouth and lit it quickly. "I couldn't sleep without you."

He looked down at the crown of her head, at the jet black strands of her hair and felt a sense of possession over her.

"I didn't want to wake you," he said almost lovingly.

"What are you out here thinking about?" she asked quickly.

"Everything."

"Well, I've been thinking about one thing and one thing only."

"I fucked you all night. You should barely be able to walk," Ivan said, spitting into the fresh snow beside him.

"Not that," she answered, sucking her teeth. "Your brother's promise. I want to tell Dorian now." She looked up at Ivan for approval.

Ivan raised his brow. "Dmitry said to wait until we arrive back in London for *obvious reasons*. We don't want a fucking war on our hands with our own men in Prague."

Arie was not happy. She rolled her eyes and sneered. "Isn't this your team? Dmitry isn't even going back with us. How will he know if we do this now or later?"

"By the gun shots," Ivan answered. "It's not a good idea."

"So now that your brother is Czar, you've become his lackey, incapable of thinking on your own?"

Enraged, Ivan turned and slapped her down into the snow. She fell without grace, hitting her butt on the ground. She quickly got up and brushed herself off. Sucking the blood from her lip, she snapped. "Fuck you!"

"Don't fucking push me," Ivan said, pointing his finger. He looked away from her with a huff. *Fucking women*. "This is my team, and you still answer to me. And I say that you wait. It's not about Dmitry."

"I doubt *that* very seriously," she said, stepping away from him. She thumped the cigarette into the snow and looked up at him. "I deserve this and you know it."

Ivan was unmoved.

"Everyone got something out of this. Dorian got over a hundred thousand dollars and so did the others. All I got was my freedom and I want it now," she pouted.

It was too early in the morning for a squabble. He scratched his eyes and bit his lip. "Fine. Go in there, look your brother in the face and tell him that you struck a deal behind his back to lead his team and put him in bitch status and see what happens. He'll put a hole in your chest with one of those mini guns, and I won't half fucking blame him. Quit being a cunt and just wait!"

With that, he turned away from her and walked towards the trees. He needed to think, and he didn't need her crowding his mind with her own family bullshit. She had put up with him for nearly eighteen years; she could handle being at Dorian's beckoned called for a few more days.

"Where are you going?" she called out as he walked away.

"To mind my own fucking business...now fuck off," he said, shaking his head. "Stupid bitch."

Arie watched him disappear into the trees and leave her in the clearing alone. Enraged, she turned and looked at the barn.

"I won't wait one more fucking minute," she said aloud as she walked back towards the barn. Pulling out the gun inside her jacket, she did a brass check, flipped the safety off and headed inside.

To be continued....

The Chronicles of Young Dmitry Medlov: Book Two (Volumes 5-8) Coming 2012

Trivi's Charities of Choice

There are so many worthy charities that need your help. Please consider making a contribution to the following charities to help military men and women and their families in their time of need.

Semper Fi Fund
http://semperfifund.org/
Wounded Warrior Center • Bldg H49 •
Camp Pendleton, CA 92055
Phone: 760-207-0887
or 760-725-3680
Fax: 760-725-3685

Soldier's Angels
http://www.soldiersangels.org/
1792 E Washington Blvd
Pasadena, CA 91104

Wounded Warrior Project
http://www.woundedwarriorproject.org/
4899 Belfort Road, Suite 300
Jacksonville FL, 32256
Telephone: 877.832.6997
Fax: 904.296.7347

Whether time or money, consider giving back to the people who have already given so much.

STAY IN TOUCH

Official Author Website
www.latrivianelson.info

Email Latrivia Today
Latrivia@LatriviaNelson.com

Follow Latrivia on Twitter
www.twitter.com/Latrivia

Blog With Other Lonely Heart Fans
www.thelonelyheartseries.wordpress.com

"Like" The Lonely Heart Series
www.facebook.com/thelonelyheartseries

Become Friends on Facebook
www.facebook.com/latrivia.nelson

Visit Latrivia's YouTube Channel
www.youtube.com/Latrivia2009

THE UGLY GIRLFRIEND

LaToya Jenkins is the quintessential woman: smart, successful, grounded and determined. She only has one problem socially - she's overweight. As the "big one" of her girlfriends, she often faces rejection from the men of their social circle because of her size and/or her dark skin. And due to a painful past relationship, she gives up on love completely until, she takes on Mitchell "Mitch" O'Keefe as a new client.

The Irish born architect needs a professional cleaning service to help him literally clean up his life after a nasty divorce, but he winds up finding a true friend in LaToya, the owner of It's An Honor Cleaning Service.

While LaToya is handicapped emotionally by her baggage, Mitch thinks she's the strongest woman he's ever seen and a breath of fresh air in his hectic life. His only goal is to prove to her that his interest in her is more than lust sparked by curiosity.

Read the story of two beautiful people in totally opposite ways who help each other see that beauty is not skin deep but soul deep in the first book of Latrivia S. Nelson's Lonely Heart Series, The Ugly Girlfriend.

First Book In Lonely Heart Series
ISBN: 978-0-9832186-4-7
Retail Price: $9.99

FINDING OPA!

What does the Greek word Opa mean? According to some it is a word or pronouncement of celebration; the celebration of life itself. It is another way of expressing joy and gratitude to God, life, and others, for bringing one into the state of ultimate wisdom.

Stacey Lane Bryant has three rules. She doesn't drive; she doesn't travel; and she most definitely will not date. From the outside, this odd-ball, thirties-something, single black woman is simply a creature of habit who has been beaten down by the tragedies of life. However those on the inside know that she's the widow of esteemed astrophysicist Drew Bryant, a highly sought after best-selling romance author and a devoted cat lover. The rules are simply designed to keep her safe and keep her sane.

However, someone didn't tell the Greek bombshell, Dr. Hunter Fourakis, that rules weren't meant to be broken. While at his favorite pub, he eyes Stacey and instantly falls under her spell. Only, his rusty moves don't get him far with the brilliant introvert, who quickly leaves just to get out of his grasp.

What is meant to be will be, and the two run into each other in another chance encounter. This time Hunter is able to convince Stacey not only to go out on a spur-of-the-moment date with him but also to consider an unorthodox proposal that would benefit them both.

Hunter's late wife was killed while serving in Iraq, and he mourns every year for two months and three days. The mourning period is usually miserable for Hunter, but this time, he wants to celebrate life. Stacey's second romance novel is due to her agent in two months but is totally lacking motivation or passion, because she hasn't gotten over her late husband. Considering that they both need someone for a short period of time to fulfill very specific needs, they agree to be each other's help mate temporarily. Only as deprived widows, pressured professionals and lonely hearts, they find that while deadlines pass and mourning time ends, love lasts forever.

Read this romantic tale about two people who fight through tragic personal loss, family prejudices and age-old traditions to find good old fashion love in the second book of the Lonely Hearts Series, Finding Opa!

The Lonely Heart Series
Book Two
ISBN: 978-0-983-28647-9
$8.99

The Grunt

Staff Sergeant Brett Black has a bad feeling that something is going to go terribly wrong. And as a Recon Marine, he pays attention to

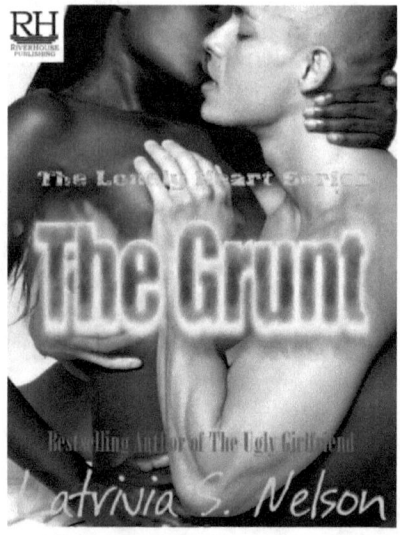

his gut. Only nothing can prepare him for what he encounters when he arrives at home from the base. His wife is leaving him, and there is nothing he can do about it.

Abandoned with a kid, the super alpha-male has to become domesticated quickly or find a willing substitute to help him with his son. Only the substitute he finds is no substitution.

Courtney Lawless is a true wild card. The budding librarian loves the classics and carries herself like a lady by day. But she also is full of life and surfs the waves of the Atlantic Ocean by night. Since her parents won't pay for college because of bad decisions in her past, the reformed bad-girl takes a job as Brett's live-in nanny to finish paying for school.

Brett has never seen a woman of such complex duality. Used to a wife who won't clean, cook or even talk to him, when he starts to live with Courtney, he realizes what he's been missing his entire life. Educated, amazing and refreshingly honest, the only thing that that this transparent beauty hides from her new boss is that she's also the Lieutenant Colonel's daughter.

Faced with another deployment to Afghanistan soon, the brooding Marine is forced to come out his shell to fight for what he loves, only this time, the war is at home.

Enjoy the interracial must-read romance of the summer, The Grunt, the third a longest book in Latrivia S. Nelson's Lonely Heart Series and today.

Third Book In Lonely Heart Series
ISBN: 978-0-9832186-4-7
Retail Price: $8.99

Dmitry's Closet

From author Latrivia S. Nelson, author of the epic romance Ivy's Twisted Vine, comes a story about Memphis, TN, a deadly faction of the Russian mafia and an innocent woman who dismantles an empire.

FROM THE INTERRACIAL ROMANCE SENSATION

DMITRY'S CLOSET

Latrivia S. Nelson

Orphaned virgin Royal Stone is looking for employment in one of the country's toughest recessions. What she finds is the seven-foot, blonde millionaire Dmitry Medlov, who offers her a job as the manager of his new boutique, Dmitry's Closet. After she accepts his job offer, she soon accepts his gifts, his bed and his lifestyle. What she does not know is that her knight in shining armor is also the head of the Medlov Organized Crime Family, a faction of the elite Russian mafia organization, Vory v Zakone.

Falling in love with the clueless Royal makes Dmitry want to break his coveted code, leave his self-made empire and start a life far away from the perils of the Thieves-in-Law. Only, his brother, Ivan, comes to the Memphis from New York City bent on a murderous revenge.

With the FBI and Memphis Police Department working hard to build a case against Dmitry and his
brother trying to kill him, he is forced to tell Royal of
his true identity, but Royal also is keeping a secret -
one that changes everything.

Who will win? Who will lose? Who will die? Watch all
the skeletons as they tumble out of the urban
literature sensation Dmitry's Closet.

Warning: This book contains graphic language, sex,
and various forms of violence. However, it will also
melt your heart!

The Medlov Crime Family Series
Book One
Available in paperback and e-book format
ISBN: 978-1-6165874-5-1
Retail Price:$12.99

Dmitry's Royal Flush:
Rise of the Queen

From the popular multicultural author, Latrivia S. Nelson, comes the highly anticipated second install-ment of the Medlov Crime Family Series, Dmitry's Royal Flush: Rise of the Queen.

For Dmitry and Royal Medlov, money doesn't equal happiness. Forced to leave Memphis, TN and flee to Prague after a brutal mafia war, the couple nestled into the countryside to raise their daughter, Anya, and lead a safe, quiet life. But when Dmitry's son, Anatoly, shows up with an offer he can't refuse, Dmitry is forced to go back to the life he left as boss of the most feared criminal organization in world. Consequently, the deal could not only destroy the Medlov Crime Family but also Dmitry and Royal.

Royal hasn't been the same since she was attacked three years ago. Where she used to be a sweet, innocent girl, she's now the jaded, bitter mistress of the Medlov Chateau. However, a reality check is in store for the pre-Madonna when Anya's new teacher shows up with her sights set on stealing Dmitry, and

Ivan's old ally shows up with his sights on killing him. Can Royal save them all? Will she?

With a family in such turmoil, the only way to survive is to stick together. Read the gripping tale of a marriage strong enough to stand the test of time as Dmitry realizes that he has the best cards in the house as long as he has a Royal Flush.

The Medlov Crime Family Series
Book Two
Available in paperback and e-book format
ISBN: 978-0-5780601-1-8
Retail Price: $13.99

Anatoly Medlov: Complete Reign

From the bestselling series, the Medlov Crime Family, comes the highly-anticipated story about America's favorite bad boy...

Anatoly Medlov is the youngest crime boss in the Medlov Organized Crime Family's history. Now, he has to prove himself to a council who thinks his legacy has not been well-earned, amidst a grueling investigation by Lt. Nicola Agosto of the Memphis Police Department and during plot to destroy him by his ex-lover, Victoria. In his loneliness, the only one he can confide in is the shop girl, Renee, an old friend who knows more than anyone about his personal journey. However, his friendship soon turns to love for a woman he knows that he cannot have because of the feared code his is bound to by the Vory v Zakone.

When his estranged mother dies suddenly, Anatoly flies to Russia to pay his last respects and discovers a jolting secret. The late Ivan Medlov's own brutal legacy still lives through his son, Gabriel, and his New York crime family. Anatoly's father and former Czar of the underworld, Dmitry, sees this as an opportunity to unite the two major families and blesses both men. However, Anatoly sees Gabriel as a threat to his empire and competition for the affection of his father. Will cousins kill because of the sins of their fathers?

Gabriel Medlov has always resented his existence. Now as an undercover DEA agent, he plans destroy the Medlov Crime Family once and for all. Only in order to get close enough to destroy the organization, he must also get close enough to love his estranged family. Will blood prove thicker than water or will one man's revenge end the Family for good?

Follow the story of one young man who fights to be king in a room full of royalty and suffers the pain of his position in the romantic suspense guaranteed to make you want more.

The Medlov Crime Family Series
Book Three
Available in paperback and e-book format
ISBN: 978-0-9832186-1-6
Retail Price: $14.99

Upcoming Books

The Lonely Heart Series:
Gracie's Dirty Little Secret
Taming the Rock Star
Unleashing the Dawg
The Pitcher's Last Curve Ball
The Tragic Bigamist
The Credit Repairman

The Medlov Series:
Saving Anya

The Chronicles of Young Dmitry Medlov:
Volume 5-8

The Agosto Series:
The World In Reverse

The Married But Lonely Series:
Forgive Me
Sexting After Dark

Paranormal Books
Funny Fixations
The Guitarist
The Pain of Dawn

The Nine Lives of Kat Steele:
Volumes 1-9

Books will be released during 2011 & 2012, but dates are tentative so please visit website for updates.

About the Author

In the last three years, bestselling author Latrivia S. Nelson has published ten novels including the largest interracial romance novel in the genre to date, *Ivy's Twisted Vine* (2010), The Medlov Crime Family Series and The Lonely Heart Series. She is also the President and CEO of RiverHouse Publishing, LLC, the wife of retired United States Marine Adam Nelson, the mother of two beautiful, rambunctious children and working diligently on her Ph.D.

When she's not busy writing novels, doing homework or running a publishing company, Nelson spends her time at princess tea parties with her daughter, Tierra, or being saved by her super hero son, Jordan, during playtime, cooking great meals for the family and watching the sunset with her best friend and real-life super hero, Adam.

Attention Future Romance Authors:

Do you have a romance novel or short story that you want to share with the world? Is it edgy? Is it romantic? Is it erotic? Is it unpublished?

Latrivia S. Nelson and RiverHouse Publishing are going to launch an **e-book only imprint** in the Summer of 2012, Love Only.

We will begin accepting submission in January 2012 and will announce the authors in April of 2012. For more information, please contact Latrivia S. Nelson via email at Lnelson@RiverHousePublishingLLC.com.

The Home of Bold Authors with Bold Statements.
www.riverhousepublishingllc.com

THE LIFE OF XXXTENTACION

THE LIFE OF XXXTENTACION

BLAZE CARTER

CONTENTS

TO ZFD

For opening my eyes to the genius of XXXTentacion. Your passion for his music helped me appreciate the layers emotion in his work. Through our conversations, I learned not just about the artist, but about the struggles and triumphs of a generation that resonates with his message. Your dedication to his artistry inspired me to dive deeper int his life and legacy. Thank you for inspiring me to understand the chaotic brilliant XXXTentacion and the connection he forged with so many.

Acknowledgement

I want to give a huge shout-out to the design collective Real Fashion Bomb and the gallery *Florida Man* for permitting me to reuse my artworks in this book. Your support means the world to me and has added so much to the stories I wanted to tell. Thanks for being a part of this journey and for championing the creative spirit that XXX Tentacion embodied.

CHAPTER 1

A Controversial Icon

The story of XXXTentacion begins in chaos, and it's a chaos he never quite escaped. Born Jahseh Dwayne Ricardo Onfroy in 1998, XXXTentacion rocketed to fame in the latter half of the 2010s as a rapper whose music was as turbulent and troubled as the man himself.

His songs, marked by a raw emotional vulnerability that spoke directly to a generation riddled with anxiety and rage, tapped into the darker corners of youth culture. Yet for every tear shed by his fans, there was a fist raised in anger and a desire for redemption.

His rapid rise to stardom came with accusations of domestic violence, brutal beatings, and a string of legal battles that left many wondering if he was the artist of a generation or a figure that embodied its darkest impulses.

In the years since his murder in 2018, XXXTentacion's name has become a byword for contradiction. He remains a figure who splits opinion, with critics focusing on his violent past while his most ardent fans maintain he was a reflection of his generation and on a path to redemption.

His popularity has only grown since his death, as posthumous releases, fan tributes, and continued cultural resonance have kept his name alive. But can we, or should we, separate the art from the artist? What can we learn about ourselves by looking at his life and legacy?

So that is the central question: can we extract the deeply personal, often heart-wrenching music from the man who, in the public eye, embodied some of the worst impulses of youth violence and recklessness? For many, XXXTentacion represents a paradox, an artist whose ability to connect with fans on issues like depression, loneliness, and suicide was matched only by his capacity for cruelty and destruction. His legacy, as much a product of his brief but explosive life as his tragic death, forces us to confront these 21st century American contradictions head-on.

In the landscape of modern rap, few figures loom as large and as controversial as XXXTentacion. The public's fascination with him is a testament to his ability to provoke people—and provoke he did, both in his music and in his actions. From the earliest days of his career, he stood apart from his peers. His breakthrough single, "Look at Me!," was a chaotic anthem of sex, power, macho violence, distortion, a raw expression of teenage angst that became an instant hit. With lyrics like: I'm like "Bitch, who is your man's?", ayy / Can't keep my dick in my pants, ayy," it was brash, aggressive, obnoxious, and unapologetically confrontational, qualities that defined not only the song but XXXTentacion himself. Here was a rapper who didn't just reflect the emotions and desires of a generation; he embodied them. At the same time, we have to recognize where this style of thinking, acting, talking and singing came from. In a country that continually glorifies and rewards these orientations, who can be shocked by this hit?

So it was the same qualities that made his music resonate with fans, however, that fueled the controversies that surrounded him. While XXXTentacion was gaining fans for his emotional openness, particularly around mental health, his personal life told a darker story. Accusations of domestic violence and assault followed him, culminating in a 2016 arrest for the brutal beating of his then-girlfriend, Geneva Ayala.

The details of the case were harrowing, painting a portrait of a man capable of terrible acts. For many, it was impossible to reconcile this image of violence with the artist who sang openly about his own vulnerabilities, who in songs like "Jocelyn Flores" and "Sad!" seemed to offer a window into the pain and suffering of a generation.

As XXXTentacion's star continued to rise, the conversation around him became increasingly polarized. His most devoted fans—many of them young, marginalized, and perhaps struggling with their own mental health—saw him as a hero, someone who spoke to their pain in a way no one else did. The context of this was in many ways the opening up of social media and other digital technologies that were simultaneously opening the world to young people while also making them feel ever more isolated and like they were never enough (a theme that would be openly addressed in Greta Gerwig's 2023 Barbie movie, where Ryan Gosling plays Ken, whose "Kenough hoodie became its own Tik-Tok fashion statement).

His detractors (and there were many), on the other hand, saw him as a danger, a figure who glorified violence and set a toxic example for his audience. And perhaps most troublingly, his success appeared to show that violent behavior could be excused—or even rewarded—in the music industry. His career, marked by chart-topping success and equally headline-grabbing scandal, became a symbol of the contradictions inherent in celebrity culture, where fame and notoriety often go hand in hand. Why this conduct by XXXtentacion garnered so much negative attention when similar, and much worse, acts by so many others were glossed over remains a mystery.

At the heart of the debate over XXXTentacion's legacy is the question of whether we can separate his art from his crimes. This is not a new question—our culture has long grappled with the separation of the artist from their actions, particularly when those actions involve violence.

Maybe it is because in the case of XXXTentacion, the stakes feel higher. His music was not just a product of his environment; it was a reflection of his inner turmoil, a soundtrack to the self-destructive path he seemed destined to walk. His songs were confessional, often deeply personal, offering a glimpse into his mental state in a way that felt both raw and real.

A related question is whether the art can stand on its own when the artist is so deeply entangled in violence? Can we appreciate songs like "17," where he explores themes of depression and hopelessness, knowing that the man behind the music was accused of some of the very behaviors he seemed to decry? For some, the answer is a resounding yes. They argue that his music should be judged on its own merits, that the emotional connection he forged with millions of fans cannot be dismissed because of his personal failings. For others, his crimes overshadow any artistic achievements, and to celebrate his music is to condone the violence he perpetrated.

In many ways, the debate over XXXTentacion mirrors broader societal discussions about accountability, forgiveness, and the role of art in shaping our culture. His life and legacy force us to confront uncomfortable questions about the relationship between an artist and their work, and whether we can—or should—draw a line between the two. Jean Genet, Flannery O Conner, Ezra Pound, Caravaggio and so many other great figures from the pantheon of great artists and writers have left a complicated legacy, as their art often stands in stark contrast to the turbulent, sometimes destructive ideas they promoted or lives they led.

Perhaps the most compelling aspect of XXXTentacion's story is the way it encapsulates the contradictions of fame in the digital age. He was, at once, a villain and a victim, a product of his circumstances and a force of his own making. His music spoke to the insecurities and fears of a generation, yet his actions often betrayed the very values he claimed to represent.

In songs like "Changes" and "Everybody Dies in Their Nightmares," XXXTentacion laid bare his own struggles with depression, loneliness, and the fear of abandonment. His fans saw in him a kindred spirit, someone who understood the pain they were going through because he had lived it too. But alongside this vulnerability was a darker, more destructive side. His violent outbursts, both in his personal life and in his interactions with the media, painted a picture of a man at war with himself and the world around him. Fame, for XXXTentacion, was both a blessing and a curse—it gave him a platform to express his deepest emotions, but it also amplified the strange times that had defined his life from the start.

In the end, the story of XXXTentacion is one of contradictions—between fame and violence, vulnerability and destruction, art and crime. His music continues to resonate with millions of fans, even as his legacy remains mired in controversy. As we look back on his life, we are left with the difficult task of making sense of these contradictions, of finding a way to understand the artist without excusing the man. In this way, XXXTentacion remains one of the most compelling and divisive figures of his generation—a man whose life and music defy easy categorization, and whose legacy forces us to confront the uncomfortable realities of fame, violence, and mental health in the modern age.

CHAPTER 2

Jahseh Onfroy

From the start, XXXTentacion was a study in contradictions. Born Jahseh Dwayne Ricardo Onfroy on January 23, 1998, in Plantation, Florida, his life began in the shadows of violence and instability. South Florida, with its strange mix of sun-drenched beauty and dark undercurrents of crime, would be the backdrop of his early years. It was a landscape of extremes, and he would come to define that in his music. Jahseh Onfroy grew up as part of a generation raised by single mothers, absent fathers, and systemic inequality, where life was often a battle for survival. His own story reads like the beginning of an American tragedy, one in which all roads seem to lead toward some kind of self-destruction.

As a child, Onfroy was restless, full of pent-up energy and aggression that could not be contained. Reports from those who knew him describe a young boy who was always in trouble—fights at school, conflicts at home. His mother, Cleo, was a single parent who worked multiple jobs to support him, and she struggled to control his temper. "He was always a difficult child," she said in a rare interview after his death, a note of weariness in her voice. "He was fighting from the day he was born." The roots of his anger, she explained, could be traced back to the absence of his father, who was in and out of jail for most of Jahseh's life. Without a stable male figure, Jahseh grew up in the rougher neighborhoods of Broward County, where violence, bravado, and chaos were the currency of survival.

By the time he reached his teenage years, the world around him had taught Jahseh some hard lessons about power and control. He learned that, in order to survive, you had to strike first and strike hard. Violence became his shield and his weapon, a way to project strength in a world that had denied him any semblance of real control. This fight-or-flight sense of survival bled into his music, where themes of violence, anger, and betrayal would become central. He never fit in, and he didn't want to. Instead, he embraced the role of the outcast, cultivating a persona that resonated with legions of disillusioned youth who saw their own struggles reflected in his songs.

Onfroy's adolescence was littered with moments of profound disruption. Expelled from middle school for fighting, he bounced between friends' houses and juvenile detention centers. By 16, he had developed a reputation for violence—both feared and admired by his peers. His behavior was a product of both nature and nurture; one of the most defining moment of his early life was his time in juvenile detention. It was here that Onfroy's identity began to crystallize. Surrounded by other young men who shared his anger and brokenness, he hardened.

Stories from this period paint a picture of a boy who had learned to use violence as a language. In interviews later in his life, he would speak of it as a necessity, a way to keep himself safe from those who would try to hurt him first. These institutional factors have shaped an entire generation of kids who, for a variety of reasons, find themselves behind walls and bars.

In the detention center, Onfroy also met Stokeley Clevon Goulbourne, who would later become Ski Mask the Slump God. The two bonded over their mutual love for music, and in this unlikely environment, Onfroy began to consider music as a potential escape from the life he seemed destined to lead. It was during this period that Jahseh Onfroy became XXXTentacion—a name that would soon take on a life of its own. "I was always violent," he admitted in one of his rare interviews, "but music became my way of channeling that aggression."

From the beginning, XXXTentacion's music reflected the lack of order of his life. His early tracks, released on Sound-Cloud, were raw and unpolished, full of distorted beats and shouted lyrics. Listening to these tracks gave you the feeling that you heard him, especially when compared to the legions of over-edited, auto-tuned, overproduced works that are commercially available. And it was this rawness that attracted a devoted fanbase. His early music wasn't just about anger—it was anger, distilled into sound. For many of his fans, who came from similarly troubled backgrounds, XXXTentacion was a reflection of their own pain, their own frustration, their own sense of alienation. In him, they saw someone who understood what it was like to be pushed to the margins, to be dismissed by society. As his following grew, so too did the myth of XXXTentacion—the anti-hero who had clawed his way up from the depths, bloodied but unbowed.

In crafting the persona of XXXTentacion, Onfroy tapped into a rich cultural history of the outsider, the rebel, the harlequin. Like the punk rockers of the 1970s or the grunge musicians of the 1990s, he positioned himself as a voice for the voiceless, an artist who didn't play by the rules because the rules were never made for people like him. And really, they weren't.

From the earliest days of his career, he presented himself as someone who stood outside of the system, unafraid to challenge authority. His appearance—a strange blend of goth, punk, and rap aesthetics—reflected this rebellion. With his shock of bleached blonde hair, facial tattoos, and somber expression, XXXTentacion looked every bit the tortured artist, the young man at war with the world. Of course, it did not hurt that he is also beautiful by almost any standards.

This persona wasn't just an act—it was an extension of Jahseh Onfroy's own life. He didn't just play the role of the outsider; he was the outsider. His early experiences with the criminal justice system, his tumultuous relationships, and his struggles with identity all fed into the image he projected. He was open about his battles with depression and suicidal thoughts, using his music as a platform to talk about the struggles that so many of his fans shared. Songs like "Jocelyn Flores" and "Everybody Dies in Their Nightmares" tackled these themes head-on, and it was this emotional vulnerability that made XXXTentacion a beacon for young people dealing with their own mental health issues.

For his fans, XXXTentacion was more than just a rapper—he was a symbol of survival, someone who had been through the fire and come out the other side. His openness about his worries resonated with a generation that was increasingly vocal about these issues, and his music became a space where they could confront their own pain. "He was the first artist I ever heard who made me feel like it was okay to be depressed," one fan wrote on Reddit after his death. "His music saved my life."

Enter "Look at Me!" XXXTentacion's breakout hit. This song that propelled him from the underground SoundCloud scene into the mainstream consciousness. Released in 2015, the track is a sonic assault—a blast of distorted bass and shouted lyrics that feels less like a song and more like a primal scream. The track's aggression is palpable, its energy frenetic and unrelenting. In many ways, "Look at Me!" encapsulates everything that XXXTentacion was as an artist—angry, rebellious, and unapologetically raw.

Lyrically, "Look at Me!" is confrontational, a declaration of independence from the norms of both society and the music industry. "Can't keep my dick in my pants," he shouts in the opening lines, setting the tone for a track that is as vulgar as it is defiant. This is not a song that plays by the rules, and that is precisely the point. XXXTentacion isn't interested in fitting in—he wants to break the mold, to tear down the expectations that have been placed on him as a young Black man in America. The song's explicit content, while shocking to some, is a deliberate act of rebellion. It's XXXTentacion's way of saying, "I don't care what you think of me."

The song's production is equally aggressive, with its distorted bass and chaotic beats creating a sense of disorientation. There's a direct texture to the sound that feels almost unpolished, as though it was recorded in a fit of rage. This lack of refinement is part of what made the song so appealing to fans. It didn't feel like a sanitized product made for the radio—it felt real, a burst of unfiltered emotion that tapped into the anger and frustration so many young people were feeling.

"Look at Me!" became an anthem for disaffected youth, a rallying cry for those who felt ignored by society. In the song's aggression, they found a reflection of their own anger, their own sense of being pushed to the margins. "He was speaking for all of us," one fan wrote on Twitter after the song went viral. "He was saying the things we were too afraid to say."

The success of "Look at Me!" was not just about the music—it was about what the song represented. For fans, it was a rejection of the mainstream, a middle finger to the system that had left them feeling abandoned. In XXXTentacion, they found an artist who wasn't afraid to be different, who wasn't afraid to express the anger and pain they themselves felt. The song's aggression was a catharsis for listeners who felt they had no other outlet for their emotions.

But what does this tell us about XXXTentacion's audience? In some ways, "Look at Me!" is a reflection of the disillusionment felt by a generation growing up in a world that seems increasingly hostile. This is a generation raised on social media, where image is everything, and yet they feel invisible. They are told to aspire to success, yet they are often left with few avenues to achieve it. In "Look at Me!," XXXTentacion gives voice to this frustration, this feeling of being ignored, frustrated, and overlooked. The song's aggression is not just a form of dissent—it is a cry for attention, a demand to be seen in a world that so often looks the other way.

For a lot of XXXTentacion's fans, this sense of rebellion, this refusal to conform, is what made him an anti-hero. He wasn't perfect, and he didn't pretend to be. He was messy, flawed, and at times destructive. But in his imperfection, his fans saw something real, something and someone they could relate to. In a world that often demanded perfection, XXXTentacion's willingness to be unapologetically himself, to embrace his own darkness, was a source of comfort for those who felt like they didn't belong.

As we look back at the making of XXXTentacion, it becomes clear that his rise was about more than just music. He represented something deeper—a rebellion against the expectations placed on young people in a world that often feels indifferent to their struggles. He was the anti-hero they didn't know they needed, and in his music, they found a voice for their own pain.

CHAPTER 3

The Rise of a New Sound

There was something different about XXXTentacion. You could hear it from the first seconds of a track like "Jocelyn Flores," where the haunting, fragile guitar loop drags you into the song's aching melancholy before you've even considered the lyrics. It was this sound, both understated and direct, that set him apart from so many of his peers. XXXTentacion blurred lines—between genres, between his own pain and public persona, and perhaps most notably, between what was real and what was performative. He made it difficult to know where the artist ended and the person began, and it was in that ambiguity where his influence, and his controversy, lived.

It's hard to categorize XXXTentacion's music without reducing it to something that doesn't quite capture what made it unique. For an artist who rose to prominence during the reign of SoundCloud rap—a genre known for its lo-fi production, distorted bass, and raw, unpolished delivery—XXXTentacion stood out precisely because he refused to adhere to any one sound.

In one moment, his voice was a snarl of anger, as in his breakout track "Look at Me!"; in another, it was a quiet whisper, as if he were speaking directly into your ear, as in "Jocelyn Flores." His music pulled from everywhere—emo, punk, rap, even grunge. He created a collage of sound that shouldn't have worked but somehow did.

To understand his rise is to understand the cultural moment that birthed it. In the late 2010s, hip-hop was evolving. Artists like Drake, Travis Scott, and Kendrick Lamar were pushing the genre's boundaries, but something different was happening on the internet, specifically on SoundCloud, where a new wave of underground artists was emerging.

These artists weren't getting radio play or major label deals, but they didn't need to. The platform allowed them to cultivate fanbases through direct connection with listeners, bypassing traditional music industry gatekeepers. It was DIY in the most visceral sense. And of all the artists on SoundCloud, XXXTentacion was one of the most compelling.

What set XXXTentacion apart wasn't just his sound, though. It was the power of his emotion. In a scene dominated by hard beats and braggadocio, XXXTentacion's music was introspective, often painfully so.

Take "Jocelyn Flores," for example. This track is less a rap song than a eulogy. Named after a friend of XXXTentacion's who had committed suicide, the song explores the intersection of grief, guilt, and depression. Over a somber, looping guitar riff, XXXTentacion's voice is low, almost monotone, as if he's drained of the energy to feel anything but numb. "I'm in pain, wanna put ten shots in my brain," he confesses, his voice devoid of the performative swagger that often accompanies lyrics like these in mainstream rap. There's no posturing here, no attempt to be cool or detached. It's pure sadness, laid bare for anyone who cares to listen.

But to what extent was this vulnerability genuine? And to what extent was it calculated, a performance meant to endear him to his young, impressionable audience? This question lingered over XXXTentacion's career and continues to follow his legacy. In many ways, he was the perfect artist for the era of social media, where authenticity is both craved and elusive. He bared his soul online, in interviews, on Instagram Live, and in his music, but there was always the sense that he was curating this image of himself, that he knew how to manipulate the emotions of his audience. "He was like an open wound," one fan said in a Reddit thread after his death. "But I think he wanted us to see the wound, to feel bad for him."

For fans, though, whether or not XXXTentacion's vulnerability was performative seemed beside the point. His music spoke to them in a way that few artists' music did. In a time when mental health struggles were increasingly being destigmatized, XXXTentacion's openness about his own battles with depression, suicidal thoughts, and trauma resonated deeply. For many young listeners, his music was not just relatable but cathartic, a way to process their own pain. "Jocelyn Flores" became an anthem for anyone who had ever felt the weight of loss or the burden of their own mental health. And for some, it was more than just a song. It was a lifeline.

Yet, for all the sincerity in songs like "Jocelyn Flores," it's impossible to ignore the more cynical aspects of XXXTentacion's career. He was, after all, a super savvy marketer, someone who understood how to manipulate the media and his audience. He knew that controversy sold, and he used that to his advantage. His violent past—including allegations of domestic abuse and a viral video of him hitting a woman—was well-documented, and yet it only seemed to fuel his fame. There's a sense that, for XXXTentacion, these moments of personal failings were part of the performance, part of what made him compelling to his fans. It's as if the line between the artist and the persona, between real life and the spectacle of his public image, was blurred beyond recognition.

Take his role in the rise of SoundCloud rap, for instance. The genre itself was rebellious, rejecting the polished, commercial sound of mainstream hip-hop in favor of something messier, angrier, more immediate. It was music for the disaffected, for those who felt overlooked by the traditional music industry. XXXTentacion thrived in this environment because he was able to embody that sense of rebellion. But unlike many of his peers, whose lyrics centered around drugs, partying, and violence, XXXTentacion's music often touched on themes of self doubt and vulnerability. He offered something more than just anger—he offered a kind of emotional release.

But how much of this vulnerability was real? Even in his more introspective tracks, there's a sense that XXXTentacion was performing for an audience. His lyrics, while raw, often feel calculated, as if he's saying exactly what he knows will resonate with his listeners. In "Jocelyn Flores," he sings about guilt and depression in a way that is both deeply personal and universally relatable. "I know you're somewhere, somewhere / I've been trapped in my mind, girl, just holdin' on," he croons in the chorus. It's a sentiment that could apply to anyone who has ever felt the weight of grief or mental illness. But it's also a sentiment that feels carefully crafted, designed to strike a chord with the millions of young people who have experienced those same feelings.

And perhaps that's the point. Whether or not XXXTentacion's vulnerability was performative, it doesn't change the fact that it resonated with his audience. In a world where so many artists seem disconnected from their fans, XXXTentacion offered something different.

So, he wasn't just a rapper; he was a conduit for his listeners' emotions. He didn't just make music about pain—he made music that felt like pain, that took the listener into the depths of his own psyche. In doing so, he created a space for his fans to confront their own demons.

It's worth considering the larger cultural forces at play here, too. XXXTentacion rose to prominence at a time when discussions about mental health were becoming more mainstream, particularly among younger generations. His music tapped into a growing movement of artists—like Kid Cudi, Logic, and Lil Peep—who were using their platforms to talk openly about depression, anxiety, and suicide.

In this context, XXXTentacion's vulnerability didn't just feel authentic—it felt necessary. He was giving voice to a generation that was struggling with its own new cultural landscape, a generation that was increasingly disillusioned with traditional ideas of masculinity and emotional stoicism.

But there's also something troubling about the way XXXTentacion presented his pain. In songs like "Jocelyn Flores," he seems to wallow in his depression, offering little in the way of resolution or hope. It's a stark contrast to someone like Kid Cudi, whose music often feels like a journey toward healing. For XXXTentacion, there is no healing—only pain. This, too, resonated with his fans, many of whom were drawn to the darkness in his music. But it also raises questions about the impact of his art. Was he helping his listeners confront their own pain, or was he glorifying it? Was he offering catharsis, or was he feeding into a cycle of despair?

The answer, perhaps, lies somewhere in between. For some fans, XXXTentacion's music was undoubtedly therapeutic. It gave them a space to feel seen, to feel understood. For others, it may have reinforced their own feelings of hopelessness. But to focus solely on the impact of his music is to ignore the larger questions about who XXXTentacion was as an artist, and what he represented.

At the heart of his music, and his life really, was a deep sense of contradiction. He was truly vulnerable and violent, both sincere and performative. His music was unsanitized and underproduced, but it was also carefully constructed. He blurred the lines between genres, between authenticity and artifice, between himself and his audience. In doing so, he created a new kind of sound—one that was as complex and contradictory as the man behind it.

And perhaps that's why XXXTentacion continues to be such a divisive figure. For some, he was a revolutionary artist, someone who pushed the boundaries of what rap could be. For others, he was a deeply flawed individual, whose personal demons often overshadowed his artistic achievements.

But regardless of where one falls on that spectrum, there's no denying his impact. In blending emo, rap, punk, and his own personal pain, XXXTentacion created a sound that was uniquely his own—a sound that continues to influence the landscape of music today.

CHAPTER 4

SoundCloud and Beyond

In the era of SoundCloud and Instagram, fame is something that can be built—or destroyed—at light speed. For XXXTentacion, the internet was both his rocket fuel and his downfall, the stage upon which his meteoric rise and violent, public unraveling took place.

He seemed to have understood, almost intuitively, how to manipulate social media to craft a narrative, one that blurred the lines between real life and spectacle, between violence and vulnerability. And for better or worse, this understanding was central to his success.

To speak of XXXTentacion's career without considering the role of social media is impossible. His rise was almost entirely predicated on it. Platforms like SoundCloud and YouTube allowed him to bypass traditional music industry gatekeepers, reaching listeners directly in their bedrooms, on their phones, late at night when they were most vulnerable to his haunting, raw sound. But it was Instagram and Twitter where he built his persona—the troubled, tormented anti-hero who oscillated between extremes of emotion, between outbursts of violence and moments of heartbreaking tenderness.

In many ways, XXXTentacion was a product of his time. The late 2010s were a period where the boundaries between public and private, artist and individual, were dissolving in real time. Social media platforms had turned celebrities into constant, living content, their every move available for public consumption.

For someone like XXXTentacion, whose life was as chaotic and complicated as his music, this was both an opportunity and a danger. I suspect this is true for all of Gen Z today.

There's an often-repeated notion that if it bleeds, it ledes....controversy sells. In XXXTentacion's case, it wasn't just that controversy sold—it became the main currency by which he traded his fame. His online presence was marked by a kind of instability that felt genuine, even if it was often unclear how much of it was theatrical.

He was often unpredictable. One day, he would post a video apologizing to his fans for his violent past; the next, he would be caught on camera in a brutal brawl. The volatility of his persona was captivating, even if it was disturbing. It was a kind of car crash fame—people watched because they couldn't look away.

At the same time, social media offered him a way to communicate directly with his audience in a way that felt personal, even intimate. His Instagram Lives were often long, rambling affairs, where he would talk about his struggles with emotional turmoil, his regrets, his fears. These moments of confession made him seem real in a way that many artists do not. "He spoke to us like he knew what we were going through," one fan recalled on Twitter after his death. "It wasn't polished or scripted. It felt like he was just as lost as we were."

But there was always a darker side to this accessibility. While social media allowed XXXTentacion to connect with fans, it also exposed him to constant scrutiny, amplifying the controversies that followed him. His frequent outbursts, his unhinged behavior, and his legal troubles became fodder for tabloids and gossip blogs, creating a feedback loop where the more outrageous his actions, the more attention he received. It didn't matter if the attention was negative; in the world of social media, any attention was good attention.

There's a moment from his career that captures this dynamic perfectly. In 2016, XXXTentacion was arrested for the assault of his then-pregnant girlfriend, Geneva Ayala, an act of violence so horrific that it seemed like it would end his career before it had even really begun. But instead of fading into obscurity, XXXTentacion doubled down on his persona as the tortured, misunderstood artist.

So, he didn't shy away from the allegations—instead, he leaned into them, using them to fuel the narrative that he was an outsider, someone who had been "canceled" by the mainstream but still loved by his loyal fanbase. He even went so far as to claim that the allegations against him were part of a broader conspiracy to take him down, painting himself as a victim of a corrupt system.

The result was a kind of martyrdom. In the world of SoundCloud rap, where authenticity was prized above all else, XXXTentacion's very public flaws made him seem more real, more relatable, than the polished, PR-friendly rappers who dominated the charts. His legal troubles, his erratic behavior, even his violent temper—they were all part of the same package. He was damaged, and that damage was central to his appeal.

But there's a danger in conflating damage with authenticity, in assuming that because an artist is troubled, their art is somehow more real. Social media has a way of flattening nuance, of turning complex people into caricatures of themselves. And in XXXTentacion's case, the line between his public persona and his private life became so blurred that it was impossible to tell where one ended and the other began.

Was the violence central to his appeal, or was it simply sensationalized by a media eager for clicks? It's hard to say. Certainly, there were fans who defended him even in the face of damning evidence, who claimed that the media was out to get him, that his actions were being blown out of proportion. But there were also those who were drawn to him because of the darkness, because his music—and his life—tapped into something primal and disturbing.

In "Jocelyn Flores," a song that deals explicitly with suicide and depression, XXXTentacion's voice is hauntingly monotone as he describes his own anguish. It's the kind of song that feels deeply personal, almost like a cry for help. And yet, it's hard not to hear the echoes of performativity in it, too. After all, XXXTentacion knew that this kind of vulnerability was what his fans craved. He knew that by sharing his heart, by making it public, he was giving them something they could relate to. But was it real, or was it part of the spectacle?

In many ways, XXXTentacion's career was a case study in the toxic feedback loop of social media fame. The more he shared, the more attention he received; the more attention he received, the more he was compelled to share. It was a cycle that fed on itself, growing larger and more dangerous with each new outburst, each new controversy.

And the media, of course, was complicit in this. Every time XXXTentacion was involved in a fight or arrested for assault, it became headline news. His legal troubles were dissected in gossip columns and social media threads, turning his life into a kind of reality TV show for public consumption.

But for all the attention he garnered, there was always the sense that XXXTentacion, like so many celebrities and ordinary people who get caught up in reality social media exposure, was playing a dangerous game, one that he couldn't win. Fame, especially the kind of fame that is built on controversy, is inherently unstable. It's like building a house on quicksand—eventually, it will collapse under its own weight. And for XXXTentacion, that collapse came all too soon. In June 2018, he was shot and killed in what appeared to be a robbery gone wrong. He was just 20 years old.

In the days and weeks following his death, social media was flooded with tributes from fans and fellow artists alike. But there was also a darker undercurrent to the mourning—a sense of inevitability, as if XXXTentacion's death was simply the logical conclusion to the kind of life in the facst lane that he had been living. He had always been a figure of risk, and in the end, that risk consumed him.

But even in death, XXXTentacion's social media presence continued to haunt the internet. His Instagram account, once a place where he connected directly with his fans, became a shrine of sorts, filled with messages of love and grief. His songs, many of which dealt with themes of death and mortality, took on a new, eerie significance. And his legacy, complicated as it is, became a subject of intense debate.

Was he a victim of his own demons, or a product of a culture that fetishizes violence and trauma? Was he a cautionary tale, or a martyr for a generation that felt just as lost as he did? Or both?

Perhaps the most troubling aspect of XXXTentacion's rise—and his fall—is the way social media not only amplified his flaws but also made them part of his brand. He wasn't just a musician; he was a figure of controversy, a character in the ongoing drama of his own life. And in the world of Instagram and Twitter, where attention is the ultimate currency, that drama was what kept people coming back.

But in the end, the very thing that made XXXTentacion famous—the contraditions, the violence, the controversy—was also what destroyed him. His life, and his career, were consumed by the same forces that had fueled his rise. And in the world of social media, where nothing is ever truly forgotten, his legacy remains as complicated as ever.

It's tempting to look at XXXTentacion's story as a cautionary tale, a reminder of the dangers of fame and avatar life in the digital age. But it's also a story about the forces of culture today and the power social media to shape not only how we see artists, but how they see themselves. For XXXTentacion, social media was both a mirror and a magnifying glass, reflecting and amplifying the darkest parts of his life. And in the end, that reflection was too much to bear.

CHAPTER 5

Violence as Style and Story

XXXTentacion's life, both public and private, was entangled with all kinds of violence—a force that shaped his persona, haunted his career, and ultimately contributed to his early death. For fans, media outlets, and critics alike, his music became impossible to separate from the acts of brutality, both physical and symbolic, he both endured and inflicted. The stark contrast between the vulnerability he often displayed in his music and the violence that seemed to trail him in his personal life is one of the most perplexing aspects of XXXTentacion's story, a tension that feels at times irreconcilable.

Born Jahseh Onfroy, XXXTentacion grew up in South Florida under conditions of instability and neglect. The violence that would come to define much of his life began at an early age. He spoke often about his abusive childhood, how his mother, Cleopatra Bernard, left him with relatives, and how he was in constant conflict with other children.

But as much as XXXTentacion's early life was marked by trauma, it was also defined by a capacity for inflicting violence on others. Nowhere is this more evident than in his relationship with Geneva Ayala, his ex-girlfriend and the woman who became the focal point of the most damning chapter of his life. In 2016, Geneva accused XXXTentacion of repeated physical and emotional abuse, including one especially harrowing incident in which he allegedly beat her while she was pregnant. Court documents detailed the brutal assault, describing how XXXTentacion allegedly held her captive, threatened her life, and assaulted her in a way that left her permanently traumatized.

This was no longer the narrative of a troubled artist struggling with internal demons—this was a public revelation of cruelty that placed XXXTentacion in a different category altogether. Geneva Ayala became a symbol of the hidden cost of his fame and the secondary victim his own abuse. She became the young woman who had suffered in silence while XXXTentacion's star was on the rise. In an interview with the *Miami New Times*, Ayala described how her life was forever changed by the abuse, painting a picture of a relationship filled with manipulation, gaslighting, and fear. "He knew how to make me feel like nothing," she said. "He made me feel like I was crazy for thinking he would hurt me."

The reaction to the allegations was polarizing, to say the least. On one side, many in the media—especially mainstream outlets like *Pitchfork* and *The New York Times*—condemned XXXTentacion for his actions, calling him a danger to society and questioning how someone with such a violent history could have a platform at all. For them, the allegations against him weren't just a scandal—they were proof of a deep moral failing. *Pitchfork* was particularly scathing in its coverage of the court proceedings, publishing detailed accounts of Ayala's injuries and the specific charges XXXTentacion faced.

Yet, his fanbase remained largely loyal, with many questioning the validity of the allegations or downplaying their significance. For them, XXXTentacion's pain—the same pain he frequently discussed in his music—justified or at least contextualized his violence. Fans flooded social media with messages of support, pointing to songs like "Revenge" as proof that he was a product of his circumstances, that his violent outbursts were simply the manifestations of a deeply damaged individual trying to navigate a world that had been cruel to him from the start. To these fans, Geneva Ayala became an inconvenient narrative, one that threatened to derail the connection they felt with an artist who spoke to their own struggles with depression, anger, and alienation.

But even beyond his direct relationship with Ayala, XXXTentacion's music was riddled with allusions to violence, both inflicted and endured. Songs like "Revenge," for instance, present an ambiguous relationship with the concept of retribution and suffering. "Revenge on my body, revenge on my heart, revenge on my soul," he sings, with a haunting repetition that seems to invoke both the desire for vengeance and the toll it takes on the self. The title itself suggests a cycle of violence, one that is difficult to escape once entered. There's a numbness to the way he delivers these lines, a kind of resignation to the inevitability of violence in his life, as if it's not just something he does but something that happens to him, a force beyond his control.

In "I Don't Even Speak Spanish LOL," a track that deviates from his typical style with its reggaeton beats and light-hearted feel, the lyrics take on an unexpected significance when viewed in the context of his personal life. While the song may seem like a playful departure, there's an eerie undercurrent to the way he moves between personas—the carefree lover in the song and the violent figure outside of the studio. It's a dissonance that speaks to the complexity of his character and the troubling ways in which he compartmentalized different aspects of his life.

What makes XXXTentacion's violence particularly difficult to process is the extent to which it was woven into the public's perception of him. His legal troubles, his public fights, his outbursts on social media—these were not separate from his music; they were part of the same life/performance. In the digital age, where platforms like Instagram and YouTube allow fans constant access to an artist's personal life, the boundary between Jahseh Onfroy the person and XXXTentacion the performer became blurred to the point of non-existence. This was a new kind of celebrity, one where authenticity was both demanded and manufactured in real-time.

His violence, then, wasn't just a scandal to be reported on—it became central to his mythos, something that both repelled and attracted his audience. This is the paradox at the heart of his career: the more violent and erratic he became, the more people seemed drawn to him. His life became a kind of spectacle, a performance of suffering and brutality that mirrored the chaotic world of social media, where every outburst and every transgression was amplified for maximum effect. We tell ourselves stories in order to live, in order to explain ourselves to ourselves and to others. And we tell ourselves stories to explain the world. Or maybe to explain it away. In the case of XXXTentacion, the story that was told—by him, by the media, and by his fans—was one of a tortured artist whose violence was both a product of his pain and a form of catharsis.

But what does it mean to consume violence as entertainment? For decades, critics have debated the role of violence in art, particularly in music. Artists from Tupac to to Fifty Cent to Eminem have faced backlash for glorifying violence in their lyrics, even as fans defend their work as reflections of the harsh realities of life. In XXXTentacion's case, the debate takes on a new urgency because the violence wasn't just in the music—it was in the man himself. When fans listened to songs like "Revenge," they weren't just hearing a narrative of abstract suffering; they were hearing the voice of someone who had inflicted real pain on others, someone whose actions had left a permanent mark on those around him.

The music industry itself has long been complicit in this dynamic, profiting off the personas of troubled, violent men while turning a blind eye to the damage they cause. In the case of XXXTentacion, record labels, managers, and promoters continued to work with him even after the details of his abuse became public. It's a pattern we've seen before—R. Kelly, Chris Brown, even Michael Jackson—all men whose immense talent was overshadowed by their violent behavior, and yet who continued to enjoy commercial success because the industry deemed them too valuable to lose.

But perhaps what's most troubling about XXXTentacion's legacy is the way in which his violence has been posthumously reframed as part of his artistic narrative. After his death, fans rushed to canonize him, painting him as a martyr for a generation struggling with mental health issues, economic violence, depression, and trauma. His aggressive behavior was downplayed or dismissed as the actions of a young man who didn't know any better, someone who was still trying to find his way in a world that had been unkind to him. It's a narrative that conveniently erases the pain of his victims, particularly Geneva Ayala, whose life was forever altered by her relationship with him.

In the end, the violence that haunted XXXTentacion was both a symptom of his own trauma and a choice he made, over and over again, to inflict that trauma on others. His music, while often beautiful and vulnerable, cannot be separated from the harm he caused. As much as fans may want to believe that they can separate the art from the artist, the reality is far more complicated. XXXTentacion's violence was not just a part of his life—it was central to his identity as an artist, a fact that raises uncomfortable questions about the role of violence in our culture and the ways in which we celebrate and consume it as entertainment.

Joan Didion once wrote, "I have already lost touch with a couple of people I used to be." In the case of XXXTentacion, it's hard to say if he ever truly had the chance to *lose touch* with the person he was. His life, from beginning to end, was marked by violence—both as a victim and as a perpetrator. And while his music may live on, it will forever be haunted by the shadow of the violence that shaped him. XXXTentacion himself indeed embodied the idea of violence as style and story, fashion and narrative, aesthetic and explanation.

CHAPTER 6

Young Fashion

XXXTentacion—he wasn't just a musician; he was a walking contradiction wrapped in fabric and ink, a kaleidoscope of pain and rebellion. In a world where fashion often serves as a flimsy veneer to mask deeper issues, XXXTentacion ripped through that facade with dreadlocks, tattoos, and an aesthetic that was as loud as it was vulnerable. He became a cultural phenomenon not merely by virtue of his music but through the totally distinct way he chose to present himself to the world—a statement on identity, trauma, and the social constructs that govern both.

The young men of his generation—those who wear oversized hoodies and sagging jeans, who boast skin adorned with artful ink—know that style is not just a fashion choice but a manifesto. For XXXTentacion, every tattoo was a verse of his life, and every piece of clothing was a chapter in a story that fluctuated between chaos and vulnerability. He wore his trauma like a badge, an invitation for the world to confront the darkness that lingered in his mind.

And designers have taken up this challenge (the collective Real Fashion Bomb, shown here, has an entire line based on his look .) Yet, here is the irony: in a culture that celebrates the rebellious outsider, XXXTentacion found himself celebrated and vilified in equal measure. In so many ways this is the quintessential mark of an A-list artist. Jean-Michel Basquiat, Andy Warhol, Damien Hirst, and Pablo Picasso found themselves in the same boat.

Fashion is a language all its own—one that speaks volumes about race, class, gender, and the unspoken hierarchies of society. XXXTentacion's dreadlocks, a crown of defiance, his face tats, serve as a reminder of the complexities of cultural appropriation. For many, his look was an embrace of Black culture; for others, it was an unsettling reminder of a society that commodifies pain without reckoning with its historical roots.

His style mirrored the wildness and chaos of a generation grappling with its identity in a world where representations of race and gender can feel like a cruel joke played on those who refuse to conform.

In America, the world of streetwear thrives on the idea of rebellion, creating a marketplace that blends authenticity with commercialism. The paradox of street fashion is that while it may rise from grassroots movements, it often finds its way into the corporate realm, where major brands exploit the very essence of rebellion for profit. Of course, the look becomes defanged i the wrong hands. Dissent is thus always a hit and run affair.

Consider how XXXTentacion's style—marked by his tattoos, oversized drapes, and a nonchalant attitude—was emblematic of a larger shift in youth culture. Brands like Supreme and Off-White emerged as symbols of status, often co-opting street style, whichXXXTentacion embodied.

Yet, unlike polished labels, XXXTentacion's fashion choices were original, raw, unfiltered, and reflective of a life lived on the edge, a life that resonated deeply with a generation craving authenticity in an increasingly manufactured world. In a way, he was the ultimate post-modern fashionisto.

This aesthetic evolution can be traced to the emergence of the "SoundCloud rap" scene, where artists like Lil Uzi Vert, Lil Pump, and XXXTentacion created a new paradigm that blurred the lines between hip-hop and punk rock, with fashion as an integral component. His influence was palpable at music festivals and urban gatherings, where fans donned similar looks—dreadlocks, face tattoos, and oversized tees—creating a subculture that rejected mainstream standards of beauty and dress. It was a powerful statement, one that declared individuality in a society that often demands conformity.

In this context, the garments worn by his fans transcended mere clothing; they became armor, protecting them from the slings and arrows of a society that often felt alien. Wearing XXXTentacion merchandise was not just an act of fandom; it was a statement of identity. The XXX hoodie, emblazoned with bold graphics, became a talisman for those grappling with their own darkness, a uniform for a generation that often felt misunderstood. In this sense, his merchandise was not merely clothing but an emblem of solidarity, a flag raised high in the face of societal indifference.

But the link between fashion and identity is fraught with tension. As XXXTentacion rose to prominence, the line between admiration and exploitation blurred. Major brands, eager to capitalize on his cultural impact, began to incorporate elements of his style into their collections, often without acknowledgment of the artist's troubled history. In a glaring example of this, a well-known streetwear brand released a collection that mirrored XXXTentacion's signature look—giant silhouettes, vibrant colors, and bold graphics—yet failed to mention the man behind the aesthetic. This phenomenon raises uncomfortable questions: when does fashion homage become appropriation? How do we honor the legacy of an artist without stripping away the complexities of their narrative?

The dynamics of race, gender, and cultural representation play a significant role in understanding the complexities of this appropriation. XXXTentacion's life was a testament to the harsh realities faced by many young Black men in America—a life shaped by systemic violence, trauma, and societal expectations. His fashion choices, rooted in this lived experience, became a rallying point for a generation striving to reclaim its narrative. However, as brands commodify this rebellion, they risk diluting the very essence of what made XXXTentacion's style resonate in the first place.

Moreover, XXXTentacion's impact extended beyond his own image; he sparked conversations about the aesthetics of vulnerability and masculinity in fashion. The traditional notions of masculinity—stoic, unemotional, rigid—were challenged by his open discussions about mental health, depression, and trauma. In this way, his style became a canvas for exploring broader themes, inviting conversations about what it means to be a man, especially a man of color, in a society that often encourages emotional suppression. By wearing his brand, fans embraced the idea that vulnerability is not a weakness but rather a powerful form of self-expression.

As we delve deeper into the cultural landscape that XXXTentacion helped shape, we recognize that the aesthetics of rebellion he cultivated are still in play today. Fashion has become an avenue for social commentary, a way to challenge societal norms and expectations. The brands that have embraced this ethos, such as Fear of God and A Bathing Ape, demonstrate the power of fashion as a medium for expressing identity and rebellion. They encourage a dialogue about the complexities of race, class, and gender, pushing against the boundaries of what it means to be stylish in contemporary society.

XXXTentacion's legacy is a multifaceted one—part musical genius, part cultural icon, and part cautionary tale. He embodied the tensions that define American society, reflecting both the dreams and struggles of a generation grappling with its place in the world. His fashion choices invite us to consider the profound impact of aesthetics on identity, and how the garments we wear can serve as a powerful means of communication.

In reflecting on XXXTentacion's vision of fashion and youth, we confront the uncomfortable truths of our society—about race, identity, and the relentless pursuit of authenticity. His life serves as a prism through which we can examine the complexities of contemporary culture, inviting us to grapple with the tensions that define our existence. In the end, the story of XXXTentacion is not just a narrative about a troubled artist; it is a mirror reflecting the struggles, contradictions, and aspirations of a generation in search of its place in the world.

As we navigate the swirling currents of the modern world, we would do well to remember that fashion is not merely about what we wear but about how we choose to present ourselves in a place that often seeks to define us. And often just as an avatar on a small screen that others, many of whom are strangers, may view for just a few seconds. In this sense, XXXTentacion's vision remains as relevant today as ever—a call to embrace our individuality and confront the complexities that shape our identities. He may have been a controversial figure, but in the end, he was also a deeply human one—his legacy reminds us that the journey toward self-discovery is often messy, chaotic, painful and beautifully authentic.

CHAPTER 7

Redemption Songs

XXXTentacion's story is not just that of a troubled artist—it is a reflection of a generation tangled in the complexities of identity, vulnerability, and societal expectations. His music strikes at the heart of a cultural moment where loneliness has morphed into an epidemic, and the hunger for connection feels almost palpable. "I don't want to be alone. I don't want to be left on my own," he sings in "Changes," a sentiment that resonates like a haunting refrain. Yet, to view him merely as another casualty of fame, another tortured soul cast adrift in the void of social media, is to ignore the larger implications of his work and persona. XXXTentacion articulated the frustrations and fears of a generation that often feels unheard, trapped in a commercial landscape where emotional honesty is both celebrated and vilified.

The digital arena serves as a backdrop to his quest for redemption. Each tweet, Instagram post, and song release becomes a fragment of a larger puzzle, a desperate attempt to connect with fans who find themselves equally adrift. In this vortex, a vital question emerges: did audiences genuinely seek to understand him, or were they merely spectators consuming the spectacle of his suffering? This dynamic is not merely personal; it is emblematic of a broader cultural phenomenon wherein vulnerability is commodified and reduced to a trend.

Take the immediate aftermath of the "Changes" music video release. The visual narrative, coupled with the confessional tone of the lyrics, led many to interpret it as a plea for help. Fans and critics alike dissected the video frame by frame, searching for authenticity in every pixel. "He's a genius," some proclaimed, while others countered with accusations of playing the victim. The need to construct a narrative—one that would fit neatly into our preconceptions of artistry—often overshadowed the complexity of his reality.

Consider "Sad!," a track that propelled him to even greater heights while exposing the core of his internal struggles. The chorus—"I just want to be loved"—resonates deeply, embodying a juxtaposition of vulnerability and bravado. This longing for connection becomes a double-edged sword, where love can simultaneously lift and tear apart. Through these lyrics, it is clear that XXXTentacion was not merely a product of his environment; he was a mirror reflecting the chaos of his generation.

Discussions around his openness about mental health often teetered between admiration and skepticism, blurring the lines of authenticity in an age dominated by social media. "The more he exposes, the more we consume," remarked one commentator, pinpointing the paradox of our time—where the act of revealing becomes a performance. In such an environment, the question of whether XXXTentacion was truly seeking redemption or merely leveraging his vulnerability for fame looms large.

The tumultuous relationship with Geneva Ayala punctuates these discussions, revealing the intricacies of gender dynamics and accountability in a culture that idolizes flawed figures. The allegations against him became as integral to his narrative as his music. Supporters waved flags of forgiveness, while critics demanded accountability. This tension reflects a disturbing tendency to overlook transgressions in the name of artistic genius. One friend remarked, "It's like people wanted to see him fail, but they also wanted to love him for it." This paradox complicates our understanding of celebrity, particularly within the realm of masculinity, where vulnerability is often at odds with societal expectations.

Media obsession with his redemption arc encapsulates a cultural fixation on sensationalism, stripping discussions about mental health of their necessary nuance. Headlines questioning the authenticity of his transformation proliferated, begging the inquiry: can an individual's past actions coexist with a genuine desire for change? XXXTentacion's attempts at redemption were scrutinized relentlessly, each move analyzed under a microscope as if everyone was waiting for him to slip again, to reaffirm their worst fears about fame and its accompanying chaos.

In examining his music, the uncomfortable reality emerges: redemption is messy and fraught. The lyrics of "Revenge" reveal a longing for understanding that transcends mere atone-ment. "I think I found a way to cope," he sings, an assertion that doubles as a personal testament and a universal acknowl-edgment of the pain that many endure.

The question of whether XXXTentacion achieved redemp-tion cannot be easily answered. His music, a visceral reflection of his struggles, articulates a yearning for connection and un-derstanding that resonates with many. Yet, his legacy is irrev-ocably intertwined with the violence that marred it. This contradiction—the tension between the desire for forgiveness and the actions that perpetuated his suffering—lies at the crux of ongoing cultural conversations surrounding mental health, celebrity, and accountability.

To disentangle XXXTentacion's legacy is to confront our discomfort with the complexities of the human experience. His music is both a balm and a challenge, inviting listeners to grapple with their narratives while questioning the societal structures that shape them. The crazy journey through fame, violence, and emotional vulnerability reflects our collective struggle, revealing that redemption is not always just an indi-vidual pursuit but a communal reckoning—one that demands empathy, understanding, and a willingness to engage with the uncomfortable truths that permeate our lives.

XXXTentacion's existence compels us to grapple with the paradox of vulnerability in an era where it can be both a source of connection and a commodity. As we navigate this cultural landscape, his music stands as a reminder that the search for redemption is intricate—a chaotic, often elusive endeavor intertwined with the complexities of the human condition. Ultimately, it invites us to confront the delicate interplay between despair and hope, challenging us to question what it truly means to seek forgiveness in a world that often prioritizes the spectacle of suffering over genuine understanding.

CHAPTER 8

Gen Z's Anti-Hero

XXXTentacion is a name that still resonates deeply with the youth culture of today, emerging from a backdrop of personal turmoil and societal unrest. He is a figure of immense devotion and deep controversy, an anti-hero for a generation grappling with complex issues of identity, loss of place, and unmet societal expectations. His fans' unwavering loyalty, despite a litany of scandals and accusations of violence, raises critical questions about what it means to be a hero—or, more aptly, an anti-hero—in the current cultural landscape.

The allure of XXXTentacion is in his unapologetic vulnerability. His lyrics lay bare the anguish of a generation struggling with anxiety and fear, navigating a world that often feels hostile and unforgiving. Songs like "Sad!" and "Changes" cut through the noise with raw emotion, connecting with listeners who feel unseen in their pain. The lyrics serve as an anthem for those wrestling with their own demons, highlighting a profound yearning for understanding and connection.

He desperately wanted to live. This sentiment is echoed in interviews where he candidly spoke about his battles with depression, stating, "I just want to be happy, man. I don't want to die."

Yet, the fervent devotion of his fans exists in stark contrast to his public persona, which was riddled with scandals that paint a picture of a deeply flawed individual. The media coverage oscillated between fascination and condemnation, presenting a unresolved narrative that reflects much broader cultural struggles. In a world where social media amplifies both voices and controversies, XXXTentacion became a lightning rod for debates about accountability, redemption, and the complexities of identity. Fans have crafted a mythology around him that emphasizes personal growth, seeing his past mistakes not as indicators of a villain but as part of a messy, human experience.

This narrative speaks volumes about contemporary American society—a landscape where the lines between hero and villain blur, especially when it comes to figures of cultural significance. The affinity for anti-heroes is not just a product of storytelling; it is a reflection of a generation's frustration with sanitized portrayals of success. In a world rife with images of perfection, the rawness of XXXTentacion's life offers a counter-narrative. He embodies the idea that growth is often nonlinear, that one can oscillate between moments of brilliance and darkness.

As fans cling to the notion of redemption, it raises uncomfortable questions about what we are willing to overlook in our heroes. The fervent support for XXXTentacion may stem from a collective recognition of human imperfection—a desire to embrace those who struggle openly with their flaws. This echoes a broader societal trend where audiences are increasingly drawn to complex figures who challenge traditional norms and expectations. In a culture that has long been obsessed with perfection, the appeal of the anti-hero lies in their capacity to humanize the experience of failure and the pursuit of forgiveness.

The implications of this devotion extend beyond personal narratives, touching on issues of race, fame, class oppression, and the commodification of trauma. XXXTentacion, a young Black man, navigated a space fraught with systemic challenges, where his talent was often overshadowed by his controversies. The scrutiny he faced from both fans and the media is indicative of a larger societal pattern that disproportionately affects Black artists. In an industry that often values marketability over authenticity, his life became a testament to the struggle for recognition amidst a cacophony of judgment.

Moreover, the conversations surrounding XXXTentacion invite scrutiny of the very structures that elevate individuals to fame. What does it mean to idolize someone who has perpetuated cycles of violence and pain? The fan devotion speaks to a larger desire for connection in a fragmented world, yet it also raises critical questions about responsibility and accountability. Are we willing to overlook harmful behavior because it resonates with our own experiences, or does that complicity reflect a deeper societal malaise?

The phenomenon of XXXTentacion illuminates the nuances of American culture, where the intersection of race, class, and violence shapes our understanding of identity. In an era marked by social media's omnipresence, the ability to craft one's narrative has never been more accessible. XXXTentacion's artistry, filled with confessional vulnerability, resonates with a generation eager for authenticity but simultaneously wary of the consequences that accompany public exposure. This complexity plays out in real-time, as fans engage with his music while grappling with cancel culture and the moral implications of his legacy.

The cultural significance of XXXTentacion's music extends beyond the individual; it invites broader conversations about the role of art in shaping societal narratives. His songs become a platform for exploring the complexities of grief, loss, and the human experience. In the wake of the Parkland shooting, his tribute "Hope" stands as a poignant reminder of the power of art to connect and heal, even as it emerges from a troubled past. It's a call to confront the pain that permeates our society, an invitation to engage with difficult truths that are often swept under the rug.

Ultimately, the legacy of XXXTentacion forces us to reconsider our notions of heroism and accountability in an age where the personal and the public are linked. The fervent devotion of his fans reveals their deep-seated desire for connection and understanding—a yearning to find solace in the shared experiences of suffering and redemption. His life and music serve as a mirror reflecting the complexities of American society, urging us to confront our own struggles with identity, violence, and the often-painful journey toward healing. And of course, XXXTentacion was not shy about pointing out the hypocrisy of American narratives associated with justice, class mobility, and equality.

In navigating the contentious waters of fame and legacy, XXXTentacion's story resonates with profound implications for a generation seeking to reconcile their own narratives with the realities of the world around them. His enduring popularity is not merely a celebration of his artistry; it is a testament to the complexity of the human experience, an acknowledgment that even in darkness, there exists the possibility of light. In a way, the inability of fans and media to domesticate the story of XXXTentacion, much less his person, is what seems to have driven his fame. And consciously or not, through his lyrics, XXXTentacion continues to challenge us, inviting us to engage with our own vulnerabilities and to face head-on the broader societal issues that shape our lives.

Blaze Carter is a passionate writer and cultural commentator from the streets of South Florida, where the legacy of XXXTentacion continues to resonate. A fan of the artist, Blaze's work explores the relationship between music, identity, and youth culture today. With a keen eye for detail and a knack for storytelling, Blaze explores the emotional landscapes shaped by XXXTentacion's lyrics, addressing themes of vulnerability, rebellion, and redemption. Inspired by the artist's ability to connect with a generation struggling with issues of identity, social justice, and authenticity, Blaze tries to provide insightful analyses that honor XXXTentacion's impact while navigating the controversies surrounding his life. When not writing, he can be found enjoying the underground music scene, engaging in discussions about the evolving nature of fashion and art, and connecting with fellow fans who share a love for the power of music. As a voice for the generation that embraced XXXTentacion's message, Blaze Carter seeks to contribute to the conversation about the artist's lasting influence and the wild cultural landscape we live in.